Selfish
AMBITIONS

A DAY IS A LIFETIME IN POLITICS

RICHARD EVANS

852 PRESS

852
PRESS

First published in 2023 by 852 Press.
Suite 12, 12 Eshelby Drive, Airlie Beach, Queensland Australia
www.852Press.com.au

10 9 8 7 6 5 4 3 2 1

A catalogue record for this book is available from the National Library of Australia

National Library of Australia Cataloguing-in-Publication entry:
Author: Evans, Richard
Title: Selfish Ambitions / by Richard Evans
ISBN: 978-0-6455544-3-4 (Trade paperback)
ISBN: 978-0-6455544-4-1 (ebook)
Australian fiction.
Cover Design: 852 Press

I haven't met a Richard Evans book that I haven't loved, and I look forward to reading more in the future. – GOODREADS

As well as being a ripping good yarn, Evans charts the course for establishing a homeland state for Australia's First Nations in FORGOTTEN PEOPLE. Compulsive reading with action, drama and a seriously provocative political challenge. – AMAZON

Wow! Richard Evans has given us his best book yet with THE KILL BILL. From the moment I picked this book up, I was hooked. I didn't want to put it down to go to work, - BJ'S BOOK BLOG

I absolutely loved it, and couldn't put it down. I would love to see your book become a movie. – IAN S.

Rich in ideas and provokes much thought about our parliamentary process, abuses of power, corruption, and the need, at times, for ordinary people to step up and take a stand in the name of honour and professional integrity. – NADINE D.

Utterly gripping thriller with compelling characters and surprising plots twists. It is a provocative read. I couldn't put it down. – AMAZON

A great read, fast paced and page turning. I found it difficult to put it down. What a great book! Well written with all political content relevant, it kept me reading till the very end. – GOODREADS

A gut-wrenching Australian based political thriller full of manipulation, deception, and greed. THE MALLEE is a complex web of a story that left me speechless, it has taken me days to process. – GOODREADS

Evans' writing is slick, tight, and unobtrusive. The dialogue is a joy to read. The characters are solid and believable. One of the best books I've read in a while, and a solid five stars from me. Recommended! – GOODREAD

ALSO BY RICHARD EVANS

For my friends who have shared my journey and continue to inspire me.

Rob, Greg, Phil, Paul, Michael, and Peter.

A MESSAGE FROM RICHARD

After talking with many men in the twilight of their careers and even their lives as research for this book, I have been struck by their feelings of leaving a legacy and their angst about if they truly mattered to others. Many of these men have wondered if they have done enough, others reflected on if they made the right choices throughout their life when asked to decide. Some had regrets, but most enjoyed their journey.

The journey of manhood can be a difficult one, full of expectations and responsibilities. As we age and reflect on our lives, it's natural to wonder if we have made a difference, if we have done enough, and if we have done the right thing by others.

For some men, the weight of these expectations can become overwhelming, leading to feelings of insecurity and doubt. I think it is important for men to remember that they are not alone in these thoughts and feelings. Many men face the same struggles, grappling with the challenges of manhood, their identity, and the impact they have had on their world.

The past can hold lessons and fond memories, but it is not a place to dwell. Some men may find themselves looking back with regret, wishing for a different path or a different outcome. But it's important to focus on the present and the future, and to strive for continued personal growth and fulfillment. By reflecting on our experiences and learning from our mistakes, we can shape a better future for ourselves, our family, and those around us.

We must balance our reflections with our vision, lest we become lost in the past and unable to see the possibilities that lie ahead. This story is about one man's journey, grappling with the angst of a late-career reflection and the weight of his responsibility. From my research, it's a familiar story, but we never hear it because blokes don't want to talk about it.

The male voice is often silent in contemporary discussions about feelings, but the integrity and honesty that many men embody is never diminished. I invite you to read and reflect, with compassion and understanding, for the silent, perhaps lonely men in our community who may struggle with their role but still strive to make a positive impact.

I hope you enjoy the read.

- R

It's important to be faithful to truth and
stand up for what is right,
even if it's difficult or unpopular.

This helps to build trust and integrity
        within us
and in our relationships with others.

RICHARD EVANS, AUTHOR.

All the world's a stage,
and all the men and women merely players.
They have their exits and their entrances;
And one man in his time plays many parts.

AS YOU LIKE IT, ACT 2, SCENE 7
WILLIAM SHAKESPEARE

You are too concerned
with what was and what will be.
There's a saying:

Yesterday is history,
tomorrow is a mystery,
but today is a gift.
That is why it is called the present.

BIL KEANE
JONATHAN AIBEL
GLENN BERGER

Growing old is like climbing a mountain;
you get a little out of breath,
but the view is much better.

MAYA ANGELOU

Life is a dream for the wise,
a game for the fool,
a comedy for the rich,
a tragedy for the poor.

SHOLOM ALEICHEM

One

4:48 AM

―――――――――

Christ, I hate my life. Every moment of it.

I wander through my life, feeling lost and aimless. Most days are now consumed by a sense of loathing and despair. Nothing has turned out the way I had hoped, and I can't shake the feeling that I'm stuck in a constant state of malaise. I feel suffocated by my own existence, and I can't help but think that everything, every single thing, is a burden that's dragging me down. *"I just want it all to end"* feels like a refrain echoing through my head, on a never-ending loop that threatens to drive me mad. Sometimes, when the darkness feels too overwhelming, I find myself standing at the edge of the bridge, staring down at the black water, wondering what it would feel like to let go. Other times, I would sit alone in my office, my hands shaking as I reach for my bottle of pills in my desk drawer, wondering if this could be the solution to my pain. The thought of ending it all is both terrifying and alluring, a way out of the endless cycle of misery that seems to consume me. I often tell myself no one would miss me. To be honest, I'm ready to quit my life.

People tell me to snap out of it, but I don't know what they mean. Snap out of what? How can I snap out of my own life and start enjoying it? It's not that simple. I lay awake in the early morning, plagued by thoughts of how miserable everything is for me, and how nothing has turned out as I had hoped.

It seems a black cloud looms over me most of the time. It's the cloud everyone talks about, but nobody ever admits to seeing. I know it's there hanging over me; I feel it most days. It shrouds my thoughts and pushes me into dark, shadowy places I don't want to be. Sometimes, I wish I could be anywhere but here, trapped in this damn life.

But like any good husband, father, and son, I keep doing what I have to do, even though it seems like there's an endless line of people wanting something from me, wanting a piece of me. It feels like nothing will happen unless I make it happen, and I'm just so exhausted from it all. Despite this darkness, I still force myself to keep going, fulfilling my obligations, and making everyone happy.

I reckon I desperately need a break, a chance to get away and think, to clear my head and consider my future. I need respite from the constant demands and a chance to be myself again. But it's just a dream, something I often think about when I can't sleep.

Most days my body niggles at me reminding me I am getting old. I need to stretch out the ache when I get up from a chair. My feet hurt. My knees sometimes buckle when I move down steps. I once tripped crossing a curb and fell, dislocating three fingers. I seemed more concerned about the damage to my phone than popping the knuckles back. Now I rarely stride out with the same confidence. My hunched shoulders crave a good massage, but I never seem to have the time for such luxury. There's just too much to do.

Sleep would help reduce my anxiety and would be a welcome gift for me, but it doesn't last long. I have too much to do and think about, especially my responsibilities at work, and I just don't have the time for myself anymore. It's getting to me, wearing me out, and I'm becoming lost.

I know I don't have the energy I once did, and I can't help but feel like I'm letting the old man in.

Two

5:32 AM

E very morning, as if on schedule, my mind rouses before my body is ready, driving thoughts of my political assignments well before mindfulness forces my weary eyes open. I try holding on to a pleasant dream, avoiding the realities of the day to come, but often to no avail. And today, the haunting melody of Elton John's *"I Guess That's Why They Call it the Blues"* has wormed into my head, adding to the already crushing weight of the blues that are already pressing upon me. Maybe I'm trying to tell myself something.

Frankly, the blues hit harder these days, and I hate it. It's not just my work that worries me, but also my family, and I reckon my friends seem to drain energy from me. I hate the way I feel and I'm beginning to question if I should continue.

And yet, there is not one reason I should feel this way, not one.

On any measure, and this is the dilemma I struggle with, I confess to having a comfortable and fortunate life. I'm employed, I enjoy financial stability, and I'm surrounded by a loving family. I'm a privileged man and I really shouldn't complain.

I do though. These days, I do it more often.

Despite this privileged life, I'm plagued by a constant sense of anxiety and self-doubt. It's as though a spinning wheel of regret, self-loathing, and a sense of loss has taken hold of me, expressing itself in a never-ending narrative of disappointment. My comfortable life doesn't diminish the tightening ball of angst sitting in my gut, squeezing me, and surging enormous self-doubt into my head.

I reckon others would kill for the life I lead. Not literally, of course, but just saying, I shouldn't complain. Yet, I can't shake the feeling that at my age I'm still not living up to expectations. I keep questioning myself during these times of funk: did I really aspire to live this miserable life?

This damn question buzzes about my head almost every day, especially when anxiety threatens me. I struggle to cope with the daily stress of everything caving in on me. So, I find myself frequently daydreaming about what life could have been like had I made different choices. To escape the angst in my life, I daydream. I often close my eyes and reflect on those sliding door moments when I could have made a different choice and changed my life.

When I compare my life to that of my father at my age, I wonder if we are similar in our values and goals. I remember him working assiduously to run his business and I question if I possess the same level of dedication. But then I recall how he seemed older with his face wrinkled, cragged with age, and always sad, probably weighed down by the responsibilities of his business and supporting his family.

His health had always been a problem, and his smoking only worsened it. The hacking cough, which seemed to cause more pain to his family than to him, was a constant reminder of his struggles. It was also possible that his financial battles also added to his worries. Who knows though because he never talked about it. Despite his worries and his stoic nature, I enjoyed hanging out with him and watching him succeed. Now look at me. They reckon I have everything, and yet I feel, deep in my heart, compared to him, I have nothing. Absolutely nothing, and I feel dreadfully lonely.

My parents did their best for my little brother and me, and they were always pushing us to prosper. They wanted us to do well and tried their best to discipline us to the path of success. While I may have received the occasional praise from them, it never truly resonated with me. Each success just seemed like another day to me. I couldn't shake the sense that their love was conditional and based on my ability to meet their expectations.

The relentless nagging to make the most of my life began when I reached twelve and started secondary school. They wanted me to excel in my studies and to make them proud, but I couldn't help but wonder if I ever truly achieved this dream for them and if those goals were really mine. I suspect I will never know.

This negative self-doubt I constantly fight often leaves me feeling like an imposter, as if I were simply going through the motions for the benefit of others, trapped in a mundane existence for others to admire. Like a performing animal trapped forever in a caged life, its freedom gone with the carnival sideshow barker calling for an audience. *"Come bear witness to the imposter and behold the emptiness of his existence, devoid of true substance or purpose."*

So, here's a question: where the heck am I this morning? My senses are awash with confusion and disorientation, leaving me a little uncertain of my surroundings in the darkened room. This is not the first time in which I've little idea where I am. The plush bedsheets cocooning me would seem to indicate that I am in a luxurious hotel, but was it Singapore, or was that yesterday? The very act of struggling to think, to make sense of my situation, nudges me from the blissful stupor of sleep, yet still the answer eludes me. Where the hell am I?

Christ, I hate my life!

Three

5:53 AM

Now I hear them. The soft, sleepy murmurings beside me sound familiar. Ah yes, it's slowly coming back, my recent international trip. It was a long and tiring journey, filled with stress and responsibilities that weighed heavily. And yet, in the hustle and bustle of everyday life, it's easy to push such thoughts aside and simply try to get through the day. My tiredness, the stress of too much responsibility and creeping to bed late, careful not to wake Wendy can be so easily forgotten. I'm at home.

It's a strange sensation, this feeling of sickness that seems to grip me in the gut whenever I allow myself a moment to reflect on the state of my life. I'm not a young man anymore, and the responsibilities that come with age burden me. Sometimes, during a long and tiring day, I find myself yearning for the carefree days of my youth, when the only concerns on my mind were where to catch the next big wave and how to impress the chickee-babes.

But those days are long gone, and in their place is a life filled with constant demands and obligations. I travel often, criss-crossing the globe and leaving behind the comfort and sanctity of my bed.

9

But even when I'm at home, there's always something that needs my attention, whether it's the stress of dealing with federal politics in Canberra, or the daily grind of making important decisions at the office, or even the chaos that seems to exist at home, it seems it's up to me to make things happen. Sometimes my days merge into one.

I recall one particularly trying evening in Sydney when I found myself locked out of my hotel room after a boozy function. Frustrated and exhausted, I stormed down to the front desk, demanding answers. The sympathetic supervisor graciously explained that they had booked me into a similar room on the floor above, and that the room I had been trying to enter - room 305 - was the one I had occupied just a week prior.

Sometimes life can become a pile of unreality like that. It was an embarrassing mistake, one that I was fortunate the media never caught wind of. They would have had a field day with it, calling for my resignation and lambasting me for days on end. Such is the nature of life in the public eye, where every misstep is scrutinized and judged.

But even without the added pressure of the media, life as a politician can be a trying and overwhelming experience. The constant demands of work, coupled with the need to always be on and ready to make critical decisions, can take a toll on even the strongest amongst us in a similar role. But perhaps these are just the natural musings of a privileged man at a certain age, struggling to find his place in the world and trying to make sense of his own maturing identity. All I know for certain is that sometimes, when the anxiety and melancholy become too much to bear, all I really want is a break from it all. Is that too much to ask?

I know I shouldn't complain, I'm fortunate to have a good job and a supportive family, and I try my best to contribute positively to the world. But sometimes the doubt creeps in, and I wonder if I'm really making a difference, or if I'm just taking up space and going through the motions. And as I approach sixty, I can't help but feel a sense of anxiety and doubt about the future. Will I have made a difference in the world when all is said and done? Will my contributions be remembered, or will I simply fade into obscurity? And as the regrets of the past creep up on me, I question the choices I've made at various stages of my life. I wonder if I took the right path at those critical moments which often makes my anxiety worse.

Like any man I suppose, I hate to confess to any weakness, but as I lie here, shrouded by a cloak of malaise and self-doubt, I find myself troubled by thoughts of the future. What will become of me as I grow old? Will I be able to find happiness and fulfillment, or will I simply go through the motions, repeating the same tired patterns of the past? These are the questions that bother me as the knots of anxiety twist and turn in my gut, some days making me feel physically ill.

It's not just at work or at home that these anxieties plague me. Even the mere thought of boarding another plane fills me with a sense of dread and feels as though the entire burden of the world has been placed upon me. And even the hallowed halls of Canberra's federal parliament cannot offer me respite from these feelings, as it is a place normally rife with combative energy and a workplace laced with hate.

The citizens of Australia are quick to decry the *"ratbag politicians"* in their midst, and they're not shy about expressing disdain through abuse, mockery, and condemnation. It's almost a national pastime to ridicule and humiliate those in the public eye. And as much as I hate it, I know I must bear the burden of such criticism when it is directed toward me and try to rise above it. However, whenever I read or hear commentary about me, I am finding it harder to ignore it.

Sometimes, I wonder if my contributions to the world have truly been worthwhile. Have I made a difference, or am I simply taking up space? Is my identity, my self-worth, and my relevance threatened by the passage of time and the regrets of the past? When I am amongst my friends and blokes my age I wonder if they struggle with the same insecurities.

Gee, I'm really a sad sack this morning.

As I stare toward the ceiling considering the choices I've made and the paths I've taken, I can't help but wonder where the carefree surfer boy of my youth has gone? Where are the lazy summer days of beach, beer, and bongs that once defined my existence?

No, I can't allow myself to wallow in these thoughts of past glory.

I must push them aside and keep moving forward, even as responsibility presses down upon me, and the regrets of the past threaten to consume me. For in the end, it is only by facing these challenges and overcoming them we can hope to find true meaning and purpose in life.

Yeah, righto. What a joke.

Four

6:27 AM

To be honest, if the truth be told, nothing happens in my life unless I'm the first to initiate action. If I don't take the first step: to decide, to act, to say something, or do something, then nothing ever gets done.

Believe it, absolutely nothing, and I'm sick of it.

I can't remember when these negative thoughts first began. It simply seems that in recent years I've been imagining what my life would be like if I had taken a different path when I came to those crossroads. Would my life be different if I had put myself first instead of doing what others expected of me? I wonder. If I chose differently, what would life be like?

For instance, what would have happened if I jumped into that smoky van?

The way I feel right now, I'm convincing myself I'm an actual victim of the life others wished for me, and why not? These days, everyone claims to be a victim; why not me?

I reckon I'm a victim of my family's expectations. My parents wanted me to step up, and that's what I did. It wasn't what I wanted, but I did it because I felt obligated. So perhaps I am a victim. My electorate is much the same with their demands, so I have little time for myself. I get scheduled for events, public meetings, constituent sessions, speeches, and business meetings without my agreement. Doing what others want and not doing what I want. Classic victim status, I reckon.

Why the heck do I have to wake up every day and take responsibility? Why is it, in my life, that if it is meant to be, then it's up to me?

These darn clichés will be the death of me.

I hate my life.

'Are you okay?' a sleepy question comes from under the covers.

'Yeah, I'm fine. Go back to sleep.'

'Nice to have you home, darling. Love you.'

Does she really? Does she, or are they just words?

'Yeah, me too.'

Damn it.

Must my life be like this? Do I really have to deceive myself and those around me by saying things I don't mean?

Expectations drive me and it starts early every single day. The male schemas implanted in my head from a young age have taken over. Be a man. Boys don't cry, never express emotion, always pay for the woman, open doors, show respect, protect others, stand up, man up; these were just a few of the little nuggets rooted into my psyche as I grew up.

The fingers of responsibility gripped me on the shoulder as a young man, and they still clench me tight as the weight of responsibility cripples me. I've lived my last three decades being too darn responsible. This is not living. My repetitive life seems to me like a monotony, bordering on frustration without allowing me to do the things I want to do. It's certainly not freedom.

Surely, true happiness in life comes from our individual freedom.

The freedom to not have to make decisions, the freedom to do things that bring us joy, the freedom from responsibility. The freedom to catch waves, and the freedom to not worry too much about who is in charge of the government. To have freedom from debt and not worry about money, and the freedom from other demanding people I encounter. Those pesky and eager individuals I encounter everywhere, every day who irritate me no end.

Truth is, the scent of freedom left me when I stepped away from that van, closed the door and let the smoky rust-bucket drive off.

I want to be free again. Free to breathe without feeling anxious, free from responsibility, free to be happy again. To live a life with little concern, with plenty of weed, and a good wave to chase. Who said we must contribute to our community? Others don't. Who said we should seek happiness through setting goals, striving to attain, and providing for others? Others don't.

Who made that decision for me?

These damn clichés are killing me.

Why do I not simply say no?

Perhaps, I just lack the courage.

However, this notion I'm tethered to my life is not right. I can leave anytime if I choose, but I decide to stay. Ultimately, that icy hand of responsibility grabs me, dragging me back, insisting we must not stray from the path chosen for us. Or maybe I'm just too lazy to try something else.

Life tells us we must not be different, that we must always comply and not disrupt the status quo. We are told that we must do what they expect of us to live a fulfilling life. Men are often told they must be responsible, provide for their families, and contribute to their community and country.

Which moron said I should do that?

Who stamped my card and said this is the life you will now live? Why me? Why am I the one who must take responsibility for making the tough decisions that affect my family? Why am I the one who must take responsibility for getting out of bed every day and facing the hordes of people who want a piece of me? Why do I have to do it?

Who is looking out for me?

"I guess that's why they call it the blues."

Good grief.

But here's the real kicker: someone should accept responsibility for protecting the family. That's what happened to me years ago, I did.

Here's what I struggle with: who has ever taken on the responsibility for providing all that good stuff for me?

Who's filling my damn bucket?

Responsibility sucks sometimes.

Oh man up, for fuck's sake.

I have everything I need in life, all the trinkets and the toys. Yet when I think about it, I feel like I have nothing. That's pathetic, really. I have all these material things and yet I reckon I have nothing.

I reckon there's no true love in my life and I truly miss it. I miss thinking about it and its romance.

There's no emotion, no joy, no satisfaction, and very little respect for the things I do and the sacrifices I make. This is what I mean about having nothing, and I hate it.

Maybe I should have gotten into that damn smoky van. What a dumb mistake that was. Maybe things would've been different.

No, not maybe. I reckon I'd be a different person, that's for sure. I wouldn't be this wimp who grumbles about everything. So, I just keep smiling and nodding, but behind my façade, I grind my teeth and close my eyes to dream about what might have been.

Stop it! This is pathetic.

I hate this time of the morning, when I think about what might have been, my regrets, and this sense of hopelessness that tightens my gut. I endlessly prompt myself to snap out of it but it gets harder for me.

I hate my life.

Five

7:06 AM

I t sounds like the children are organising breakfast, I can hear muffled voices, music and rustling coming from the back of the house. I should probably get up and join them for a chat. Maybe I'll even make Wendy some tea. Swinging out of bed I comb fingers across my scalp trying to motivate my mind to rid itself of life's regrets.

'Hi Dad, when did you get back?'

Fraser sounded excited as I padded into the back of the house, turning on the morning radio and the music off as I pass the media wall.

'I've got a big game today. Do you want to come?'

'Hey Buddy, what's happening today?'

'We're playing Hurstbridge at the sports centre. It's the grand final. Wanna come?'

'Umm, let me think about it.' I'm not too enthusiastic about watching a kids' game of basketball after spending so much time away, I had plenty to do at the office. 'How are you, Peewee?'

Peter, for a moment, checked me out over his chunky, black-framed glasses sitting on the end of his nose. It was difficult to tell if he was acknowledging me or just contemplating the physics of his breakfast. I fussed in the kitchen because I didn't know what he was thinking, nor did I really care.

I still don't really know how to brew teapot tea, expected whenever we have guests. Wait, we never have guests, so that expensive teapot that Wendy purchased sitting on the shelf collecting dust is yet another example of my money just being wasted on her whims. I set out a cup and saucer for her, Wedgwood's finest of course, and a huge, cheap supermarket mug with a couple of heaped sugars for me with a tea bag in each.

'How was Germany? Did you bring me back anything?' Fraser is his usual chatty self. It doesn't seem like much has changed over the past five days.

'I didn't have time son, but I did get your favourite Belgian chocolate at the airport.'

'You're awesome Dad, you never forget us,' he said, his eyes sparkling with appreciation.

A whimsical smile crept across my face at my youngest's observation. Maybe life isn't so bad when you have a twelve-year-old who thinks a block of airport chocolate is the best gift a father could give, even if he must share it with his siblings.

I gambled with the other one. 'Peewee, tell me mate... what's happening, dude?'

'Nothin' much.'

'How's school?'

'Okay.'

'Done anything exciting?'

'Nah.'

'Achieved anything this week?'

'Nuh.'

'Doing anything on the weekend?'

'Nuh.'

'Want to do something with me?'

'Like what?'

'Maybe catch a movie.'

'Maybe.'

'I'll come,' interjected Fraser.

'Of course, you will. What do you want to go see?'

'The latest Bond movie,' Fraser said, his eyes lighting up as he karate chopped an imaginary enemy operative.

'Sounds good. What about you Pete?'

'Maybe.'

'Come on bro, snap out of it. Dad's takin' us to the movies.'

'Yeah, so?' He looked tired.

'If you don't want to go, I won't force you.' I challenged him for a response.

'Okay.'

'Okay, what?'

'Okay, I won't go.'

'What's wrong with you, son? Am I missing something?'

He looked at me as if not knowing what to say. 'What do you care? You probably won't be able to go, anyway. Something will come up... it always does.'

The kettle clicked, interrupting the tense exchange and I poured the steaming water, keeping my back turned to the boys as I tried to process what's going on with them. Sometimes it's so confusing dealing with the boys. Was I like this with my dad?

'Hey Daddy, if the boofhead doesn't want to go, can we still go?'

'Sure, does anyone need a lift to school?' I walked around the island bench and rested against it.

'No, I'm right, Dad. Nick's mum is picking me up. Thanks for offering.'

'No worries, Buddy. What about you Pete?'

'Nah.'

'What's wrong son, anything worrying you? You seem a little distracted this morning.'

'Nuh.'

'Everything okay at school?' He pushed back in his chair with palms on the table, panting deep through his nose as if in extreme pain. 'You want to share anything with me?'

'Noooo.'

It's like trying to extract a confession from Bond. 'Are you sure? You know you can tell me anything.'

'Stop hassling me, will ya?' He struggled to get the words out as he snapped at me.

'Just wondering. Nothing to worry about.' Maybe he does have something bothering him. 'If you want to talk, let me know.'

'Sure.'

The conversation is interrupted as Sarah stumbles through the glass door from the back patio, looking like she had a good night. She reeked of smoke and alcohol, eye makeup smudged, her hair is a mess, and her clothes are strewn about her body.

'Hi gorgeous.'

'Don't talk to me,' my daughter groans as she raises a silencing hand, drops her bag, and walks past the kitchen on her way to her bedroom upstairs.

'Look what the cat dragged in,' Fraser tries to joke, but it falls flat.

'I said, don't fucking talk to me.'

'Hey, ease up. Don't talk to your little brother like that.'

'I say whatever I damn well feel like.' She sways as she stops to challenge me, placing a hand on her hip.

'Where have you been?'

'None of ya goddam business.'

'Don't talk to me like that, please.'

'Who the fuck are you to tell me what to say?'

'I'm your father.'

'Ha,' she bellowed. 'What a laugh that is. You're never home long enough to be called a father.'

'Lower your voice will you, you'll wake your mother.'

'Oh, we mustn't do that, must we?' Sarah baits me, raising her voice almost to a yell.

'Maybe you should just go to bed and sleep it off.'

'Sleep what off?' She stood before me, still baiting me, legs apart, both hands clenched on her hips, just like her mother. 'You think I don't know what's happening? You think I'm way too smacked to know what I'm saying? Is that what you think?' she asked, seeming ready for a fight. 'Look at you, standing there with that smug expression thinking I'm just one of your many encounters you must deal with in your magnificent day as you go about solving the problems of the world, with your head up your arse. You think sleeping it off will fix everything, just like Mum.' Sarah ends with a shout toward the front bedroom. 'Isn't that right, Mummy dearest?'

'All I'm saying is that you may have had too much of a good time, and perhaps you need to go to bed before you say something you could later regret.'

'What makes you think I don't have regrets right now?'

'Give it a break will you, sis,' Peter interjected, seemingly annoyed by the noise.

'Have you asked him yet?' Sarah turned on her brother. 'Or are you still the dipstick scaredy-cat you've always been?'

Peter glanced down, averting eye contact with Sarah and me.

'Ask me what?' I wanted to know what was going on between these strangers.

Sarah waited for Peter to say something. When nothing seemed forthcoming, she turned to me. 'By the way Daddy dearest. I'm not going to university next year and may not even go at all.'

Her pompous attitude was getting on my nerves, and I couldn't help but think how she was still young enough to have the fly swatter spanked across her backside. 'Yes, you will.' I tried to remain calm, speculating where the swatter might be.

'It doesn't matter what you say, Mum has already said yes.'

'What do you think you'll be doing?'

'I'm doing a gap year and going to London.'

'No, you're not, young lady.' The prospect of that idea seemed ridiculous. 'Where do you think you're getting the money to do that?'

'Mum's giving it to me.'

'Your mother?' I could feel myself about to explode as my gut tightened, so put the island bench between us as I finished preparing the tea. 'Where do you think she'll get the money?'

'She has her own.'

'Which I gave her.'

'So, fucking what? You have little say in this family anymore.' Sarah walked to the bench. 'You act like you're the lord and master with all the old-man privileges when you're here, but you're only the occasional caller. You know nothing about what's going on. You don't even know what's going on with Peewee.'

Peter stood, almost charging at her. 'Sis don't, please, I beg you.'

'What's going on?' asked Fraser.

'I told you,' Sarah jabbed a finger at Fraser. 'Shut the fuck up.'

'Let's just remain calm, please?' I usually try to be the peace maker to avoid challenging and difficult emotions, now I'm having to placate another ranting woman in my life. I still considered her to be my little girl, but she was still a woman in my life. A ranter, just like the others. 'Now tell me, what's going on with Pete?'

'Nothing is going on with me,' Peter insisted.

'Tell him,' Sarah said.

'No.'

'Tell him or I fucking will.'

'No, please don't Sarah. Please don't.' Her brother burst into tears.

'You see.' She turned to me. 'You have no fucking idea, and it's your fucking fault.'

'Please say nothing, I beg you, please don't.'

Sarah, her eyes now wide and ready for a fight, seemed placated by Pete's words, crumbling her hostility toward me. She gathered her bag, storming off to her room. 'You mean nothing to me anymore.'

After the silence of morning drifted back, once the stomping feet and slamming door above stopped, I poured milk into the tea and threw the tea bags in the sink.

'Whatever it is you need to tell me, Peter, it's okay. You can.'

'It's not okay.' Another child stormed off upstairs, minus the prima donna act of defiance.

I turned back to Fraser, raising an eyebrow.

'Well, that was interesting,' he sniggered, a cheeky smile filling his face. 'I bet you weren't expecting that so early in the morning.'

I chuckled at his witty observation. Fraser was a great kid always making light of the most serious disputes. The family seemed to have a lot these days. His schoolbooks were not as good as his siblings, but he was more street smart than anyone else in the family, including me. He was a great little kid.

'What about the game? Do you want to come?'

'Of course, son, I'll be there.' I knew getting to the game could prove problematic. My first day back after a trip is always hectic, and I suspected Fraser already knew that.

'That'll be great, Dad. I love you.'

'I'll just take this tea into your mum. I'll see you before you leave to go to school, okay?'

'Do you love me, Daddy?'

'Sure son.' I scooped up the tea and headed off.

'How come you never say it?

Six

I gnoring Buddy's flippant line, I tottered off down the hall with tea rattling in the saucer, kicking open the bedroom door, placing my mug on the side table before cautiously navigating the darkened room around the bed and setting the tea on the latest book club offering. 'Wendy.' I whispered, 'cup of tea, gorgeous.'

I drew open the drapes, eliciting a sharp protest from under the covers.

'Good morning darling, a cup of tea for you.' Slipping back into bed, I added one of the many pillows scattered on the floor to prop myself up against the wooden headboard.

Wendy's over-bleached mane of hair spilled out from under the covers, wild strands strewn like a shaggy dog across her face, a stark contrast against her tanned skin. Despite the dangers of doing so, Wendy seems to have once again indulged in the burning sun lamps during her spa session. As a mother of three, cancer health risks did not deter her in the pursuit of beauty treatment.

I've always considered her to be a good-looking woman, but I remain puzzled by her insatiable need for the constant self-improve-ment, whether it be in the form of blonde hair or the small Botox enhancements her consultant insists upon. I had drawn the line at breast augmentation, feeling that it would set a poor example for Sarah. Wendy agreed but warned that the moment Sarah turned twenty-five, she'll be getting what she considers her saggy breasts done.

'Three kids have ruined my tits, and it's your fault, so you can pay.'

I was not sure how the birth of our children could be considered solely my fault, but then, I struggled to understand many of the things Wendy said these days.

Where do women find the motivation to reach an unattainable level of adoration? Is it the *"toxic"* patriarchy setting impossible standards, driving women to alter their appearance? To be honest, I have no idea why, and I suspect that most men didn't. It's a social construct I have little patience for, but if it kept Wendy happy then so be it. *"Happy wife, happy life"* is the advice given to me by blokes my age when I complain. 'Do whatever you can to make her happy, and then you can do whatever you want,' my friend Roy Harper told me when I was younger. So that's what I have done, but at what cost?

Why do girls and older women feel the need to wear makeup? I simply don't understand. In my opinion, if a woman felt the need to wear makeup, it should enhance her natural style and beauty, not mimic some retouched advertisement in a magazine. In my youth, I dated girls who preferred the sun, surf, and sand, and we would often mock girls who caked on greasy makeup. Once a girl left a smudge of gunk on my shirt, I wasn't happy. Makeup smudges on your best tees meant the relationship wouldn't last. But that's just my preference, which is possibly an ignorant male point of view.

I took a swig of the now lukewarm tea, sweet and welcome, before reaching for my phone to scan the early news headlines.

'Good morning darling,' Wendy groaned as she struggled to get comfortable, reaching for a pillow to nestle into. She placed her tea on her chest and stretched her arm back to grab her phone, scrolling through Facebook notifications and checking in with friends. While I sometimes find Facebook useful, I often wonder why it has such a devoted following. It seems to be an addiction with questionable benefits. If you want to communicate with your friends, I think you should just call them. 'Thanks for the tea, sweetheart. What time did you get in?'

'I don't recall. Around midnight, I reckon. I tried not to wake you.'

'I thought you were landing around seven. I tried to stay up, but once it gets past nine, I get tired.'

'We landed later than expected.' I sipped my tea still scrolling my feed. 'I dropped into the office to organise some papers for what is going to be a hectic day.'

'You work too hard, darling.' She took a sip and sighed. 'How was your trip? Successful?'

'No, not really. The Germans want us to give them more money. I won't know until I speak to the boss this morning to see what her final decision is. I tried to get a hold of her last night, but she wasn't available.'

'What's your plans today?'

'I'm obliged to make an statement about the German jobs. There's a lot of folks waiting for the news.'

'Buddy has a big game this afternoon. He's been asking about you. It would make his day if you could go. It's at the sports centre near the city.'

'I'll try. Are you going?'

'No, I have our dinner tonight. I need to be at the function centre early to help prepare.'

'Of course, you do,' I said, feeling annoyed that charity dinners seemed to be all she ever did.

'What's that supposed to mean?' Wendy asked, immediately on the defensive. 'You remember about tonight, don't you?'

'Yes, but I can't just drop everything to get to a game. I'm busy.'

'It will mean a lot to him if you drop in for a few minutes, even if you can't stay for the entire game.'

'What?' I stopped scrolling. 'Doesn't he care if you don't see the game, just me?'

'He misses you darling and wants you to watch him play.'

'I'll try, but I can't promise anything.'

This is how it happens so often these days, me feeling frustrated that it seemed to always be up to me to make things happen. I'm so tired of it all. How did I end up like this? I blew a heavy sigh feeling overcome by a sense of negativity and sadness.

I understand that the decisions I've made in my life have led me to this place, and it's my fault. I wanted to be relevant, but it's not what I expected. I wish things were different, but they aren't. My decisions have made me who I am, and I don't like who I've become.

Do other blokes struggle with these same pressures of life? Like me, do they wish their lives were different? Or am I just a sad sack complaining about my life that most blokes would love to have?

Today, for instance, I'm required to make a decision that will affect the jobs of numerous people. Do I deliver good news or bad news to these worried individuals? Indeed, should I be the one to make the decision, or should the boss step up and make the announcement? I can't help but wonder why I am the one tasked with this difficult duty of breaking the news to these hardworking families. It's not my fault, but apparently, it's my responsibility.

The stress of this decision has been dogging me for weeks, like a metal vice squeezing my chest that makes it sometimes hard to breathe. It's no wonder I can't sleep. Why can't someone else decide for a change?

And that there is the answer to my ongoing stress, I reckon.

Decisions must be made, and it seems no one can make them but me. It's the same stress and tension with every damn decision, whether it's work requiring an answer, or my family wanting me to be somewhere. This is what my life has come to and I'm sick of it.

I hate my life.

Why can't someone else do it for a change?

'He needs his father. They all do.' She paused and took a sip. 'I'm worried about Peewee. He seems to get more and more distant. I found a strange, small tin in his bag the other day. What do you think that might be used for? I think he's taking drugs.'

Around this time, most mornings when I'm home, Wendy seems to think it's a grand idea to lecture me on the many problems in my family and what I should do about them. Today's ear-fucking seems focused on the children, thankfully not me.

'He never leaves his room, and he's always on his computer? Doing what? I'll never know because he never talks to me. His room stinks like a football locker room and the housekeeper has trouble putting his clothes away. He insists I not enter his room, and he only lets Anna in to clean when I nag him. You need to have a talk with him. Tell him about the standards expected if he is to live here.'

'Why do I need to do it?' I wasn't surprised, but I fancied hearing her answer.

'You're the dad.' Her argument didn't convince me.

'What happens if he doesn't comply with your standards? Do we throw him out on the street?'

'Don't be ridiculous. He's wasting his life. He's not doing anything to better himself. He's given up sports, doesn't go to any of his friends' houses anymore, and he hardly ever has anyone over. When he does, they lock themselves in his room and play on the computer. I think he needs a father-son talk as soon as possible, or else I'm worried that he's putting his grades at risk. We can't have another one causing problems for us. I mean, you've let Sarah get away with way too much. Now Peter is heading down the same path. I don't mind saying it's your fault.'

'My fault?' This should be good.

'You're always away. I don't have control anymore. They never listen to me. They aren't the babies I raised, almost on my own I might add.' Of course, she would add that, she always does. 'It's your turn to step up and take control. I don't know what will happen if you don't. If you continue not to control them, they will leave us with nothing. They'll leave us and never come back. If that happens, it'll be because of your neglect, I promise you. They could even turn to crime and maybe end up in jail. If they do, how would you feel then? Will you have any regrets?'

The tea was great. If I just close eyes for a few moments, then maybe my ears will get a rest as well.

'Sarah has been misbehaving again. She needs you to decide about next year's study.'

There was no chance of me getting a break because it seems the whole family will get an opinion about them this morning. I'm grateful that it isn't me.

'She's just told me you've allowed her to take a year off and go play in England.'

'I've done no such thing. I insisted you make the final decision.' Wendy always passed the blame to me.

'Do you want her to go?'

'No, of course not. It would be the worst thing for her. What control will we have? I can just imagine what sort of trouble she'll get into. Why would I let her go overseas? I didn't have that opportunity when her age. Why would I agree with her going by herself?'

'Why not tell her then? Why would you let her think you'll pay for the trip, and you agree?'

'This is your decision,' Wendy persisted.

'So, you let her think she has your support?'

'You don't have to deal with them every day. I do.'

'Why can't you do it?'

'Because you're paying for it. You must decide.'

'Nice one, thanks.'

'Darling, this is what fathers must do. You're the man, so you decide. The children come to me afterwards for love and the support they need. I'm the nurturer. You're the wallet.' Wendy's chuckle didn't convince me as she slid out of the bed to visit her bathroom.

The great home designer insists on her own bathroom, claiming I make too much man mess and take up too much room. Plus, it allows her to set out all her bits and pieces, so she can easily access her creams and potions when she needs to work up a storm of creative remodelling.

The other bathroom downstairs is my space shared with occasional guests invited for dinner. The kids have their own enormous one upstairs. Wendy has a rather large ensuite which contains a deep bath. At least a tonne of candles and other scents creating an oasis of female splendour and sophistication. I still don't get it.

I watched her tiptoe off. The fitness classes seem to be working a treat as she looks great, with tussled blonde hair cascading almost to her waist, and a subtle, tiny touch of red lace bringing a sly smile.

She has changed little in twenty-five years other than the intervention of medical procedures. She still looks as tanned and fit as she did when we first met at a pool party one year between Christmas and New Year. It was hot, and we took an immediate shine to each other splashing by the pool. It just came easy for me to join her life.

Before I met Wendy, I travelled on surfing safaris in Bali most years and spent my weekends down the coast, but I barely have time for surfing anymore. Now I feel like I'm just going through the motions of doing what other folks want me to do. Wendy has worked hard to make our life comfortable, but I sometimes wonder if this is the life I really fancied. I feel like I'm just the financial breadwinner for my wife and three kids, with the burden of responsibility stressing me.

My younger brother is completely useless and lives a totally different life. He takes no responsibility for anything, let alone our mother. Unless I step up as head of the family, nothing gets done. I love my mother dearly, but she rarely thanks me for the things I do for her, and it's wearing on me. Just an occasional thank you would be nice.

I think she begrudges me for selling the family business for a tidy profit. It was the right thing to do, as my brother couldn't manage it, but I reckon my mother wishes we kept it. Wendy and I sold our first home soon after I sold the business and we moved to the bayside, spending a lot of money renovating the house into a beautiful home that has even been featured in magazines. My mother still refuses to come to dinner and calls it my *"blood money house"*. It hurts to think she believes the money is hers and not the wealth I have since created. It still upsets me, but hey, she's my mum and she can say whatever she likes to her oldest. She still lavishes my brother with gifts and food, but never acknowledges me for the things I do for her.

'What's your plans for the weekend, darling?' Wendy returned to bed and snuggled close.

'I suggested to the boys we go see a movie. Buddy mentioned a Bond movie.'

'Can I come?'

'Sure, if you want, perhaps we can go Saturday afternoon?'

'Nope, no good. I have a book club at the library. This is the only time we could manage it with this specific author, apparently.'

'Sunday is out since I have church with mum in the morning. She also wants me to do a few odd jobs.'

'Can't Jim take care of those chores for once and give you a break?'

'Mum prefers me.'

'Why? Because she knows you'll do it?' she scoffed.

'Let's not go there Wendy, please.' I breathed a terse sigh. 'What about late afternoon after your meeting?'

'Let me check.' Wendy reached for her phone, flicking through to her calendar, and checking availability. 'It looks like you have another dinner scheduled for Saturday. I keep asking Fiona not to schedule weekend dinners.'

'Who's it with?' I already knew the answer.

'She didn't say, it's just blocked out and marked as dinner. So, I think I'll pass on the movie. Sorry about that.'

'I'm sorry too, gorgeous.' I wasn't entirely sure I meant it.

'No, that's fine. I can get a spa treatment done on Sunday now.'

I pondered on what she said and the work she does on herself. 'We should make a date sometime. It would be nice to spend some quality time together.'

'How do you mean?' Wendy glanced at me, distracted from updating her phone.

'We don't get a lot of time together. It would be nice to have a romantic meal.' Wendy leaned over and put her telephone back, picking up the connection from the floor. 'You've got scratches on your back.'

'What? Where?' She flopped back into the bed, pulling the covers up.

'On the back of your shoulders. They look as if you have scratched yourself recently, maybe stretching or something.'

'Oh probably, I hadn't noticed.' She scooted closer and placed her head on my chest, draping her arm across me, trailing her fingers against my arm. 'I've missed you.'

I kissed the top of her head. 'It's good to be home.'

'When are you going away again?'

'I'm not sure. I think around two weeks. I'm headed to China.'

'For how long?'

'Could be five or six days, maybe longer. I haven't seen my schedule. Why do you ask?'

'Oh, just curious. That's all. I might head for the holiday house for a few days.' She gazed up, then stretched to my mouth to give me a warm, welcoming kiss. She pressed harder. I retreated into the bed, wrapping my arms around her, responding as she liked.

Abruptly, a whooping alarm from my phone blared, signalling time for me to get moving. I stretched to turn it off, giving Wendy the opportunity to slip her hand into my underwear. 'Would you like a quick romp?'

'No, thanks darling, I have to get going.'

'It's been a while, are you sure?'

Before my body could respond, I rolled out of the bed. 'I have a busy day and it's not the time right now, sorry.'

'Your loss, sweetheart. I want it in the minutes that I offered.'

'So, recorded, gorgeous. Can I get you anything?'

'No, thanks. Are the boys up?'

'Yeah, and Sarah just got home.'

'She had a sleepover with Sam.'

'Boy Sam or girl Sam?'

'Girl Sam, of course.'

'She smelt like it might have been boy, Sam.'

'What are you suggesting?'

'My girl is no longer a girl?'

'You can't say that.' Wendy recoiled back into the pillows.

'Why? How old were you when you jumped into the world of randy boys?'

'Younger than her, as you well know. It was different back then. She hasn't done it yet.'

'How do you know?'

'She would tell me.'

'Did you tell your mother?'

'No, but Sarah and I are friends, and you tell friends everything.'

'Don't kid yourself. I'm taking a shower. Can I get you anything?'

'No, thanks.'

Seven

7:51 AM

As I stepped into the shower, the icy water took me by surprise, causing me to lose my footing and stub my heel on the tiled gutter. A sharp pain shot through my foot. 'Geezus Christ!' It was clear someone had used the shower while I was away and had not bothered to reset the temperature. How dare they invade my personal space like that?

I gritted my teeth and waited for the water to warm, then stood under the stream, letting it wash away the grime and stress of travelling. I couldn't remember the last time I even showered in Wendy's bathroom, and I smirked as I reflected on the effort and expense it took for her to look good. I just don't get it, maybe it's to do with feeling good about herself.

As I dried off, I took a good look at myself in the mirror. It had been a while since I had really examined my body, and what I saw was not pretty. I couldn't help but let out a sigh of frustration. The rolls of fat on my stomach seemed to have multiplied, and my once strong fit frame had been replaced with a softer, less toned version of itself. No one else seemed to think I had a weight problem, but I knew the truth. The stories of cardiac arrest and blocked arteries were always at the back of my mind every time I indulged in that extra fried chip.

But I refused to let this get me down. I took care to groom myself, trimming the greying beard and applying lotion to my skin to combat the drying effects of age.

After frisking product in my hair, brushing the fangs and swirling mouthwash, I poked my head through the door to see and listen if the coast was clear. A quick nudie run to my dressing room behind our bedroom. Today, I think dark blue. Cuff linked, crisp starched white shirt and navy blue, hand crafted, fine woollen suit with a multi blue stripped silk tie, deep maroon slip on Moreschi Italian leather shoes, and a complementary orange silk kerchief for the top pocket.

I may not be the surfer I once was, but I can still present myself as a fashionable and put-together man. And as I made my way out of my dressing room, I couldn't help wondering why more men don't take the time to invest in their appearance. Denim and sneakers may be comfortable, but they do nothing for one's identity. It's not hard to look good, and the effort is well worth it.

Hang on a second, am I being a hypocrite?

What am I trying to prove?

I just thought, that in my own way, I'm actually seeking the same validation as Wendy. We just go about it in different ways. While she indulged in creams and treatments to keep herself looking young, I took pride in my appearance, spending time and money on grooming and dressing well. We really are both the same when it comes to our vanity, and I am a total hypocrite.

As I sat on the bed next to Wendy, who was snoozing away, I gave her a quick peck on the head before announcing that I had to leave.

'Have a good day, darling. I love you,' she mumbled.

'I'll try to get to Fraser's game, but I can't promise. I'll text you my movements, okay?'

'Do your best, honey.'

'I will, I promise.' I tucked in the covers just as she liked them, soft around her to snuggle in, securing her. 'I don't suppose you know why my water temperature changed, do you?'

'What water?' she whispered.

'My water. When I showered, someone changed the temperature to cold.'

'Must have been one of the kids,' she murmured.

'Never mind, I'll check with them later. Have a great day gorgeous.'

'I'll see you tonight, darling.'

Not paying any attention to what she said, I closed the door quietly. When there is nothing else to do other than sleep, what else do you do? Oh, to be so lucky. I headed to the back of the house to grab my bag and say goodbye to Fraser.

'You look sharp today, Dad,' Fraser said, giving me a once-over.

'Thanks, son. You're not looking too shabby yourself.'

Fraser rolled his eyes. 'I'm just wearing my school uniform.'

'Well, you wear it well.'

'So, are you going to make it to my game today?'

'I'll certainly try my best. What time is it again?'

'It's a 2 o'clock start, but don't worry if you can't make it,' Fraser said with a shrug.

'I'll do my best to be there. I don't want to miss seeing you in action.'

'Okay, cool.'

'You know, son, I'm really proud of you.'

'Thanks, Dad.'

'No, seriously. You're a great kid, and you work hard. I admire that.'

Fraser looked down at his shoes, a hint of a smile playing at the corners of his mouth. 'Thanks, Dad. That means a lot coming from you.' Fraser gave me a playful shove. 'Now go get 'em, tiger.'

'Thanks, son. See you.' I collected my bag and headed for the front door, knowing my car would be waiting.

'Good morning, Minister.'

'Good to see you, Guy.'

Even as I stepped off into a new day, I couldn't shake this feeling growing within me that I was being a charlatan, trying to maintain a persona that may not be entirely authentic.

Eight

8:16 AM

———————

'How was your trip Minister, successful?'

'A little unsure at this stage.'

'Oh well, I'm sure it assisted you.'

The limousine was reversed into the driveway. Guy took my case, opening the back door, allowing me to slip into the warmed leather. A national newspaper lay ready to read on the way to the office, almost thirty minutes away. I checked back to see a smiling Fraser waving from the *"Do Not Enter"* front sitting-room window, so I returned a smile and managed a wave. What a great kid.

'What's the bridge traffic like this morning, Guy?'

'Roadworks again I'm afraid Minister, so I thought we wouldn't risk it and take the long way. Traffic is light, and we should make good time. Madam Fiona has requested you on time this morning.'

'And we obey she who must be obeyed, don't we?' I chuckled, flicking open the sports section.

'She asked me to request you call her once you settled in.' Guy's eyes engaged mine from the rear vision mirror and I imagined his sympathetic smile. Not even in the car five minutes and others are demanding me to do things.

'I'll call her soon enough.' Trying to ignore the nagging voice in my head, I settled into a story about a star player rupturing his knee. Good news for my club as we play his team soon.

The phone in front buzzed.

'We're on our way now,' Guy said. He listened for a moment before adding. 'Yeah, told him.' Silence again. 'Yeah, will do. See you.'

'Am I in trouble?'

Guy's eyes creased in the mirror reflection. 'I suspect you are.'

My phone buzzed. I checked the screen. It was Fiona. As always at her desk too early in the morning, finalising my day. Organising me. I let it ring out, but she persisted.

'Hello?'

'Good morning, Minister. How was your trip?'

'I think it was a waste of time.'

'Did you get to meet the Chancellor?'

'Oh yes, I spent about an hour with her. The embassy people did a terrific job in arranging it on such short notice, so can you send a note of thanks? I also met with their trade minister and lunched with Dietmar Schoenmakers to discuss a compromise, but we came to no resolutions. They just won't budge. So, I'm not sure about what our position will be. It's precarious I reckon.'

'Did you meet with the company?'

'I enjoyed two days with them, Dietmar arranged it. They stressed the point that they wanted to do business with us. I had a tour of their plant, and I've got to say, they're an impressive unit. Fantastic.'

'Outcomes?'

'They want the government to toss money in. Otherwise, they'll close all Australian operations before Christmas, starting with the

Melbourne plant within a week if the government doesn't support them.'

'Oh, no,' her exclamation jolted me a little.

She was right. I either approve the government funding they want or send their workers to the unemployment lines, and I must make that announcement today. Cabinet instructed me to resolve the policy challenge and take full responsibility, but I still don't know what the right choice is. I care about the fate of these families, but I'm not sure how to balance that with the needs of the company and the country. No other cabinet colleague seemed to care.

The prime minister wanted me to ignore the community's concerns and not approve government funding, but I knew that would mean countless people losing their jobs and struggling to make ends meet. On the other hand, if I approved the funding, it would mean going against the prime minister's wishes and possibly jeopardizing my career.

This is the political dilemma I'm struggling with, adding to the anxiety gripping and tightening my chest. Maybe this worry is boosting the whimsy about my past which is also torturing me.

'Their ultimatum was: give us the funding or we close operations.'

'Did you leverage our investment in their Antarctic project?' Fiona asked.

'Of course, but Dietmar seems to have had the hard word thrust upon him by his financiers. He advised he must accept nothing less than a full bailout as proposed by the Bundestag.'

'So, it's over?'

'Unless the PM changes her mind that is the case.'

'She wants to talk to you. I received a message from her early this morning.'

'Christ, doesn't she ever sleep?'

'She's the prime minister. I guess she needs to be on top of everything.'

'The last bloke didn't ring ministerial staff during the middle of the night.'

'Maybe it's harder for her,' Fiona sighed before adding, 'maybe she's trying hard to prove herself amongst all you men.'

'Yeah, I wouldn't have thought so.' I squinted, forcing a grimacing smile unconvinced the prime minister is performing poorly because she is a woman. 'She's never on top of her brief and it takes too long to get a decision from her office.' I supported her elevation to leadership, now I speculate if we made a mistake. 'I'll call her. I tried last night, but it went straight to message bank.'

'I wouldn't bother. She's on a plane and wants to see you at 10.30. I've asked Guy to ensure you get here on time. You weren't thinking of going elsewhere, were you?'

'No,' I razzed her, not sure what she was suggesting. 'Did you say she is flying down just to see me? Is she not seeing anyone else in Melbourne?' A morsel of anxiety crept in as she rarely left Canberra.

'Not sure about that, but I think you're her first engagement.'

'I wonder what she wants?'

'Ryan, she just needs reassurance. This issue is important to her. She just needs to know you have her back. She needs to know you'll do what she's asked and not make mistakes.'

'By mistakes you mean going against her by approving the bailout?'

'She needs to know you're with her, that's all.'

'We've spoken about this funding many times.' The prime minister micromanaged too often. 'I'm not sure I can support her any more than I already have. I keep reassuring her I'm going to do what she wants. She doesn't need to threaten me with a muzzle. Doesn't she trust me?'

'The latest poll numbers show she may be in trouble. The primary vote is down, and her preferred prime minister poll has blown out. You're in today's press, polling much better.'

'You're kidding, which poll?'

'Hancock Limited took a poll over the last few days. It seems you're the preferred prime minister by a very long way.'

'What page?'

'Front page, have you not read it?'

'No, it's here. I have a copy. I haven't looked at it. I thought I would ring you first.'

'Oh, aren't you nice?' Fiona sassed me with a sweet, girly voice. 'But you forget Minister, I rang you.'

'Yeah, well, I thought I could at the very least drive out of my street before clicking into political mode.' Is there no let up from people wanting things from me? 'What else have I got on today?'

'I've moved the union back until this afternoon. The PM wasn't flexible.'

'Have they confirmed who's coming?'

'Their national secretary Lionel Brereton and Michella Franklin, their on-site representative.'

I knew Michella. She worked with me when she first left university and we have been having regular social meetings over a coffee. 'We'd better get someone in from the department. Try to get Margaret Hodgeman. What else?'

'It seems we've had a breach of security within our email server. The federal police want to meet with you later this morning.'

'Did they identify what type of breach?'

'No, only that it's serious. They would prefer to talk to you rather than with the CIO.'

I gazed out the window at the passing traffic. 'Not sure what that means. Did they provide any clues?'

'Only they insisted on talking with you.'

'What time?'

'Eleven.'

'What time has Jo planned the press conference for the announcement?'

'She hasn't.' Fiona is my greatest asset, always reliable and across every detail. 'She's decided to wait until after your meeting with the PM to make sure there are no problems.'

'Probably a good move. What are your thoughts?'

'Have you decided what you are going to do?'

'I can't move against the PM. It would cost me my job.' I gently prodded my forehead. 'At this time in my life, I can't afford it.'

'You amaze me with how selfish you are sometimes,' Fiona snapped.

I couldn't believe what I just heard and duck-faced my lips. 'You what?'

'You're about to make a decision affecting twenty-five hundred workers and their families, and all you can think about is your own job?'

'It doesn't have to sound like that.'

'How should I make it sound?' Fiona was always up for a debate.

'It is more complicated than that.'

'I would hope so. Never forget why you're doing this, Ryan.'

'You know me better than anyone. You ought to know why I'm doing this.'

'Sometimes I wonder if your mind is fixed on other priorities with some of your recent behaviour. Speaking of which...' Oh no, not another opinion. 'I noticed there is a double booking for tonight, so I confirmed you at Wendy's dinner. Is that the most appropriate thing to do? You still have your dinner booked on Saturday with the other party.' She knew it wasn't appropriate.

I thought through the implications gnawing on my bottom lip. 'Have you let her know?'

'Nohoohoohoo. That honour should fall to you.'

'Don't sass me, Fiona. I'm not in the mood.'

'I suppose you know what you're doing, although I question your motives. You are making strange choices, Ryan.'

I scratched and rubbed the back of my head pausing for a moment. Surely, we could talk about something else. 'Do I have any free time this afternoon? Fraser wants to see me.'

'Nothing for lunch, although there are several requests. Given you've been away, I decided to keep your day open as much as possible to catch up with the issues that are around the place and maybe you can call local party people.'

She knew me and my needs after travelling and always planned space in my diary. I needed to refocus and think through politics and issues without the stress of performing elsewhere.

'You could squeeze sometime this afternoon, but remember we need to clear time for your Symonds' announcement.'

I sighed and rubbed my chest, feeling the burden of the day already bearing down on me. It seemed like no matter what I did to be co-operative, I couldn't please everyone. I just hoped I could find a way to make the right decision today and keep everything together.

'So, no time for me again. When do I get my life back?'

She scoffed. 'Depending on your decision you may have more time on your hands.'

'Hilarious.' She was cute sometimes when she joked with me. 'Have you had luck tracking down details for the history project?' I checked Guy in the rear vision mirror who seemed not to be paying attention.

I could hear Fiona sigh, followed by heavy, unimpressed breathing. 'Again, this is what I'm talking about, Ryan. I don't know what goes through your head sometimes.' Fiona didn't support my little history project and resisted requests to get on with it. 'But yes, I've had some luck.' I could feel her sarcasm dripping through the phone.

'What have you got?'

'A number.'

'You're kidding me.' I smiled broadly. 'How recent is it?'

'Confirmed as of yesterday. I'll give it to you when you get in.' She didn't sound enthusiastic. 'I really think you should focus on the PM today and not this flight of fancy back into your past.'

'I'll be the best judge of that.' I grinned. 'That's terrific news that you've been able to achieve that.'

'You are the industry minister. Evidently, for any reason, you can find information on anyone who is employed in Australia. It was a matter of making a few formal requests to the tax and welfare departments to match data. I've confirmed a contact number. I expect it's a work number.'

'A Melbourne number?'

'I presume it is,' she retorted.

'Amazing, thank you so much. I really appreciate it. That's great.'

'As I said, Minister, focus on the main game. These old memories you've been phaffing with over recent weeks should not be distracting you.'

'I'll take that as a comment, Fiona. See you when I get in.'

I studied my trembling hand, pumping fingers, balling them into a fist. The news of a telephone number shook me, literally. I could feel my chest tightening, shortening my breath.

'You okay, Minister?' Guy said, checking through the rear vision mirror. 'You look a little disturbed, bad news?'

'Quite the opposite, Guy, quite the opposite.'

My conversation with Fiona had left me on edge as I gnawed at a fisted knuckle, and I couldn't shake the feeling that something major was about to happen.

Nine

8:27 AM

I gazed out the window and watched as things passed and snorted a little, then sighed, when I realised it seemed a perfect metaphor for my life. Things pass me by, and I have little say.

I wonder if I could make simple decisions without the cold, bony hand of responsibility squeezing me. Deciding about the small things in my life again would bring me tremendous pleasure. Decisions like watching my son play basketball.

As I surveyed my surroundings, the realisation that I was a phony hit me like a ton of bricks. I had always preached honesty, integrity, and selflessness, but lately, I had been anything but. This feeling of self-loathing has grown inside me, and I grimaced as I looked around, seeing nothing that brought me joy or satisfaction. The thought of giving it all up, of ending everything, flashed through my mind like a lightning bolt. For a moment, I felt the weight of despair bear down on me, and my heart raced with the possibility of escape. But as quickly as the thought came, I shook my head, willing it away.

The squawk of my phone then startled me. I almost dropped it, fumbling to stop the noise. The screen displayed Larry Matthews. No doubt after something. 'Larry, what's up?'

'Hello to you, you pompous prick. Why does something have to be the matter?'

I rolled my eyes. 'Maybe when you call it always does.'

'Got time for a coffee? I need to talk to you.'

'What a surprise.'

'What's that supposed to mean?' Larry seemed offended. 'Geez, I'm only wanting to talk to you about your trip and other things you've discussed with me. I'm concerned enough to call you, and this is the crap you give a mate.'

I pinched the tip of my nose. 'Yes, well, it just seems you want something from me every time you call.'

'Well, if I don't call you, we would never talk.'

I couldn't help but feel a little frustrated, 'Why is it always about you, Larry?'

'Are you able to enjoy a coffee before you get to the office?'

I hesitated for a moment before responding, 'I need to be in early. Perhaps we can manage a quick one, same place?'

'Yeah, that'll be good. I'm already here. See you soon.'

'I'll be twenty minutes. See you.' I pushed the end-call. 'Guy, can we stop at the M Bar for a coffee before we hit the office?'

'Sure, we can do that.'

As we drove, I couldn't help but reflect on the irony of my life. It was my first decision of the day, and it seemed ironic that someone else made it happen. I'm a politician, and yet others seem to regularly dictate my schedule and the decisions I need to make. Everyone is at my beck and call, doing things for me, that's a given. But it's not as glamorous as it seems. It's a demanding job, always being *"on"* and never really having a moment for myself. I sometimes wonder if I would be happier if I weren't a politician. Who knows? It's just one of those unanswered questions I have been asking lately.

As I thought about meeting with Larry, I couldn't help but question if he was even a true friend. We go way back to our surfing days along the coast and getting mixed up with boyish shenanigans. We once spent six months together in Bali, carousing and surfing every day with an endless line of ladies seeking an exotic taste of the carefree Bali lifestyle.

Nowadays, it's fashionable to seek spiritual enlightenment in Bali. I blame the romantic novelists who go there searching for something missing in their lives, then write a book about their experiences. The book then attracts a whole group of disillusioned tourists seeking something different, like a spiritual awakening or an exotic romance. Who was I to deny them their experience?

Larry and I were low rent scoundrels during our days in Bali, but that was the life we wanted. We would surf all day and then go to clubs and bars at night, pretending to be whoever we wanted to be. Our fabricated stories of wild adventure and romance would captivate women of all ages and give them a holiday memory.

We provided our new friends a vacation I wager they still talk about, and we always treated them with respect. They guessed we were rogues, but they didn't seem to care. What a fantastic time for two young Aussie blokes like us. I recall just that one incident with the Swiss cousins that didn't end well; but more often than not, everyone had a great time.

Larry remains my only link to that carefree period of my life, and maybe that's why we still hang out together. Perhaps I just want to hold on to those memories. Do friends cling to each other to reminisce about the good old days? Maybe they do, I'm not sure. I just know I had a great time back then. What would this pain-in-the-arse life I now live be like without those memories?

And now the best thing about that carefree life is that Fiona, my magnificent Fiona, has provided the prospect for me to step right back and maybe relive it. She's given me a connection to my past, with a treasured telephone number. What awesome support Fiona provides for me. I must remember to pick up some flowers to thank her.

Larry wouldn't remember this because it happened over thirty years ago. One hot summer, I fell head over heels in love with the most beautiful woman I've ever met. I think about Selena and those romantic moments I shared with her more and more these days. I still fantasise about it, wondering what life would be like now if I had made different choices that summer.

The weird thing is, in all the years since that time, I've felt nothing like those emotions with anyone else, not even Wendy, which I'm uncomfortable to admit. I made the foolish choice not to get into her rickety, smoky van and lost everything and I have been regretting it since. For me, that summer was a wild emotional ride and I miss those feelings we shared.

I often think back to her cheerful brown face and broad, toothy smile. I cherish the memory of her frizzy hair with a flower I plucked wedged behind her ear. She closed the door and drove off in a cloud of smoke, never to be seen or spoken to again. It pains my soul to think about not jumping into her van when invited.

I wonder about her. What is she doing? I speculate if she ever thinks about me the way I think about her. Maybe joining her on her glorious adventure would have taken me to a different place, in a different life with very different outcomes. Instead, I listened to my father and helped build the family business. Now I look back with regret with maybe a tinge of anger about what happened after she left me.

Who knows? If I had jumped into the van, perhaps I would be happier than a pig in muck right now. But the company might not have survived, and it may have killed Dad earlier. My responsible decision to support my family meant ignoring my own youthful needs.

Mystical moments of the past can be haunting when you long for an easier life. That summer and my feelings still draw me back to what could have been, and I miss it.

Now I have her telephone number.

Selena was the most gregarious girl I ever met on my travels. On a February afternoon, watching mates work their magic on my surfboards changed my life forever. She emerged from the water like a Bond movie, wearing an O'Neil wet suit top with a six-foot gun under her arm. She hooked me then like the proverbial catch of the day.

'Man, I was jammin'. It was epic!' she shouted to her friends as she trotted up the beach. 'I'm so stoked.' She squealed and jumped a little. 'How good was that?' She dropped her board and another girl, who sounded French, passed her a towel to wipe her face.

I couldn't help myself, so-called over, 'Ya ripped good rads out there, girlfriend. Impressive.'

Selena glanced at me, a little miffed by the interjection. 'I ain't your girlfriend, moron.'

There wasn't much enthusiasm in her voice, so I knew straight away I needed to work harder. 'No moron here.' I then gave her my irresistible Kennedy smile. I could swear a glint sparkled from a tooth. 'And not yet you're not.'

She laughed and then looked out into the surf while she worked the towel through her hair. 'Why aren't you out there?'

'My quiver is.' I pointed to the waves.

'Your what?' she said, snorting. 'Man, you are such a moron.' Her intoxicating laugh knowing I was full of it drew me closer. 'Talk English, will ya?'

'My boards are out there. Take a look.' I pointed to the surf. 'The aerial guy on the red fish is mine.'

'Pfftt, he hogs waves. I don't like guys like that. Smart arse boy of privilege would be my guess.'

I wasn't sure Larry would have appreciated being called privileged, so I pointed to the surfer out the back of the break. 'And the tri-skeg retro, the green one, is mine as well.'

'Why aren't you on one of them?'

'It's a zoo out there.' I pointed to the young kids on the beach. 'Grommets are still on holidays, and they're everywhere, and anyway...' I tried never to waste my charm. 'You're here.'

'What's your name?'

'My mates call me Rat.'

The intoxicating laugh seduced me again. 'Why do they call you Rat?'

'My charming personality, I suppose.'

'Well, Rat, I'm feeling hungry. Do you want to buy me a burger?'

Her boldness flabbergasted me, but I went with it. 'Only if we get chips. Nothing better than tons of salty hot chips after a day in the waves. I know just the place.'

'Where're you staying?' She stood before me, hands on hips, almost as if she owned the beach.

'We're camping down the coast a way. Sociable campfire with plenty of JD, and a bag of candy, if that takes your fancy.'

She checked her friends who nodded. 'I could be in the mood after a great sess like that. Do you mind if my friends come?'

I scanned her friends and reckoned four chicks hooked up with three desperados could be the start of a great party. 'Sure, let's go eat. I'll get my boards in.'

Was it that easy to smooth talk the woman of my dreams?

Yeah, maybe not.

My memory has faded a little, and it might not have happened exactly like that. Maybe I even exaggerate a bit. I remember paying for the burger and chips, though. We sat by a fire for three nights.

We surfed massive waves over four days; and we fell in love, at least I did. She still is the girl of my dreams and has become central to the memories I've been missing. She and her friends were traveling the coast and begged me to come with them; *would've, could've, should've*, have been my stark reminders of not jumping in that damn love-shack.

Those summer memories remain my escape from my real world as a politician, husband, and father. My real world often forces me to do things that go against my values and character, causing me tremendous inner conflict. Being a politician especially means making decisions I don't always agree with. It's the constant compromise of being a minister in the government and it often demeans me, and I feel it deep down.

Fiona advises me to give up these memories from too long ago and focus on my job, but I can't. They comfort me when things get too hard, so I close my eyes and go to the beach, thinking of Selena. I don't want to give them up.

As I gazed at the passing streetscape, a sense of emptiness and regret washed over me. The desire for freedom from the shackles of my political career and the mistakes of my past consumed my thoughts. I couldn't help but think that the only way out was to give it all up. This idea of being a fraud weighs heavily on me, and I grimaced at the thought of my current situation.

And then, as if from nowhere, another suicidal thought flashed through my mind, causing me to shudder. But as quickly as it came, it passed, leaving me feeling more lost and hopeless than ever before with my gut roiling.

It was then that I realized I needed to make changes. My commitment to my career had come at the cost of my personal life, and I knew I had to address that if I ever wanted to have a shot at happiness and overcome my loneliness. As the thought of Selena crossed my mind, I couldn't help but acknowledge that I needed to express my true feelings to Wendy. It was a risk, but I knew deep down that it was the only way to move forward.

By confronting my past mistakes and acknowledging my need for change, I could finally find the freedom and happiness I had been searching for. I'm a minister, a politician, a husband and a father and these things should make me proud, but they tighten my chest. The anxiety and dread seem to disappear when I drift off to the beach.

Ten

8:41 AM

'Looks like it could rain, Minister.'

'What?' My lovely memory of the beach flashed by as reality struck.

'It could rain, sir.'

'I suspect it will only be a shower. Even if storm clouds open later.' I swiped and tapped my phone to get the details I wanted. The call answered almost immediately. 'Good morning, Madam Director. How is your morning?'

'Not as good as yours, darling. Have you seen the Hancock papers?'

'No, not yet.' I flipped over the paper to read the headlines. 'I've heard about them.' I smirked as I read the line about me being the preferred prime minister. 'I suspect they're being provocative. The PM is flying down to see me this morning.'

'Are you okay? What is she seeing you about?'

'I reckon it concerns my statement today. In fact, I'm sure it is.'

'Are you worried?'

'There is nothing I can do now to change her mind. She is the prime minister, after all. We'll take a hit in the polls. The media will make a story of it, they always do. At least we continue to be civil to each other and work together.'

'Is there anything I can do to help? I want to make sure you're okay.'

'I appreciate it, Rose. I truly do.'

'It was a shame you had to leave so early last night. It's always good to share quality time with you, if you know what I mean,' she purred into the phone, sparking my neck hairs to tickle. I rubbed the back of my neck.

'Oh well, I think I explained it to you. Family things to do.'

'I'm looking forward to having more time over dinner tonight.'

'That's proving to be problematic.' I felt uncomfortable as a rush of heat embraced me. 'My day is full, and I'm double booked for a function with Wendy tonight. A charity dinner.'

'Fuck Fiona, she knows not to do that,' Rosemary said, in that tone that sometimes scares me. 'She will do whatever it takes to finish us.'

'I don't think that's the case.' I again tried to soften her aggression. 'It's just a double booking. Saturday remains confirmed.'

'Do you have time today? There are several things I want to run past you.

'I thought you were in court all day?'

'I've had a judge call in with Covid, so they have moved my cases to another day. I want to see you. I need to see you,' Rosemary insisted.

'I will call you when I get to the office and check the diary. The PM is at 10.30, I think. We plan the statement for this afternoon, after I meet with the union.' I checked my nails as I paused for a moment to allow space for a change of topic. 'The Feds want to speak to me.'

'What about?'

'A breach of security. Someone has been in the email system.'

'Say what?' Her long pause washed anxiety over me. 'You deleted those photos I sent, didn't you, hon?'

'Sure.' I swallowed and then cleared my throat stumbling over my words. 'I delete everything you send me.'

'You don't sound certain.' I wasn't. 'I can't afford for them to get out. They were just fun things for you to look at and remind you of me.'

'I deleted them.'

'Look,' she snapped with a change of tone that shifted me in the seat. 'I want to see you today. I won't take no for an answer. Make time, or I will.'

'I'll see what I can do.'

'Do better than that, Ryan.' The line went dead, as Rosemary always does when making a point.

I dropped the phone to the seat feeling my heart race. It seemed like every time I try to focus on something, another call or message comes through, demanding my attention. I try to keep up, answering as many calls during my day as I can, but I still felt frustration mounting with each interruption and I'm still to get to the office. It's like a constant barrage of noise and demands, and I didn't know how much longer I can keep up the facade.

The most influential person in my life is my mentor, Rikki Alvarez. At our monthly coffee meetings, I haven't raised my anxieties with him. I feel embarrassed when I talk about my needs with him, but I reckon I need to talk to someone about these issues I struggle with. Maybe Rikki could offer a solution to my angst before it gets out of hand.

Our relationship started when I bowled into his crammed office to sell the benefits of Kennedy Transport. His business specialised in wholesale produce, operating a fleet of twenty-two trucks and vans. I pitched him the idea of contracting Kennedy's to transport his produce to retailers.

Initially, he remained hesitant and turned down my generous offer. But after a year or so of negotiation, plenty of beer and the occasional meal, he agreed to shift all transport logistics to us under a long-term subcontract agreement. It set Kennedy Transport up with significant revenue growth without altering our business model. Our deal allowed Alvarez to grow his profit, motivating him to expand into other wholesale categories, and eventually branch out into importing, invest in gold mining, and even buying gaming licenses at the ten-yearly auction.

Rikki became my business mentor after my father died, almost a father figure, offering me sound business and political advice on various issues. Although, now I sometimes question his advice, as I'm not sure if he gives it to me unbiased or if he promotes his own interests. I remain cautious around him when discussing policy to avoid any appearance of impropriety.

He remains a tough negotiator and although it assisted our companies, it was no simple relationship. He taught me the importance of providing value and I still use his negotiation tips. When he learned my family planned to sell our transport company, he submitted an offer we could not refuse. He had a unique caveat when negotiating, he wanted me to head up the Transport Industry Association which he chaired.

Funny how things work out.

After five years of rattling the cages of politicians, getting them excited about transport, protecting the nation's supply chains, and advocating for its importance to nation-building, the party approached me offering preselection for a safe seat. The rest, as they say, is history. I am now a minister who has never really had political ambition with a preferred prime minister rating higher than the PM. Strange how things work out.

Oh, and now I'm bonking his daughter.

'We're here, sir,' Guy said, pointing ahead. 'I'll wait in the loading zone just along the street.'

'Thanks, Guy. I won't be long. I'll find out what my friend wants and be back with you very soon.'

Eleven

8:50 AM

―――――――――――

Stepping into the M Bar, I couldn't help but feel a sense of enjoyment. The owner knew how to present a café that was popular with the city crowd, even in the pandemic's aftermath. They opened early for the slow breakfast trade, but also offered on-the-go food for busy folks with little time to enjoy life. Already it seemed busy with people chatting, drinking and eating. The combination of chunky framed mirrors and provocative artworks of naked abstract human forms helped the ambiance, plus the smooth, easy listening background music added the perfect touch to the sensory system. I felt comfortable for a moment as I ordered a latte and fruit toast, then looked around for Larry.

I spotted the big greying bloke perched in a back corner, hunched over a laptop, staring at the screen. A transactional sales agent without peer, always on the lookout for a deal to feed his gambling and alcohol habits. He relied on making daily sales.

'Lunch box?'

He glanced up and smiled. 'Gidday Rat, thanks for coming. Grab a seat.'

'You've got five minutes.'

'Christ, you're a wanker,' Larry said, shaking his head. 'Grab a seat and have a coffee, for fuck's sake.'

'I've already ordered. How can I help?'

'Mate, why do you assume I need help?' Larry said, tidying papers, then pushing them into a leather satchel. 'Is it possible to just have a coffee with a mate?'

I wasn't sure if Larry was really a friend. He calls me his best friend, but I don't really feel the same way. He has never really done anything for me I truly valued. He is high energy, needing a heap of attention, but I just don't feel the love he claimed he has for me. I'm still waiting for him to step up and support me when I need it. He offers to help with my local election campaigns, but never does. A headache can do that to you. Larry has given me more than a few headaches over our journey together.

'What's happening, brother? According to the media it seems your career has hit the stellar button.' He grinned and wobbled his head. 'This morning's papers have you as the next prime minister.'

I didn't want to get caught up in political conversation with him. 'Don't believe everything you read in the paper.'

'Why wouldn't you be happy about that news? It means you're in line for the top job when that dopey bastard gives it up. You'll then be the next drop-kick leading our country.' He laughed until he coughed. I couldn't help but smile as I watched the old bloke enjoying a good chuckle.

'Contrary to what you may think, being a politician is serious business.' I wanted to get things moving. 'We get enough crap from the whingers and whiners in the media and the cynical public as it is, without having to put up with the same crap from friends.' I rubbed my face and my eye as I grimaced.

'Hard day?'

I dropped my head and brushed my fingers through my hair

before straightening 'No, it's still early.' I shifted in my chair; it just seemed the negativity was never-ending. 'No one seems to appreciate the work we do. It's a national joke to shit-can politicians, and everyone gets a laugh out of it. It matters not that we politicians are required to make tough decisions which either help or hurt people.' I searched about for my coffee and toast. 'To be honest, mate, I'm sick of the angst having to justify myself, and I especially don't need my fucking friends to add to the stress.'

Larry gawked at me, leaning back in his chair, a mix of confusion and amusement as he frowned shaking his head. His once handsome features now ruined by alcohol and abuse, leaving him with a pudgy red face. 'Are you happy?' he asked.

I checked for the coffee again. 'Why do you ask?'

'You don't look happy.' He shook his head, as if in surprise. 'In fact, you look like a bloke who has the weight of the world on his shoulders and not an ounce of happiness inside of him.'

'What do you mean?' I shook my head, smirking rubbing the hair around an ear. It was feeling like a therapy session but Larry ain't no psychologist. 'What are you suggesting?'

'Mate, you just don't look happy. You're not your usual self. What's wrong?'

I gazed at him, screwing my face sinking my overbite into my lip trying to figure out how to respond. 'Oh, I don't know Larry. It just feels like it's all too much for me.'

'What is? The job?'

I blew out a sigh as I rested my chin on my fingers. 'No, it's not the job, I actually enjoy it. Although maybe not today.'

'What's happening today?'

'I have to make a statement about Symonds.'

'Haven't they already announced their willingness to retool to build an aeronautics business?'

I nodded a squint. 'They have the support of the German government as their first client.'

'So, what's the problem?'

'They want two and a half billion dollars.'

'And so, the problem is?'

'The PM is under extreme political pressure to say no.' I smirked wondering if the big fella even understood any of this exchange.

'Who from? The banks?'

'Nuh, the Chinese.'

'Why would the China want to stop us building an industry in Australia? Christ, since Hawkie they have captured most of our manufacturing. They stole our clothing and textiles and took our cars. Do they want us to starve?'

'Since we signed the free trade agreement, they have considerable policy input into what we can do.'

'Why should we follow what they want us to do?'

I raised an eyebrow at Larry's question as I shook my head. 'They take our iron ore, coal, and gas. Without China, our economy would tank, and then we lose our standard of living. We could not withstand the downward adjustment. My reality today is this: we must keep China happy. If we want to keep our schools and hospitals operating, I have to lay-off twenty-five hundred jobs.'

'That seems like a bit of a stretch.'

'It's what the prime minister wants me to do.'

'Crumbs, that's tough, mate. Why do you have to do that?'

'I'm the industry minister. Lewis wants me to protect her position as prime minister.' I searched again for the waiter, now approaching with my order. 'So, if her leadership rival, according to the media, kills Australian jobs, he also kills his leadership aspirations.'

'What happens if you refuse to do what she says?'

'Not sure, but it won't be good for my career.'

Larry leaned forward with a chortle, his thick neck jiggling. 'Well, I take it back. You do have a few challenges.'

I gazed over the rim of my glass and sipped the coffee. It was good. 'Yeah, so that's my day. How's yours looking?' I plastered soft butter on my toast, taking a bite, not caring about his answer.

'Oh, I have a few deals to be done this afternoon. Still try to scratch a living. How's Wendy and the kids?'

'Good, I suppose.'

'What do you mean, you suppose; what's happened?' His cynicism was getting on my nerves.

'Oh, I don't know. I just seem to feel restless and it's not the same with her anymore.'

'You've been complaining about that for years. What's changed?'

'I just don't feel good anymore. It's just not giving me what I need.'

Larry raised an eyebrow. 'Well mate, maybe it's time you figure that out. What do you need?'

An excellent question and I studied him as I chewed on a piece of toast. 'That's just it, my friend. I just don't know.' I sipped my coffee before turning away checking to see if anyone could be listening.

'She's done an incredible job with the kids. They're terrific,' Larry said.

'I didn't have a hand in that?'

He studied me as I stuffed more toast into my mouth and took another sip of coffee. I tried to avoid looking at him.

'Still banging the lawyer?'

'Ease up, Larry.'

'You're crazy if you think she's the answer.'

'She gives me what I want.'

'Which is what, besides a regular screw?' Larry said with a little snigger. 'You can get the same anytime from a takeaway store, and it's cheaper. Plus, mate, there is no ongoing stress. They all love you no matter how you perform, and they don't talk back.'

'That's a little unfair.' I felt his comment a touch ironic, as I probably was thinking the same years ago. 'We're making plans... well she is.' I smirked at my comment.

'You're kidding me, mate. She only sticking around because of what you are, not who you are.'

I shook my head. 'You wouldn't know.'

Was he right? He's known me the longest. Maybe he is right. I don't know. Maybe there's some truth in what he's saying. It's all very confusing. I scooped froth with my spoon, avoiding his glare.

'Mate, you have way too much invested in your family and I'm not just talking about money. You have a long history together. You can't just give it up so you can get your rocks off with some bimbo for a few years. It'll cost you a fortune. You don't think Wends will take you to the cleaners? And the kids will side with her. You know they will,' Larry said, leaning forward.

'It won't be that bad.' I tried reassuring him, and probably myself.

'You're kidding yourself. What does Rikki think about all this?'

'I doubt he knows.'

'You're kidding. He will literally kill you if he finds out you've been screwing his daughter, or at the very least cut your gonads off,' Larry said, as he broadened his grin shaking his head. 'You're fucking crazy, man.'

'No one knows.'

'You can't be screwing a woman for two years with no one knowing.'

I scoffed as I looked down into my coffee, then glanced up at him. 'It's been five.'

Larry fell back into his chair, glancing around the café. 'You're kidding me? When did this start? You dirty, sly bastard, Rat.'

'At a conference in Madrid. She was an adviser with the European Parliament, and we bumped into each other.' I grinned. 'How can anyone else know if you don't?'

'You sneaky dog.' Larry chuckled, then frowned. 'Trust me, though. This is something you shouldn't be doing.'

'Maybe you're right, but it just keeps me from thinking about the nightmare at home.'

'You had the chance to give Wendy up early, so why didn't you?' Larry asked.

'Oh, I don't know. Maybe it was just easier for me to keep doing what I was doing.'

'You're a wanker, mate, truly,' Larry said, shaking his head. He had my best interests at heart, I suppose. 'You have a life most folks would kill for. A beautiful wife, fantastic kids, and a job which transforms you into a media rockstar, and apparently, you're likely to be the next prime minister, and still, you're not happy?'

I took a deep breath and let it out slowly, trying to calm my nerves. 'To be honest mate, I don't really want to talk about it. It's just...complicated, you know?'

'What do you think the lawyer will give you?'

'I don't know.' I really needed the conversation to end and shifted in my chair avoiding his gaze. 'It has to be better than what I already have.'

'You want more kids?'

'No, she doesn't want any. She is too invested in her career to want kids.'

'Have the snip then. I bet she won't let you,' Larry said.

'I don't have to do that; she's already said she doesn't want any.'

'And like a fool you trust her.' Larry tossed his hands in the air before leaning in closer. 'Mate, she doesn't want you. She wants what Wendy has. Which means you continuing to do what you

71

already hate. Starting over again providing her with a house and family.'

'I'm not so sure about that.'

'Ask her. I bet she says she wants it all.'

'How do I ask her? She'll deny it. She's a prosecutor, after all.'

'Tell her you're going to get the snip,' Larry said, with a smile. 'Better yet, tell her you're about to get the sack, then watch her reaction. I bet she goes ballistic.'

'She's not like that.'

'They're all like that, Ryan, and you know it. We've known that since we were kids.'

The coffee was perfect. I rebuffed Larry's jaundiced view, given his two divorces and ongoing alimony challenges. 'Speaking of our wayward days, do you remember Selena? The girl we met down the coast... you fell in love with her kinky French friend.'

'I need more information.'

'We were with them for a few days down south. Your girl was a hippy.'

'Vaguely. The memory is hazy these days. Sometimes I wonder if we actually did do half the things we say we did,' Larry said, smirking.

'Mate, you will remember Selena and her friends. We had an awesome time together one February about thirty something years ago. I may have mentioned her once or twice since then.'

'What, the Polynesian girl?'

'Yes, now you've getting it.' I smiled and glanced away.

'The girl you've been wet dreaming over since we were lads?'

'Yes, her.'

'I vaguely remember her friend, but not her,' Larry said. 'We were a bit out of it those days.'

'I've found her.'

'What do you mean you've found her?'

'I have her number.' I straightened with a broad smile.

'Wait up,' Larry gestured with his hand. 'After thirty-plus years of pining over a mystical Fijian, you now have her phone number?' He flopped back in his chair. 'Tell me you aren't thinking about contacting her?'

'I'm calling her this morning.'

'Why, you stupid bastard?' He tossed his hands onto his head.

'Because I want to see her.'

'You're the most irresponsible person I know. As if your life isn't complex enough.' Larry dropped his head, shaking it. 'You have a beautiful family. An occasional screw who is the daughter of your patron. Now you want to explore a relationship which never existed thirty years ago. You're fucking crazy, man.' He circled his finger about his ear. 'Insane.'

'I can't explain it. It's important to me. I've been thinking about her for a long time.'

'You remember the acres of diamonds story don't you, Ryan?'

'No, let the brilliant salesman tell me a parable.'

'Don't get snarky, my friend.'

'Sorry, go ahead.' I crossed my arms and leaned back in the chair.

'The acres of diamonds story is about a farmer in South Africa who had a fertile, high producing cattle ranch but could not get ahead financially. He'd heard stories of the great riches others achieved by searching and finding diamonds in the wilderness. So, he sold up everything and left the farm to prospect for his fortune. After many years of toil and nearly losing all his money, he came back to his old town much poorer than when he first left. And do you know what he found?'

'No Larry, what did he find?' I checked my phone.

'Don't be a smart arse.'

'Sorry, please, go ahead. What did he find?'

'His farm was now a rich diamond mine, and the manager

advised him they found acres of diamonds. The moral to this story, Ryan, my old friend is this... work your own farm before going to look elsewhere.'

'I'm not sure I want my current farm.'

'Madness,' Larry said, shaking his head.

I checked my watch and tapped it. 'So, what do you need?'

Larry seemed uncomfortable as he shifted in his chair. 'I have some financial troubles, serious troubles. I need four grand today to solve them.'

'What have you done?'

'Not much, suffice to say someone wants his money back. Otherwise, I'm going to be seriously manhandled.'

'What do you need?'

'I need two grand. The other two are already covered. I need it this afternoon,' Larry said, sounding desperate as he wiped his upper lip.

'When do I get it back? I don't want to chase you for it, not like last time.'

'I can get it to you in two weeks.'

'I'm not a bank and frankly, I'm tired of helping you out whenever you get into trouble.'

'Ryan, we're mates, and this is what mates do for each other.'

'Mates? What have you ever done for me?'

'Don't be like that. This will help me out,' Larry said, staring at me, his face twisted. 'Don't make me beg for it.'

'I just love the fact you think I have money stashed away whenever you fall on hard times.'

'You're my last resort.' He said, steepling his fingers in front of his face. 'And anyhow, you owe me.'

'Owe you?' I was more than a little surprised. 'How do you think for one moment I owe you anything?'

'I took you to the pool party when you met Wendy. Now look at you.' He opened his arms as if he was preaching. 'Mate, despite what you reckon, she has been good for you. She kept you on the straight and narrow.'

'I'm not sure I should be in your everlasting debt.'

'Come on, Ryan, I need your help. Will you help me?'

'I just wonder when I get the help I need from my friends?'

'What do you want?' Larry seemed prepared to get me whatever I wanted. Trouble is he had nothing I wanted. 'Let me know what I can do for you.'

Taking down the last of my coffee, I wiped my hands and tapped my mouth with the paper serviette, stood ready to walk from the table. 'Stop asking for favours would be a good start.'

'Are you going to help me?'

'I should have something for you this afternoon. I'll text you.'

'Thanks Ryan, I appreciate it,' Larry called after me.

I was already gone.

'I'm sure you do Larry, I'm sure you do. Just like everyone else.'

Twelve

M y office foyer is a far cry from the grand reception areas of other ministers. There was no impressive reception or imposing corporate decor, just a simple coat of arms decal on the back wall. As the deputy prime minister, I didn't expect any special treatment. In fact, my team preferred it this way. We were all on equal footing, and I regarded my staff as my most valuable asset. They were the backbone of my success, and I encouraged them to speak their minds freely, without fear of retribution, plus I made sure they could go home at a decent hour each night hoping they turn up the next day.

Fiona was the standout member of the team, my right-hand woman. Her work caught the attention of other politicians, who offered her lucrative positions in their offices, even that of the prime minister. But she made a commitment to me when promoted to the front bench, and I intended to return that loyalty. I knew I could trust Fiona completely; she knew everything about me, and I was confident she would share none of my secrets. In return, I made sure the department rewarded her for the dedicated work. I also provided her with the emotional support she needed during her tough times at home. She was a reliable ally who always had my back.

'Minister, I've received an update from the PM's office. She is now seeing you at ten. It's confirmed she will come here for the meeting. It seems easier that way, apparently. I also confirmed the union meeting at four o'clock. You'll have to decide when and how to handle the media conference. Do we do it after the union?' I winced as I considered the options. 'Do you need anything before the meeting?'

'Have you got the phone number?'

'I've had second thoughts about giving it to you.' A second woman this morning standing defiantly before me. 'Don't dive into that murky water you want to play in. Perhaps you might consider playing your games later this week. You need to remain focused on today's announcement.'

'You're probably right, but give it to me, anyway.' I held out my hand, waving my fingers. 'Please.'

'I hope you know what you're doing.' She tossed a crumpled sheet of paper on the desk.

'Can you ask Joanne to step in? I'm gonna need speaking points for the media. I better see Jordan as well to go over strategy for tomorrow.'

'Can I get you anything? Do you need a coffee or a tea?'

'Actually, I do need something,' I leaned back in my chair. 'I'm not sure how best to handle it.'

'What do you need?'

'I need two thousand dollars in cash.' Fiona made a few notes. 'I think a bank cheque will suffice, but it needs to be made out to cash.'

'Not sure the banks deal in cash anymore. Modern technology has made it irrelevant. I'll give the local branch a call and ask if they can help us.'

'It would be better to have notes. I just need twenty hundred-dollar bills rather than a bundle of smaller notes. Will you need my cards?'

'I had better take them, just in case. Why do you need the money?'

'A friend has an urgent need.'

'I'm not convinced Mr Matthews is the right friend to have around you at the moment, especially given today's media reports about your leadership ambition.' I smiled and screwed my face into a *What can I do?* expression. She was an excellent judge of character and always seemed right about most things. 'If you're linked to anything dodgy, the media will come hard against you.'

'Hence the reason for cash.' I passed her my credit cards. 'Let me know when you have it. When the others arrive, send them in. Thanks Fiona.' I watched as she retreated after taking a final note. 'Oh, how's your mother?'

Fiona turned and smiled, seeming thankful for the question. 'She came home the other day, and she's moving about, which is great. She's looking good.'

'Good news. That must be an enormous relief?'

'Yeah, she'll be fine,' Fiona said. 'I'll go get the others now.' She left the room.

With the crumpled note in hand, I carefully smoothed it out, tracing the elegant handwriting with a finger. Selena Tatupo, her name written with a flourish, and her phone number, 7555 9484, right before me. Folding the paper twice, I slipped it into my shirt pocket, patting it gently as I imagined what was to come.

My thoughts drifted to Selena, and the excitement of finally being able to reach out to her after years of nostalgia. I couldn't help but grin, drumming my fingers on the desk as I imagined the possibilities. While my mind raced with the prospect of a rekindled relationship, I glanced out over the city skyline towards the bay suburb where my wife may still lay asleep, oblivious to my plans. With one hand still on my chest, I let out a small sigh and turned back to the work that lay ahead.

'Hi boss, you wanted to see us?' Jordan and Joanne walked in, interrupting my musing.

'I have the PM in fifteen minutes. What should I tell her?' I gestured them to sit.

'You know my opinion. I think we should invest the money and save the jobs.'

'Jordan, I can't do that, you know it. The PM won't approve it, especially since the Germans made negative statements about the government's process.' My staff seemed disappointed but not surprised by my response. They knew I was wrapped tight in the prime minister's power grip.

'You know it's the right thing to do, boss. Cabinet have already approved the money. Why not do what they want and go for it?'

I liked Jordan. He was such a hipster but without the beard, with a massive opinion on most things in life, often conflicting with mine. But that's what I liked about him. He challenged me to think outside my comfort zone, and kept me on edge, thinking through issues one more time to ensure I remained on track.

Joanne gazed at me for a moment, then weighed in on the discussion. 'I recommend you play your cards close to your chest, Minister. Wait and see what the prime minister is thinking.' I valued Jo's differing view. 'She'll want an outcome that positions her high above all this mess. She'll want you to take responsibility for any hit in the polls, weakening any thought of an immediate challenge.'

The corners of my mouth dropped. 'I'm not thinking of a leadership challenge... or am I?' They didn't respond, their faces telling me nothing.

'What will happen if you change your mind and save the jobs?' Jordan asked.

'I lose my job, and no doubt so will you.' I tried nibbling an irritating piece of nail from my thumb.

'Hmm, let me think.' Jordan said, beginning to sass me. Just add him to the list of folks who have a go at me. 'Two jobs versus two and half thousand jobs. What a dilemma. What do you think, Jo?'

I glanced over at her. 'Yes Joanne, what would you recommend?'

'I would do as the prime minister wants you to do. If she says cut them loose, then cut them loose.' This is what I like about her; always prepared to speak her mind, delivering advice with confidence.

'That's crap,' Jordan said, shaking his head and glancing at Joanne as if she just farted. 'Since when do we do what Lewis wants?'

I gawked at him and smiled, shaking my head. 'Well, young man, she is the prime minister. She wants me to deliver a positive result for the government. Which paradoxically, is her decision.'

'Why doesn't she do it then?' Jordan snapped.

'Whilst she's prime minister, I do what I'm told.'

'You have numbers in the party room. She knows it,' Jordon said. 'That's why she's forcing you to make this announcement.'

'Wait up?' I shifted in my seat frowning and wincing, leaning forward. 'What's this decision today got to do with my numbers?'

Jordan crossed his legs and relaxed back in the chair as if talking to his professor. 'If you force the sacking of the workforce today, you'll lose some of your supporters in the party room. It may just be a tad too difficult for you to recover.' This now added an extra dimension to the decision. According to Jordan if I do what I'm told by the PM, I will lose my crucial support in the party room. 'In my view, you should ignore the PM and do the right thing by the workers.'

'Which is?'

'Do the deal and keep the workforce employed.'

'Minister, the right thing for you is to do what the government wants,' Joanne interrupted. 'It's not possible for you to go rogue on this issue. The PM and your colleagues will misrepresent you if you do, and your leadership ambition is punctured. There will be even more potential votes lost if you go against her. It's a no brainer on this. Give the PM what she wants.'

'I have a meeting with the union this afternoon. I'm going to advise them of the government's plans. Then I'll do the media to announce the government's decision. Can you prepare some speaking notes and perhaps a brief speech for me?' Joanne nodded as she took notes. 'Maybe we can organise a live cross and break into the television news broadcasts.'

'That'll mean an after six o'clock media conference. Are you happy with that?'

'I'm scheduled for a dinner tonight with Wendy. We can do this media conference before I leave. Can you arrange the press room, please Joanne? Jordan, can you attend the union meeting?'

'Whatever you say, boss,' Jordan said, his energy now seemed flattened.

'Okay, Joanne get a speech and notes done before two.'

'Sure, just let me know the key messages she wants to put out to the community.'

'What are the chances of the PM changing her mind?' Jordan asked.

'I doubt there'll be any chance of that happening.' A thought crashed through my mind. 'Well... not while the company and the Germans continue to want her to throw taxpayer money into the project.'

Jordan shook his head. 'She's gutless. This shouldn't be happening.'

'The prime minister is not gutless.' I smirked at my disappointed staffer. 'It takes courage to say no.'

'This is not courageous. It's sad that we have a PM more interested in polls than good policy.'

His statement stopped everyone in their tracks for a few moments. We glanced at each other not wanting to respond. Perhaps he was right.

I broke to silence by standing. 'Right folks, thank you. I appreciate the work you're doing. This is a tough announcement we're going to have to make. I know it must be hard on you, but let's stay focused.'

As they stood to leave, Jordan lingered to share a quiet word and as Jo left, he said, 'Why do you keep me here if you don't want to follow my advice?'

'You're here because I need you here. I rely on you, Jordie, and I appreciate the passion you have for your opinion.'

'But you always do what others tell you and never follow your head or heart on what you want to do.' He moved away. 'You know it's the right decision to save those jobs. You have the ongoing commitment from the Germans, so why not grow some balls and do it?'

If he wasn't a valued adviser, there would have been a sharper response from me. 'I'm doing what's best for Lewis. My job is to be her loyal deputy.'

'Your job is to serve your constituents and your country, and you aren't doing that very well at the moment.'

'Jordan, everything will be okay. Trust me.'

'I do trust you, boss, but I just wonder where your head is sometimes. The government needs you to make tough decisions if we're going to win the next election. You need to step up and show leadership on these many challenges in cabinet and take a strong stand for us,' he said, his words hitting me like a punch in the gut.

I gazed at yet another person standing before me, telling me what I needed to do, and I wondered if this was as good as it gets. 'I'll see you this afternoon.'

'Let me know the outcome of your meeting with the PM.'

'As always you'll be my first call.'

'Sure boss, of course.' Jordan smiled and moved off.

I swung back to the window and gazed out over the city, my mind racing with doubts and insecurities. Jordan's words echoed in my head, questioning whether I was true to myself. Was I really the leader of my own life, or was I just an appeaser, suppressing my own views to please others?

As I pondered these thoughts, I couldn't help but wonder: what was wrong with me? Was I really the servant to others around me, doing their bidding and neglecting my own needs? Larry has me running errands for him, Fiona is constantly cautioning me against doing anything foolish, and my family all have their own expectations of me. I felt like I was being pulled in a million different directions, and it was no wonder that I was feeling so unsettled.

I stepped closer to the window, dropping my forehead against the glass with a thud that echoed through the room. The chill of the glass against my skin made me quiver, but I pressed my head harder against it, trying to make sense of my jumbled thoughts.

Who was I, really? I had everything I could want, but still felt like something was missing. Maybe it was time for me to take control of my own life and start making decisions based on what I truly wanted, instead of trying to please everyone else. And maybe it was time to let go of the past and the things I never had and focus instead on building a better future for myself.

But even as these thoughts ran through my mind, I couldn't shake the feeling of uncertainty that plagued me. Who was I, really? And did I have what it takes to find out?

Fiona was at the door. 'The PM's waiting. Are you okay?' Fiona's concern for me etched into her face as she stood at the door. My mind was still reeling from earlier thoughts, and I hesitated, unsure how to respond. Was I really okay? Did I even know what that meant anymore?

As she stepped away, back to her desk, I felt a sudden impulse. I needed to do something for myself, something that would give me a moment of clarity amidst the chaos of my life. Without thinking, I snatched up the telephone handset and unwrapped the note from my pocket. The number scrawled across it beckoned to me, daring me to make the call. I punched in the digits, my fingers shaking with a mix of nervousness and excitement. It was as if I was transported back to a younger, more reckless version of myself, a time when calling a girl seemed like the most important thing in the world. I wiped a clammy palm on my trousers and waited anxiously for the connection to go through, wondering if Selena would even remember me after all these years.

'Good morning, Selena speaking. How can I help?' The voice on the other end sounded soft and velvety like chocolate, smooth and rich, taking me straight back to the beach. 'Hello?'

But then I dithered, second-guessing my choice to call. I quickly put the telephone back in the cradle, collected my briefing notes and began the trek to the meeting room and the waiting formidable prime minister.

Thirteen

———————

P rime Minister Freya Lewis sat at the polished jarrah table, head bent low over briefing papers as Fiona and I took our seats opposite. I nodded to the chief of staff on her right, casting a quick glance at the new policy wonk on her left. A chill in the air seemed obvious and had nothing to do with the air conditioning of the windowless office. Politics can be brutal, almost animalistic in the way colleagues treat each other, and it was no secret that Lewis had never cared for me. She considered me a rival and was forced to accept me has her deputy. She assumed I had an ambition to replace her rather than support her and each dialogue we have is always tense. I could almost smell her anger as I sat back and swivelled in my chair, flicking open my trusty leather folder and switching my phone to silent then tapping my chest through the phone note to my heart.

Fiona leaned in, scribbling a quick note, and sliding it across:
Let her get all her issues out first, including today's polling.
It seemed like sound advice. We sat in silence as Lewis tried to

assert power over me by not responding, and I must admit, she was doing a good job with her icy silence.

Her hair now shorter than the last time we met, styled in a very short, masculine cut. She dressed in a power suit, the only thing missing was a silk tie. She wore no makeup and little jewellery, just a gold band on a middle finger. I assumed the papers in front of her were related to the policy issues she needed to address, but for all I knew, they could have been the lunch menu from a local cafe.

So, we waited.

'How was your trip?' She didn't look up.

'A little tiring, Prime Minister. You, more than anyone, would know that.'

'Who did you see in Germany?' she asked, even though she probably already knew the answer from her department. Such is the dance of power politics.

'I met briefly with the Chancellor. She urged me to ratify the deal with Symonds. She reassured me of her government's commitment to procuring product from them if the deal could be done.' No response came from her. Her staff took notes as the silence lingered like a shroud. 'She says hello, by the way.' I smiled, hoping to get a reaction.

'What would you have expected her to say?' she said, continuing to read her notes.

'I take her at face value. She seemed sincere.'

'She's a two-faced bitch.' Lewis spat out, fixing me with her celebrated withering stare. 'She will no sooner throw me under a bus than do a deal with me.'

'But she is not doing a deal with you, Prime Minister.'

'She wants me to give two and a half billion to a German company,' she countered, not breaking her stare. 'She will say anything to coax me to guarantee the investment. It doesn't mean she will buy their drones.' The policy wonk passed her a note, which she quickly checked. 'What has the company said?'

'They will close all operations before Christmas and the Melbourne site immediately. I expect they'll ensure they do it in December, causing as much political grief for us as possible.'

'How many people will be affected?'

'Last count it was two thousand, five hundred and forty-three at the Melbourne site.'

'What do you want to do?' Lewis said, glancing back at her notes.

'Prime Minister, this is your call.' I followed Fiona's advice.

After a few moments, Lewis closed her briefing folder and glanced up with a death stare that had me immediately on the defensive. 'You slimy little toad,' she snarled, crossing her arms.

'Freya, you're better than that.' I tried placating her, with a raised peaceful hand.

'Who leaked today's story to the fucking papers?' Her stare had not shifted from my and I took in deep breath.

'What story?'

'The one online from Hancock media, suggesting I directed you to sack the entire Symonds workforce.'

'Not sure what you're talking about.'

'Did you push Hancock to do a preferred prime minister survey?'

'Of course not.' I shook my head. 'I've been in Germany for the last week.'

'I suppose you think you benefit from a leadership story in this morning's papers. Quite the political beauty queen, aren't you?'

'Wrong gender.' I've always used humour as a disarming, charming device to smooth over touchy situations. Maybe that's where Fraser gets it from. But just like him, I wasn't sure my timing was working this morning, so I smiled.

'You know what I mean. You're such a celebrity, both you and your wife are store-bought.

'Ease up, Freya.' I shifted in my seat and caught the corner on my bottom lip with my teeth.

'Like a fucking show pony. So neat and tidy and ready with a toothy grin and political comment on television. A regular on FM radio talking to the hipsters with your wisecracks about politics, such a funny bastard. Never out of the social pages. This is the reason the party will never elect you as leader. You live your life like a rat with a gold tooth.'

'Anything else?' Fiona may have been mistaken about this let-her-speak strategy.

'I know you've been working the numbers to get my job for months.'

'That is a complete fantasy.' I knew my staff hadn't been, but I wasn't sure about my colleagues.

'You have another think coming if you reckon you'll nail me with this German fiasco.'

'Well, Prime Minister, give them the money and save the jobs.' I assumed what her response would be.

'You know that can't happen. Did you tell the Germans that?' She paused for a moment, staring at me, drilling through to the back of my skull. 'I bet you didn't.'

I breathed deep as I nodded looking around the room then leaning into the table to face her, jaw and lips taut. 'Your mates in the union will not be thrilled.'

'Why should I worry about them?' Lewis lay back in her chair, pushing it away from the table crossing her legs, confident and in control, arms crossed over her chest.

'They influence caucus and control your support base.'

'So, what?'

'What happens when we decide to end all outstanding government contracts with the company? They'll close all their operations in Australia, which means five other sites. The union will then come after you. What will you do then?'

Lewis ignored me and grinned. 'Caucus didn't vote for you in the last ballot. They won't vote for you next time. They know intellectually you're as deep as a thimble. Your policy work across all portfolios is weaker and more elastic than a rubber band.' She always took the argument to a personal level, every time. 'They can't trust your word. In fact, no one can, can they, Ryan?' She looked at me like she knew something that I didn't.

'What do you mean?'

'How's the family, Ryan?' she drawled in her vicious, sinister tone.

'They're good.' I gulped, hoping it wasn't obvious, my tongue licking my lips. 'How's yours?' I mocked her knowing she had none, trying to deflect the conversation. She glanced away, as if knowing the discussion was getting too personal.

'Take me through your plans,' she said, abruptly switching the focus back to business.

And just like a burst balloon, we were back cooperating in a discussion on the biggest policy decision facing the nation since the collapse of the Asian money markets. The closing of Symonds' manufacturing was a topic of discussion among most political commentators and politicians of all parties and persuasions, especially the independents who were very negative toward the government's management of the decision. They used every media opportunity to express their thoughts on the matter and it seemed most nights, on all channels, a negative government story tied to the policy drove the news cycle.

For over fifty years, Symonds manufactured in the Australian market, but their decision to withdraw, whilst expected, had proven to be political kryptonite. Cabinet voted me the authority to decide whether to assist the technology company, specialising in IT systems for heavy duty motors and manufacturing trucks. The Opposition party encouraged populist rhetoric about saving Australian jobs, and the media, sensing the potential for a change of government at the next election, had been happy to flay us.

In negotiations with their technical senior executives, we advocated they diversify resources into the growing aeronautics industry and encouraged them to research the unmanned drones' market as a cheaper alternative for unmanned strike fighters. It was figured new technology could be a game-changer to warfare, allowing greater first strike options. The Australian government wanted the company to remain and develop the new industry, but in order to consider staying in Australia, the company wanted two and half billion dollars funded over ten years.

Lewis sided with China, arguing the region would not welcome the intrusion of a new era armed air fleet. Her plan was to reallocate the proposed money into social welfare policies, especially focusing on the hot topic of domestic violence against children.

The government had a straightforward choice: save existing jobs or redirect spending into vital social services. Jobs or a social welfare program, some choice.

The juicy political battleground in front of the media had two senior politicians facing off. A prime minister who endorsed social issues to dominate political discourse and with that the government's policy agenda, versus an industry minister, her deputy, who preferred to save Australian jobs, the best social welfare program of all.

The prime minister's demeanor didn't show signs of weakening as I struggled to explain what I wanted to achieve. She would have nothing of it and seemed focused on the no funding option. I just wanted it all to end and maybe it was my recent travel, but it seemed my energy was waning. It was clear my role was to remain loyal to the PM and increase her favorability in the polls. Frankly, right now, I would rather be surfing.

'A meeting with the union is scheduled at four to advise them of the government's decision. I then have a media conference planned for a little after six, with live crosses into news programs. I can then do the early morning media unless you want to do it.' Lewis shook her head, typically ducking responsibility. 'I then have a scheduled luncheon with the Business Council where I'll make further announcements about the new direction for government industry policy which you may recall was agreed at the last cabinet meeting.

Lewis tilted her head, the light casting shadows on her face. 'What say you, Kennedy? What path do we take with this decision?'

'I think we should save the jobs.' It just blurted it out with little thought.

Fiona coughed, and I glanced at her. I got nothing from her, making me shift in my chair which moved on its castors. Maybe I surprised her.

'We don't have the recurrent expenditure to sustain it.'

'Yes, we do Prime Minister. We can adjust funds through the annualisation of specific defence revenues and reallocate them to the defence industry portfolio. This allows us to invest capital to establish a substantial aeronautical industry capable of developing defence equipment for countries in our region.'

'China has vetoed the idea.'

'Why should they have a say in our decisions? This decision has nothing to do with Beijing. We are a sovereign government, with loyalties to no-one.'

'This is the reason you will never be the leader of the party, Ryan. You're too dangerous in foreign policy.'

I leaned forward. 'Prime Minister, why don't you explain to me why the Chinese will care if we recalibrate our outdated heavy vehicle industry into a defence aeronautics industry?'

'Who do you think they're concerned about in the region?' Lewis asked, her tone that of a schoolteacher leading a failing student.

'Obviously, the Americans, possibly the Japanese and the Russians to the north.'

'What about their interests in the South China Sea?'

'They've established bases for the last decade. I'm sure they're not threatened by anyone.'

'What about the Indonesians?' Lewis' voice was low, almost a whisper.

'Why should they worry about Indonesia? They don't have the military might to take on China and have little interest in expanding their territories.'

She seemed to enjoy her questions, as if playing some sort of intellectual game, trying to expose me as a fraud. 'If Indonesia had long-range bombers, what would happen in Beijing?'

'Maybe they would be a little concerned, but no more than we would be to the same threat.' My mind grappled with her line of enquiry try to understand where she was going.

'And who can supply Indonesia with these long-range weapons of destruction? A strike force capable of posing a significant threat to China.' She leaned forward, her eyes locked on mine.

'We wouldn't.'

'Of course not, but would the Germans?'

'The Germans, why would they? They have no connection to Indonesia.'

'To recoup their costs from investing with Symonds?'

I didn't believe such a proposition could be treated seriously. 'The Germans would never get involved in East Asia politics again. They have no relationship with Indonesia.'

'Huh, do you think so?' she asked, her voice rising.

'You know China and Germany share resources such as oil and

gas. China now manufactures German cars for the European market. It seems unlikely Germany would risk all that by selling strike fighters to Indonesia and threatening their economic relationship with the biggest market in the world.'

'Yes, but I do wonder about the Germans and their ambitious chancellor,' she said, leaning back, a sly smile on her lips.

It was an amusing idea but intellectually stupid. 'Do you think China beating Germany in the world cup pissed them off?'

'Is that supposed to be funny?'

'I'm not laughing.' My voice now a little tinged with disbelief. 'But I do reckon the idea of Germany selling strike fighter drones to Indonesia is hilarious.'

'You, Kennedy, are what we call a morality snob,' Lewis said, moving into the table, leaning forward. If she could have ripped my head off, I think she might have. 'With your highbrow commentary and your lowbrow wit. You think you're so sophisticated and wise, but anyone who doesn't agree with your views is stupid in your eyes. But, you are so dumb.'

I leaned back in my chair, frustration brewing as I wiped a palm across my forehead. I felt a slight touch on my thigh from Fiona under the table. Another withering opinion of me. What have I done to merit such treatment today? What words did I utter to attract such personal condemnation? Is it my appearance? My odour? What sets them off, I wonder? I was just so tired of it all.

'Prime Minister, this is a grave matter.' I shook my head slightly as I studied her. 'We should remain focused on policy. You're better than this.' The leadership issue must be causing her grief as her preferred prime minister rating continues to drop. 'You're not happy about today's press reports. I get that. But these media reports have nothing to do with me. I want to achieve the outcome you want. I'll support your decision, but please understand, this is your decision.'

'What do you think, Robert?' Lewis said, turning to her chief of staff.

'I think we should not fund the company under any circumstance, Prime Minister. It has nothing to do with defence or the new technology.' This should be interesting, as they were the issues, I considered important when shaping the decision. 'We are five points behind in the polls and the electorate does not want their government to provide taxpayer funds to big business, especially multinationals. We will take a huge hit in the polls and never recover if we gift Symonds the funding. Meaning, we all lose our jobs at the next election,' he finished, a smirk on his lips as he stared at me.

Lewis would have already known what he would say, and I dare say she probably provided him the script. 'An interesting perspective, Robert, thank you.' She gazed at me, waiting for a response.

Slowly, and ever so slightly, I shook my head, closing my eyes, gnawing at my bottom lip wondering what the surf was like. It's always best to back self-interest if it is running in any political race because you would be damn certain it will be the one trying the hardest. The prime minister was backing her self-interest.

I dropped my head into my fingers and rubbed my forehead. Just for a brief bizarre moment, my imagination had me getting up from the table, storming out, slamming the door, grabbing my bag, and leaving the office forever. They may have considered my scowl as a smile when I looked back at them.

'You know, Ryan.' The prime minister scrapped her bottom lip hard against her teeth her voice low and menacing. 'I know we must work together, but I don't like you. I never have.'

Did this childish statement, like we were kids fighting in the school yard, warrant a response? I took a few deep breaths to calm rising anxiety and gave her my best passive-aggressive stare.

'Freya, politics doesn't suit you. I mean, you struggle with policy unless it is for your leftie mates. You struggle with leadership of the party, and it seems polling indicates you have lost the voters. Hell, you even struggle with stringing words together. You are, as sure as Armstrong was the first man on the moon, not the smartest book in the library.' I took a quick breath keen not to give her an opportunity to interrupt. 'But I must hand it to you. You have fucking gumption. That's what the party hard heads like about you and that's why you still sit in the chair. It's truly a sad fact your leadership doesn't rate in the polls anymore because you don't provide any.'

I could feel Fiona fidgeting beside me, her discomfort unmistakeable.

I leaned forward, my voice steady but stern. 'Unless you accept the challenge of communicating policy in a way that resonates more effectively with voters, we are stuffed at the next election. If you think history will document you as one of the better prime ministers, then you're sadly mistaken. You have achieved nothing whilst you have been in the chair. Australia needs leadership and when voters come to your well to drink it, they find it empty. Unless you provide our people with dreams for the future, your government will be their recurring nightmare.'

The prime minister might have been shocked, though it was hard to say from her expression. She'd cultivated a formidable reputation as a tough cookie and would have heard a worse rant throughout her career. She naturally attracted that type of political narrative behind closed doors from any colleague with the courage to defy her. They say if you like Freya Lewis then you don't know her, and it seems according to the polls voters were beginning to know her.

'Like any stale, pale male Kennedy,' she retorted with a soft growl, 'your remarks are a deliberate attack against me as a woman to force me to feel cheap and insecure.' She tugged at her ear. 'It's a typical form of male bullying, bordering on the misogynistic. This type of abuse toward women is common among old men like you, especially in politics. You just can't help yourself, can you? It's the same repugnant abuse that domestic violence victims endure every day.'

I braced myself for what was to come not entirely sure I should have turned her switch on.

'You're a man who uses his toxic male privilege to denigrate women. Your smarmy language is how you violate them. You are a right bastard. You prove time and time again that you are nothing but an abuser of women, Kennedy, we all know that.' She paused for a moment to sneer at me. 'I have it on good authority you'll soon be exposed to the disgusting person you are.'

I narrowed my eyes as I watched her. What was she talking about?

'The media will no doubt soon launch a major investigation into you, exposing your dishonesty and your corrupt ways to the electorate and to yourself. You are a shallow man, Kennedy, with nothing other than a glib line and a cheesy smile to satisfy your media fans. If you ever wondered why you sicken me? These are just a few of the many reasons,' she continued, her voice rising.'

'Freya, I just want to do my job.'

'Well then, do it for fuck's sake!' she yelled, slapping the table. 'Announce the Australian government will not be financing big business.' She stood and leaned across the table; fists planted forcing me to lay back in my chair. 'Because let me assure you, mister, if you don't, you'll be out of cabinet and this glorious office before midnight.'

'If that is what you want, then that is what you'll have.'

The prime minister heard what she wanted and stormed toward the door with her staff scrambling to follow. 'Ryan, be a good boy, and do what you are told,' she growled before disappearing without a goodbye, or a good job, without even a salute to Fiona.

'Well, that was interesting. Is she normally that rude?' Fiona asked as the silence became uncomfortable.

I reflected on the meeting, my head resting on a hand, drumming my other fingers on the other arm of the chair. 'I've witnessed worse.' I spun my chair toward her, and smiled, but remained a little dumb-founded as I pulled at the hair under my lip. 'I reckon it's because she understands she is out of her depth and uses assertiveness like that to shut down any contrary opinion.'

'Abuse you mean,' Fiona retorted, a sceptical lift to her brow. 'Don't sugar coat it, that was awful.'

'No, I don't think it's abusive. It's just poor communication skills. She needs to be protected from the media, and indeed government policy decisions, because she really doesn't understand this thing called politics, so uses bluster to get her way.'

'Yet, she is the prime minister,' Fiona said, shrugging, a hint of disbelief in her tone.

'Yeah, go figure.'

'That is the worst meeting I've ever attended.'

'You haven't been to a cabinet meeting.' I laughed to release accumulated stress. 'There are others in the ministry worse than her.'

'Why are you sticking up for her after she just abused you like that?'

'Maybe I deserved some of it.' I shrugged. I could tell Fiona didn't believe me. 'No matter, we have much to do. Well, at least I have. What time are the Feds coming in?'

'Eleven. Have you used that number I gave you?'

I cupped my heart knowing the number was safe. 'No.'

She probably knew I lied; she always does. 'Just be a good boy and defer all that silly stuff until next week, otherwise you could get yourself into serious trouble.'

'Cheeky possum.' I grinned as I stretched out of the chair and headed back to my office, with a toss of my head to indicate playful-ness and not taking the meeting outcome too seriously.

Fourteen

10:36 AM

Many folks don't understand politicians. They just declare them all to be liars, and normally that ends any rational political conversation. Where do you go after having your honesty questioned?

We have a coffee shop near home by the water which is a cosy and inviting space. The aroma of freshly brewed coffee wafts through the air, mingling with the salty tang of the sea whenever we are there. The wooden chairs and tables were worn but sturdy, and the soft rustling of newspapers and murmurs of conversation created a warm and welcoming atmosphere most weekends when Wendy and I visit. She was once reading a newspaper article at the café soon after my election, declaring, 'All politicians are liars.'

I looked at her and smiled. 'Your husband's a politician, gorgeous.'

'Of course, not you, darling, but everyone else is,' she replied tapping the news article.

This is the ongoing dilemma with my identity since I was elected. Every day, I want to be truthful, to explain how actual policy issues work, to speak my mind, but many folks just assume I'm a liar. I have spoken to groups of citizens within my electorate over the years, and I just get a nagging feeling they don't believe me, which adds more stress to the churning gut I have.

Honesty is a value I hold dear, in my mind at least. Political lies exist, sure they do, but they're different from other lies. We need to tell political lies to get the news broadcast we want, to get the policy decision we want. It's not really lying; it's just the political system and how things get done. The media scrutinise every word I say, so I often need to prevaricate and be very careful when questioned so as to protect myself. I sometimes appear uncertain with my ums and ahs, but what I'm really doing is scrolling my mind searching for the right word.

That's the truth of it, but when leadership issues arise, that's when it all gets a little tricky. I try my best not to lie to my colleagues about who I support, because once you get caught telling a political lie to a colleague, all credibility and respect vaporises. Colleagues will never trust your word and take you into their confidence again. In the party we have a collective group of ambitious politicians trying to get ahead who garner support by dancing around the truth whenever asked a question. In this game of political dark arts, the sad truth is that you can trust no-one.

The paradox for me is that I value political honesty, but in my personal life, I live a hideous lie. So, I'm a hypocrite. I spruik honesty about family values whilst breaching my matrimonial commitment to Wendy. It's a deceit that leaves me feeling tainted every day. I peddle this deception of being a good husband and father when I know I'm not. Being true to myself and my family whilst having my need for love unfulfilled and seeking it elsewhere sits in my gut as a lie and squeezes it tight most days.

As I pondered the prime minister's constant flagellation of my character, Fiona's observation about the PM's abuse creeps into my mind, stirring up an uneasy feeling within me. Despite the discomfort, my emotions remain lukewarm and benign, lacking the fiery rage needed to stand up for myself in these confrontations with her. I simply accept the verbal lashing and let the words sink in.

My responses to these situations are bizarrely contradictory, as I defend the prime minister against criticism from my staff, even though she continually tears me down. It's almost as if I am numb to the situation, unable to fully comprehend my own feelings or react appropriately. This internal struggle leaves me feeling lost and confused, unable to understand why I'm unable to stand up for myself in the face of such harsh treatment.

I don't know if I've lost the drive to be a politician or even to be a man of honour. I wonder what's become of me, that I can't stand up to someone who abuses me. When did this meekness wash over me? Has politics desensitised me to the constant negativity in my life? Is that why my brain is always off with the fairies, wishing I was surfing or in some delusional relationship with someone I haven't seen in thirty-odd years?

I shake my head at what I've become when I can't stand up to someone who abuses me. The vitriol comes every day in politics, from everywhere, especially in the parliament. It's the media's constant haranguing that gets to me, questioning my character and trying to catch me out in a 'gotcha' moment, which seems to be a national sport these days.

The media never forgets and will use a past indiscretion to damage your reputation, always on the hunt for their next kill. This is why politicians are so damn vanilla these days and probably why we have the prime minister we have. They are too afraid to speak the truth, worried a mistake will be twisted and skewered on social media.

It's just not as it seems living my life as a politician. My friends remain supportive of my career, but they often joke about the alleged expense rorts, the lies, or the oversubscribed benefits of life as a politician. No one believes me when I try to explain. The latest political stuff up is still the hilarious joke at most social events. The constant negativity within the media and indeed with family and friends is such a grim cross to bear for me, adding to my mental anguish.

Why do I do what I do? There's always a constant demand from someone, anyone, to deliver a benefit for them or someone else. Look at my day so far. The demand list is getting longer as the day continues, and it is a never-ending torment for me. And sure, it's my job to meet the demands of others. I'm a volunteer, no one forced me to enter the parliament. But these demands, they add to this increasing lament I feel, which is driving me to distraction.

I question why I even do what I'm supposed to do. Just exactly who is looking after me and meeting my demands? Why do I put up with all the crap dished out, especially from my colleagues and party members? And yet I keep coming back every day with a bigger smile. Truth be known, behind my smile is a mask of despair, wanting to get away.

Everyone goes hard at me when I act in a way they don't like. They challenge me, call me names, shout abuse and question my ethics. No wonder the merit argument for politicians entering parliament gets a going over when we have a prime minister who ducks, dodges and weaves staying out of the way of criticism to keep her job. Is that the type of politician we really want to lead the country?

I look around at the people in my life and I can't help but feel like they all want something from me. Wendy wants me to contribute to her community work. Sarah is trying to establish herself and find her own identity. Rosemary, well, she has her own libidinous needs that I can barely keep up with. Freya, with her overt political strategy to bring my political career to heel. Fiona, with her mother-hen need to protect me, even from myself. Even my dear mum who seems to rely on me for everything.

It's interesting how all these people who want something from me are female. I wonder if it's some sort of karma for my past naughty boy indiscretions. When did my life become so molded by everyone else's needs? What happened to me that I can't seem to say no to them anymore? What mirror cracked during my life to deserve such a laborious existence?

As I think about it, I realise that this has been my life for so long that I can't even remember when it started. It's like a heavy weight that I carry around with me all the time. The constant demands and expectations make it hard to find any peace. Is it self-indulgent to think this way?

I realise I have a ridiculously warped perspective of the world and what is actually going on in my life. Maybe I should just get over myself, grow up and accept this is the way life is mapped out for me. My constant lament about how bad I have it is becoming boorish. But the truth is, I can't keep living like this. Something has to change.

Staring out into the distant vista doesn't help. My thoughts were racing off everywhere and I can feel tension building inside me. It's as if a dark cloud is hovering over my head, threatening to burst at any moment. I need help, but the thought of seeking professional help only adds to my anxiety. I rub my temples, trying to calm my racing thoughts, but it's no use.

I start to think about my journey, about the choices I've made, and the paths I've taken. What if I had made different choices? Would my life be different? Would I be happy? I shake my head, trying to clear my mind of these thoughts. They only lead to more questions and more uncertainty.

Politics is addictive, and the rush of being close to power is almost intoxicating, but it's not what I want. Am I punishing myself for something I didn't really want to do? I need to rid myself of this feeling of remorse, but how? I close my eyes and take a deep breath, trying to center myself.

Punishment is such a harsh word for a relationship. Am I being punished for feeling guilty about wanting to rid myself of this life? To rid myself of the guilt, the responsibility, and the indifference I show for others who affect my day. More and more these days, the only way I can sense getting rid of this sponge of malaise is to give up.

I either change my life or I take my life.

There seems no other way.

'Get over yourself.' It was a mumble, but I said it to him, inside. I wonder if he was listening.

Fifteen

10:43 AM

I've made some interesting decisions in my life. None more stupid than waving goodbye to that damn van. In recent months I have been lamenting about that decision and perhaps dreaming of what my life with Selena could have been. The fact I walked away from that potential relationship just adds uncertainty within me. Is my life unfulfilled from the affection I desperately need because I made the wrong decision that day? Is that it?

It's so damn confusing.

My head again drops against the window, seeking an answer from the streets below. I can't keep doing this. I drop my hands into my pockets and stare out toward home.

I breathe deep through my nose, filling my lungs, seeking relief.

No one likes a whinger.

This is my life, so suck it up princess, no one cares. The folks out there have their own lives to worry about. I'm just a bit player, just passing through so get on with it.

A mist of heavy rain increased across the city, thrashing the streets below as I reflected on those scurrying about, wondering if they enjoyed their lives.

Such a boring and self-absorbed thing to be doing. I shook my head staring out the window. I remained deep in thought about the Symonds' workers, ignoring my reading file. There was plenty to do but I just didn't seem in the mood or have the energy. That's when Fiona interrupted, bursting through the door with a vase of vibrant violet tulips, which she dumped on my desk. I turned away from the window and smiled at the unexpected display.

'How nice, who are they from?'

'There's a card. I would wager they're from your lawyer friend,' Fiona replied with a shrewd grin.

I took the card from the arrangement opening the envelope, sliding out the card, allowing the envelope to drop to the desk. The message was brief and cryptic.

Anytime, anywhere.
12.30 upstairs at the Continental.

'Was I right?' Fiona asked, reading my expression. 'She's a dangerous woman, Ryan. She'll end your marriage if you're not careful. If that's what you want, then end your marriage. But if you don't want that to happen, you must end this relationship with her.'

'Thank you, Fiona. I'll take it from here.'

'Mark my words, it'll be the worst mistake you'll ever make if you end your marriage and give up your family for this woman. Be true to yourself.'

'That'll be all, thanks.'

'The Federal Police will be here in fifteen minutes.'

Watching her leave, a question popped into my head. Is she right?

Would it be the worst mistake to leave my family and give up my political life? Would the outcome be that bad for me? The thought of it sent a shudder though my shoulders. I picked up the phone and punched in familiar numbers then waited for the answer. Amazingly a quick response, usually it takes ages.

'Hello darling, how lovely to hear from you. What's up?'

'Wends, I'm just thinking, do you need me tonight? I'm double booked.'

'It's important you come along. There are only a few speeches and an award or two. They're looking forward to seeing you. You won't have to speak. I would like you to be there.'

'I have a couple of important media things to do this evening, and wondered if I could get a leave pass?' I screwed my face, hoping for a friendly response.

'Fiona told me about your business meeting, but she told me she rearranged it to suit the other party.' Wendy sighed. The type of sigh with frustration writ large, as she often does these days. 'But if you can't manage it, then I guess it'll be okay.'

Why does she have to be so nice about these things? She never holds back on me if she has an issue with the children? It confuses me. I just don't get it. Is she supportive or sarcastic?

'I would love to have you there, darling,' my wife continued, her tone dripping with honeyed sarcasm. 'If you think your work needs you more than me, and it's more important than me, then do what you have to do.'

There it was: the zinger. Whenever she wants to get what she wants, the guilt jibe comes into her conversation. She uses words like a wilful dagger.

The barbs and jabs began early in our marriage, maybe even before, but I let them pass, dismissing them as the small irritations of a long-term partnership. Now they are thrown out frequently, leaving me feeling rotten for not putting the family first. I hate it when she does it. I hate she needs to shame me. I hate her for doing it to me.

'I'll check with Fiona, but if she's moved the conflicting meeting, then I guess I can come.' She'd won again. 'I will let you know if things change.'

'We have a seven for a seven thirty sit down. Try to get there for a pre-dinner drink,' she said, her tone crisp and no-nonsense.

'I'll try. How is the rest of your day looking?'

'I have lunch with the girls. My hair and nails are being done this afternoon,' she replied casually, with a hint of self-satisfaction.

'Of course, you do.' I tried not to sound sarcastic. I didn't want another sigh of frustration, not from her. 'Have you spoken to Sarah?'

'No, I told you, that was your job,' she said, the disdain clear in her voice.

It's always my job. The hard stuff of parenting is always my fucking job. I wriggled a finger in my ear and sighed as I waited for more.

'Are you getting to Fraser's game?'

'Oh geez, I've forgotten about it. I'll try.'

'Try harder darling. You know it's important. Move things around, make it happen. You're the minister, for gosh sakes.'

'Okay gorgeous, I've got to go. Have a great day.'

'You to sweetheart, love you.'

'Me too.'

I tried not to think about how long it had been since I'd said those words 'I love you' to anyone, not my wife, not my son, not even Rosemary. Do I tell anyone I love them anymore? Maybe I don't and I and I don't know why.

I didn't say it to Buddy, and he called me out on it. Now I failed to respond to Wendy. Do I actually love her? That's the question that should be answered. On cue, Fiona walked in with a stack of files needing my signature, and informed me the police were waiting, so I asked her to escort them in.

Sixteen

I swayed around the desk over to the door, my heart pounding, as I waited for their arrival, unsure of what security breach they wanted to notify me about. These departmental blemishes have a habit of splattering themselves all over the media, leading to all sorts of ministerial scandals. It seems nothing is ever trivial to the media with politicians, especially ministers. I suppose that's why I'm always checking over my shoulder who might be within earshot when at a café with Wendy when I'm usually reduced to speaking in hushed tones just in case.

As the heavy-set men entered, I gestured for them to take a seat in my lounge, offering refreshments. Both declined, not even wanting a sip of water. They introduced themselves as Deputy Commissioner Ceglar and Commander O'Brien and I received a faint waft of cologne from one of them, I recognised it as one of mine. I asked if I could have a staff member present, and their response only heightened my anxiety.

'It might be more appropriate if we kept this meeting confidential if you don't mind, Minister.'

Fiona glanced at me, shrugged, then stepped away, closing the door behind her.

'Alright then, how can I help you?' I tried to sound cheerful, but my throat was tightening, and I needed water, I ringed my collar with a finger before straightening my tie. 'I'm advised you've discovered a breach of the department's email system. Is this right?'

'Partially, sir.' Ceglar opened his compendium and scribbled a few notes on a yellow legal pad, worrying me a little as I hadn't even said anything. 'Minister, we've been tracking a breach of your email system for about a week now.'

'My system? How do you mean?'

'The breach has been isolated and they accessed your department and private logins with most metadata scans working through your private emails.'

'Right.' A cautious gulp squeezed my throat, my mouth dry. 'How is that possible?'

O'Brien responded. 'It's possible if the hacker gets your login and passwords, otherwise the system is secure.'

'Who would have these details? I don't have them written anywhere.'

'Hackers reason most folks with logins and passwords go for codes they can remember, such as birth dates, pet names, that sort of thing.' Mine were a little more sophisticated than that. 'In your case, the logins are very secure if the hacker doesn't know your personal details,' O'Brien explained.

'What were they after?'

'We picked up the hack because our regular security scans identified unusual activity, specifically, activity in your private correspondence.'

'I don't understand. You scan my server?'

'Standard procedure Minister, especially when you're travelling internationally. We're just looking for unusual activity.'

I struggled to swallow, wiping my palms on my knees as I shifted in my chair. 'How often were they in?'

'They seemed to hover over your private files for a few days and they downloaded material.'

I cleared my throat. 'Do you know who came in?'

'Yes, we do, and we met with them yesterday afternoon,' Ceglar responded.

'More than one?'

'The hacker had a guardian.'

'A kid?'

'He made a full admission.'

'What did he get access to?'

'Most things, including many of your very personal files,' said Ceglar, his expression turning grave. This concerned me because my personal files were, well, personal. If these files were compromised, they could cause significant angst for me and others. 'I must say, Minister, some of the material is not appropriate for a government system. We would encourage you to delete them.'

'Yes, I'll get rid of them.' I averted my eyes, shifting in my chair, crossing my legs.

'That sort of material could get you into significant trouble if ever it was made public,' Ceglar said, his tone seeming to want me to feel embarrassed, and he succeeded. 'I'm sure you're aware, even though it's personal and private.'

'Did the hacker copy it?' My voice was barely a whisper, so I cleared my throat.

'We are aware images have been downloaded. He denied downloading them but told us he was only trying to find information.'

'About what?'

'About you,' O'Brien said, his eyes never leaving mine.

I didn't understand. 'Where did you find him?'

'We could track the metadata activity to a computer he used, and that surprised us.'

'Why?'

Ceglar shifted in his chair. 'Sir, this is very difficult. The security breach came from your house.'

'My house?' I coughed, now confused.

'To be specific, Minister, it's your son, Peter.'

'Peter?' I sat back not knowing what to say or how to respond. I could feel an emotional lump rising from my gut and I spread my knees seeking relief. The officers watched me, waiting for the right moment to continue.

'We met with Peter and your daughter Sarah yesterday. He made a full admission.'

'Did he explain why?'

'He told us he was concerned about you and the manner you have been behaving lately. He assumed something was stressing you because he said you were rarely home. He went searching for anything that may have been bothering you. He moved through most of your personal files, but claims he downloaded nothing, although we detected activity confirming downloads have been done.'

I didn't understand. Why would Pete worry about me? Was that information shared with Sarah? Does Wendy know? Who else knows? Fuck! I could feel my chest tightening from a strong surge of emotion and anxiety. 'What happens now?' I said, coughing again, and sitting forward, trying to relieve my discomfort.

'We would normally charge him with breaching government security and illegal entry into your department's IT systems. As you know, we now have strengthened laws to allow severe penalties for security breaches, including significant jail time.'

My head dropped as the emotion of the news took shape, exposing itself as I tried to talk, 'And ah, what um, what is the likely, um ah, the likely outcome of your, ah, meeting with, with my son?'

'We thought we would first refer the matter to you. We are meeting with you today to seek your formal direction.'

I gazed into Ceglar's eyes looking for a sign to understand what he meant. 'How do you mean, formal direction?'

'Minister, the breach is in your department, and it has compromised the system. The department's email system, your private files, and your personal email system secured by the government. It's your decision if you want us to come down hard on this hacker and charge him.' Ceglar remained unclear. Will he charge Peter or not? 'This needs to be your decision.'

'Our suggestion is that we provide you a report of the breach with notes of our interview with your son. You can then direct us to act by charging him or you can withhold any further action.' O'Brien said, now more specific. 'Understand this, Minister, our hands will be clean on this procedure. If you decide not to press formal charges and it comes out, we took no action because of the relationship between you and the hacker, then it will fall back on you. Our files will note our conversation today and your direction following our advice within the report. You will be responsible and if there is any blow back, then it will come to you, not us.'

'What do you think I should do?'

'Minister, it's not our job to advise you, only to report. We are seeking your direction.' Ceglar said, his tone clear that if things went pear-shaped, this wouldn't return to the Federal Police.

'When do you need an answer?'

'Before the end of the week,' Ceglar responded.

'If I chose to not press charges, how safe is the report?'

'If it leaks, it will only come from you,' O'Brien affirmed.

'Thanks, gentlemen.' I stood, ending the meeting by walking to the door. 'I'll let you know tomorrow.'

'Good luck, Minister,' Ceglar said, as we shook hands.

'Thanks for dropping by.'

Fiona led them from the office. I closed the door behind them.

So, at the very least one of my children knows I've been having an affair with Rosemary and seen graphic evidence kept as a trophy memento to titillate me when I needed it. How damn stupid of me!

Seventeen

11:22 AM

Could my day get any worse?

No wonder he didn't want to talk this morning. I paced back and forth across the room considering the police briefing. This could even explain Sarah's outburst. Is this what the prime minister was referring to when she said there was information about me out and about and the media will expose me? How could she know?

I returned to my desk considering the evidence that exposed me as a fraud and an imposter, my greatest fears seemed to be realised. Life had bowled me a cruel blow, and I couldn't help but wonder if things could possibly get any worse. The thought of facing my son after this was unbearable; how could I look him in the eye with any respect ever again?

My mind was racing with questions, and I felt my chest tighten as anguish washed over me. What was I to do now? Was this the end of everything for me? Had my secret life finally caught up with me and was now disembowelling me?

I slumped back into my chair, suddenly feeling unwell. Surely, this was not the way my marriage was supposed to end. With this revelation, Wendy could use it as an excuse to cut my gonads off, and no one would come close to supporting me. My marriage was over, this was it.

I ran my hands through my hair, feeling lost and helpless. How could I have let it come to this? The weight of my own deception and this exposure felt crushing, and I couldn't escape the sense of shame and guilt that consumed me.

I stared out my window seeking alternatives. If walking away from this angst in my heart was critical to me, then this disclosure can deliver it. This could be the catalyst for a separation from Wendy. I shook my head not knowing whether to feel sad or happy. Mind you, I couldn't help but reflect on the financial hit I would take if she divorced me, as if it was the most important thing to worry about. Pathetic really.

My family is important to me but where is the love? Unfortunate with its poor timing, but now there is a reason for everyone to end it. I massaged my temples as I thought about what to do.

To leave the family for another woman. To give it all up, counting on starting afresh. Ending the past and creating a different future with someone and yet being shamed for doing so. Does the last twenty years mean nothing to me? Am I that shallow?

Oh, Christ what a day. I buried my head into my hands, running fingers through my hair to get relief from the angst trawling through me.

What have I done?

Overwhelmed with self-doubt and despair, I gazed out over the city, feeling like a complete fool. How could I have been so blind to the consequences of my actions? What will Peter think of me now that my true colours have been exposed? Can our relationship ever be repaired? I've been nothing but foolish and selfish, and now I must face the consequences of my recklessness.

My throat tightened, and tears threatened to spill down my

cheeks as I struggled to hold them back. I couldn't believe how care-less I had been with the safety and security of my own family. How could I have been so thoughtless and self-centred?

Lost in my own sense of worthlessness, I dropped my head and scootered my chair to the window, feeling sick to my stomach. The tightness in my chest returned, more intense this time, and I felt like I was suffocating. What could I do? Where could I turn for help? I needed someone to talk to, but who would be willing to help someone like me?

Desperate and alone, I leaned forward, resting on my knees as I gazed out to my home. Should I confide in Rosemary? What would she think of me now? Would she demand that I leave Wendy and expose our relationship to the world?

Oh, my God. What have I done?

Then Selena popped into my head and those memories I have been having. They're gone now. Fuck me. What a stupid moron to think there was ever a chance of meeting her. Why would I do that? I must be nuts. How self-indulgent must I be to wish my life were different? Geezus, hasn't dreamtime been so damn stupid?

Does Wendy know?

She couldn't know or the locks would be changed by now. She knows she can continue her cosy lifestyle without me. What were those scratches on her back? Is there something going on with her? What about the water in my bathroom?

Jesus wept. What am I thinking?

I jumped up out of the chair and thundered my hands onto the window and leaned into it. Am I trying to shift the blame to her? Did I just think she's having an affair to justify my miserable behaviour? What is going on with me? What's rampaging through my head? How could I be so stupid?

What to do, what to do?

I eyed the tulips on my desk, wondering how I should broach

this news with Rosemary? Feeling my chest tighten further, I dropped my hands to my knees for a bit of relief. Should I tell her? Or is that just creating another problem? She'll no doubt go ballistic knowing her photos have been found. Christ, why did I keep them? What an idiot? I let out a sigh, rubbing my forehead, trying to distract the tension from me and started pacing. When she knows Peter has seen them, my god, my balls will be wrenched off. What happens if Rikki finds out? Oh shit.

I flopped back in the chair, feeling overwhelmed. Still rubbing my forehead.

The door opened after being knocked, and I glanced over. 'Hey boss, are you alright, you look terrible?' asked Joanne Sicily as she stepped into the office. 'I have the speech notes for you, but I can come back later.'

'No, come in, Jo. What have you got for me?' The interruption was exactly what I needed. As she talked, I nodded, but not really listening, trying to rid my mind of my mistake. Should I ring Peter, or go see him? What do I say to him?

'I thought you could speak about the years the company invested in Australia, benefiting from government policy and funding. Then question why they would abandon their long-standing workforce, or do you think it's too harsh?'

'Yes.' I nodded.

'Yes what? Too harsh or yes put it in?' I didn't hear her, my mind elsewhere. 'Boss? Are you okay?'

'Jo, I think we leave it in. Nothing is harsh enough when bastards mistreat their families like this.' I seemed to be vocalising my own condemnation.

'Like what? I don't understand.'

I dithered a little trying to regain political focus. 'Sacking staff without a care for the welfare and security of families is stupid and a moronic thing to do. They should be made to feel shame. They deserve a strong rebuke from the government.'

'They are providing a generous payout scheme, but I get your point. I'll toughen up a few lines.'

'You're doing a great job. Is the media conference set?'

'All set for a little after six,' Joanne said, as she checked her notes. 'It'll be the perfect time for them to do their lead story on the closure and then cross to your announcement.'

'Great, well done. Now, I need to do a few things.'

'Sure boss.' As she left Fiona replaced her, bringing more files for my signature.

'What did the police say?'

I tried to avoid her gaze. 'Nothing much.'

'Nothing much?' She said, sounding cynical as she placed the files at the top of my desk, her bangles tapping the wood.

'You look like crap and the police told you nothing much. Yeah right, who are you kidding?' Fiona faced me with hands on hips. I wasn't sure what to do. 'Is there anything I should be concerned about? Anything I can help you with?' Fiona asked. I didn't know what to say.

'Have you been able to get the money?'

'All done. Should be here around two. Anything else?'

Ignoring her, I texted Larry to come by the office at two thirty to pick up his cash. Then I began flicking through the files, signing where a yellow sticker indicated. As I worked my way through the pile, Jordan Whitecross joined us.

'I hear the meeting with the prime minister was not as expected.' He sat at my desk, prompting Fiona to do the same. 'Do you want to do or say anything within the network about it?'

'It was a little ugly.' I didn't look at him.

'More than a little ugly,' added Fiona. 'More like a feeding frenzy at the zoo. She picked his bones like a hyena.'

'I heard you gave as good as you got,' Jordan said.

'Who did you hear that from?' My eyes shifted to him.

'I have connections with Foreign Affairs. It seems you're a hero over there.'

'I'm not sure I want that information to circulate.'

'Do you want to do anything?' Jordan asked.

'No, let's just wait until tomorrow and gauge the response to the announcement.'

'Sweet. I want to get a sandwich. Can I get you something?'

'No, I'm out for lunch, and I need to go very soon.'

'What about you, Fiona?'

'No thanks Jordie, I brought my own today.'

'Sweet. I'll see you at four, boss.'

'You're stepping out?' Fiona asked me.

'Just for an hour or so. I should be back before two.'

'Nothing special I hope, not today,' she said, sounding a little uneasy.

'Everything is fine.' I tapped my chest and felt the paper. 'I haven't called her.'

'I wasn't talking about her. I was talking about the flower girl. Don't stuff it up, Ryan. You have too much to lose.'

'It's an old record you keep playing, Fiona, and I'm sick of hearing it.' I passed her the completed files. 'Give it a rest, will you?'

'What time are you leaving?' She took the files and stood before me.

'In about thirty minutes.'

'I'll see no one disturbs you,' Fiona said as she left the room.

Pulling over my leather compendium, I made a few scribblings and wriggly lines on a page, diagrammatically getting a plan in place to manage the crisis. Sketches and diagrams are my usual source of creative thinking. If the right arrow pointed to the right doodle, then my troubles would be resolved.

But who was I kidding? It's never that easy.

Peter exposed me. Who has he told? Has he told Wendy? Sarah knows. Has she seen the photos? What do I say to him about hacking into the government system? Where did he get my login details, and what else does he know? A jagged arrow led to a stick figure with a short triangular skirt, Rosemary. Does Wendy know? I leaned back dropping my pen and linking my hands behind my head.

How do I feel about Wendy knowing about Rosemary? Should she know? If she knew, would it make a difference? Why would a secret be kept from her? Hey, here's a clue to my dilemma. If I wanted her to know about Rosemary, then why haven't I told her? Damn good question, as I've kept it a secret for five years. The only reason I could think of would be that I didn't want to leave the family. So how do I feel about that?

What a bloody mess I've found myself in. So many damn questions.

I scrawled a picture of Wendy linking it to Rosemary with a question mark through the arrow link, which I thickened again and again almost tearing the paper. Then a doodled stickman to complete a triangle, named Selena, with a question mark next to it. In the centre, a dollar sign with a small design of the parliament underneath, linking Wendy and Rosemary, but nothing to Selena.

I leaned back in my chair, studying my artwork. It was obvious Selena meant a new world to me. Rosemary would only be more of the same. What did Larry say? Something about Rosie wanting to replace Wendy. He told me to bullshit her about getting the snip and suggest to her the PM would sack me to bring the real Rosemary out from her cover. Fucking stupid thing to do. I don't need another ear-fucker in my life. I chuckled as I scrawled a bag and scissors.

This doodling prompted me to think deeper about my decision, needing to be announced this afternoon. If the tables were turned and I went against the prime minister, then I would get the sack from my job. This would mean my career was over. This could mean Selena comes into the picture. Interesting, so I added a giant work boot kicking beside the money symbol with a squiggly line back to the stick figure.

Then two sad faces were drawn under Wendy, one with pigtails the other with glasses. Then a smiley face with freckles was added, representing Buddy. What was required to turn my children's sad faces into smiles? I worked through my diagram and notes, trying to work out an answer. No question Peter needs to be spoken to. This would solve a few of the riddles about our little secret, and whether he told Wendy.

My heart needs to tell me if I care about what Wendy thinks. I leaned forward, resting my head in my hands. If the marriage was over, it didn't matter if she knew. The real challenge before me was to confront the angst of uncertainty in my life. I need to decide if I transition to live a different life or not.

The pressure would be on now, and I suspect I was being forced to decide. Another damn decision. This is where the exquisite Selena comes into the picture. Would I give up everything for a chance at happiness with her? Is my affection for Selena just a silly delusion or a reality?

I thought back to the last thing Selena said to me. 'In our hearts, we are together forever. What we shared cannot be stripped away or bettered by anyone, and the depth of our connection will never be matched.'

I shook my head and smirked. I reckon she must have read it somewhere.

It was such a romantic thing to say, and she was right; no one has ever come close to expressing anything like that to me since. Which is the fundamental problem with all my relationships since Selena. Nothing has ever been better than that summer. I have been searching ever since for that romance she spoke about, and I felt.

Selena was a romantic and expressed herself selflessly and I loved the way she seemed to say the right things to me about us. The search for that same romance we shared has been a failure in my life, so I wonder if she remembers.

I pulled the crumpled note from my pocket, my fingers trembling as I unfolded it and spread it out before me on the desk. I stared at it for what felt like an eternity before finally mustering up the courage to dial the number. As I waited for her to pick up, my heart raced with anticipation and anxiety.

'Good afternoon, Selena speaking. How can I help?' came the voice on the other end.

My mind went blank for a moment, unsure of how to proceed. I cleared my throat, 'Hello, Selena.'

'Yes hello, can I help?' she asked, her tone professional and polite.

I hesitated for a moment before saying, 'Yes hello, it's Ryan here.'

'Ryan? Ryan who?' she asked, her voice tinged with confusion.

I took a deep breath. 'Look, I'm sorry, let me start again.' I stood up and walked by my desk, stretching the cord. 'My name is Ryan Kennedy. We met some years ago surfing down the coast, on a holiday.'

Silence hung heavy on the line for a beat before Selena spoke again. 'Ryan Kennedy?'

'Yes, we were surfing and camping together one February. You were with three friends on holiday.'

'When was this?' Selena asked, her voice betraying a hint of scepticism.

'I'm sorry to have to tell you this, but it was over thirty years ago. We were only kids,' I chuckled, trying to case the tension. 'We spent three or four days surfing and camping together. You suggested we go looking for better waves further along the coast. I parted ways with you and your friends in that battered blue van of yours with the huge smoky exhaust plume.'

'Oh yes, I think I remember,' Selena said, her voice growing warmer.

'You may recall my name as Rat.' I rubbed my chest.

'Rat, not Ryan?' Selena sounded surprised.

'Yeah.' I laughed at the absurdity. 'We had a great time together, surfing, smokin' and drinkin'.'

'Were you that kid with the tattoo?' Selena asked, her memory seemingly returning.

'Yeah!' I could feel her memory returning and was delighted she remembered.

'It was an angel or something across your shoulder.'

My fleeting moment of delight dismissed itself very quickly.

'You had blond hair and a beard, am I right?' Now joyful, she oozed that gushing warmth I'd been dreaming about. 'We camped and smoked dope, and we were in love.'

'Yeah, sort of.' I grew uneasy, wondering if I was making a huge mistake, she had no idea who I really was.

'So, what do you want? How did you get my work number?' Selena asked, her tone shifting back to business-like.

'You've been on my mind, and I thought it'd be lovely to catch up.' I could feel my heart racing with the lie.

'Oh, how sweet, sure we can catch up. What was your name again?' Selena said, her voice growing warmer again.

'Ryan, Ryan Kennedy.' I felt a pang of guilt.

'You're around my height, am I right? I remember you. You were a great kisser. Yeah, let's catch up. Are you still smoking, or do you prefer playing with anything stronger? I don't mind a sniff or two, as you know it gets me going, if you know what I mean,' Selena said, her voice dripping with innuendo.

I felt a lump form in my throat. This wasn't how I imagined our reunion. 'I'm not certain we're talking about the same guy.' I realised she had no memory of me.

'Hey, wait a minute,' Selena's tone changed, like opening a freezer. 'You rang me, so let's catch up, no matter who you are.'

'You don't remember me, do you?' The energy just seemed to escape from me.

Selena didn't respond, but her breathing confirmed it. 'Over thirty years is a long time ago. I've travelled and done a bit, but if it means a lot to you, then let's catch up. Hopefully I'll remember,' Selena whispered into the phone.

'Selena, thanks for the memories. Let's leave it there.'

'That's a shame, Ryan. You sure Selena can't do anything for you?'

'You were lovely back then. That's what I would rather remember.'

'Call me anytime, Ryan. I'm here if you need me.'

'Bye.'

Dropping the phone back into the cradle, my stomach lurched as if to expel the lump which had hit me earlier. So, I positioned myself head down over my rubbish bin just in case. What a fool, to yearn for something that never really existed. Well, it did for me, but it didn't score any goals with her. What a moron I've become. Not even a morsel of recollection. Though, I suppose it was a spur-of-the-moment call. Perhaps I caught her unawares.

I believed love could only exist with her; from an imaginary moment frozen in time. Not with Wendy, not even with Rosemary. Now, I'm not so sure what the heck I've been thinking about over all these years. The flame of love and happiness I thought flickered between us was now extinguished. My musings, my silent wishes, are now nothing more than ash. This shallow man the prime minister alluded to earlier now believes her presumptive words. I am without character. Can life get any worse for me?

How stupid and shallow I've become, and how bleak the future now appears. I gazed at the diagram before me, and with a swift motion, I marked a cross through the stick figure, crumpled the paper, and chucked it into the desk drawer with a sigh.

'What a fool I am.' No one was listening.

Eighteen

12:15 PM

The crisp, after-rain air whispered wellness to me as I emerged from my oppressive office, where I had been under immense stress. Despite my son's serious problems, I couldn't help but focus on my own troubles. Not the greatest parental value to exhibit. I felt disheartened in myself for not prioritizing my family.

My father was a loving and hardworking man, but he had difficulty expressing his emotions to his family, a trait that I seemed to have inherited. So maybe I have become my father. I wondered why I kept seeking something better instead of accepting life as it is.

I strolled along the crowded street, the peak lunch crowd in full throttle as pretenders struggled through the crowd to important lunch meetings. The barons of the brassiere with their insatiable appetite for free meals were out and about. The absurdity of conducting business over a meal was not lost on me, yet it remained a crucial part of the culture. No lunch, no deal.

I made my way to The Continental, a fancy three-chef-hat restaurant known for its extensive wine list. The owner, Roberto Palagressi, greeted me at the door, 'Minister,' he said with a nod,

'Madame Alvarez has yet to arrive. Would you like to wait outside with an espresso?' I took the opportunity to call Peter.

'This is Pete. Leave a message.'

'Hi, son. It's Dad, all's good. Look, I would like to catch up before five if you can. Call me. My preference is for you to drop by the office on your way home. Let me know, thanks.'

As I pushed the end call button, the phone lit up with the ID of a journalist. I tossed up whether to answer, deciding to take the call. 'Hello, Phillip, nice to talk to you.'

'Minister, glad I could get you. Do you have time for a couple of questions?'

'On the record, or off the record?'

'Let me know once you hear them.'

'Shoot.'

'Can you confirm if you met with the prime minister this morning?'

'Yes, I can. We discussed various issues.'

'Was leadership discussed?'

'No.'

'Can I quote you?' Phillip asked, his toned seemed too clever.

'No.'

'Are you able to comment on reports you received an old-fashioned dressing down from her?'

'What reports?'

'We have a comment from the PM's office. There may have been heated words between you...'

'I have no comment.'

'... and you were told in no uncertain terms you're required to do what the PM wants you to do regarding Symonds.'

'And what does she want me to do, Phillip?'

'I'm just trying to get your side of the story,' he said, trying to sound innocent.

'I don't think you have a story. You're trying to build one in your normal unsourced way.'

Just then, Rosemary swept past. I waved an acknowledgement as she stepped into the Continental, disappearing with Marco the head waiter, her blue pleated skirt swaying around her brown knees as she danced up the stairs. The red stilettos didn't trouble her.

'I know you had a meeting. I know you had words, and I know you discussed the polls.'

'Then write your story.'

'I don't have one yet.'

'That's what I thought. Nice talking to you, Phil. Anytime, see you.'

I finished the coffee and then bound up the stairs, adjusting to the darkness to find Rosemary with a glass of champagne with what appeared to be two mouthfuls down.

'Hi, darling.' I pecked her proffered cheek before taking a seat opposite in a booth overlooking the street.

'I'm not sure I know what's going on. Do you want to stay together?' Rosemary asked, her voice filled with hurt.

'Whoa, wait up.' I knew Rosemary for being brutal and blunt in court. 'No hello darlings? How's your day?'

'How do expect me to feel after tonight's snub?'

I took a deep breath and tried to choose my words carefully. 'Rosemary, you know how I feel about you. You're being unreasonable. If I could get out of this event Wendy has organised, I would.' She didn't seem satisfied, frowning then turning away. 'I tried again about an hour ago. I still can't seem to wriggle out of it. Last night was perfect and we have dinner on Saturday, so ease up, will you?'

She looked at me skeptically. 'I'm numero uno, or I'm not.'

'You are a priority, Rosemary. You always have been. But it's not that simple. You know that. I said we need to wait until Fraser is a little older.'

'How old?' Her expression would have scared anyone. 'You've been suggesting that notion for too many years. I'm not getting any younger.'

'Why is your age an issue?' I wanted to gauge her reaction.

She didn't respond and opened the menu. 'Let's order, and you can tell me about your meeting with Lewis.'

It's much easier to let go of the challenges from other people's mindsets, rather than argue their point of view. You can never change their view on life. You just change their opinion of you, that's all. So why argue? Why seek to voice an opinion?

I did when I was young. When I thought of any idea or opinion, tramping through my immature brain was always right I would always express it. I had little time for folks who did not share my point of view. My excuse then was my youth. Now I'm fascinated by folks who still think their point of view should be everybody's truth. Just like Rosemary.

'She threatened me with my job.'

'She what? She can't do that?' Rosemary stretched out her hand and I dutifully reached for it. 'You must be having a rough day, sweetie.'

'She can sack me if she is in the mind to do so.' It continues to baffle me how little folks know of the parliamentary process. 'The prime minister provides the patronage of promotion to the cabinet. She can do whatever she wants whenever she wants. If she wants to sack me, she can.'

'Why does she want to sack you?'

'It's complex. Today's preferred prime minister polling has something to do with it. I'm well ahead, and it doesn't placate her conspiracy mindset.'

'You're not challenging. At least, not yet, are you?'

Was that a question or a statement? I wondered. 'I have the numbers, but I'm not interested. The timing is not right.'

'When do you think you might challenge? Before Christmas?' Her eagerness seemed too obvious.

'Why do you ask?'

'I have a few projects to finish. I have plans to travel to Europe early next year, so I don't want to be away when you are appointed prime minister,' Rosemary said, with a grin.

'Why should that bother you?'

'I want to be with you, darling.' She beamed. 'I want to support you, to help you move into Kirribilli. It would be such an impressive achievement.'

Has she already moved in? What's all this about? She's the mistress on the side, tasked with keeping me happy and satisfied, and now she's moving into the prime minister's residence. Am I again in someone else's plans?

'Can you stop her from sacking you?' she asked. Her mind seemed to be already moving on to the next step.

'If I terminate the Symonds' workers today, I'm safe.' I wasn't sure Rosemary knew of my Symonds' dilemma judging by her, *what the hell are you talking about,* expression. 'If I do what she wants, she'll not discharge me.'

'Then you must,' she said, her tone matter of fact.

I winced, opening my hands. 'No thought about the workers' lives, mortgages and repercussions in the community?'

'They'll get over it. Keeping your job is the most important thing for you.'

'Not doing the right thing?'

'Sacking them is the right thing for us, darling.' She snapped the menu shut and signalled the waiter.

'I'm having a salad. Do you want to share?'

'No, I'll have the fish.' I hate sharing. If you want the salad, order the salad. Why would I want to share a salad? I don't get it.

'I'll have the green salad, thanks. He'll have the fish, butter fried with vegetables, and no chips. Can we also have a bottle of the Meursault Chardonnay, the seventy-eight, if you have it chilled?' She passed the menu to the waiter who scurried off. She then smiled. Again, a decision where I had no input.

'Not sure I can drink more than a glass, darling.'

'No matter, just drink what you want, the Department of Public Prosecutions can pay,' she replied with a wave of her hand.

'How is your day shaping up?' I tried to change the subject. 'Oh, thank you so much for the flowers. They're beautiful. I appreciate the thought.'

'They're nothing, my love.' She thrust her hand out again and smiled. I obediently reached for it. 'You know I love you. You know that don't you?'

As she pulled my hand to her face, I wondered if anyone could hear her. 'Yes, of course I do.'

'I've had a dreadful day,' she said, her eyes darkening. 'Aside from you cancelling dinner this morning, I had to speak to my staff about their attitude. There are too many mistakes in court documents because they spend too much time gossiping. I had to tell them to maintain proper hours and cancelled all personal time. One girl cracked it storming from the office. Unbelievable.' She drained the remaining champagne. 'Then the HR manager turned up advising me I acted inappropriately, and I should apologise. Me? Apologise? For what? Asking for a more professional attitude? I'm looking forward to the day when I can leave that pit of incompetence.'

'What are you hoping to do if you leave?'

'If you take over the leadership, then I would support you every day,' she said, her eyes fixed on mine.

I reached for the water as an excuse to pull my hand away. It seems Larry may have been right? 'Have you got any cases coming up?'

'They have given me a few files. Which reminds me, when are you off to China? I want to come this time.'

'Not sure that would be appropriate, darling.'

'Why not? I miss you when you travel. I haven't been to Beijing,' she said, her voice taking on a hint of frustration.

'The Chinese take a dim view of infidelity.'

'The land of concubines has a dim view on infidelity? You are kidding me, right? Don't you want me to come? I can take a low profile and meet up when you're free of the pomp and ceremony. I thought you said you loved me?'

If I closed my eyes, I would swear it was Wendy talking to me. 'It's not that. I just need to be unhindered in case I need to travel to another city at short notice. Maybe we can have a holiday another time.'

'You don't want me to come. Is your wife going, is that it?' she asked, her voice cold.

'Do we have to get into this discussion again? That record must be worn out by now?'

'You either love me or you don't. I'm sick of being your other woman.'

'You aren't the other woman, you know that.'

The waiter arrived, and we fell into a hush. He went through the wine tasting protocols, then poured. I raised my glass toward this crazy woman, with a fiery red lipped pout before me, and smiled. 'Here's to the most beautiful woman I've ever met.'

'When's she arriving?' She laughed her eyes sparkling. 'I must look terrible today, after what you did to me last night.' She swayed in her seat, trying to get a reflection in the window behind me. 'Anyway, I wasn't a woman when we met.'

'I didn't see you when we first met.' She was only a girl back then.

'I thought you were the most handsome man I'd ever seen.'

'Those were the days.' I smiled at the memory of my youth and took a sip. The wine was chilled and full of the oak flavour, an undeniable feature of the French.

She leaned forward, her voice low. 'When you kissed me at my twenty-first birthday party, my pants were so wet.'

I raised an eyebrow. 'I don't remember. I remember the party, and the birthday girl, but I can't remember kissing you.'

It's curious how some folks remember significant moments differently. Just an hour ago the love of my youth was telling me she didn't remember me. Now it seems the love of someone else's life can't remember their first kiss. Is that how it works? Memories become selective, depending on meaning. Does my family have different memories of their lives? Peter's anxiety this morning was obviously painful for him. Maybe he is hurting more than me. Did I cause that?

'That was the first time I knew I would never be happy without you.' Rosemary refocused me and reached out, taking my hand.

I pulled my hand away. 'You've had plenty of relationships. What about that chap from Russia?' Did she not love those boys she dated? Rikki believed she did. 'I'm sure you've had other men. A Frenchman or two, perhaps?'

She shook her head. 'Of course, you know that, but only ever to progress my career. They never shared my affection like the love I have for you; I can assure you.'

I leaned back in my seat, surprised by her remark. 'Really?' We've been lovers for five years and this is the first time she said that.

Do folks marry to improve job prospects, or their social status? Maybe they do. I suppose I might have done given half the chance. I thought I loved Selena. Whilst holding onto that dream I married Wendy, because it was easy for me. So maybe it's the same with Rosemary. I turned away and sipped a generous amount of wine.

'Things will be different. We will have a glorious life together.'

Rosemary flicked back her rich black hair and brushed it with her fingers.

The waiter arrived with our meals, positioning the barramundi fillet before me, and tabling the tapa sized salvers of root vegetables, and a silver dish of beans. It was a generous serve, too much for an appetite now abruptly lost.

We worked our way through our meals, Rosemary nibbling like a rabbit on the green weeds they serve as salad. Me flicking through my fish barely touching the vegetables. The wine was going down a treat.

She looked up, her eyes scanning my face. 'Anything wrong darling, you seem distant?' She crunched a sliver of carrot with her goddam perfect teeth.

'Nah.' My nonchalant answer didn't seem good enough for her. 'I have a lot on my mind.'

'I think I know what you need.' She smiled the subtle, demure thing she always gave me when feeling flirtatious, always at the most inappropriate time. Rosemary thought a place to a man's heart was through his loins. She used this strategy throughout our relationship as an effective weapon to get whatever she wanted.

'What would that be?' I engaged her eyes, knowing exactly what was ploughing through that sexually active mind.

'Dessert.' She licked her lips, and I almost weakened.

'Not today, darling, maybe later in the week.'

She snatched at her glass, fierce black eyes reminding me of her impatience. She drained the glass. 'Too bad, such a tragedy for you. You may come regret it one day.'

I let out a sigh. That's the second time today after being offered pleasuring and rejecting it I have been told I would miss out on something special. Maybe, I am missing out, because whenever sex happens, I never think it to be the best thing in my life. Maybe I'm missing something.

I then thought of Selena who held my heart and provided me with sexual, loving memories. Well, not anymore after telling me she couldn't remember who the heck I was. How could she not remember those three days? I don't understand. I thought we were eternal lovers.

'You haven't asked me about the police?' I sought to change the subject.

She leaned back. 'Oh, I'm sorry, how neglectful of me, what happened?' Rosemary mocked me. She had a habit of treating me with overt disrespect. She called it teasing or being funny. I call it contempt, but let it go, yet again.

'They sent a couple of senior officers to see me. It seems my son has hacked my email system.

'Why?'

'Not sure. I'll talk to him later today.'

'Fraser?'

'No, Peter.'

'Why am I not surprised?' Rosemary quaffed a mouthful of wine from her refilled glass. 'You know, I just don't trust that kid. He always looks at me funny. It's very creepy.'

'What do you mean?'

'He makes me feel uncomfortable whenever we see each other. He has a look about him I don't like. Just like his mother. Is he yours?'

She is kidding. She has only met him two times, three tops, at Rikki Alvarez' events. How could a kid make a woman feel uncomfortable? 'I'm not sure you should feel that way about him.'

'Oh, so now you know how I feel?' Again, she confronts me.

I sank back into my seat, bewildered by the conversation. It seemed very tense. Not untypical of the way we sometimes talk to each other. There is no love, no respect, just an entitlement dissertation from the prosecutor. I pulled the fine cotton cloth serviette off my lap and dumped it on the half-eaten fish.

'I need to go to the bathroom. Please excuse me.'

She looked up, her eyes scanning my face, a sudden hint of concern in her voice. 'Is everything okay?'

I admit I remained a little irritated by her observation about Peter. She seemed shaken by my unexpected strut from the table. I needed a break from her. 'Everything is fine, won't be long.'

Palagressi knew the standard of washrooms often distinguished restaurants. Clean bathrooms added to their reputation, meaning diners would come back; too many restaurants and bars cannot provide clean, well-resourced bathrooms. The Continental out classed themselves with delivering elegance.

I escaped into the silence of the men's lounge. A wood panelled, rich green, dimly lit room, with soft cotton towels stacked on a timber shelf, whilst offering over twenty colognes placed alphabetically along the shelving. It was a pleasant, elegant touch, which I suppose helped justify the prices.

The room seemed a mile away from my day. It provided a sanctuary to spend a few moments away from my life. The pristine marble benches with perfect white basins and gold tapware welcomed a visitor, and I soaped and washed my hands, then brushed warm water across my face, then again, and yet again, trying to reinvigorate my day. Resting on my forearms, my eyes stared up into the mirror, gazing at the person before me. Really looking deep, searching for an answer or even the hint of the personality others see in me.

I saw nothing.

Picking up a towel and wiping my face, still trying to comprehend and categorise the challenges rushing before me, I questioned why today? Others want me to fit in with their mindset. There are too many decisions to make. Too many disappointments. There remain too many stark realities about my life. It was exhausting.

Why me, why now? There is an urgent need to make decisions. Major decisions. Yet I'm stuck in this swamp of self-analysis, which is a dreadful indulgence. I need to change my life. How to precisely go about doing that muddled me.

Today was not a day for reflection. I didn't have the time. These unwanted revelations being forced upon me more often these days drained me, but not now, not today.

My family is at threat and needs protection. But it's me threatening them. Exposed today as the impostor, I am in the embrace of a woman who seems to have little interest in my brood. I'm not sure what I should do. Either I go down a path of destruction and self-interest or choose to protect my family. Either way, it's me who misses out again.

I stood before the mirror, my thoughts a jumbled mess. The happiness in giving up everything lays within me. So why not reach out and grab it? Why am I in this funk? Issues of the heart have failed me for years. Even on my wedding night I knew I'd made a mistake. Yet, I did nothing about it. I know what I must do to remedy this malaise. Yet, I vacillate on taking action.

Man up would be my father's advice.

The man in the mirror gave no clue, but the man up refrain beat into my brain.

What a day. Could it get any more challenging?

Shrugging on my jacket, straightening my tie, and leaving the sanctity of the lounge, I stepped out to encounter Rosemary leaning against the wall opposite with a broad flirtatious grin. She dangled a cloudy plastic bag of white powder from her fingers.

She looked at me with a naughty grin. 'Want some dessert, darling?'

Nineteen

1:15 PM

'I'm not in the mood sweetheart. There are too many things to do this afternoon.' I tried to push past. 'Come on Rosemary, be reasonable, please.'

'Just let me have a line. It won't take a minute.' She took my hand and led me toward the larger washroom designated for ambulant access. 'Quick, come in here,' she whispered, her voice low and seductive, pulling me into the suite.

The room seemed similarly appointed and warmer, but I couldn't shake the feeling of unease creeping over me.

'We don't have time for this. This is silly. Why do you do this?'

She shrugged. 'Like you often say, I do it for the kick. You didn't complain last night,' she replied, a hint of a smirk playing at the corners of her lips as she locked the door. She moved to the marble counter, dropping a small amount of powder on the pristine bench. Using her credit card to prepare it into lines. 'Are you sure you don't want any, honey?'

'Just hurry, will you?'

She took the familiar glass tube from her clutch and bent over,

143

using it to sniff the powder along the lines. She dropped the tube and the small bag back into her clutch, pinched then rubbed the tip of her nose, and applied a finger to the remnants, rubbing them into her upper gum.

'Much better, thank you, darling. Now, can I have a kiss?'

She flung her arms around me, pushing her lips onto mine with her tongue working into my mouth, and I couldn't help but responded to her warmth and eagerness. What a great kisser. She pushed into me, and we hit the wall harder than I expected, her body pressed against mine. I was feeling for her, squeezing her. She pulled her mouth from mine and moved to my neck.

'Come on darling, let's do it,' she whispered, her breath hot against my skin.

'Not here, not now.' I tried to step away.

'Don't tease me Ryan, I don't like it,' she said, pushing harder.

'I'm not.' I now tried pushing her away.

'Don't you want me? Is that it? Not good enough for you?'

'Don't be ridiculous.' She cut my words off as she latched onto my mouth, working hard.

'I need you now. I must have it,' she whispered, her breath coming in gasps as she worked my ear. 'You know you want it, don't you baby?

'Rosemary, please stop.' I tried to push her away as she bit hard into my lip. 'Stop.'

She stepped back with wild eyes, filled with desire. I checked for blood from my lip, and she stepped forward, slapping my hand away kissing me again, this time with even more intent.

'Come on, baby, you know you want it,' she said, her voice low and husky.

'Not here, stop it. Rosie, please.'

'Not man enough, eh, Ryan? Not good enough for you?' she

taunted, stepping back then punching me hard in the cheek before rushing to kiss me again. 'Come on, give it to me.'

'Stop it.'

'Baby, you're driving me wild.' She gripped me between my legs, squeezing hard on whatever she could find, pressing her lips wildly against mine and pushing me further into the corner, stifling me, causing panic. 'Punish me, hit me. Punish me,' she pleaded, her eyes glinting.

'Stop Rosie, this is too much.'

She gnashed at my face then her teeth sunk into my flesh as she then licked and nibbled at my neck. 'Do it!' she pleaded.

My mind clouded with lust and anger, and I couldn't help but give into her demands. I gripped her neck just wanting her to stop, swinging around and slamming her hard against the wall stretching her upwards. 'Stop it.' My growl intimidated me.

But she only smiled, her eyes alight with pleasure. 'Go for it darling, punish me. You know you want to do it,' she gasped, a sly smile playing on her lips as I squeezed harder. Her eyes revelling in it.

The violence excited her, and I couldn't help but be drawn in. I knew I was crossing a line but couldn't stop. But then, as she gasped approval, I realised it wasn't passion I was feeling, it was pure brutality. I dropped her, backing away until feeling the marble bench resting against it, disturbed by my ferocity and viciousness, and trying to regain control of my emotions.

'I can't do this.' I lightly fingering my forehead, my throbbing face buried in my hands.

Rosemary wasn't done yet. 'Hurt me baby, do it,' she said as she came to me, lifting my face, kissing passionately, and I weakened, responding to her touch. She squeezed my trousers, fumbling with the zipper. She worked her hand into my trunks, kneading, and pulling at me. She groaned into the nape of my neck.

She slumped to her heels, deftly unfastening my belt, dragging my trousers and trunks to my ankles, then took me. I grabbed her hair, yanking at it, trying to pull her away, wanting to get away, wanting her to stop.

'Stop. Not here. Please stop.'

She only continued, her teeth grating against my skin as she increased the pressure.

'Rosemary, please stop. Stop. This is wrong.'

She stood, studying me, then smirked a greedy smile. Stepping to the wall she flicked up the pleated skirt over her hips and bent over, splaying her legs providing a provocative view with no strips of cotton lingerie. She leaned against the railing, watching back over her shoulder. She stretched a hand, her red-tipped fingers working, revealing she was ready.

'Punish me, Ryan. Please punish me for what I have done,' she said, her voice low and seductive as she pulled at her hip. 'Front or back, your choice. Come on darling. Give it to me now.' She sounded desperate. 'I need to be punished.'

I couldn't resist her. I did want to punish her, to make her pay for her disrespect and constant demands. I shuffled toward her, my trousers still around my ankles, and I pushed into her. She squealed with pleasure, begging for more and I gave it to her, punishing her for the contempt and then I pushed even sharper with thoughts of Freya Lewis entering my mind. She responded by pressing back harder in rhythm.

'That's it, honey. Give it to me. Be a man and punish me.' She squealed with surprise and pleasure when I slapped her. 'Harder. Slap it harder,' she begged.

She licked her lips, leering in the mirror, watching as she ran her fingers through her tousled hair. 'I'm almost there. Give it to me, harder.' Rosemary weakened against me. 'Punch it.'

I convulsed unable to hold on any longer, in a frenzy, grunting and clawing at her with no ability to control myself any further. She pawed at the back of my head, arching her back, gasping in pleasure as she found release. When done, she broke free, kissing me, all passion gone.

'You are just the best lover. I love it when you do me like that. You had so much intensity. I could feel your love.'

As I looked at her, I couldn't shake the feeling that what I felt for her wasn't love.

'I'll see you back at the table. I'll just go fix myself.' Rosemary grabbed her clutch and disappeared.

I straightened my clothes and fixed my appearance in the mirror, trying to shake off my feeling of unease. I examined my reflection. The emergent face welts were growing, but there was no obvious evidence of bites, thank goodness, although my lip looked red and felt a little tender. I tossed a few handfuls of water across my face and patted it dry; it was aching. I straightened my hair, buttoned my jacket, and checked the image.

'Well, minister, you have been well and truly fucked today.' I mocked my mirror image and left the room. Rosemary was signing the account and jumped up when she saw me approach, kissing me.

'That was great, thank you. Let's go have coffee outside,' she said, linking her arm in mine.

Marco led us to a table. We ordered espresso and water. Rosemary leaned her head on her hand and gazed at me. 'I can still feel you,' she murmured. I'm throbbing like crazy.' My eyes checked over my shoulder. 'I want it noted that you were a willing participant,' she said with a smirk.

'I'm not so sure about that.' I tapped the corner of my mouth.

'Okay, you were eventually,' she giggled.

'It made me feel uncomfortable. I didn't like you hitting me.' I tried to keep my voice steady.

'It was only play, Ryan,' she snapped. 'Give it a break, will you?' She straightened and pushed back into the chair.

'No, it was more than that. You were trying to hurt me.'

'I was trying to get a response,' she said, shrugging.

'No, you were punching me.'

'Oh, did I hurt little Ry-Ry?' Her cutesy tone grated on my nerves and didn't interest me. 'Little Ry-Ry turned into Jack the Giant Killer, and he stabbed the evil monster. Hard and many times... yummo, that was so good.'

'Rosemary, you know how I get when you push my buttons. It's not the first time. This time you got me furious enough to choke you.'

'Oh, you choked me alright, you were so ready.'

'Stop it. Just stop it.' I slapped the table raising my voice. 'This is serious.'

'Come on Ryan, I'm just playing, baby,' she dismissed me and stretched out a tender hand. 'I love you. It's okay. I wanted it.'

'I didn't.'

'What do you want to do about it?' Her tone turned cold, eyes narrowing. She pushed back into the iron chair, crossed her legs, and spooned a half teaspoon of sugar into her coffee.

'I'm not sure. But I know this is not the way normal folks express love.'

'Normal? Darling, we're far from normal.' She seemed condescending. 'That's what makes us so perfect for each other. Our passion, our fire. That's the way I like to express myself with you.'

'I can't do this anymore, Rosemary. I can't keep pretending that this is love.'

'Since when? You've never complained before,' she said, her eyes flashing with anger.

'Since, around fifteen minutes ago.'

'What does that mean?'

'I'm not sure. I'm going to reflect on it for a bit.'

'Are you thinking what I think you're thinking?'

'What am I thinking?'

'You can't get rid of me that easy, you bastard.' She leaned into the table, pointing a finger. 'I've given you five years and I expect more from my investment than that. It's not over until I say it's over.'

'I can't give you children.' Larry suggested it, so I dangled it out there.

'Why not?'

'I had the snip before I travelled to Germany.'

She scowled at me for a moment, her lips working as she tried to hold on to her tears. 'Why didn't you tell me?'

'You said you didn't want children, so I made sure.'

'You bastard.'

'Why should it matter? You don't want them. I already have three. We can make do with those.'

'You're kidding me, your children?' she sneered, her disdain clear.

I started feeling anxious, as if a public slap might be on the way. Her hand clenched a few times as I waited.

'You know something, Mr Kennedy? I love you. I will have you. And I'll make damn sure you will get me very, very soon. I think it's time I spoke to Wendy to make sure we can manage it before you leave for fucking China,' she said, sneering at me, her voice filled with malice. 'Let me tell you something. I will go to China with you. I will be beside you when you are prime minister, and we will make Kirribilli our home. It's all I've ever wanted since I first met you twenty years ago. You will not deny me that now.'

'Do nothing you'll later regret.'

'Like you've just done to me, do you mean?' She stood, gathering her clutch. 'Never threaten me again. Who the hell do you think you are?'

'It's over, Rosemary.'

'It's not over until I say it's over.' She leaned in and seemed about to slap me. Perhaps she thought better of it as I raised a guarded hand. 'I'll find out where you are partying tonight, and I'll be there to have a chat with your wife.' She then strode off. 'See you tonight, darling.'

Twenty

1:40 PM

I watched and smirked as Rosemary strode away, her confident gait and purposeful manner a reflection of her father. I snorted a chuckle as the absurdity of her asserting power over me in the washroom upstairs flushed through me. She was right. It wasn't the first time we played rough, but always consenting. On many levels, I didn't like what happened. But carnal reflection flicked through with a guilty twinge of admiration to her cleverness to get me to do whatever she wanted. Maybe I did ask for it. I could have walked away.

'Front or back? What a card.' I chuckled.

The waiter glanced at me and grinned as I waved him away.

Guessing Rosemary had already paid for the coffees with lunch, I collected myself, straightened my stiffening body, strolling back to the office, perhaps a little reluctant to address the challenges ahead.

Life as I know it is falling apart. Oh really? I shook my head. Falling apart may be a little dramatic. Pathetic, that an old man like me can think I can be the stupid kid, free of the worries of living. I've spent way too much time playing with this woe-is-me mindset.

I touched my sore lip, checking for blood. Mind you, how many fifty-five-year-olds are having lunch time sex in a washroom? Not many I'd wager.

Reality has come knocking today.

The consequences of my couldn't care less behaviour are coming back to haunt me, and I can imagine what the fallout will be from my infidelity with Rosemary. Wendy will no doubt leave me once she finds out, and if my current feelings for Rose are valid, then it's over as well. A sadness and defeat washed over me. I imagined there was a better life elsewhere and blamed everyone in my life for missing out on it, now the shit from my disrespect is going to hit the fan in a huge way.

So, with very little effort from me today I've lost my wife, my lover, and the girl of my dreams all within a few hours. Yeah, nice one, Minister.

Walking into the office, Fiona spotted me and scooped up several files and papers then followed, waiting for me to hang my jacket. When I faced her, her mouth dropped open as she scanned me. 'What happened to you? Have you been in a fight?' she asked.

'No, why?' I touched my tender lip, feeling a twinge of pain.

'You look hurt. Are you okay? What happened?'

'I tripped over and fell on my face on the stairs at the Continental.'

'Do you want to see a doctor? Maybe you should. Your face is swollen. Your lip is huge.'

'I must have bitten it as I landed. As I said, I went face first into the carpet. I suppose it'll be okay.' She knew me too well and smirked a look of doubt. 'I have the media conference at six, so maybe I'll need a makeup touch-up, but I'll be okay.'

'I'll get a cold towel for you, or maybe some ice,' Fiona offered, but I cut her off.

'Don't fuss, please. What have you got for me?'

'I have your money.' She passed me an envelope. 'I've also got bits and pieces for you to consider, but on reflection, I think I'll wait until tomorrow.'

'That's a good idea.'

'A Selena Tatupo called. She insisted on seeing you this afternoon. I slotted her in after your meeting with the union. She said you approved it this morning, is that right?' Fiona retained a hint of suspicion in her tone.

My heart skipped a beat. Selena tracked me down? Was she telling me the truth? Is this for real? 'Yes, I spoke to her this morning, and it's good she's coming in.'

'I suppose you know what you are doing,' Fiona said, her tone filled with disbelief.

'I do Fiona, thank you. Is that it?'

'You have a busy afternoon, and your evening looks rather hectic. Do you want to talk about tomorrow?'

'I would rather not think about tomorrow. What I do this afternoon could affect what I do tomorrow.' I was impatient to call Larry about the money as I fingered the envelope.

'I would prefer we map out what we're planning to do, so I can help you prepare.'

'It's ironic, isn't it?'

'What is?' As expected, she seemed perplexed.

'The future and not knowing what it will bring. A metaphor for my life.'

'Amen to that, Minister. I have been telling you it's time for you to take control and stop living in other people's mindsets,' Fiona said.

'How do you mean?'

'You allow too many people to control your day,' she replied, with a touch of insight and relevance. If only she could tell me what to do, I thought, feeling a sense of hopelessness.

'Jordan wanted to see you when you arrived. Do you want to see him?' Fiona asked, interrupting my thoughts.

'Umm, sure, why not?'

As Fiona disappeared, I picked up my phone to call to Larry, but it pinged a message.

DAD R U COMING???

Crumbs, Fraser. I'd forgotten. I jumped up, feeling a pang of guilt, thinking about dropping everything and getting to the game. It was only down the road.

'Where are you going?' asked Jordan.

'I have a meeting for about an hour. What do you need?'

'I need you to change your mind about the announcement,' Jordan pressed, his tone filled with urgency.

'We lose our jobs if I do.' It was a glib answer. 'I suspect I'll do as the prime minister wants me to do.'

'This is not you, Minister.'

'What are you saying?'

'You know this decision is wrong thing to do. You know this will cost you with your future leadership ambitions.'

'How the heck would you know?'

'Minister, I have known you for almost a decade. We fought a lot of battles together and I'm sure we can win this.'

'We?' I stopped moving. 'You mean me, don't you Jordan? You mean I can win this?' Then reaching for my jacket, I started to move out. 'I'm the one out at the front line getting kicked to death every day. I don't see many people standing beside me fighting the good fight.

'You've always been a conviction politician, Minister. Now is the time to become one.'

'Life must be pretty good from where you stand, Jordan. I don't see you taking the hits, yet you still get promoted when I do. Why is that? Why is it that you do well out of me when I'm taking the political hits?'

'I want you to run big on this. It'll change your status and focus will switch to you as the next leader.'

'Just make sure I have my speech from Jo before I see the union.' I ushered him out and stood before Fiona's workstation. 'I'm popping out for an hour to see Fraser. If you need me, message me.'

'If I need you, I will call you,' Fiona said, with a touch of annoyance. Is there no relief from the women in my life? Every single one of them seemed to want to take total control of me.

Walking into the elevator lobby, I texted Larry to meet me for a quick coffee at the cafe nearby. Not as grand as his hideaway where he spent his days, as this place served coffee with limited chairs and stools to deter long stays. He replied he was already there when the doors opened on the ground floor. Perhaps he was waiting for the two o'clock deadline to come to my office.

Twenty-One

2:00 PM

'Have you got a black eye, mate? Did someone take a swing at you?' the big guy asked as his beady eyes scanned my face.

'No, I don't, and no. Is this mine?' I pulled a latte toward me and ripping a sugar sleeve.

'No wait, let me guess,' Larry continued, a chuckle rumbling in his chest. 'You opened a mirror door, and it caught you. Am I right?'

'Get stuffed, will you? It's nothing.' I tightened my lips, wanting to move on.

'I've been hit enough to know when someone's whacked you. Who was it?'

I sighed, feeling defeated. 'Rosemary.'

'Bitch!' Larry almost shouted it, drawing the attention of a few folks nearby, turning to look.

'Don't be like that, Larry. She didn't mean it.'

'She looks as if she got in a few good licks,' Larry scoffed. 'Did you slap her or anything?'

'No, of course not.'

'So, why'd she hit you?'

'I don't want to talk about it.' After taking a sip, I pulled the envelope from my jacket. 'I have your money.'

'No, wait up, let's not be so hasty. Tell me why she did this to you.' Larry's eyes gleamed with interest.

I grimaced, taking in a deep breath, avoiding his gaze. 'We were engaging in sex at the time.'

A slight smirk crept across my lips. 'When was this?' he asked, now wide eyed, leaning in.

'About forty-five minutes ago.'

'Where?'

'In a washroom at the Continental.' I savoured the shocked look on his face.

'You sly dog.' Larry laughed. 'Was it good?'

'No! She punches like you. She bloody hurt me.' I touched my cheek.

'Why did she punch you?'

'I didn't want to do it.'

'She raped you?' His jaw dropped, then his smile widened.

'I wouldn't go so far as to say that.'

'Let me see if I get this straight. She tried to coerce you into sex, and you said no?'

'Well, yes, in a manner of speaking, I suppose.'

'She hit you until you said yes. Is that right?'

'Sort of.' I looked down at my hands.

'During this time, were you saying no?'

'Maybe.'

'Mate, you lucky dog.'

'Why?' I shook my head a little perplexed.

'You're the only bloke I know who can say he's a rape victim.' Larry seemed to celebrate the idea. 'What are you going to do about it?'

'Nothing, as I said before. She didn't mean it.' I sipped my coffee. 'She just blew a line and perhaps she had a bit too much alcohol.'

'No means no, Ryan.'

'Can we stop talking about it?'

'Was it good? Did you cum?' Larry pressed on.

'Leave it will you?' I wanted to leave.

'You did, you dirty bastard.'

'No, means no, Larry.' I shrugged his arm off my shoulder as he tried to pull me into a friendly embrace.

'Still the Rat, you old dog,' Larry laughed, his rough voice filled with nostalgia. 'I'm proud of ya.'

'Larry, I'm a little embarrassed by it all. I have this face and need to do media. So, can we stop talking about it and get this deal down?'

He wanted to make one final point. 'I told you she was no good. You should get rid of her.'

'Maybe.' I gestured to the envelope of cash on the table. 'When will you return this to me?'

'Four weeks at the latest.'

'Can I trust you with this?' My eyes narrowed

'You have in the past. Why do you doubt me now?' Larry asked, a hint of hurt in his voice.

'Because, in the past, you've failed to meet the deadlines you set.'

'I promise you, Ryan, I won't let you down,' Larry said, his hand over his heart.

'And we do not associate my name with this?'

'Of course not. What do you take me for?'

'This is some nefarious payback for debts, isn't it?'

'Look, you don't want to know,' Larry said, his eyes shifting away from mine. 'Suffice to say, unless I deliver the funds today, I'm in serious bother. So, thanks for your help. I appreciate it.' A hint of desperation crept into his voice.

'Larry, you have to stop this shit.'

'It's what I've been doing since I was a kid. If you hadn't gone all goody two shoes on me, you would be doing the same right now.'

'I'm not so sure about that.'

'Listen to yourself, will you?' Larry said, a hint of annoyance creeping into his voice. 'You've been banging on about how bad your life is, but if you want to know what it would have been like, just look at me.'

We paused to look at each other, both of us lost in thought.

'What a joke,' Larry laughed, then coughed hard. 'You would have been worse than me. Fatter than me, and you would have hair in some form of outdated Rastafarian state and stink of dope.'

'Maybe.' I thought he may have had a point.

'Mind you, you would have to kiss women goodbye, like the lawyer and your wife. Forget about those overseas holidays you've had every year, except maybe an occasional magic mushroom holiday in Bali,' Larry continued, his tone more serious. 'No, Ryan, you made the right decision. It's just a shame you couldn't convince me to join you. You gave me plenty of opportunities, especially with your dad's business and the association. I just keep stuffing up.'

His sadness seemed obvious and uncomfortable, so I changed the subject. 'Hey, my dream girl is coming to see me.'

'No way, when?'

'This afternoon.' I smiled and ran my tongue along my bottom lip.

Larry smiled. 'Why is it you that gets all the luck. You have more women chasing you than the average bear and I can't even meet one,' he said, shaking his head. 'It's been a long time between drinks.'

'Don't be too harsh on yourself, Lunchbox. You've done okay.'

'You're my best friend, and you support me, but I think I've let you down way too often. You're always there for me when I need you.' He dropped his head and stared at his coffee.

'Even though the timing isn't good, I have to leave.' I slapped him on the shoulder and moved off. 'Thanks for the chat and the coffee.'

'You're a good man, Ryan. Just remember that.'

'Yes, well, I suppose you're right, but maybe not today.'

'Go do what you must do. See you, and thanks. You have literally saved me.'

'See you, Lunchie.' I left the cafe to catch a tram toward the sports centre. Time was running out.

Lunchbox, what a name. He's been called that since we were young and long lunches were popular. He was the man who got the deal done. Lunchbox and the Rat. We were a pair of young tearaways. More interested in good times than responsibility. We overindulged back then and had fun, yet it seems neither one of us enjoys life anymore.

Twenty~Two

2:39 PM

━━━━━━━━

I had little time to do this, but Fraser seemed keen to for me to watch him play. After today's clash of opinions with everyone in my life, maybe it's a good idea to gain some sense of connection with someone who loves me. The sports centre was a short tram ride from the city, and I walked into the stadium thirty minutes after leaving Larry.

The energy from the enthusiasm of the cheering fans surprised me. I couldn't quite remember what game Fraser told me it was. The stadium provided no ticketed seating, so finding a seat proved problematic amongst the blue and white colours of Patterson College fans who seemed excited with their team leading the game by two points. The Hurstbridge Grammar boys scored two quick baskets as I searched for a seat and were now in front with five minutes to play in this, the last period.

I spotted a seat in the last row and made my way up to it. I focused on the game, trying to pick out Fraser, who wasn't on court, but on the bench, looking up at me. When he recognised that I saw him, he waved, and my fist pump provided him a broad smile. I pointed two fingers to my eyes and then the game suggesting he watch. The timeout hooter sounded. Fans in front stood to stretch legs, so I joined them, searching the crowd trying to identify anyone. I saw no one I knew.

As the crowd resettled, Fraser was now on court, bouncing around as a guard, trying to block a huge kid with facial hair. The College boys appeared a lot smaller than the Grammar men, which seemed an unfair contest. The blue shirts were jumping about, creating chaos for the lumbering boys in yellow. Fraser's mop of hair was bouncing everywhere, looking like a wild beast who shouldn't be on court. It seems the use of head bands had not been raised with him.

A loose ball and Fraser swooped, weaving his way down court, flicking it to a taller boy who tried to dunk, as kids do, tossing the ball up against the backboard and it circled into the hoop, creating pandemonium in the stands. Hey, this is good.

The Grammar boys walked the ball back and flicked it about encouraging the tight defence to open up the key, so they could attack the ring. Suddenly, a steal by Fraser. He scooted off to the other end and jumped backwards as he floated the ball into the ring. I jumped to my feet shouting and fist pumping, watching him wave to me as he scrambled down the court to position.

It was my first game in four years. I swore never to come to another after the last was a waste of time. Fraser hammered me for years to come along, but I resisted. If this was the usual excitement, then perhaps I should have listened when he nagged me. Maybe I should have paid more attention to his sporting endeavours.

The game seesawed its way through timeouts, foul calls, and substitutes until there were just forty-five seconds left. How a forty-minute game can take two hours is beyond me. Forty-five seconds left and the College boys were two points ahead of the hairy gorillas.

I began thinking about leaving and perhaps saying a quick goodbye to Fraser. What a champion.

A gangly Grammar boy, who must have been six feet tall, all arms and legs, ran towards the basket with only Fraser to pass just outside the key. The brave little bloke planted his feet and stood his ground as rules permitted; arms tight across his chest. The yellow grasshopper leapt for the basket using Fraser's shoulders as a stepping-stone and continued his way to air the basket.

'Foul!' A man-eater just devoured my son.

The ball rimmed the basket for at least one full circle before sinking in, sending parents and friends nuts with enthusiasm as scores drew level. Whistles blasted from the two referees running into the court to call a foul against the Grammar boy. But as arms waved and fingers pointed it became obvious. They called a foul on Fraser, now prostrate on the floor, knocked into next week. This had me on my feet flaying the referees for the poor decision as the Grammar boy stood at the free throw line waiting to put them in front. I was incredulous and so it seemed was everyone else.

Teammates picked up Fraser, helping him to the bench as his coach called his last time-out. Buddy had blood on his towel from wiping his face. The coach pointed to Fraser, pushing him in the chest and gesticulating to the other boys thumping a clip board. I thought it seemed a bit over the top, blaming Fraser for the foul. At least this is what the scene looked like. I considered going down to the sidelines to have a quiet word.

Time-out finished. The boys resumed their positions around the key, waiting for a conversion for an extra point with twenty-three seconds to play. Enough time for the College boys to track the ball down court and score a two-point basket and win by a point. Fraser looked up as he took his place and gave me a cheeky smile amongst smeared blood and smashed nose.

The gangly boy came to the line. He glanced at a team mate to his left, who nodded. Something seemed planned and about to happen. Other players surrounded the key, waiting for the ball in case the gangly boy missed, but with these free throws they seldom do.

Gangly boy set himself for the free throw at the line, bounced it once, then twice as the NBA stars do to steady themselves. He looked up at the ring with the ball above his head. But then he took a sharp step back from the line, and instead of shooting he hurled the ball at the back board, whacking it hard sending it straight back to him, over the heads of the jumping boys under the basket. The boy then flicked it off to his teammate who tossed the ball high and straight into the basket, taking only the net, two points. Like everyone else caught unawares, I admired the nous to try the play. The Grammar bench erupted with excitement. Now two points up with seventeen seconds to play for a College lay-up to score a draw, and force extra time. If the Grammar thugs stop the lay-up, they win, the bastards.

The Grammar boys applied a full court press, blocking all the College players from taking the ball at the restart. Unless they could get the ball in court within five seconds, they lose it. If the yellow boys took possession from this premeditated set play, they would run the ball until the hooter and win. The bastards.

The College boy with the ball didn't know what to do so tossed it high to the big teammate standing at centre court, who fumbled the contest, providing an opportunity for Fraser to swoop and dribble the ball toward the basket to lay-up for a two-pointer, too easy. Extra time seems now a formality.

But Fraser didn't perform as expected and ran through the key, slowed, and went to a corner, checked the clock, and waited, settling himself, five seconds remaining. His teammates were in position waiting but were now covered by the bigger boys. He needed to move to the key for a shot, but seemed anxious as he bounced the ball, frozen in his position not knowing what to do. Precious seconds ticking away. Then he was free as the guard dropped back, and now open to go to the basket. Instead of dribbling to the paint of the key, he jumped like a ballet star with graceful arms and hands, tossing the ball high toward the basket. As it reached its pinnacle of trajectory, the hooter sounded. The stadium was deathly silent as everyone, including myself, watched in spellbound excitement. Like slow motion, all eyes were on the ball. It spun as it came to the ring, smashing hard against the back edge, which sent it into the air. The Grammar boys were leaping, trying to touch the ball away. It dropped back and hit the front edge, popping up again. It hit the back board, then ringing the metal before tumbling into the hoop.

'YES!'

I jumped to my feet as the three-pointer gave the College the win. Fans rushed onto the court to congratulate Fraser and the other players, lifting them onto their shoulders and carrying them around in celebration.

My admiration increased as I watched Fraser hoisted on shoulders, basking in the glory of his game-winning shot. What a moment in his life. He won the game with a three pointer after the hooter. I screamed so much I was almost in tears. He scrambled from the shoulders, making a dash for the stairs, crashing his way through the congratulatory crowd until he got to me and jumped into my arms.

'I'm so happy you made it.'

'Fraser, you were sensational. How's your nose?'

'Dad, you gave me the confidence for that shot. I wouldn't have done it if you weren't here.'

'Not sure I follow son, that was all you.' He needed another hug.

'You give me confidence to do things. It's you I think about when I play.' He hugged me harder. 'Seeing you today gave me the confidence. I love you.'

I was at a loss for words and kissed him on the cheek a little embarrassed by the outpouring of emotion. 'How do you want to celebrate?'

'The Bond movie will be great. I have other plans with mates this afternoon.' He patted me on the arm. 'Don't worry.'

Who was this kid?

He's very special. I just didn't realise how special until now. Glancing up at a beaming Peter and excited Sarah waiting to hug their little brother, I let him go, and they crashed in for a piece of him.

'You were fantastic little brother,' Sarah shrieked.

'What a goal!' Peter agreed. 'You were brilliant.'

'He was terrific, wasn't he?' I stuck my arm around him.

'Dad, I just need to get my gear. Wait for me.' Fraser leaned in and kissed me. 'Do you guys want to visit the rooms?'

'Sure,' they both said.

As they walked off, jumping and squealing with excitement, I grabbed Peter by the jacket. 'Can I have a word?'

He appeared anxious. 'Sure. You guys go. I just want a chat with Dad.'

Pointing to a quiet spot nearby, I ushered him to a seat. 'Is there anything you want to tell me?'

'Nah,' Peter said, shaking his head.

'I had a visit from the police this morning.'

We looked at each other. He became fidgety and seemed to want to leave, and began rocking back and forward in his seat, avoiding my gaze. I reached out and held his hand.

'Everything is alright, my boy. Just tell me what's going on.'

'Dad, I know it was a mistake. I'm sorry.' He choked out, tears beginning to stream down his cheeks. 'I just needed to know.'

'Know what, son?' I ran my hand over his head, trying to soothe him as he struggled to regain control of his emotions, pulling a tissue from his pocket.

'If you and mum were splitting up.'

'What? Why would you think such a thing?'

'Miss Alvarez,' he said, glancing at me with distress in his eyes.

'How do you mean?'

'You don't get emails and photos from a stranger like you do from Miss Alvarez.' Peter glanced at me. 'I began to believe you might leave us.'

'Son, I have no intention of leaving your mother. Why would I ever do such a thing?'

'Other dads do. Why not you?'

'Do what?'

'Trade their family in for a new one. Tim Rogers' dad left last year and married a young girl.'

'Is that what you think I want to do?'

'Do you?' he demanded, looking at me anxiously 'You, see? You can't even say it.'

'Son, no matter what happens we will always be a family.'

'So, it is true,' he said, his anger growing.

'These are issues I don't want to talk about here. We will talk about it another time.'

'Just a typical bloody politician.' He stood, trying to squeeze past me.

'Don't speak to me like that.'

'Don't treat us like fools, Dad. You go do what you want to do.' Not knowing what to say, I moved my legs to let him pass. 'The police told me it was up to you if they charge me. What have you decided?'

'I haven't.'

'You see, this is so typical of you.' He shook his head. 'You're never able to make a decision.'

'Peter?' He never turned back as I watched him go, unsure of what to say or do, so I left.

As I reached the exit door, Fraser called me to stop. I waited just outside to allow him to catch up.

'Dad, thanks so much for coming. It meant a lot to me.'

'No worries, Buddy. I enjoyed it. You played a great game.'

'Don't worry about Peter, Dad. He's a moron and worries too much, just like Sarah.' He took my hand. 'I know you work real hard for us, and I know you'd rather be at home than working all the time. It must be tough for you, and even though you don't say it a lot, I know you love us. I really do. Thanks for coming.'

'Who are you? When did you get so wise?'

'I learned from my father. I love you.' Fraser hugged me, hard.

'Buddy, go enjoy your celebrations. I'll see you when I see you, but we will do Bond on the weekend.'

'Bond. James Bond.' The young lad's Scottish impersonation, though not perfect, was not without some charm. 'Thank you, Moneypenny.' Then he laughed. 'Or is that Mr Moneybags?'

I hugged him, kissing him on the cheek. 'See you, son.'

As I walked away, I mused on all the moments in his life that I had missed. The regrets of a father, wishing for more time with his children, are a common one. My father had often expressed similar regrets, and now they were mine to bear.

'Hey Dad?' Fraser called after me. 'Have a brilliant afternoon.'

'Take care son and put some ice on that nose!' I shouted back, waving goodbye.

Twenty-Three

3:44 PM

The union officials were early, sitting in the lobby, glancing up as I strode through casting a cursory wave in their direction and informing them that I would be with them very soon. Fiona was waiting for me outside my office, like a cat ready to pounce, with news and papers.

'The prime minister's office called,' she said, handing me a stack of papers to sign. 'They want to be kept informed about any media you're planning. Joanne has your speaking notes ready and a draft media release for review. She's wondering if you'd like to make a longer speech.'

'No, I don't think so.' I finished scrawling my signature across the pages detailing staff leave, allowances, and a third I didn't bother to read.

'The union folks are here; do you prefer to see them in your office or meeting room?'

'Take them to the meeting room and give them tea and a biscuit.'

Fiona raised an eyebrow. 'Why so generous?'

'They're comrades, Fiona.' A mansplaining moment was now

before me as she shook her head. 'They have been fighting for a smoko for years. Who am I to deny them that opportunity?'

'Not sure a biscuit is a healthy cigarette replacement.'

'Occupational health and safety regulations would deny them the opportunity of drawing on a smoke, but a biscuit is still okay.

'Chocolate or cream?'

I couldn't help but laugh, 'Are you seriously asking me that?'

'Come on, Minister,' Fiona urged, with a hint of sarcasm. 'Make a decision.'

I rubbed my temples wearily. 'This is, I reckon, the first decision I'm about to make today. What flavour biscuits to offer the union before delivering bad news.'

'Let's make it chocolate then,' Fiona said.

'And even then, I wasn't able to make it.' I chuckled. 'Can you let me know when Hodgeman arrives, please?'

'How was the game?' Fiona asked, her tone softening.

'Oh, it was fantastic.' Enthusiasm rose within me. 'Patterson won with my little boy sinking the winning point on the hooter.' The beaming smile must have impressed her. 'Fantastic result. The crowd went nuts.'

'Nice boy, your little one.' Fiona smiled. 'He knows what's going on.'

'A wise head on young shoulders.' I smirked.

'I think he's been here before. Sometimes you should listen to what he says.' Fiona began her hocus-pocus spiritual energy crap again. 'He won't know what it means when he says it, but he'll be giving you a message.'

'Is it a full moon?' I tried to be funny, but it probably came across as an inappropriate quip.

'You don't have to agree with my thing, Ryan.' Fiona replied, her voice now tinged with annoyance. 'Sometimes it might be a good idea to just listen. I don't need the commentary.'

'Thanks Fiona. I appreciate it.'

'Don't give me the irrits,' Fiona warned, beginning to depart with the signed papers. She wasn't happy.

'I'm trying not to.' Another validation of my poor communication skills. 'It's just that today seems to be full of people offering advice.'

'Maybe you should accept it.'

The union representatives came to mind as she closed the door. They won't be happy either. My dad always drilled into me about the company's staff being the most important asset and making sure they were happy.

I sat at my desk, staring out the window at the western suburbs, where the bulk of the Symonds workforce lived. My father's words echoed in my mind, reminding me of the strain of dealing with people. He was always a block of ice with feelings, especially with his sons. But his advice seemed more relevant to me during my years managing the company and then the industry association. I could almost hear his rumbling voice telling me what to do.

'If they don't turn up for work in the morning, you have nothing.' He would often say.

I stood at the window, thinking through my troubles. My dilemma is simple enough. The prime minister and media populists demand I save government money by rejecting the company's request for subsidises. Simple enough. Don't pay taxpayer funds to keep folks employed. The decision was even more single-minded for me: if the government does not guarantee company funding, then the workforce will be retrenched, changing the lives of thousands of families.

Not my life, though.

Unions fight hard for fair work conditions. Their success for their members over the years has meant the cost of manufacture increased thus forcing prices up. Now consumers favour cheaper imports. The pendulum of fairness in the workplace has now swung too far away from skilled labour as machines replaced lifelong jobs. Machines rid the workplace of dispute, but locally manufactured goods prices remained high. As a consequence, we now see investment capital moving to countries with lower taxes and lower labour rates. Go figure.

Modern nations like Australia are developing technology creating fewer jobs for our citizens, and yet the unions still maintain the rage to fight for higher living standards we can't afford.

Symonds is the perfect example of how modern capital works. They are moving their operation to a country with cheaper labour rates, closing old plants with inflexible workforces. The company's chairman, Dietmar Schoenmakers, understands my dilemma, but advised unless the government subsidised redevelopment, they would not stay in Australia.

I let out a sigh as I looked out my window. It was my *show me the money* moment. I had to explain there was no money to show him.

What a day.

It already seems like hours ago I had my run-in with Rosemary. The basketball game got me back on track. Fraser was just too good. It was great Sarah made the effort to get along with Peewee. Maybe they thought Wendy wouldn't be there so wanted to support Fraser. My track record not attending games is well known. What other things have I missed in their lives? I must admit I really haven't put the effort in. Who can blame the children for thinking poorly of me?

Sarah doesn't enjoy talking to me anymore, let alone seeing me. She used to love spending time kidding around with me. Now it seems I'm more trouble to be seen with me, and she avoids me. I'm not sure what went wrong between us. Not being around when she needed me has been an issue I suppose, or it might be a teenage phase. Maybe it's girls not wanting to deal with their dad's discipline and my tendency to say no to any request. I just don't know and haven't bothered to find out.

I admit for years I haven't been engaged at home. When I've been there, it's easier to let them do their own thing rather than imposing upon them. It must be a sacrifice for many blokes to do a job that doesn't get him home. I reckon that could be a reason distance exists between us, I'm never home. I wish it were different, that I was different. Yet here I am doing nothing different.

I'm such a moron.

What is going on with me? Do other blokes my age struggle with a life unfulfilled and battle against this angst I feel?

Am I the only newcomer to this angst of age? I can't be the only one who feels this way? Does any other bloke try to understand themselves a little better? Or am I the only moron struggling with life and getting old?

There are never stories highlighting the struggles old men suffer during the finale of their lives. No stories of their dignity and relevance being ripped from them like mine has today. Maybe this angst I struggle with doesn't exist with other men. Maybe it's just me and my failure to commit to the important things in life. Maybe it's because I'm such a selfish bastard, or maybe I'm just an imposter.

Peter was right. Tim Rogers's dad did marry a young woman. Someone he met at a bar who was his student fifteen years earlier.

This whole notion of starting again is obviously wrong, given my privileged position and the power I retain. How could a bloke in my position, with all my privilege and success, with the trinkets accumulated, still consider life not good enough and need to start again? Excellent question.

I haven't been able to shake this feeling of being a fraud. I still fear being called-out for the fake I think I truly am. Is this the idea that the prime minister mentioned? Am I an impostor in the world he lives? How is that idea even possible? But maybe it is for me.

For a long time, I considered myself to be out of my depth in parliament, especially when promoted to the front bench. I still get worried and admit to nervousness when in question time. I hate the anxiety I feel when my opposition comes to the despatch box to ask a me question. It is much worse when the prime minister is overseas and I'm acting as prime minister. I literally feel ill when my stomach tightens and churns. Yet there I stand at the despatch box with a disarming smile, a witty remark and then a rousing attack on opposition policy. I still feel I am a fake though, waiting to be exposed. Maybe today is that day.

I need to get away from it all to end this negativity that troubles me every day. I still fight this notion of why it is me who must step forward all the time.

Why can't others step forward occasionally and protect me? To stand in front of me and deflect the angst coming at me every single day? This is why there will be no leadership challenge from me against Freya. I could never cope with the anxiety. Why put myself out there as a leader to be rated, criticized, and never having a private life to do the things important for me?

I wandered the floor back and forth in front of the window. This is probably the reason I resist making decisions. It's just too easy to allow others around me get what they want. This anxiety has been overwhelming for years and I just couldn't bring myself to change my personal life. It's just too easy to let strong women like Wendy, Fiona, the Prime Minister, and even Rosemary have their way. I just don't need the aggravation added to my stress.

I stopped pacing and let out a sigh, staring outside. Larry is right. Maybe I don't appreciate my life and the many benefits it provides. I began rubbing my temples. Maybe I'm too blind to see what goes on around me.

I'm so damn confused. I shook my head, trying to clear the fog.

Rosemary isn't the answer for me, that's for sure. She showed me today what it might be like. There's no future with her, I'm sure of that. It surprises me I hadn't seen it earlier, just as Fiona pointed out. I let out a bitter groan.

Selena became my perfect fantasy because I wished I could see her again, and yet she didn't even remember our treasured moments together. I wasted so much emotional energy dreaming about her, which has ultimately stuffed me about. Perhaps I've missed living my future by only ever thinking about the past and dreaming about what might have been. Would my life have been different with Selena? Probably not.

I could never shake this feeling that I missed out on something with her, and now poor me. I've never truly felt the buzz or the same warmth and love with anyone since Selena. How could she forget those three glorious days? Or does she? Why else would she want to visit me? How did she know how to get hold of me unless she remembers? Maybe she could help me sort myself out? Maybe she and the love we shared really is in my future?

Oh Christ, I don't know. And that has been my damn problem for years. I just don't know what to do. As I searched the horizon, I stretched my hands behind my head. I'm such a moron. Pathetic, really.

They say sixty is the new fifty, stuff that for a joke. I reckon sixty will be the new thirty for me. That's where I want to live, back when I was young and carefree. Maybe that's why Rosemary hooked up with me. How is it I can almost get to my sixties and still not know what my life is about? Bizarre really that I haven't sorted myself out, and yet here I am.

My parents just wanted the best for me as most parents do for their children. They insisted their oldest son become a man and take responsibility. I couldn't help but wonder, how did Wendy persuade me to take the road of responsibility?

Just a few short years later I'm a minister with dirty work to do.

How did this happen? Charisma can't be the answer to my political success. When challenged to do the right thing, I usually shrivel. I really should be saving those jobs today, but I am too weak.

I slapped a palm against the window, rattling it.

As I thought about the hardworking Australians who were at risk of losing their jobs, I couldn't shake the feeling that I could save them if I had the political will. I could save them if I had the courage to stand up against the prime minister's wishes. Sure, it's likely I'll lose my job, but the jobs of those hard-working Australians would be saved. Surely that's worthwhile.

I bit down on my lip and grimaced. Here I am succumbing to the will of another woman. This is something I don't want to do anymore. I've had enough.

I cupped the back of my neck and gave it a rub as I shook my head. I've sat on my fat arse for years and years, expecting my life to be different, wishing for romantic love, searching for life's happiness. Now it seems I'm incapable of deciding to bring about the things I want. It's a total mystery to me. Courage has left me and allowed me to become a hollow man. Perhaps it's just easier to quit, just give up and leave.

I felt a sense of hopelessness wash over me. The thought of leaving everything behind crossed my mind. Leave everything: my job, my family, my life, and just vanish. I let out a sigh.

There is way too much responsibility in my life and it's crushing me. It demands me to be present every damn day. It's becoming too much of a burden. I can't stand the way I feel. No one truly understands me or really cares. Why waste my time doing things for people who don't appreciate my efforts to do the right thing? I reckon no-one would miss me if I took off and ended it all. I breathed deep and then dropped my head and let out a moan.

This is what hurts so much. The bleak loneliness of my life and it's overwhelming. The shame of failure bullies me and follows me everywhere, every day, and no-one fucking cares.

My eyes welled, so I brushed a cheek.

I couldn't help but reflect, no-one cares about men. Not even men.

What drives men to give up on life by taking theirs in such high numbers? Do they have an angst they can't control which they suppress with no-one to talk to? Do they struggle with who they have become and their relevance? Are they lonely? Why don't they call someone before they do it? Like me they probably think no one cares. Don't they realise we love them?

The staggering statistics of men taking their lives makes a startling statistic. For every woman who commits suicide, three men do the same. Yet, we hide these figures and seldom talk about them. I have thought about these things over the last few days and accept it will be my fault if one Symonds employee ends their life. Will anyone care if they do?

I will, and it will be an extra burden for me.

As I gazed out the window, my mind wandered.

A larger than normal brown coloured bird glided in the distance, playing on the air streams as it circled its way down then floating up again. Was there prey about or was it living the carefree life? No rigid system out there. The bird's effortless movements were a stark contrast to the weight of responsibility that hung heavy on my shoulders.

Floating with the breeze; no cares, no stress, no demand, just a whisper of air, heading in a different direction. Floating on air. Would you feel the air if you were hurtling down to the street? To give up and just... let... go. What would it feel like? When would I stop thinking I was floating? When would this angst leave me? At the window? Or would the friggin' thing follow me all the way down?

I read somewhere, maybe it was yesterday on the plane, the highest incidence of men ending their lives is in my age group. Fuck. Does that mean these blokes who kill themselves feel the same as I do right now? Just wanting to give up on their life and exit the stage after getting to the juncture where they can't cope with what's going on around them. Losing all control and reasoning by wanting their angst to end, so they just decide to end their life.

Something needs to change because this thinking is becoming morbidly dangerous for me.

'Minister?' Fiona was standing at my desk. 'Are you okay? Didn't you hear me?'

'Sorry Fiona, I was miles away. What did you say?' I continued gazing out the window, fixed on the bird as it dipped and soared.

'Margaret Hodgeman is here. She's with the union reps with their tea and bickies waiting for you.'

'Call Jordan to join us, please.'

'Shall do. Do you need anything, a tea perhaps?'

'No, thanks. What time is Miss Tatupo coming in again?'

'I have scheduled her for five. Is everything okay? You look a little pasty?'

'It's been an interesting day.' I felt a little pasty with this sense of defeat washing over me. 'My travel over the last few days has been hectic. No doubt it's catching up with me. I feel a little drained.'

'I don't know how you do it sometimes.'

'Neither do I, that's my trouble.' I couldn't help but let out a sigh.

'How do you mean?'

'I put all this work and travel in trying to do the right thing, yet today unless I do as Freya Lewis wants, I lose my job.'

'Be true to yourself, Ryan.' Fiona's words were a familiar comfort. And she's been telling me that same cliché for years. 'Do what is right for you and your family. Focus on them for a change.'

Easy to say, harder to do I'm afraid, but I appreciated her senti-ments. 'Thanks Fiona, always good advice.'

But as she left to call my senior policy adviser, I couldn't shake the feeling of being torn in multiple directions. The weight of responsibility, the expectations of others, and the fear of failure all pressed heavily on me. It was a difficult balance to strike, and the thought of giving up and letting go, like the bird outside, was a tempting escape, but not right now.

Scanning the few notes Fiona had left, I tried not to focus on the challenges thrown at me today. Peter's police issues, Sarah's international trip, Freya Lewis, Larry and his money. Rosemary and her crazy demands. Symonds, Wendy's scratches, and what about that cold shower? Selena came to mind, and those damn wasted years thinking she was a goddess. Regrettably, now realising she wasn't.

Now the union was pounding my head like a headache. Maybe I just don't enjoy my life anymore. Crumbs, that's a step in the right direction by admitting I don't enjoy my life. I hate it and now admit it. I shook my head as I thought about the day. Christ, I'm a troubled soul: hopefully, it'll get better tomorrow.

'Hi boss.' Jordan stood in the doorway. 'Is there anything you want me to do?'

I let out a sigh, rubbing my temple. 'No, let them get their issues out.' I collected my favourite folder. 'Let's give them a good hearing. We'll tell them we tried to meet their demands. Blame the Germans and give them the blah, blah, blah.'

'Not sure they will accept government chitter-chatter spin.' Jordan moved aside, motioning me to pass.

'Let's see how it goes. I suppose we need an agreement not to take strike action.'

'Yeah, well good luck with that one,' said Jordan as he trailed after me.

Twenty-Four

4:04 PM

The delegation stood as we entered. Indeed, most folks do when I enter a room as if in reverence to some sort of grand deity. I can't help but wonder if it's the man they're venerating, or the position I hold. This is maybe the reason why many of my political colleagues misunderstand their true status in the community. It's not them but the job they do that brings the esteem. I so hate this job and the dills I need to be associated with. It needs to end.

'Lionel, nice to see you again.' I offered my hand. 'And Michella, you are as radiant as ever.' I sat with Margaret Hodgeman on the opposite side of the table. Jordan lurked in a chair in a shadowed corner of the room. 'I see you have a tea. Did you manage to secure a chocolate biscuit?'

'All good Minister, thank you.' Lionel smiled, taking his seat. 'Thank you for seeing us. We appreciate the opportunity to speak with you again so soon after your visit to Germany.'

'I'm afraid my trip was not as successful as we would have hoped.' I shrugged, knowing full well they were aware of the company's decision. 'They clarified that unless government stumps up the cash, they're out of Australia.'

'As to be expected,' said Lionel with a sympathetic nod, seeming to understand my predicament. 'They've been bleeding the Australian operations dry for years. It's time for them to step up and support their workers. The bastards have stepped down and backed away at the first sign of trouble, typical bloody Krauts.'

'That is not welcome news for our members, Minister,' Michella said, her tone heavy with sadness. 'What will the government's message be to them?' Her face etched with gloom.

'They've agreed to meet the national standards on retrenchment. More generous than anything being offered in Europe.' I tried to inject enthusiasm into the conversation. 'They agreed to provide four weeks' extra pay for all the factory staff. Not administration, though.'

'Factory admin?' Michella asked, scribbling notes.

'That's a good question. Their specific response was administration staff at the corporate office.' I turned and nodded to Jordan, taking notes. 'Let's check it, Jordan. I assumed all staff in the factory would be compensated, including on-site office staff.'

'Is there nothing we can do, comrade?' Lionel asked, his voice heavy with concern. 'My members are keen to keep working.'

'The company has requested the labour rate be reduced to twenty-five dollars an hour, with limited penalties for additional work beyond standard hours.' I expected a reaction. Michella's pen began tapping noisily on her notepad. 'They want the entire workplace wage system based on units produced, not hours worked. They're offering annual bonuses to bring the rate back to normal award rates, if production numbers and costs are within budget.'

'How very generous of them.' Michella's sarcastic tone suggesting she didn't agree.

'Is the government prepared to do anything?' Lionel asked, his voice tinged with hope.

'As I've said in previous meetings, no.' I paused, the silence emphasising my point. 'The government has been clear about its policy. We will not provide subsidises.'

'Why not?' Lionel's voice filled with frustration, broke the silence.

'If we do it for one, then every business will expect the same treatment when faced with similar financial circumstances. Plus, the government can't afford it.'

'How did it come to this?' Lionel asked, heavy with disappointment.

'I suspect it's the convergence of a lot of issues.' I knew he would not appreciate this next comment, so I braced for his reaction. 'The simple fact is your members have the highest labour rate in Asia. They are two times the rate of Europe. No matter the proximity to their major market, Symonds can manufacture and ship cheaper from their German base than what they can make it for here.'

'It's unacceptable.' Lionel said, now tight with anger. No one would disagree with him.

'It's just another example of the bosses screwing the workers,' Michella chimed in, her bitterness evident.

It surprised me to hear such an antiquated cliché. I had thought I had enlightened her in a more balanced view of industrial relations when she worked with me at the peak industry body. Maybe that philosophy is why she resigned to organise for a union. Working for an employer group as an IR adviser was not to her liking. I followed her career with interest and thought of her as a protege. I liked her and rated her family highly.

I forced a smile, shrugging. 'That argument might have been relevant fifty years ago. We now operate in a free market where capital and labour compete. In this case, labour has lost.'

'So, my members suffer the consequences,' she snapped, dropping her pen, crossing her arms as she leaned back.

'It seems so.' I kneaded my hands as I gazed at her. 'At least they're receiving a generous payout. Which, if I'm right, is a record settlement.'

'Big deal,' Michella said, full of sarcasm. 'I think my members would prefer to keep their jobs.'

'Then why not accept the company's offer and take a pay cut?'

'Would you?' Michella shot back, challenging me.

'If it was the difference between me starving and being able to pay my bills... yes, I probably would.' I knew full well I had never had to make that decision.

'What would you know about starving and job loss?' Michella turned it personal. 'You weep for us comrade, but you have no idea how we suffer with the uncertainty, with the never-ending fear of losing your job.' She wouldn't know I have that feeling most days. 'When you tell us to accept less than half of what we're worth, we lose more than just money... we lose identity and dignity.'

I sat with my hands entwined, gazing at her, conceding the distress she seems to be suffering. 'It's unfortunate, I'm sure, but this is the world in which we live.'

'It shouldn't always be about money,' she said, her mouth taunt with a hint of defiance. I admired her spunk to speak out, but reality had a way of biting hard in business. Perhaps I should have spent more time explaining profitable business models to her. 'We need to do something. You need to act to save their future,' she pleaded.

'Michella.' I fanned open my hands, trying to reason with her. 'Many working people in this world already have a future. In this case, your members do not have a future because their union is inflexible with the wage rate.'

She flipped open a file of what seemed to be 10x8 photos and placed the top one before me, a smiling woman with two kids. 'This is Marion Breust, a single mother of two. This unskilled line worker has been with the company twelve years.' She dropped the next photo on top, an older couple. 'This is Benjamin Langford. He's sixty-three and has been with the company for nearly thirty-five years.' She placed another. 'Rita Hale has an adult disabled child and a husband with dementia. She has worked for the company for two decades.'

'Are you planning to go through all two thousand?' I frowned, wanting her to stop. 'What's your point?' I detected nothing of the relationship we share.

'My point is Minister,' she said, her voice rising as she jabbed a finger at me. 'These union members have families. They have responsibilities and at the end of their shift today they will be told they don't have a job and there is nothing they can do about it.' Her voice dropped to a near whisper as she added, 'my point is Minister, why aren't you taking responsibility and saving their jobs? In many cases their lives?'

'That's a little unfair. We've tried to help.'

'Have you?' she sneered as she gazed at me through watery eyes.

Lionel touched her arm. 'We would've preferred the government to provide funds and continue operations. At least offering them a tax incentive.'

I studied them, trying to remain calm. 'They want the government to fund retooling and transition from manufacturing heavy-duty trucks to first strike drones.'

'What's holding you back from giving it to them?' Michella asked.

'Are you serious?' I breathed in and sighed. 'You want the government to save jobs, but you do nothing to save yourselves. You folks would not negotiate about reskilling the workforce, and yet you plead for us to pay.'

'They wanted to cut numbers,' Lionel said.

'For heaven's sake, Lionel. You don't want reskilling and you aren't prepared to reform working conditions. You either want to save jobs or you don't?'

Lionel slammed his hand on the table. 'We've worked too damn hard to gain those conditions for our members.'

'Yes, but the reality is your recalcitrance means twenty-five hundred workers lose their jobs and Australia loses another manufacturing company to our trading partners.'

'You can subsidise the wage bill. You've done it before with vehicle manufacturing,' Michella suggested.

'Free trade agreements with our regional partners now hamstring the government. There are limitations to what we can do. And we don't have any vehicle manufacturing anymore. Another industry where the union priced their members out of a job.'

'You can do whatever you want. You're the government, not some Asian monarch who may want to trade with us,' Michella said, sounding dismissive. 'They'll always want to trade with Australia, Ryan, you know that,' she added with a hint of annoyance.

I looked at her, then shook my head. 'Not necessarily.' I tried not to antagonise her but could not let her point go unchallenged. 'We take our obligations seriously.'

'No one else does,' Michella almost yelled, her voice rising in frustration. Another woman barking at me today. 'You just don't have the balls to do the right thing.'

'Please don't shout.' I felt a twinge of guilt. Maybe she was right. The thought of being a weak leader without the courage to make difficult decisions came to mind. I gazed at her, considering how to finish this distressing discussion. 'Let's try to keep the meeting civil.' I wasn't sure appeasement would work. 'There is nothing I can do to save this deal. If you aren't prepared to save your members, why should the taxpayer help you?'

'What a surprise. No doubt a commentary on your department. You are always promising but never delivering, eh, Minister?' Lionel chimed in.

'We have done what we could.' If they only knew what I just claimed wasn't true. I should have been tougher with the prime minister. 'I have done what I could.'

Michella's scowl of disappointment suggested she wasn't convinced. Lionel leaned forward to make a point. 'You have not impressed us during these negotiations, comrade. We will reflect on your future in the parliament over this ministerial inaction. If you know what I mean,' He said leaning back, rocking the chair, not taking his eyes from me.

It was an obvious threat. He was threatening my preselection. Unlikely he could influence it as he didn't have the numbers. I did. His threat still sent a tremble across my shoulders. I leaned back in my chair, stroking the hair on my chin taking a moment to reflect. 'I'm not sure I can help you with anything further.'

'This is typical of all you dickheads,' Michella snapped. 'A little taste of challenging political times and you forget where you come from. You use us when you need us. Then you just throw us away like some disposable nappy when it gets too hard. You're all a bunch of loser bastards,' she added, her voice filled with anger and disappointment.

'No political ambition?' I grimaced, accepting her emotional outburst. 'You said you wanted to make a difference.'

'Not likely now,' Michella responded, she almost spat the words. 'Having to compromise my values and what I stand for is not the job I want. I shall leave that to the spivs and fakers like you, Minister.'

'We are all here to make a difference.'

'Crap! You're here for your own self-interest. You don't care about the Symonds workers. You'll still sleep tonight. Me, on the other hand, will be doing what I can to support my members,' Michella said, her voice filled with conviction.

'Lionel, it's been a pleasure.' I stood, ushering them to the door with a grin, leading them through to the lift lobby. I firmly shook his hand, but Michella didn't bother acknowledging me. 'Michella, I'm sorry this hasn't worked out for you. You, more than anyone should know I've done my best.' She didn't look up. 'Say hello to your mum for me.' I watched her as the doors slid closed, hoping for a response, then shook my head when I got nothing.

'Well done, Minister. I think you handled that quite well.' Margaret offered her words dripping with politeness. Jordan, on the other hand remained silent.

'I'm not sure what they expected me to say. I suppose they expressed what they needed to say. It could have been worse.'

'A little respect might have been appropriate.' Margaret collected her things, making her way to the door. 'I shall brief you tomorrow on the offshore gas project. We have a fracking decision to be made in a week. I need your direction, but it can all wait until tomorrow.' She opened the door, and as she left, said, 'Very good meeting, Minister.'

'She must be joking,' Jordan said once the door closed. 'To have your preselection threatened like that is unbelievable.'

'You heard that too?'

'They may come after you. Although they haven't got too many supporters within the party.' Jordan sat opposite at the table. 'We can fix it.'

'Jesus, don't you ever give up?' I wasn't happy with what he was implying. 'Doesn't anyone ever give up?'

Jordan stared straight at me and without hesitating said. 'Minister, you are the best thing going for the government. You just need to put up a fight.'

'Michella had a point, though.'

'What's that?' Jordan asked, looking confused.

'We change as a person as we accept more responsibility.'

'How? I don't understand.' Jordan seemed perplexed.

'We stop making decisions when we compromise our values.'

Twenty-Five

4:35 PM

My chest felt tight again. I sighed, rubbing my hand over my breastbone for relief. Over recent months, the tightness has become more of an issue for me. Wendy insists I should visit my doctor and have tests to understand why the tightness would appear only at certain times. There was no pain, so for me there was little to worry about. Just an occasional feeling as if my chest was being hugged. Frankly, there was no time to visit the doctor. I should visit her though, I know. I thought it could wait until the tightness got worse or was replaced by pain. This time though I just think it's anxiety. It has been a tough day and maybe the increasing tightness of my chest is from what's been going on. Gone were those casual days where nothing would upset me.

I relaxed back in my chair for a quiet moment. After a few deep breaths, my eyes closed, and I felt my body start to relax, heading for sleep. I took another deep breath, trying to steady my racing mind. The demands of the day have taken their toll and I could feel myself drifting off.

Did I just hear myself snore?

Which is impossible because I wasn't asleep, but my eyes are closed, with my arms comforting me across my chest. My body relaxing more and more with each deep breath.

The surf was up, and I felt good, wrapped in my woollen jacket and my woollen boots driving warmth into my frozen feet. A blanket wrapped around, tucking into hot salty chips and smooth fat-dripping chicken in the front seat of a panel van. Watching the other crazies out in the surf on a cold winter's day. Nothing could be better than that. The memory brought a wry smile as I remembered Larry and the idiot he was in my life. He still is in many ways.

We took family summer holidays on the coast; the beach was often crowded with people who thought surfing was some sort of follow the sun adventure. After a few years of fighting for camp site space, we began staying at a lodge. Then we started renting a holiday house. Rather than waste money renting, we purchased a house beachside off the coast road. The kids would play on the beach and sometimes watch the amateurs struggle with the shore breaks while I was out the back trying to tame the bigger swell.

The children were never interested in hitting the surf. It never excited them. Too rough and they hated the idea of sharks, or even drowning. They didn't know the joy of standing on a board and cutting a big wave. Summer holidays for me soon became working holidays once I became a minister. When a cafe opened, breakfast and lattes got me start4d early to fill the days with work. Eventually, the kids stopped wanting to travel to the coast and the house now stands vacant most of the year. Wendy spends time down there by herself searching for whatever she needs in her life. Candles are everywhere, and it's set up like a health retreat for her girlfriends. I keep promising myself I'll take a sabbatical for a week or two at the house and write the brilliant novel, but this too becomes a squandered dream. Me and my damn dreams never seem to come together. Life just seems to get in the way.

No one else ever wanted to share my passion for the water, except for Selena. Wendy didn't like the sand and salt against her face. It damaged something apparently and triggered something else. I never took much notice. The kids now prefer technology and watching television, so I just leave them to it. I live in a house with little meaning or love, within a family full of strangers.

Over thirty years later, eating that dripping scrumptious chicken with a beautiful girl still seems real to me. Those days have never been thought about with as much romance and joy as I do now. Those were the days is a cliché riddled with meaning for me now. No doubt I hang around with Larry because he remains a link to those surfing days.

Does Rosemary love me? My sore lip may show she doesn't. She says she does, but only a bit I reckon, and for her own selfish reasons. She obviously wants the lifestyle I can provide.

Does Wendy love me? She could have left the marriage years ago and taken the kids with her and we all could be better off. We don't seem to do family activities as we once did, there's not much fun anymore. Wendy seems so involved with her community group she just doesn't have time for me anymore. The horrible fact could be that no one loves me and perhaps no one ever has, nor cares. I don't even get the love from Mum anymore.

How shallow is this veneer of my life I portray, living this loveless lie? I shook my head and gently touched my lip. Get over yourself, will you?

When I was young, life meant something to me. I had a lot of enthusiasm for what I did. Now I'm just going through the motions of being a husband, a father, and a politician. Always playing a role and never expressing my true feelings to anyone. It disappointments me not to be listened to, and I feel vulnerable, as it seems no one cares about me. So, I just don't want to be here anymore, as it just seems so bloody pointless.

'Boss, are you okay?' My eyes opened. Jordan was looking at me. 'Jet lag kicking in?'

'No, I'm fine. Just taking a moment to recharge.' I forced a smile and swung into my desk. 'Do you have the speech?'

'Yes, Jo has done a great job,' Jordan said, holding up a stack of papers. 'She covered the need for economic certainty, and we need to invest in new industries, as old manufacturing and infrastructure are no longer affordable. We cannot fund them for the sake of prolonging the inevitable.'

'Sounds fine.'

'She also said it's not government subsidy which helps the community. It's funding education, training, and providing a growing market where entrepreneurs can build businesses employing new skills in the community.'

'The media may not go for that. They'll be looking for a scape-goat.' I grimaced. 'How does she cover the request for funding by the Germans?'

'She doesn't,' Jordan said, flipping through the pages. 'What she wants you to talk about is the free trade agreements. The need for the world to reject the populist push for protection.' Jordan read from the speech. 'Business welfare is never any good for the econ-omy. It must be avoided if we are to maintain an open and free trading world. She recommends avoiding saying anything about Germany.'

'I suspect avoiding the Germans may be risky.

'That's the risk we have gotta take,' Jordan said. 'It's the right thing to do.'

'Yeah, I know.' I felt a twinge of guilt as I paused for a moment. 'It's hard to shake the feeling that my life as a minister is just this shallow veneer. I think I am just playing a role without much depth and never expressing my true feelings about political issues like this one.'

Jordan gave me a weird unsympathetic look. 'Where did that come from? That sounds a little strange if you don't mind me saying.' He shook his head. 'We all have our struggles, boss. It's important to remember that we're doing this for the greater good, but it's never too late to make a change.'

I nodded. 'Yeah, you're right. Sorry about that.' I grimaced and drummed my fingers on the arm of the chair. 'These free trade arguments just don't work' I sighed and shook my head. 'Other countries provide support for their entrepreneurs especially their farmers and manufacturers.'

'We do as well for Australian brands. Symonds is not a national company. Its origins are European.'

'Okay, leave it with me. I'll get across it and ignore how I really feel about it all. Do we expect many journos?'

'The networks and press will be there. I'm not sure who is coming from radio,' Jordan said referring to notes. 'This is a big deal, isn't it?'

'Jordan, bigger than we will ever know.' I scratched my face. 'The populist view could go either way. The public were with us months ago, especially after the PM started talking about jobs going to China. But it seems to have clawed its way back to the other side.'

'Senator Granger has called a media doorstop after your media conference,' Jordan added, a hint of concern in his voice. 'I suppose she will demand the government back local jobs.'

'No doubt.' I stifled a yawn. 'What do you expect from a xenophobe? Will we take a hit in the polls?'

'Of course, but thankfully it'll be seen as the PM's fault.'

I remain unconvinced that Lewis would take the popularity hit. 'It's my decision. So, it'll be seen as my fault.'

'It's not your fault. You're doing what your prime minister asked you to do.'

'If the polls go up, she'll claim it as her decision, proclaiming to be the greatest leader of our era. Which she isn't.' I never enjoyed stating the obvious. 'If the polls go down, believe me, it will be my fault. Do we have a focus group listening to the announcement?'

'Yes. The PM's office organised it.'

I couldn't help but roll my eyes. *That'd be right*, scampered through my brain.

'We will have the first results about an hour or two after you finish the media. We start selected polling the day after next.'

'Okay, leave it with me. I have a meeting at five and I've got to prepare for it.' I felt the tension across my shoulders and tightness in my neck, but it was only my troubles still gripping me.

The only thing keeping me sane these last few months was my belief I was getting closer to Selena. Now, in a few minutes we meet for the first time in over thirty years. Let's hope my reality fits my dream, although it rarely does.

Twenty-Six

4:58 PM

'**M**inister, Miss Tatupo is here. Would you prefer the meeting room or here?'

'In here will be fine, thanks Fiona.'

I stood, fumbling with my jacket, and checking the window reflection. I turned back as Fiona led Selena into the office.

It was bizarre. I couldn't help but feel a sense of unease. I didn't recognise the mature woman before me in an elegant, yet out of fashion black suit and I gestured her to sit in the lounge, before taking the hard chair beside it. Tea was offered and rejected, so Fiona left, raising an eyebrow as she closed the door.

I cleared my throat, feeling a sense of awkwardness wash over me. 'Thank you so much for coming to see me.' My tone polite yet guarded.

'Minister, I'm a little unsure if I should have come,' Selena replied, her sultry voice tinged with nerves. 'I didn't know what to think after your call this morning. It confused me. I had no idea what was happening. I thought we should meet face to face to talk. You look different on the web than you do in real life.'

'I must apologise for putting you on the spot this morning. It was inappropriate of me and I'm sorry.'

'I'm happy you did.' Selena seemed tense and appeared uncomfortable sitting on the edge of the couch, the seams on her trousers getting a decent stretch. 'As I said this morning, I remember little from my days in the sun. Your call startled me a bit.'

'Yes, I'm sure it would have puzzled you. Again, I apologise.' I tried to read the expression on Selena's face.

'Why did you call?' she asked, her eyes fixed on mine.

I hesitated for a moment, unsure of how to answer. 'Well, that's a tough question. It's very complex. Do you ever wish your life was different?'

'Not really,' Selena said with a shrug. 'Life is not about the past, eh?'

'So, you have no regrets?'

'You've got to be kidding me.' She laughed. 'There are huge regrets about the things I've done. But they are done. I can't do anything about them now, eh?'

'As I recall, we met around thirty years ago and spent a few days, maybe a week, together. We travelled along the coast, but you were heading further south, and I had to return to the city.'

'Shame, man. Why didn't you come?' she asked, her eyebrows furrowed.

'They needed me at home. I'd planned to catch up but things got in the way.' A sense of regret washed over me.

'Life is like that, eh?'

'What are you doing with yourself these days?' I wasn't sure what to ask, but I felt sure we would get to the reason she came to visit. Selena's complexion was like any other woman with plenty of sun and surf in her past. A short straight, modern comb-over replaced her once thick luminous long hair, with one side shaved back and coloured pink. Like me, weight for age caught up, with her shirt buttons fighting not to pop. Her silver jewellery seemed modern and corporate, although I noticed too many studs in an ear.

'I've worked in sales most of my life,' Selena began, her voice touched with a hint of nostalgia. 'It's all I know, doing a deal. It's what I learnt when young. I seemed good at it as the commissions rolled in, although the young ones are now getting the jobs I used to get.'

'Did you get married?'

'Three times,' she scoffed a laugh. 'Yeah, nah, marriage is not for me. It took three rotten failures to get that gem of wisdom. It's much easier hooking up using technology these days. What about you?'

'I have been married for twenty years.'

'Are you happy, man?' Selena gazed at me. 'I mean you have swelling on your face. Did your wife hit you this morning?'

'No, why do you ask?' I was a little surprised by her question.

'You look like a woman punched you,' Selena said, pointing to my face. I touched it. It didn't feel as puffy as it did. 'I know it was a woman. When a man hits you, there's bruising, teeth missing, or even a broken jaw. I can tell you; it hurts when you get hit by a man. When a woman hits you, it's a stinger and only lasts a couple of hours. You've got a stinger right there.'

'No, I fell over at lunch. I bounced up carpeted stairs and clipped a step, crashing into the carpet.'

'Yeah, sure you did. Don't kid a kidder.' Selena smiled. 'Don't take that shit from her, man. Toughen up.'

'I'm sorry to disappoint you, but it was an accident.'

'Once they hit you, they don't stop,' Selena said, her voice serious. 'I can tell you that from personal experience. So, get out while you can.' Selena drew in a breath and gazed at me. 'Is that why you called me?'

'No.'

'Then why did you call? Are you hoping we could get back in the saddle?' Selena asked, her tone mocking.

'I rang to talk to you and maybe discuss the summer we shared.' This was now embarrassing. 'I just needed to talk to you.'

'So, after all these years, you just called to talk about surfing?' she asked, her voice sceptical. 'Yeah right. What did you really want to talk about?'

Gazing at this stranger before me, I pondered what to say, bit my bottom lip and shrugged. She seemed smart enough to figure out what the creepy phone call was about. She surmised I was keen to reconnect. Well, that was then, but not now. 'No. I just wanted to catch up and reminisce about those holidays. I enjoyed that summer. I've been thinking about it, so I thought I would find you, and have a chat.'

'Like a stalker?'

'Nooohohoho, it is not like that.' I felt awkward and now uncomfortable with this stranger. 'I only wanted to catch up.' She needs to get to the point of why she came. 'How can I help you this evening?'

'Can I call you Ryan?' Selena asked, her voice soft. I nodded, unsure of where this conversation was heading. 'Let me be honest, Ryan, life has beaten me, literally. I've struggled to enjoy what it offers. I seldom see my children, and I haven't met my grandkids. I live in a one-bedroom apartment at the back of a house, and I'm relegated to telephone sales these days. Me? The queen of the deal. Now I can't get out on the road anymore to earn the big bucks.'

'Why are you telling me this?

'I haven't been in a relationship for a long time. I miss the sweat and smell of a man. All I get is the pawing morons I hook up with on Tinder.'

'What's your point?'

'You tell me we had a great time together,' Selena continued, a hint of longing in her voice. 'I'm sure you're being truthful. So, I think about that. I try to recall that summer you talk about, but I can't. I don't remember you.'

'So, why are you here?'

'I'm here to meet you, to remember. I'm here to tell you I would like to learn more about you.' Her gaze fixed on mine. 'We might build on your memory and perhaps we can recapture what you think we had. I can see by your face, and your energy tells me you are troubled. I think I can help, eh?'

'How?'

'Oh, I don't know,' Selena replied, her voice playful. 'Spend some time together. Go down the coast and check out what it's like. Maybe share a wine, perhaps a meal, maybe a bed.'

'I'm not sure that would work, Selena.' Is she suggesting what I think she's suggesting? 'I'm married.'

'You aren't happy, obviously. Eh?'

'I'm okay.'

'Then why did you ring me? A summer screw from way back?'

'I enjoyed our time together.'

'You need to man up, I reckon, Ryan, honey.' She sat back in the lounge. 'You need to live in the now, not the past.'

'Thanks for the advice. I'll take it on board. Anything else?'

She paused for a moment as if thinking about what she wanted to say. 'I need help.'

'What sort of help?' I dreaded asking.

'I need money. A weekly amount to help pay my bills.'

'Why have you come to me? There are government agencies which can help.' I felt uncomfortable.

'Government agencies can't help,' she replied, her tone dismissive. 'Anyway, I already use them when I can.' She smiled at me, her expression suggestive. 'No, what I want sweetheart, and I suspect what you also need is a good hard work-out once a week.'

'Say what?'

'I need someone to soak my sheets, and I think you can do it.'

'Are you suggesting what I think you're suggesting?'

'I reckon you remember what it's like to be with me. That's why you tracked me down. I can assure you; I've lost none of my skills.' She licked her thick lips, and I remembered. 'Sure, I may be bigger and perhaps not as agile, but you are no beanpole either. I think if we have a weekly... let's call it lunch, then we would both be satisfied.' I was taken aback, almost shocked. She was soliciting me. 'You could re-live your youth every week. I can assure you it would be worth your time, and very much welcomed by me. Plus, I can pay my bills. Are you excited enough to be interested?'

I didn't know what to say. I raised my eyebrows and smiled. 'I don't think so, Selena.'

'Come on, Ryan. This will be good for your marriage as well. You can get a happy ending once a week and the little woman will stop hitting you.'

I steepled my fingers, wondering if I should laugh. 'I'm not interested. Thank you.'

'You really are a pussy, Ryan, aren't you? I looked you up. That is the common view out there,' Selena said, her voice now heavy with disdain.

'Can we just end it there if you don't mind?' I stood and walked to the door.

'You want to live with my memory and the romantic things we did together, but you don't want to thank me for it. Typical fucking man,' she sneered, following me to the door.

'I'm not sure selling yourself is an offer I can accept.'

'I'm not selling myself, honey. I'm just suggesting we hook up. Selena can bring the best out of you. That's something you want, isn't it?' she said, closing the deal.

I smiled and shrugged my shoulders. 'No means no, I'm afraid.'

'Just like the media says about you,' she retorted, her eyes flashing with annoyance. 'They say you're a wimp. I'm guessing from the energy in this room they're right.'

'Thanks for dropping by. It was great to see you again.'

'You'll regret this, and when you do, honey, then call Selena.' She leaned in for a kiss. 'Let me take you to a different world.' I baulked away. 'You truly are a pussy, aren't you? Can't handle a real woman.' She left with the grace as if she had just closed the deal.

After a few moments, Fiona poked her head around the door. We then just sat at my desk and gazed at each other. Eventually, she said, 'What were you thinking?' We burst into a loud hysterical laugh.

'I don't know what I was thinking. That was the wake-up call from hell.'

'What did she say?' Fiona asked, still trying to catch her breath.

'She doesn't remember me. But that didn't stop her from offering herself to me. For a price, of course.'

'Sometimes Ryan, lives don't turn out the way we want them to. So, let's not judge her. Just savour the memory you shared with her all those years ago,' Fiona said, her voice soft.

'I suspect it's a waste of time to be thinking about the past. What she said, which got me thinking, was that we must live in the now, not the past.'

'How come you're just learning that now? Haven't you been listening to me?'

'She did also say I was a bit of a wimp?'

'I like this woman.'

Twenty-Seven

———————————————

The personalised ring tone squawk jolted me from my peculiar musings about my meeting with Selena. Thinking about her and our past has been a total waste of time. My memories of her, once treasured and held close, now seem to fade like a dying ember. I picked up the phone.

'Hey Rat, I just wanted to thank you again for helping me out. Everything is resolved. I'll get the money back to you as soon as I can, at the very latest, when we agreed.'

'Thanks Larry. I'm glad you sorted it. Can I just suggest you give up the gambling and concentrate on growing a pot of money for yourself?'

'Easy for you to say, given you have everything,' Larry retorted, with a trace of bitterness. He just doesn't get it. No one does. I have nothing. 'Hey, speaking of which; how did your meeting go with the islander?'

'Weird, would be the word I would use?'

'Why? What did she look like? Still the same with that gorgeous hair?'

'I thought you didn't remember?'

'I do, kinda. She and the French chick jerked us around for a few days. I remember you were in love. I recall her friend telling me the islander was just a flirt in a skirt,' Larry said, with a touch of nostalgia.

'Why didn't you tell me? You could have saved me years.'

'Did she still have a tight bod?' Larry asked, his mind immediately jumping to the physical. He never fails to disappoint me. 'I bet she did.'

'No, I wouldn't call it tight. Comfortable would be more like it.'

'Like all of us, then? What did she want?'

'Money.'

'Really? She hit you up for cash after all this time?'

'It was more of a transaction for regular action if you get my drift.'

'Crap! No way!' He almost deafened me. 'No one hooks up after decades and does a deal like that. Surely, you're pulling my lariat?'

'It was truly bizarre. She didn't remember me at all. Not one memory. She Googled me and thought I might be cute. She assumed a weekly workout would be fun and help with her bills.'

'What did you say?'

Why is he even asking? 'No, of course.'

'Why, of course? You're still bonking the lawyer. So why not get a bit on the side of the girl you already have on the side?' He laughed.

'Don't be ridiculous.'

'Me? Ridiculous? You're the one putting everything at risk because you've been hanging onto a memory which doesn't exist,' Larry retorted, his comment slicing right through me. 'You're the moron here, my friend.'

If I'd gotten into that van with Selena, I'd be nothing more than a fleeting memory, a ghost of the past.

'You need a good kick up the arse,' Larry said, his words as sharp as a whip crack. 'You must get your act together and stop worrying about the past. You should concentrate on what you have. Otherwise, you'll lose it all.'

'I'm not so sure about that.'

'Mate, your lawyer screw kicked your arse today. She showed you what she's really like. Is that what you want?' he asked, his tone tough and obstinate.

'That's a little harsh. You weren't there.'

'Did you ask about kids?' He seemed eager to make his point. 'I bet she wants them. Am I right?'

'Sort of.'

'Yeah, thought so. I also reckon if you weren't in your job right now, she would drop you like a hot potato. Am I right?' he asked, his words a pointed barb.

'Maybe.'

'Then what the hell do you think you're playing at? You've been spruiking this crap for years, that you're not fulfilled and how you deserve love. Dreaming about something you missed out on decades ago,' he moaned, giving me little sympathy. 'Well, that's crap, Rat. You've got to get over it. You also need to get over yourself.'

I sort of agreed. 'I think I am, now.'

'Well, hallelujah to that brother,' Larry declared, his voice full of sarcasm. 'You already have great things in your life. Just focus on them. Go live your life for fuck's sake. Stop dreaming about the past and start living in the future. You've got to focus on Wendy and the kids.'

'I thought I was. She gets what she wants.'

'Leadership is a verb, Rat, not a noun,' he said, sassing me again. 'You need to lead and stop taking this crap from others, especially the lawyer. Get rid of these daydreams that never existed from your past. Take a stand brother and see what you can achieve.' Curiously, he seemed to make sense. 'Wendy and the kids are fantastic and they're your biggest asset. Don't toss them away because you're distracted by a wasted dream of a few days one summer.'

'Thanks Larry, I'll consider it.'

'There you go again, you fucking moron. Treating me like some political flake. Get over yourself, will you? Start being the person I know you to be.'

I sighed. 'Okay.'

'Yeah, sure mate, at least sound engaged,' Larry retorted.

'Sorry, Larry. I just have my mind on a media conference I must do at six.' I ran a hand through my hair.

'I'll let you go then. Let me just leave you with this... take control, mate.' I was about to ring off when he continued. 'And just before you go. I gotta ask. Is there any chance I can get her number?'

I cocked an eyebrow. 'Who's number?'

'The islander.'

'Selena is her name. Why do you want it?'

'Mate, I haven't had a relationship with anyone in years. She might remember me.'

'You what?'

'Christ, mate, do I have to spell it out for you? Can I have Selena's number, so I can call and perhaps go see her?'

'You're kidding me?' My disbelief surely evident to him.

'No, I'm not. You mean nothing to her. She can't even remember you. You say she doesn't even look like the girl you remember. If she needs financial help, I might be able to assist.'

'You're unbelievable.'

'Hey Rat, help out a mate.'

'I thought I did this afternoon.'

'If you believe there is nothing you need from her. Then there is no reason you wouldn't let me catch up,' Larry said.

Maybe he was right. Selena was not a memory I wanted to keep.

If I passed on her phone number, then there would be no going back. She could always decline. It's only a work number. He wouldn't be able to harass her. She would be in control. It might lead to something good for them both. 'Got a pen? It's a work number. Selena Tatupo, 9555 94 84.'

'Thanks Rat. You're a champ. Trust me, I won't talk about you at all.'

'If she agrees to see you, make sure you never raise it with me. Ever.'

'No worries, my friend. See you.'

I hung up the phone and let out a sigh. Now I'm a matchmaker. I'm sure Selena could look after herself and Larry needs to meet someone his own age, but what a cheek. At least it gives me closure to this fantasy I've carried for far too long.

Jesus, this is a complicated life. I don't know if my imagination ever wished for this complex one. What a moron I've been. Years of dreaming about something that didn't exist. It distracted me from being a proper husband and father. Maybe, as Larry suggests, that Selena fantasy led me to Rosemary.

I crushed the paper and tossed it in the bin.

Twenty-Eight

5:38 PM

T he setting sun tossed streams of light through the city to startling effect, the growing darkness in the east cast a vivid contrast across the scene below as folks rushed home to be with loved ones. Meanwhile, above them a government minister plotted the demise of two thousand, five hundred and forty-three fellow citizens for the sake of keeping my job. Traffic snaked away to the east, red taillights offering continuous lines on the major highways. If only I could join them. I really need to go see my family.

My phone shrilled again. It was the prime minister.

'I just wanted to make sure we're still on the same page... are we?'

'Yes. I haven't changed my mind.'

'That's good Ryan. I became concerned you might go solo after the news of the incident this afternoon,' the prime minister said, her voice seemed a little suspicious.

'What incident?'

'Haven't you heard? A unionist rammed a car into the front doors of the Symonds Group downtown.'

'What? Are you kidding me?' My mind now reeling with disbelief.

'No. She sacrificed herself for the cause to make a statement against the government's decision. Bloody idiot, if you ask me.'

'What happened?' My heart now pounding in my chest.

'She smashed into the front glassed lobby area. The car flipped over stairs and dropped a floor to the food court. No-one injured except for the driver. She is under arrest in the hospital as we speak. The prognosis is not optimistic.'

'You're kidding me. Did they release a name?'

'Franklin. She was the union's onsite representative.'

'I know her.' What was she thinking? My heart now heavy with worry and I heaved my chest. 'I've known her for years. She worked for me. I'd just met with her earlier.' What would have pushed her to do such a wild, stupid thing? My mouth dried and my throat constricted as I tried to swallow. This was crazy, madness pure and simple.

'Ryan, let's talk later this evening, after I've seen the polling.'

'Sure, see you.' My voice was now barely audible, as I pushed the button and tossed the telephone onto the desk my thoughts buzzing with confusion, anger, and despair.

What was Michella thinking? Surely, she could understand there was nothing that could be done to save her members. Why would she do such a thing? What outcome did she hope to achieve? The resentment she expressed earlier about the decision must have been too overwhelming for her. This campaign of hers to save her members' jobs must have meant an awful lot for her. It's not personal, it's business for fuck's sake, I kept telling her that. To do this is... to do such a thing; to take such a drastic measure, is just unbelievable.

As I sat at my desk, my mind raced with thoughts of Michella, a young woman I mentored, encouraging her to dream big, to reach for the important things. I remembered the day she introduced me to her family, and how I protected her as best I could within the workplace. I attended her engagement party, and we recently initiated monthly chats over coffee about her career and her life. I know she was sad about the decision and my involvement, but I thought she understood I had no choice.

But now, she had taken a drastic and unimaginable step. Why? I couldn't understand what would have driven her to such a desperate act. I felt a weird surge of energy through my body, rushing to my head, forcing a wild grimace, almost forcing me to shout. A pain in my chest made me feel flushed and uncomfortable. I tried to regain control by panting, but I could feel a sheet of sweat across my back and shoulders. I stretched back into my chair, but only to duck my head back between my knees for relief.

'Boss, are you ready?' Jordan interrupted; his voice showing concern. 'We're scheduled to start in ten minutes.'

'Have you heard about Michella Franklin?'

'Yes, a tragedy,' he replied, his face etched with sorrow.

I stood, grabbing my jacket. 'We should go see her, maybe tomorrow. At the very least, let's send flowers. Can you arrange it?'

'Why?'

'It would be nice to reach out. Let her know we are thinking of her, that I am thinking of her.'

'Boss.' Jordan stepped forward, looking anxious. 'She died around fifteen minutes ago.'

And with those words, my world came crashing down, as I realized the full extent of my failure, my inability to save her, to protect her, to be there for her. And I knew, in that moment, that I could never forgive myself for my shortcomings, my inadequacies, my cowardice during this negotiation. I felt a wave of guilt wash over me, wondering if I could have done something differently. I could have prevented this tragedy. But it was too late now.

I couldn't move or breathe. A pain ripped at my chest. My mouth opened to speak, yet no words came out. I steadied myself with the desk before sitting on its edge.

Jordan rushed off to the cooler, returning with a plastic cup of refreshing water. Fiona hurried in to see what the fuss was about. She fretted over me as she steered me to a chair.

'We should delay the media conference,' Fiona told Jordan.

'We can't. The boss needs to do this.'

'I'm okay. Just give me a minute.' I downed the water.

'Jordie, you can't let him face the media. Look at him. He's about to collapse.'

'I'm okay. Seriously. I can feel myself coming good.' Though I was not so sure I agreed.

'I'll go tell them we will be there in ten.' Jordan rushed off.

Fiona stood over me and touched my forehead. 'Ryan, you look as if you've seen a ghost. Are you okay?'

'Please, just allow me to sit. I just need a few moments to get back into politician mode.'

'What caused this? Has something happened to your family?'

'Michella Franklin. The girl from the union who saw me an hour ago. She's had a fatal car accident. She's dead.'

'Oh, no,' Fiona exclaimed, her hand covering her mouth.

'Jesus Christ. Why did she do that?' I dropped my head into my hands. It's just a decision of the government. It's business, never personal. Fuck! Why? What possessed her to do this insane thing? To end her life like that? Why didn't she call me? When you don't agree with someone, you don't do this. You don't give up. You don't take your life. You keep fighting. That's what Michella should have done. So young, so passionate, and so stupid. What's the point she made by doing this?

I coursed my fingers through my hair, my mind consumed with questions. What else could she have done? Changed her job?

Worked with her members to get them a better deal? There were many things she could have done instead of doing this insane act. But she gave up. Never give up. Those who fight for what is right have this creed of never giving up. This is what that young lady, my dearest Michella, should have done.

Why didn't she call me?

Twenty~Nine

'Whenever you're ready, boss.' Jordan handed me the speaker's notes in a plastic folder, a hint of deference in his tone.

'Right, all good, let's go.' I wiped my eyes and moved off, my mind already on the task at hand.

'Be true to yourself, Minister, and you'll be fine,' Fiona said, her voice soft and sincere as she touched my shoulder.

Once at the media room, I stepped up to the podium, preparing my notes. I could feel the dark cloud on my shoulders. The lamps flickered on, illuminating the faces before me. Camera operators bustled about, readying their equipment, while journalists scribbled notes in their pads. A producer counted me in using sign language.

'Ladies and gentlemen,' my voice was now steady and measured. 'I want to talk about the death of Michella Franklin earlier this evening, in what appears to be a horrible car accident. Miss Franklin is an organiser for the union representing the workers at Symonds. She had just been to see me to argue her case regarding the ongoing dispute. We had fruitful a discussion. I last saw her leave the building just over ninety minutes ago.'

'Michella worked for me in the past, and I was proud to call her a colleague and a dear friend. We discussed many things over the years, and we often clashed over issues of policy, like today.' My voice trailed off as I stared at the lectern. 'Now she is dead.'

I clenched my teeth, fighting the movement in my lip. This was difficult for me, and I raised my head and drew in deep breaths as I fought for control.

'We lost a great young Australian today. I grieve for her family and her friends, and I know she had many. We also lost a potential mother and grandmother, and with her, a generational line of Australians who could have built upon the significant body of work she has already achieved.'

I quickly wiped away a tear as I blew out my cheeks.

'Australia is a land of opportunity for those who want to work with us to build the communities that will benefit us all. Michella lived in the belief we built our great nation from the sweat of those employed in factories, in mines, in fields, and even in the great towers now adorning our cities. Michella wanted the best for her country. She said that a great nation needs to look after its people in return for their efforts.' I paused for a moment, glancing at the ceiling, and took a deep breath before referring to my notes.

'This is very true for Australia. The way of the modern world is different. Free Trade agreements have meant our primary industries now have access to markets in foreign lands. We distribute our products all over the world. Australia is a quality, reliable brand. But this is not what it was like over fifty years ago when we operated under a tariff regime protecting our companies, our communities, and our citizens by ensuring there was no threat from cheap imported products. Governments over the years have said we must compete internationally. If that means industries sought cheaper options offshore, then so be it. From these policy decisions over the years our economy flourished and by doing so, so did our people.'

'This is the way of the modern world. We are seeking to adapt to the demands of this modern world. It may not seem fair to local manufacturers who plied their trade in Australia for decades. But this is what the market demands and therefore Australian companies need to innovate if they want to continue to do business. Those that do will be rewarded. This government promotes innovation for the future, so the jobs of the future will provide for our citizens with a future.'

'We must say goodbye to the past and the manner we have done business. We must welcome the future by building on from what we already have.' I stopped for a moment and briefly reflected on my words. Stop dealing with the past and embrace the future. An epiphany struck.

'Rewards lie in the future and not in the past.'

'The Symonds Group has been a fixture in our nation for decades, but times have changed. For over three decades, they paid their share of taxes and provided employment for many people in various business enterprises. They helped build community infrastructure and they remain significant donors to many community charities, including sponsoring the annual national breast cancer telethon appeal. They have been good citizens and good for Australia.'

A murmur of agreement rippled through the gathering. 'But their manufacturing systems are no longer relevant in the modern world. The products they manufacture are too expensive for our market and indeed our export market. In fact, they can land a heavy-duty vehicle manufactured in Germany at a local dealership for fifty percent of the total cost of producing that same vehicle in Australia. This means they cannot sustain their current operation, and the government agrees.'

I paused, letting my words sink in for those listening. 'Symonds, at their head office in Germany, suggested a change in direction and asked the government to support retooling, retraining, and help with developing new markets for a modern aeronautics industry. They want to focus on drone technology and pilotless aircraft for defence and commercial use. They requested the government's support. Not only in tax subsidies and access to investment funds, but they also requested the government provide a two and a half billion dollar grant over ten years to help build an Australian investment asset.'

'The government doesn't provide welfare for new business. Governments of all persuasions have followed this same policy approach for over forty years. We do not provide money by picking winners as once was the popular government policy, especially within my own party. In the past, we have seen the government pick too many losers. Using scarce taxpayers' funds to benefit a few entrepreneurs lucky enough to squirrel away money before their company's collapse. So, our policy is not to continue to support such activities.'

I leaned forward, my gaze locking onto the journalists. 'I travelled to Germany this last week to meet with the company and discuss with the German government our intention. We will not be providing subsidies.'

The collective murmuring within the media surged as they took notes and prepared for questions, but I hadn't finished.

'However, I also learned today that the government is more than distributing funds and allocating taxes. Sometimes politicians forget the principle of being of the people and being for the people.'

'Government is not easy. We are required to make decisions every day which could take away the livelihood of our citizens, and we can ruin a life with a policy decision.' I paused for a moment closing my eyes as I swallowed. 'Or even take a life.'

'Government should make decisions that benefit the community.

Government should not be an institution which commands its citizens. Rather, we should be an institution which leads. Leadership is not about accounting, it's about dreaming. It's not about having citizens' supporting plans, it's about having citizens embrace the dream and pushing forward.'

'Tomorrow morning, I will draw up legislation to put to the parliament next week.' I announced a new direction, my voice ringing with authority. 'It will be an Act confirming an agreement with the Symonds Group for the development of a new aeronautics industry. I will explain to the parliament that the future lies in the air, and we must be part of it. I will argue that we will fund the creation of jobs for our people and the region. We will bring science and the skills of an educated workforce together to make Australia an aeronautics leader. It starts with the retooling and re-education of the Symonds workforce keen to deliver on those dreams. The best social welfare for Australians is a job and under my watch in this portfolio I will deliver jobs.'

'This is a time for the future.' My eyes scanned the room. 'It's a time when we should put aside our differences about debt and deficit. To build, together, a nation walking into the future with confidence and playing a significant role in the development of this new and exciting industry.'

I paused for a moment, then gazed down the barrel of the central camera.

'We have the skills. We have the people. We just need motivation and money. The government will provide the money. Now I ask all Australians to provide the motivation.'

With that, I left the podium, journalists firing questions at me as I walked away. A smiling Jordan passed me, keen to manage the media barrage.

Thirty

6:19 PM

A s I swung into my office, the darkened sky seemed to mirror my mood. Fiona having listened to the broadcast followed close behind with a glass of water. 'That was the most authoritative thing you have ever said. I'm very proud of you.' She seemed on the verge of tears. 'Our country needs a leader like you.'

'The irony is, Fiona.' I sunk into my chair, accepting the water. 'I'm unlikely to have a job tomorrow and the government may never keep those public promises I just announced.'

'They will, you'll see. They'll have to.'

'I'm expecting a call from the prime minister soon. If not tonight, then certainly first thing. I expect her to discharge my commission. So, I'm a little uncertain what will happen to the team.'

Fiona's beaming smile never wavered. 'Don't worry about us. Enjoy the moment. You've made countless people happy this evening, Ryan, including yourself.'

'I do feel a little dazed. I feel as if my speech has lifted an enormous burden from me. It's been that sort of day.'

'You're finally being yourself. So, can we see more of him?' Fiona asked, a twinkle in her eye.

I couldn't help but laugh. 'Perhaps.'

Just then, Joanne hurried into the office. 'Minister, sorry to interrupt. What should I do with the media tomorrow?'

'I'll do the early morning media if I still have a job. Explain to them we'll need to confirm first thing. I should know by then.'

'It's a bold move, Minister.' Joanne seemed flustered. This announcement was not what she planned for her evening. 'I am worried about what might happen. You've taken a tremendous risk.'

'It is the right thing to do, Jo.' I nodded. 'I want to make sure we communicate that message to the community.'

'Boss, what do you think you're doing?' Jordan rushed into the office. 'You could at least have told us this is what you planned.'

'I didn't figure it out until I talked about Michella, and how it all related back to me.'

'How?'

'I'm sick of living in the past and trying to be someone I'm not.' By saying it, I felt a sense of liberation. 'I reckon this is the right decision.'

'I have been trying to tell you that for some time now.' Jordan was not sympathetic and shook his head.

'Not now with the *"I told you so's,"* please, Jordan.'

'This will mean huge anxiety in the prime minister's office,' Jordan said, his voice filled with urgency. 'We had better get to it, Jo.'

'I want to talk about jobs. I want to talk about the future. Put that line into everything we do.'

'I'll have media talking points ready for you before your interviews tomorrow,' Joanne said, stepping away.

'I'll keep the political wolves at bay,' Jordan said, now filled with eager determination. 'It could be a turning point for the government and you. I'm pumped about it.'

'Jordan, just keep focused on jobs, not mine.'

'Right boss, I'll get speech notes prepared for the invitations you'll no doubt get tomorrow.' Jordan moved to leave and then paused at the door. 'You did something prime ministerial today. Congratulations.'

I couldn't help but feel a sense of excitement about the future. This is what is so damn seductive about politics. The adrenaline pumping through you at moments like this is almost addictive. I leaned back in my chair, contemplating the possibilities.

'Do you want a coffee?' Fiona stood by the door. 'What time are you leaving?'

'I have some calls to make.' The worry of accountability, along with other minor issues from my day, are still on my mind and bothering me. 'I'll leave after that. A tea would be nice, thanks Fiona.' I felt a little weary and in need of a nap. It's been a rough day. The future seemed different from what I planned this morning.

A text pinged. It was Rosemary.

WHAT THE HELL ARE YOU DOING?

THIS WILL CREATE PROBLEMS FOR US.

CALL ME!

I tossed the phone on the desk and looked out at the city, feeling drained. Breathing deeply, I took a long draught of chilled water. It felt good. I picked up the phone, scrolling through numbers to resolve the issue which had been troubling me since the morning.

'Hello?'

'Hi son, how are you?'

'Okay.'

'Goodo. I wanted to say that things don't look like the way you think they do.' There was no response. 'I had a talk with the police, and they have left me to decide if the issue should go further.'

'What did you decide?'

'Of course, I will not press charges against my son. It was a mistake, and you were confused about what I said.'

'What do you mean?'

'I mean it will not go any further with the police or anyone else. It was a mistake. I'll take responsibility for your actions.'

'Why would you do that?'

'I'm your father, and that's what fathers do.' I could hear his heavy breathing, but he gave no response. 'As to accessing my emails. I just want to assure you I don't intend to be going anywhere.'

'Why did she send those gross pictures of herself?'

'It's just what older folks do, I guess.' What else I could say? 'Look, son, I'm embarrassed about this. What I thought was private obviously isn't as private as it should be.'

'You're embarrassed because someone knows?'

'Son, sometimes we make decisions which don't line up with our values. Crazy stupid decisions. When these secret decisions get exposed, we get embarrassed and feel shame.' I paused, wondering if I should continue. 'I feel shame right now.'

'Dad, you did the wrong thing.'

'I know. I regret it, but sometimes we get swept up into the mindsets of others. We enjoy the moment, which leads to other moments. Then we are doing silly things we shouldn't.'

'How old are you?'

'Yeah, I know, son, I know. When you get to my age, you'll realise that the things we thought were important throughout our lives are perhaps not that important anymore.'

'What do you mean?'

'I've tried to hang onto my past for far too long, which affected my recent decisions at home. I thought I was younger than I really am. When indeed I'm not, not anymore.'

'But you're not old.'

'I know, it's one of life's paradoxes. I still think I'm young. I still feel things the way I did when I was young. I still want to do the things I did when I was young. But I'm not young, not anymore. Life has moved on and I haven't moved with it, hence the reason for my foolishness.'

'What happens now?'

'Nothing, except I live for the future, rather than living in a dream from the past.'

'No, I meant with your girl.'

'It's over.'

'Do you promise?'

'With my life.'

There was a long silence as he considered my words. What happens next was his call, so I waited for him to decide.

'Can I see you tomorrow?' He finally asked.

'Yes, that would be great.' A flicker of hope in my heart touched me.

'Can we go to the movies together on the weekend?'

'That would be terrific.'

'Okay, see you, Dad.'

'Bye son.'

'I love you, Dad.'

'You too, son.'

Tossing the telephone to the desk, I pushed back in the chair, brushing my hands through my hair, frisking it trying to relieve myself of the emotion from the call. It surprised me, as I almost came close to tears. I tried to compose myself by rubbing my eyes.

'Here's a nice, soothing cup of tea for you.' Fiona placed the Wedgwood before me. 'It looks as though you might need it.'

'Thanks Fiona, grab a seat. I think your advice is needed.'

'Now you're asking for advice?' Fiona asked, seemingly filled with amusement.

'I suppose you're right. I've been making peculiar decisions these last few years.'

'Ryan.' Fiona became serious when she started a lecture with my name. I suspected this could be difficult. 'I can say this to you because I know you very well. It is time for you to grow up.'

'That's harsh.' I wriggled my shoulders at the thought of someone thinking the same as me.

'You just don't realise how good you have it.'

'You, see? This is where we differ. I don't think I have it that fantastic.'

Her jaw dropped. 'You're kidding? Tell me why you think that?'

'I don't know.' I was now slightly embarrassed, and a little cautious. 'I wanted so much from my life, and I just don't think I have got the rewards I need from my achievements. I mean, I've done well, yes-yes, but is it what I wanted? This is what I struggle with. What have I done? What's my legacy?'

'You think you lead an ordinary life?' She seemed sceptical.

'No, of course not. Looking in from the outside, anyone would agree my life is wonderful. But is it me? I don't think it is. I never asked to be a politician. It just happened and now I'm a heartbeat from being prime minister.' Then I recalled the media conference. 'Well, maybe not after today. The ironic thing is this, I don't think I ever wanted it.'

'You do it so well, Ryan.' Fiona smiled.

'I suppose, but a lot of things come too easy to me. But what I really struggle with is that I sometimes feel I'm an impostor.' The tea was sweet and addictive, so I sipped again. 'When I was young, I didn't want any responsibility. Now look at me.'

'Goes with the job.'

'But that's it. I didn't seek the job. It just came to me.' I sighed, running my fingers through my hair. 'When I need to escape from the stress, I go back to those days when I didn't have any responsibilities. When I could do whatever I wanted. Now I'm dreaming about what might have been if I didn't take this road I have been on.'

'Ah, hence your meeting today. How did that go?' Fiona pried, her voice soft and curious.

'Not well as you may have guessed.' I scoffed a smile, turning to face her. 'It readjusted my thinking, though, I reckon. It seems I need to get over myself and not be so scared of doing things.'

'What have you got to fear?'

'Becoming irrelevant. Being passed over. Becoming too old.'

'You're not old, Ryan.'

'Sometimes I feel as if I am, and I've let the old man in. It just seems to happen more these days when I sit and think about my life. I worry about life passing me by and not giving me much.'

'What do you want?'

'There was an awful moment this afternoon when I thought I wanted to go back in time.' I shifted in my chair struggling to rein in the sudden rush of wild emotions. 'Then I realised there was no going back.'

'Not what you thought it was?' she asked, her voice held a delicate hint of worry.

'You know, Fiona, I've been very lonely over the last ten or so years. The responsibility of caring for my mother, my family, my job, and folks everywhere expecting things from me is killing me. No one seems to look after me, and no one cares.' A teary sadness washed over me. 'I'm lonely for the love in my life I thought I should have by now. I've been searching for it, hoping to get it.'

'You won't find it with Miss Alvarez,' she said.

'You might be right.'

'She wants what you have, not you.'

'You know you're the second person who has told me that today.'

'Well, maybe you should start listening,' Fiona said, her voice sharp. 'This idea of no one loving you is just pathetic. You have a loving family. Wendy loves you like no other.'

'I suppose.' I was now overcome by a profound feeling of despair.

'You have dedicated staff who will cross a desert without water for you.'

'Did you say eat a dessert for me?' I laughed, trying to lighten the mood. Fiona didn't.

'Joke all you want, but we stand by you because you're our leader and we want to follow you. The reason we do that is because of you,' she said. I felt embarrassed and a little silly. 'The problem with you is that you don't respect what you have, nor the impact your decisions have on others. Just stop occasionally and take a look around. You have all that you need within your grasp. Yet you keep searching for an impossible dream in all the wrong places.'

'Today, I've come to realise that.'

'Ryan, you're a man, not a boy. It's important you respond to challenges like a man. You must step up and realise what you are looking for is right in front of you. Ask, and you shall receive.'

Ask and you shall receive. Why should I have to ask? Surely after all this effort I shouldn't have to ask. 'My father was never that close to me. Maybe I'm replaying his relationship with my own children. I mean, we're what our parents train, guide and show us to be, so maybe my parents weren't the loving folks I should emulate.'

'Isn't that what you're doing with Wendy, replicating your parents' relationship?' Fiona gently asked.

'They loved each other.' I had a nostalgic moment and smiled. 'They worked together, raised us. My father built a solid foundation for all of us.' I admired and cared for my dad. 'My gosh, his own father died young, so he never got the chance to learn from him. Indeed, I'm now older than dad when he died.'

'If you're becoming your father, isn't it time to reflect on what's important to you and change this uncertainty about your life you're living?'

'Now I come to think about it. They shoved my old man into providing for the family at a young age due to my grandfather's death. Maybe he didn't want the responsibility, either. When I sold the business, Mum didn't speak to me for months.'

'You sold her security and the legacy she and your father built together.'

'Surely we are more than just an identity living our lives through something spurious, like a company, or in my case a prestigious job?'

'Let me ask you this: what is your identity and how do you see yourself?'

'Crumbs. You're asking all the challenging questions.' The telephone pinged. It was from Rosemary.

WTF CALL ME NOW!!!

I tossed the phone back to the desk. 'I suppose I don't see myself as a loser, or a winner. I just see myself as unfulfilled. Someone who desperately needs love in his life but isn't getting any. Someone who needs appreciation for the things he does but isn't getting any. Maybe someone who just needs a holiday.'

'The good book tells us that as we sow, so shall we reap. The question I will leave you with is this: what have you been sowing?' Fiona began leaving. 'Call me if you need me.'

Thirty-One

6:44 PM

———

S ow and reap, ask and receive. It just makes little sense to me. I
work hard. I respect what I do, yet I never get what I want.
There must be more to life... why should I have to ask? I picked up
my phone and pushed the reply button and tapped in and sent a
message, then waited. Within moments, the telephone shrilled.

'Rose?'

'What do you mean it's over?' Aggression in her tone.

'My job, my marriage, us.' My voice, barely a whisper.

'Hang on a second. What do you mean we're over?'

'I remain distressed by what happened at lunch.'

'Come off it, you loved it.' She chortled, her mood changing with
every sentence. 'I know I did. Yummo, I can still feel you.'

'To tell you the truth, I didn't, and I can recall telling you I
didn't.'

'Get over yourself, will you? We've done it before. You've done it
before,' she hollered over the telephone. 'What's going on?'

'It's over.'

'Your job is, but we shall work through that and guarantee you don't lose your status. We know your marriage is over and has been for a long time. We have spoken about that.'

'I mean us.'

'No! No, it's not. You can't blow me off after five years. Not after what I've done for you.'

This will be good, I was curious. 'What have you done for me?'

'How dare you? she screamed; her voice filled with anger. 'You fucking prick. I've put out for you. I've been there when you needed me. I shared your dreams. I've advised you. I've made plans with you. Don't you dare ask me what I've done for you. Don't you dare ask, you bastard.'

'It's over Rosemary. I don't want to do it anymore.'

'Look here, you arsehole. It's not over unless I say it's over.'

'You can't be serious?'

'You want to muck me about, then get this straight,' she said, her voice dropping. 'I'll be your worst nightmare. I will be your fatal attraction. I won't just boil the fucking bunny. I'll shove it right up your arse.'

'Don't threaten me.'

'You know something, Ryan.' Now her voice moved more threatening, deeper, and slower. 'I'm now booked into your little shindig tonight. I'll come up to you during the evening, and you had better have a different point of view about us. Otherwise, my first words will be to your scrawny, skinny, botoxed wife. You can kiss goodbye to that cosy relationship you have with her. Remember this: you are mine until I tell you. You aren't going anywhere unless I tell you. Never forget that.'

The telephone went dead.

Larry's sage words ricocheted back.

She is dangerous. How did I miss that?

I really didn't know what to do. I was in her bed last night committing myself to her. Now the gates of hell seem to have swept open. A path toward destruction was now out of control, threatening me.

The telephone shrilled again. I didn't want to answer but picked it up when I recognised it was Sarah.

'Hi gorgeous, how are you?'

'Dad, did you speak with Mum about my year off?'

'I asked if she knew about it. Why?'

'She told me you said no. She also said you will not subsidise any travel anywhere. Does that mean the end-of-year break down the coast? I thought you said I could go?'

'You can. I didn't tell your mum there was a problem.' Why is this suddenly an issue? 'All I asked was if you had talked to her about this far-fetched idea of taking a year off.'

'Why do you think it's far-fetched? A lot of my friends are doing it.'

'I would prefer you do a university degree first, then travel. Then maybe work in your chosen field overseas.'

'I plan to do just that, but I want a break first,' Sarah said, sounding frustrated. 'Why is this so difficult for you?'

'I haven't said no. I just want to discuss it.'

'Which means no,' she harrumphed. 'I know what you mean.'

'I actually mean I want to discuss it further with my daughter.' I sat straighter, rubbing my temple.

'Mum says you said no. So that's it. End of discussion,' Sarah retorted, her voice sharp. 'I just want to know if I can go to the coast with my friends once the semester ends.'

'It doesn't mean no, Sarah. I'm not sure what your mother is talking about.' What are we talking about? 'I just think you're too young to be travelling overseas.'

'What are you afraid of? Daddy's little girl might get laid or something?'

'Ease up, Sarah. I'm not one of your mates.'

'Well, tell me: what are you afraid of?'

I couldn't think of anything to say other than a superficial answer. Plenty of kids head for Europe. Why shouldn't Sarah? 'I'm just going to miss you too much, that's all.'

'You're kidding me, right?' Sarah said, her voice thick with disbelief. 'You hardly see me now. So, what's this idea of missing me?'

'At least I know you're safe, and you're warm, and you're fed.' I felt the sting of her words. I already miss her. 'If you're by yourself somewhere, I won't know if you are safe.'

'Daddy, sooner or later we have to say goodbye,' Sarah said, her voice softening.

'I know.' I could feel a lump form in my throat, so cleared it. 'It just seems I've not had enough time with you.'

'Whose fault is that?' she asked with sadness.

'Mine, I guess. I had to do what I had to do to provide a secure life for you and your mum and ensure I looked after you.'

'You've done a great job, but we need to grow up one day. I want that growing up to happen before I go to university.'

'Why?'

'Because I know my studies will mean more because of it. I'll be more focused. I won't be dreaming about something or being some-place else. I would have already done it. I can then concentrate on getting the best from my time at university.'

It just struck me what a bright girl my daughter was. No longer the teenager with all her angst, but a seriously bright young lady. Why should I be so surprised?

'Let me talk to your mum about it.'

'Can I go to the coast?'

'Of course, you can. Just don't hit the credit card too hard.'

'You know I won't, thanks Daddy.'

'I'll try to talk to your mum tonight about what we might

arrange. After talking to her this morning, I wouldn't hold high hopes.'

'I don't, but thanks anyway. See you.'

'Bye honey.'

Why is it the females in my life seem to rule me? They manipulate me and mould me into their little puppet to get whatever they want. Maybe they want the best for me, but they usually want something from me. I don't know. Should I care?

Jordan had returned. 'Boss, Hancock Media wants an interview tonight. I told them you were not available until tomorrow, so I thought I would check.'

'You would be correct. I'm doing nothing until I talk to the PM. I haven't yet heard from her.'

'She is most likely waiting for the polling.'

'In the meantime, I'm out of here. Email me the speakers' notes and times for interviews. I'll check them when I finish this function.'

'What's it about?' Jordan asked, looking at me with interest.

'My wife booked me in.' I shrugged and rolled my eyes. 'I suspect it's an arty-farty dinner. Not sure what I'm walking into.'

'Stay on message if anyone raises the media conference,' Jordan advised.

'And what would that be?' I laughed.

'Jobs and growth, of course.'

'Yes, of course, your job, and my job,' I mocked myself, shaking my head. 'How could I forget?'

'I'll see you at your first media tomorrow. I should have a schedule for the rest of the day by then.'

'When are my holidays due?'

'No holidays for you, Minister, you know that.'

'Tell me why I do this job again?'

'You do it because you love your country, and you want the best for it.'

'Gee, and I thought it was for the money. Goodnight.' As I walked past Fiona's desk, she was tapping away at a computer I stopped for a moment. 'Why aren't you going home?'

'I will soon. I'm just finishing your China schedule. It seems like you'll be very busy. The department has you working hard.'

'That all depends on the prime minister. You had better brief me on that tomorrow. Is anyone else travelling with me?'

'The trade minister said she would like to go,' Fiona said, as she scrolled the computer. 'I've had a request from AMG to have a representative join the delegation.'

'That could be a good idea. Maybe they can open a door for us with the mining secretary.'

'Enjoy yourself tonight,' Fiona said, looking at me with concern. 'Try to relax a bit. You've had a hectic few days.'

'What's it about do you know?' Fiona knows everything.

'Mrs Kennedy didn't say other than it's a dinner and an award will be presented.'

'I'm not speaking?'

'Correct. You are there as the designated partner.'

'Should be fun. Alright I shall see you whenever I get in tomorrow. I shall talk to you early. Get home and get some sleep.'

'Good night, Minister.'

She works too hard that one. Invariably first in and last out. I'm not sure what would have happened to my career if I didn't have her to help me. The elevators were fast at this time of night. I took it to the basement where my car was waiting.

'Been wanting long, Guy?'

'Not long, Minister.' He opened the door, and I sunk into the warm leather seats, looking forward to a few quiet moments to rest my eyes.

Thirty-Two

7:23 PM

The brief trip to the function centre, an extension to the government funded National Art Gallery, took fifteen minutes through the rain forecasted to soak the city overnight. Guests congregated in the foyer enjoying pre-dinner cocktails, chatting to old and new friends, colleagues, and acquaintances. I helped myself to a glass of wine and glided through the crowd looking for Wendy. I finally spotted her talking with dignitaries and official guests. I sidled up, slipped my arm around, and leaned in to kiss her cheek.

'What happened to your face?'

'I slipped going up stairs and landed headfirst into the carpet.'

'Have you been to the doctor? You could have hurt yourself.'

'No time today. Too busy. If it's still looking bad tomorrow, I'll go, promise.'

'How was your day other than for that trip on the stairs? Everything okay after the few days away?'

'Everything is fine. I even had time with Fraser. It was an exciting game, and he scored the winning basket.'

'That's great. Let me introduce you to these folks.'

Wendy showed little interest in my day, just another confusing reason not to engage with her. I shook hands exchanging pleasant chit-chat with guests, with only one referring to my media conference. She congratulated me for my political courage but doubted my reasons. Politics was not on everyone's cultural radar. There were always complaints though when policy or behaviour went pear-shaped. So many people ignore the governance demands of their country yet complain about politicians when things go wrong? It still perplexes me.

Wendy had her hair styled up which suited her slim figure, draped in a backless black number with a simple gold jewellery combination. She looked fabulous. The scratches on her tanned shoulder were almost invisible, which confirmed I got my conspiracy theory totally wrong.

A deep bong of a cymbal advised guests to enter the dining room. Wendy took my hand, hers warm and soft, leading the way to our table. The elegantly dressed room looking as if this was more than just a standard awards night. Following Wendy, moving around tables and chairs, it surprised me we moved toward the head table. At previous dinners, we were often placed at the back, or by the kitchen door. I thought they directed this disrespect at me for being in opposition. Not tonight though, things obviously change when in government. It also seems Wendy will not be ensuring guests enjoy the evening as she usually does.

Like all other tables, we had name plates and mine displayed Wendy Kennedy Partner. I smiled at the irony of not having my name printed, validating my typical unreliability. I never enjoyed attending these events, which reinforced my view about the lack of commitment toward Wendy, never knowing when, or if, I would be available. This dinner it seems was a late acceptance by Fiona. Too late to change the name plate.

As we sat and settled, Wendy placed her hand on my thigh and leaned in for a quiet word. 'Thanks for doing this tonight darling. I know you're busy. I appreciate it,' she said, her voice low and sweet.

'Happy to be here.'

'Can we enjoy ourselves then, and let's at least appear to be happy together?' Wendy asked, her eyes searching mine.

'Not a problem.' Why wouldn't we be happy together? I was a little gobsmacked by her request. 'Should we kiss or something?'

'No, it'll smudge my lipstick. Kiss me later,' Wendy whispered a hint of a smile on her lips.

'You look great.'

'Thank you, I feel it,' Wendy said, as she switched to speak to the president who sat next to her.

The other guests were settling into our table. A glamourous woman sat next to me, promptly tearing open her bread roll and shoving a piece into her mouth.

'Hungry?'

'Famished.' She held her fingers to her lips seeming embarrassed. 'I didn't have time for lunch. My name is Maureen. How are you?' She held out her hand. I took it, giving my standard political shake. 'What do you do?'

'I'm in the government.'

'Oh really? What department?'

'Industry.'

'It would be a tough job these days. Most industries are now in Asia. You can't get anything of quality these days. Not like we used to,' she said with a frown.

'You can if you're prepared to pay for it.'

'We even import fruit these days. What are we becoming? A dumping ground for other countries? The politicians should do something about it,' she said, shaking her head.

'Maybe they will.' I smiled.

Glancing back to Wendy she seemed rivetted in conversation, so I took the opportunity of venturing to the bathroom. A few moments of quiet time might help me get my mind off work and focus on why I am here. Why am I here?

Thirty-Three

7:52 PM

The washrooms weren't hard to find. I ducked in, alone and in peace. As I tugged out paper towels after washing my hands, Rosemary burst in. It's not every day a woman would have the courage to burst into a gentleman's washroom. Rosemary never lacked chutzpah in taking whatever she wanted. Men's private space did not seem to worry her.

'What do you want? Can't you see I'm busy here?' What else could I say in that situation?

'I want to know what you intend to do about us.' There is no question she was a desirable woman, standing before me with her hair out, thick like a flamenco dancer, a red frock clinging to her curves. Her fiery stance, with hands on hips made it clear that this was going to be difficult.

'There is no us. It's over.'

'Why?' she demanded, her eyes locked on mine. I hesitated, then turned away. 'See you are unsure. You want me, I know you do.

'No. I don't.'

'Tell me why? I deserve that.'

'It's not you, it's me.' I almost laughed at using the cliche.

'What's wrong with you? What has changed your mind in the last few hours?'

'You attacking me didn't help.'

'Bullshit, you loved it,' she grinned. 'I loved it.'

'No, I didn't. That's the point.' I challenged her. 'You know nothing about me. You only want what I bring to the table, not me.'

'That's crap,' she sneered.

'You were nasty toward my son this afternoon.'

'He's a weird pervert,' she retorted.

'No, he's not.' She riled me as I raised my voice. 'That is a basic no-no with me. You would know that if you knew me. But you don't.'

'I will not waste five years being fucked by you to let it go now.'

'What are you planning to do? Kiss and tell? How would that complement your career?'

'Oh, trust me, it won't be me who will kiss and tell, darling. I'll have someone release juicy gossip. The way you mistreated and betrayed your family by indulging in a secret long-term relationship. By the time I'm finished with you, everyone will know you are a bullying sexual pervert,' she said, her words hitting me like a punch to the gut.

I squirmed a little. 'Nothing you say will hurt my career. That's over after today's announcement.'

'You think so? You don't think having your family dragged through gossip magazines and you exposed as a lecherous pervert will not harm you?' she asked, her voice now full of malice.

'There is nothing you can say that would hurt me. I'll deny it.'

'That's good. That will be fantastic. Denying you have a mistress.' She took a couple of steps toward me with a clenched fist, forcing me to feint a step back. 'But when your cards and notes are released along with your dick-pics, how do you reckon that'll play out in the media?'

'Why do you want to do this?'

'Because I love you, baby. I want us to be together.'

'You don't love me. You just want what I can bring you.'

Rosemary softened, sashaying toward me, her arms extended, her eyes smouldering with desire. wanting a hug. 'I love you, Ryan. I need you and you know you want me,' she purred, her voice low and seductive as she stroked my hand. 'You know you want me. Come on, you know you do.'

I pulled away, trying to sidestep her and putting some distance between us. I wanted to make my escape before things got out of hand. 'Rosemary, it's over.'

'No, it's not,' she snapped, her eyes flashing with anger. 'If you don't tell that slut wife of yours her time is over and to leave the bed, then I will. You'll be exposed as the liar you are.'

And then, as if on cue, Wendy walked in. 'Tell me what?'

'Hi honey. This is a colleague, Rosemary Alvarez.'

'Oh, I know who this skank is. Nice to see you.' Wendy walked between us, standing tall before Rosemary. 'What is it you want to tell me?'

Rosemary seemed flustered and nervous, her eyes darting back and forth between Wendy and me. 'Mrs Kennedy, I'm sorry, this is a discussion between your husband and me.'

'You've got that right. He is *my* husband.' They both stood with hands on hips. 'Now what is it you want to do with my husband?'

Rosemary backed away. 'There seems to be a misunderstanding. Your husband was trying to explain what we should do to resolve it. I think I'll do as he suggested.'

'No, you won't, you skank, and I'll tell you why.' Wendy took a few steps closer, her voice dripping with contempt. 'Ryan doesn't always know what he needs. Especially in the difficult situations his cock leads him to.' This sounded a little ominous. 'He thinks too much with the wrong head. He has let his wrong head do the

247

thinking about you for far too long. He thinks he's in love with girls from the past and tries to relive that past with skanks like you. Don't you, darling?' she said, turning to me. I couldn't respond. I could feel an anxious quiver building, my knee was wobbling. 'The thing is, and this is where you and I are so very different,' Wendy continued. 'I know him better than he knows himself. I know what he wants, even if he doesn't.'

'And what's that?' Rosemary challenged.

'His family, and not a crazy bitch like you.'

'I'm getting a little tired of you abusing me and calling me names,' Rosemary retorted. 'You don't know what your husband wants.'

'And you do?' Wendy sneered.

'I know every lump and bump he has. I know when he is hot for it and when he needs space. He does not need you and your artificial body.' Rosemary didn't back off. 'This is what he wants.' She patted her pubic groin region. 'I want you to reflect on that and make it easier for all of us.'

Wendy's eyes blazed with resentment. 'You've got a hide, haven't you? You are nothing but a cheap tramp worming your way into my family, trying to destabilise it for your own benefit. You have no ethics, no morals, and no thought for my children. No thought about screwing a man behind the back of another woman. You really are a piece of work.'

'I'm tiring of this conversation,' Rosemary snarled, her eyes flashing with annoyance. 'You either let us live our lives, starting right now, or I start a campaign which will destroy you both.'

'You're the deputy public prosecutor, aren't you?' Wendy asked, her voice cold and calculating.

'So what?'

'How would it look for the media to discover photographs of the

DPP in what I would call... compromising poses?' Wendy said, with a sly smile.

I could feel the blood drain from my face as I realised where this was going. I could see the concern in Rosemary's eyes as she began pacing back and forward like a panther ready to strike. 'What photos?' she asked, her voice tight with tension.

'Oh, just some of you in various, let's just say politely... revealing poses.'

'Like what?' Rosemary pressed, her voice growing louder with each word.

'Stella Artois bottles in imaginative, suggestive places. Some at the same time. You're such a flexible girl who enjoys a beer.' The penny dropped. Wendy had access to my files.

'The hell you say,' Rosemary said, her eyes locked onto mine. The weight of her stare was so heavy that I could feel it.

'I like what you can do with a cucumber, very accommodating. I bet you could do wonders with a watermelon,' Wendy taunted.

'What do you intend doing with them?' Rosemary asked, her voice barely above a whisper.

'Not a thing, whilst my family is not under threat. But say one word. Gossip just once. Compare my husband's cock to some else and every-one, and I mean everyone, will see the real you. All of you, if you know what I mean?' she said, her voice low and menacing with a sinister smile.

'I see.'

'Do you, skank? Do you really?' Wendy was not done, her voice cold and full of disdain. 'You've had a few good years. Now it's time for you to back off and leave my family alone. Do we understand each other?'

The only sound I could hear was a drip from a tap as the tension silenced everything. The uncertainty of what may happen scared me a little.

'You're a prick, Ryan. I'm happy to be rid of you.' Rosemary spat at the floor before me, then turned on her stiletto before storming off.

I didn't know what to do. I just stood there frozen like a bunny in the headlights, waiting for another crash.

'Oooo, how good was that. I've been looking forward to that moment, I can tell you. It felt so good.' Wendy turned, facing me with a devilish smile. 'Ryan, you have been a rather naughty boy, haven't you?'

'Wendy, I can explain.'

'No, you damn well can't,' She scoffed at my words, holding up her hand to silence me. 'Nothing you could say would explain why you have been screwing that slut for years.'

'How long have you known?'

'About a month after you started banging her,' she coolly replied, her eyes flicking over my face. 'I spotted you sharing more than a word with her at Rikki's place once, so I knew then. By the way, he'll have your balls if he ever finds out.'

'Why didn't you say anything?' I gulped, confused, still scared.

'At the time it suited me not to say anything,' she said, her voice laced with scorn. 'You never committed to her, did you? Just a bit of fluff on the side to recapture your youthful ways. Then I got into your emails.' Wendy too? How many others get into my private stuff? 'When I read there was a little more happening than I expected, I thought it was time to act. Plus, Fiona told me a few things, so I thought it was time for you to end it.'

'Fiona knows as well?'

'She is closer to me than you think,' she replied, a knowing smile playing on her lips. 'I reckon you should let her help you more. She is your best asset, not those other morons in the media unit.' Air was coming from me like a pricked balloon, slowly deflating my thinking. I shook my head, wondering what to do. 'I figured the bitch was coming tonight when I saw a ticket sold late this afternoon. Then when I saw her follow you in here, I thought now was a good time.'

'I was telling her it was over.' My voice is now barely above a whisper.

'So I heard,' she said, her smile growing wider. 'Ryan, what you must understand is that you have all you want sitting at home waiting for you. We may not be glamorous like that bitch, but we're yours, and you are all we want.'

'I can't believe this is happening. Why are you taking this so well?' I bent, placing my hands on my knees, trying to get my body operating. Tightness gripping my chest again.

'Oh, I've had a lot of sessions with a counsellor to understand and get over it by focusing on our joint priorities. Plus, I don't mind saying that I've even had my own little bits of fun on the side over the years. Sorry about this morning. That could have been embarrassing.' She laughed. 'I could have exposed you earlier for the creep you are, but I realise I need you just as much as you need me. Even if I must fight for you, I want to keep us together.'

'That's one hell of a knockout punch you just landed.'

'Maybe. I've been waiting to do it for a long time. I knew what to do,' she replied, her tone now matter of fact.

'What happens now?' I straightened, with various thoughts smashing through my head. Where do I sleep tonight? What happens tomorrow? Do we tell the kids? What will Wendy do?

'You have a lot of catching up to do. I want you focused on us and not these boys' games you want to play all the time. A bit of arse kissing from time to time would be a good start. Starting with this dinner. Let's go back to the table and be pleasant to each other. In the morning, let us resume discussion and start afresh.'

'You're unbelievable.' I shook my head.

'I told you that when we first met,' Wendy said, her eyes locked onto mine. 'I knew then we would make a great couple. I always knew you were a boy at heart. The fact is, Ryan Kennedy, I love you. Always have, always will.' She moved in closer and put her arms around me, kissing me like she hadn't done for some time. It launched a rush through me, reminding me of years ago on a beach.

'Now, let's go enjoy ourselves,' she said, pulling away and smiling at me.

'Yes, dear.'

'Can I just ask? Can we get rid of the condescending, yes dears? I'm your wife, after all.'

'Yes, darling.'

'Much better,' she said, letting me go and wiping lipstick from my lip. 'Sexy man.' She took my hand and led me out to dinner.

The entree was already at the table, the guests were just finishing their scallops. I helped Wendy with her chair and then pulled a bottle from the centre ice bucket, pouring her a wine before topping up Maureen's and refreshing mine before tossing the bottle back with a clunk.

'My husband tells me you're a little more than a public servant, Minister. You cheeky thing,' Maureen chirped, keen to engage. I shoved in a scallop as I nodded. 'Well done on the announcement. What does it mean?'

'What announcement?' Superhero hearing next to me joined the conversation.

'I committed two and a half billion dollars to establish an aeronautics industry.' Shoving another scallop into my mouth, I hoped the conversation would end.

'I thought the prime minister already announced the government wasn't providing funding?' Wendy seemed concerned.

'Yes, she told me this morning what I should do.' I took a mouthful of sliced vinaigrette vegetables, hoping she would get the message. She didn't.

'You went against the prime minister's wishes?'

'Hmm.' I didn't want to engage, not at a crowded table.

'What does that mean?' Wendy asked.

'She will sack me sometime tonight, or maybe in the morning.'

Wendy stared at me, her face morphing from concern to delight. 'Good for you darling, well done.'

'What? About losing my job?'

'No. Finally standing for something. You should do this all the time. Be who you are, not what you think you should be.'

Who is this woman?

'Lewis said she would get back to me once polling was in. She wants me to take the fall for the decision. I thought I may as well go down making the right decision.'

'This is why I love you.' She leaned over and pecked me.

Wiping a piece of bread roll to sop up the lovely dressing, I finished the plate and looked forward to the next course. The baked barramundi was tasty, the wine going down a treat. Maureen and her husband Billy were a hoot. Along with an occasional reassuring thigh stroke from Wendy, the evening was becoming more and more enjoyable. I was relaxed and enjoying myself, not even checking my telephone. Before dessert, the president moved to the podium for his speech and presentation of awards.

Thirty-Four

9:32 PM

———————

T he auditorium moved to a respectful silence, as the president checked the microphone, clearing his throat with a small cough. Service staff continued clearing tables with hushed efficiency.

'Thank you, ladies and gentlemen,' he began, 'I thank you for your support this evening as we recognise and thank our great benefactor, someone who, over the years, would not allow us to fail in providing services to the most vulnerable within our community.'

Billy began straightening his tie whilst Maureen brushed lint from his shoulders.

'Domestic violence is a continuing menace in our society. We now know it remains a complex issue of personal and collective responsibility.'

The president paused, scanning the audience with a serious gaze. 'Too often debate revolves around gender politics. This debate befalls to the obvious perpetrator which statistics show is the male. We rightly vilify all perpetrators. Yet, from study after community study, questions are raised challenging this notion of culpability, the notion that domestic violence is only the man's fault, and that toxic masculinity plays the primary role. Our organisation now plays an important and incisive role in attaining balance within this debate.'

The president gestured toward the guests. 'The ongoing Dunedin study exposes weaknesses of government policy focusing on just one gender as the root cause of the violence. Subsequent legislation has been expanded to now recognise the role of coercive power no matter the age or the gender within families. Strong advocacy for a balanced policy debate on this issue has led to more focused government funding for services. From this focused policy, we have been successful in gaining funding to support displaced children and victims of domestic abuse within our respite centres.'

He paused, a small smile creeping onto his face. 'But it's our signature education program that has truly made the difference. Without question, education is the answer to reducing family abuse. We want safe homes for our women and children. We want safe homes for our elders, and we seek recognition that all family members have a role to play in reducing abuse and violence. But we need to recognise what abuse actually looks like before it turns to violence and that the perpetrators can be in every generation or demographic of the family. We as an organisation remain committed and indeed obligated to protecting children. If parents can't do it, then the community must act. We see family education as the vital tool to help all adults within a family understand their responsibility and their impact toward other family members.'

The president took a deep breath. 'I must admit an education program was not on our planning radar. That is, it wasn't part of our strategy until the person we recognise tonight provided a strong case to consider it. It was their incisive argument to develop community support programs for all types of families and the diversity within them which motivated us. Then it was their proficiency to secure funds to build the education platform, which drove us to new high-level outcomes for families and children. Without their efforts, it is fair to say our organisation would not exist. We would have continued to struggle financially, and we would not be providing services as we now do. It's also fair to say that without their leadership we would not have achieved success across Australia and now internationally without the guidance and diligence of our award recipient.'

The president's voice grew louder, more passionate. 'All people caught up in abusive relationships no matter their family status, be they child, parent, or even grandparent, can now access the support we offer. To us it's not just about gender and the government now recognises that after many years of gentle persuasion. We would not be in our enviable financial position without the person we recognise tonight. Ladies and gentlemen, I have the pleasure of presenting our inaugural outstanding achievement award.'

The president moved to a podium side table, a glint of pride in his eyes, and picked up a beautiful glass sculpture. I smiled and nodded at Billy who smirked in return.

'Ladies and gentlemen,' the president began, his voice rich and commanding. 'Please join with me in thanking Wendy Kennedy for her outstanding achievements for us and indeed the manner domestic violence policy is now managed. I ask her to come forward to accept her award from a very grateful organisation.'

The room erupted in acclaim and stood to recognise Wendy, their energy overwhelming. Struggling to my feet, I was more than a little astonished by the accolade. I fair dinkum did not know about her work for them. My wife was beaming from the tribute. As I bent to kiss her, she cupped my face and kissed me.

'I love you,' she whispered, before dancing off to the podium.

Watching her excitement, I reflected on how foolish and selfish I'd been not to have known what she was doing on those apparently lazy days away from the house. What I assumed were latte lunches with the ladies was a little more than that. It seems she was working hard to secure the organisation's future. I remained baffled by it all, yet full of admiration.

The guests settled down as Wendy came to the lectern holding the statue. She didn't have any notes, so I speculated on what she would say. I hoped she would relax and not forget those within the organisation who helped her achieve her astounding outcomes. I was anxious for her, but she seemed happy and relaxed as she surveyed the room.

'Thank you so much. This is an enormous, unexpected privilege, and I feel humbled by the recognition. I thank you all for awarding this to me.'

She stopped for a few moments, seeming to collect her thoughts.

'Five years ago, when I strolled into the office of my local community group looking for information about family relationships, I didn't expect I would still be here years later, accepting this award. My local group supported families in trouble, providing counselling for families that may have been on the edge.' She looked at me and smiled.

'What I found was an office with no resources. They had very little money in the bank, very little furniture, and whilst volunteers were passionate and keen to help, they could not support most of their clients, including me.

'I recall having my first meeting with then president, Tony Sicily, who is here tonight.' Wendy continued, waving toward the former president. 'I remember listening to his angst about funding and the overall strategy and values of the group. He told me domestic violence and family breakdown was a significant issue for the local community and that unless his group could improve its service delivery, then there would be little government and community support to continue. Once Tony understood my background, he convinced me to join the board. I did, thinking I could bring basic planning skills to the organisation.'

'Sadly, the skills of the board focused only on service delivery. Whilst they were passionate about services, they could not articulate their vision into a plan. So, I stepped forward and helped them develop a strategic and operational business plan.'

'We recognised the dire need to establish education services. We set about developing simple communication products, which then developed into training programs. They were baby steps at first, but then we saw our baby grow. We now sell these programs under license internationally. We secured our first sale just a few months ago. We also established an online education platform, allowing greater access for those wanting access, especially for young children. It's a great tragedy to learn that children are the most at-risk family category from abuse from both their parents. The second highest category is elder abuse, which continues to astound me when the media seems so fixated on an errant father.'

The audience broke out in applause, but Wendy held up her hand to quieten them.

'Our family education programs designed years ago needed funding. At first, we were tempted to go cap in hand to the government for money. But our plan was to always be independent of government, so we instead established a philanthropic program extending into significant corporate investment.' The audience listened, captivated, as Wendy spoke of the organization's growth and success. 'And let me tell you, it paid off in a huge way, especially for corporate sponsors as they were concerned with productivity downtime caused by family breakdown affecting workforces. So, these corporates, like many others saw the need for these types of programs and supported us. Now we have beautiful premises, with professional staff providing quality counselling and support programs,' she continued, her voice rising with pride. 'We now have the biggest agency within the nation, with branches in most states, including regional centres. And five years later we are now confident to work with government and have secured vital funding for our administration which has proven its worth.'

A burst of applause echoed through the room, and Wendy paused, allowing the sound to wash over her. This was amazing. Why didn't I know about this? Surely, I could not have been so ignorant and deaf. Perhaps I've been absent for far too long.

'It has been hard work for our dedicated volunteers, and it was only in recent times that we saw the strategy which was developed in a workshop I facilitated five years ago come to fruition. Whilst they have asked me many times to stand for president, I have never been interested as I remain focused on process and implementation. I thought I would let the leaders in our group brawl over decisions, allowing me to get things done. But I must emphasise it wasn't just me who made this happen,' Wendy continued, her voice now touched with humility. 'Our current president, Robert Gunston and Executive Officer, Mary Tuck, have taken our brand and services to a new level of corporate governance. We are now considered internationally as best practice for similar types of not-for-profit community service groups. So, I feel a little embarrassed accepting this award given the work everyone has done.'

A sudden burst of contradictory applause echoed. Wendy, embarrassed, paused, waiting for it to end.

'I must also say. I'm proud of the work we have done,' she said, her voice firm and resolute. 'If I'm to be recognised, then let it also shed light on everyone involved in the development of our organisation, for I stand on the shoulders of giants.'

'In particular, I want to recognise four people who deserve special recognition. Susan Frawley has been the engine behind our growth. Without her doggedness and her dedication, nothing would have happened, and I thank her for sage advice and support.'

The guests clapped enthusiastically.

'Also, I want to recognise Billy Duryea, for his business development effort. He has changed the way many not-for-profits go about obtaining vital corporate and philanthropic funds. As we speak, we know other organisations are adopting his business development model and we should recognise him for his efforts.'

Even more enthusiastic support from guests, as Wendy smiled at Billy, and I leaned across Maureen to shake his hand.

'Margot Spangher also needs recognition for the manner in which she has cajoled and motivated the board to accept some of my off-the-wall ideas.' Margot received generous support as well, and the room filled with the sound of clapping and cheers.

'The last person I want to recognise is my husband, Ryan Kennedy,' Wendy said, her voice soft, filling with emotion as she glanced over at me.

I glanced up in admiration a little surprised and a touch emotional.

'Without his support during the last five years, allowing me to do the things I wanted to do, then perhaps we would not have achieved what we have done.'

'When I first met my husband before he became the George Clooney of politics with his suave sophistication,' the audience rippled with a few laughs, 'I saw him as a truck driver. As his family business grew and his industry career developed, his ability to get things done fascinated me. This attitude rubbed off. I learned from him that nothing could happen without leadership. When I came to our organisation, this is what I brought with me. Leadership with a capital L is what I learned from my husband. I'm proud to be his wife and I look forward to sharing the future with him.' The audience clapped, and she nodded a few times. 'Once again, thank you for this honour. I am humbled by it. Thank you.'

Wendy paused for a few photographs with the president. She

left the podium to strong applause from another standing ovation. This time I struggled, as I felt embarrassed, shamed, and humiliated. Not from what she said, but from the manner I treated her over recent years. Not overtly, but more sinisterly within my mind. I had made up my mind about her and now I was shamefully proven wrong.

When she made it past the congratulatory guests, she placed her trophy on the table and looked at me. My eyes welled, and a trickle leaked from a corner. It embarrassed me to look at her as she came in for a hug. But as she embraced me, she felt good, and her energy transferred to me reinforcing my neglected admiration for her.

I realised then that I was truly a lucky guy.

Thirty-Five

———————

The limousine's windscreen wipers beat a steady rhythmic cadence against the glass as we pushed through the city's late-night traffic, a storm drenching those outside. Wendy nestled into my chest in the back seat, her head resting on my shoulder as she used to do.

'Hey, Wends,' my voice was low and contemplative. 'Can I talk to you about a couple of things?'

'Sure darling.' She sat up and turned in her seat to face me. 'What's troubling you?'

'That was the most incredible evening I've ever experienced. Well done.'

'Yeah, it was good, wasn't it?' she said, a small smile playing at the corners of her lips.

'Why didn't you tell me about what you've been doing?'

'Oh, you're always busy,' she said, shrugging. 'I thought you may not even come along, although Fiona kept your diary clear.'

'But it's not just the dinner. Why didn't you tell me about the award?'

'I thought you wouldn't be interested,' she said, her voice tinged with sadness. 'To be honest, you have never shown an interest in what I do.'

I felt a pang of guilt and awkwardness. 'You mentioned you went to the local community centre around five years ago.'

'I wanted to know what my options were if we went belly-up,' she said.

'You were taking soundings on what you could do to end our marriage?'

'You had already started your affair. I wanted to know my rights,' she said.

'Why didn't you talk to me about it?'

'What difference would it have made? I wanted to know what I could do since you were doing what you wanted to.'

Her words silenced me. I gazed out the window. 'I've failed you.' I brushed my cheek.

'No, you haven't failed me, darling. You've mainly failed yourself.' She seemed rather matter of fact about it. 'You have always been a dreamer. You wanted to hang onto your youth. Why not let you have it?' Wendy laughed. 'Mind you, I didn't expect you to take so long to wake up. It was turning into a potential nightmare for me.'

I shook my head a little, ashamed, feeling the weight of my actions. I watched folks rushing about on the pavement, avoiding puddles and the splashing cars.

'Look, you provide a secure and comfortable life for me and the children,' she continued. 'Most of the time, you work hard and you are often exhausted. You have never dangled your amorous adventures in my face, and I never thought you were being a naughty boy because of it. You're brilliant like that.'

'That doesn't make me feel good.'

She didn't respond. I glanced at her. 'And nor should it. You've been a right bastard, and you deserve to be punished.' Wendy was right. 'Once I understood your relationship with the woman wasn't what you wanted, then I wasn't anxious about what might happen. I assumed you would never leave the family. It's just that you never knew you wouldn't. So, for the sake of our many more years together, I let you explore who you really are.'

'I'm sorry for disrespecting you. I feel so stupid and selfish.'

She glared at me her eyes filled with anguish. 'You hurt me,' she said, her voice low and filled with pain.

I turned away, feeling guilty. 'I know. I'm sorry.'

'Don't do it again.'

I looked at her, pausing before saying. 'Who are you? I mean you shouldn't forgive me for what I have done. I wouldn't forgive you if I were in your shoes.'

'Darling, it took two years of therapy for me to understand our relationship,' she said, her voice softening. 'I just had to wait for you.'

'Why?' I glanced away. 'I've acted shamefully.'

'Yes, you have. As I say, you hurt me, but you're my husband, and the father of my children. I wasn't going to let you go so easy.'

'I don't deserve you.'

She laughed. 'You're probably right,' she said, her eyes sparkling with amusement. 'Darling, the important point to remember is that I deserve you,' she said, a hint of a smile on her lips.

'What happens now?' I rubbed my chin a little unsure what I should do.

'You tell me, as you could soon become the backbencher.'

'Oh shit. I forgot about that.' I pulled out my phone. 'Jesus Christ, there are thirteen missed calls, seven from the prime minister.'

'Call her now. We should know what she is going to do before we get home. We can tell the kids if they are awake.'

'They won't be.' I stubbed the recall button and waited for Freya Lewis. 'I want to discuss Sarah as well.'

Wendy nodded and gazed out the window, dropping her hand into mine. I felt confused about my emotions and took in a few deep breaths to prepare for the prime minister.

'Freya Lewis.'

'Prime Minister, it's Ryan.'

'Where the heck have you been? I've been trying to get hold of you?'

'I've been at a dinner. Wendy received an award.'

'For her work in domestic violence, no doubt. Well-deserved, I'm sure.'

'How do you know about that, and why don't I?' A sense of embarrassment rushed through me as a cackle came from Lewis. 'What did you want to discuss, Prime Minister?'

'You're kidding me, aren't you?' Lewis said. 'You're sassing me. Are you sassing me?'

'Settle down Freya. I have no idea what you're calling about.'

'I bet you don't.' She sounded cynical.

'I suppose I have some idea. You are about to admonish me, put me through your hoops, then yell a few expletives at me, as you normally do. Then you're going to decommission me.'

'Really?'

'You threatened me with the sack if I didn't do what you wanted.'

She paused for a moment, and I squeezed Wendy's hand. 'Before I start, I just want to know why you changed your mind. Why did you change government policy after we spoke this afternoon? You made up policy on the run after we agreed on a position. Why?'

'As you may remember, I met with Michella Franklin, and she advocated for her members.' Pausing for a few moments, Wendy now squeezed my hand. 'She died soon after that meeting. I wanted to leave her a legacy.'

'How generous of you.' Lewis' toned tightened.

'Freya, it's the right thing to do. If you don't think so, then so be it. I'll move onto something else.'

'What? You think I'm going to turn you into a martyr?' Freya's voice was laced with derision.

'Hardly a martyr. I hardly consider a sacked minister a martyr.'

'You always were a pompous goose, Ryan. That's the reason you didn't know your wife was getting an award tonight.' Freya chided me like everyone else in my life. 'No, I will not sack you. Not after your media conference and the immediate impact your announcement had on the polls.'

I shook my head, confusion creeping in. 'I don't understand.'

'You've provided the government an immediate seven-point lift. My preferred prime minister rating has me at fifty-three percent. So well done, you,' she chuckled, her words sending a wave of relief washing over me.

'I'm confused. What do you mean? Am I not sacked?'

'Not on these figures you're not,' Lewis said, laughing. 'Next time you intend to go rogue just keep me advised. I want to be on the same page when the media calls.'

'You're kidding me.' I could feel my chest tighten and my eyes welling with tears. A dose of anxiety working its way through me as I tried to shift in my seat.

'Ryan, get the message out early and sleep well. This little revolution of yours may just turn around the government's fortunes. Well done.'

'Good night PM.' I dropped the telephone to the seat. The day keeps getting stranger and stranger.

'What did she say?'

'Polling has gone up, and my job is safe. Such an enormous relief.'

'There you go. If you do what feels right, everything will be okay,' Wendy said, her voice filled with warmth and understanding.

'It has been a weird day. Unbelievable really.'

'Tell me what happened?'

'Too many things to reflect upon now. Suffice to say I'm looking forward to when it's over.'

'And then it all starts again tomorrow,' Wendy sighed. 'You must be happy with the PM?'

'Yes, I am. It also makes me think, perhaps I should do more in the parliament and put my marker down.' I remain muddled about it all, but maybe Jordan urging me to raise my leadership status should be listened to.

'Only if it feels right for you, darling. Try to be who you are rather than what others want you to be,' Wendy counselled, her words ringing true in my heart.

'Wise words. I've heard them a few times today.'

'Oh yes, from who?'

'Larry told me this morning. He said I should stop being a moron and grow up.'

'Larry Matthews said that? The old man who thinks he's twenty and still acts like it. You're taking advice from him?'

'He's your greatest fan.'

'Really? What did he say?' Wendy asked, curiosity piqued.

'He said you are a beautiful wife and mother, and I should concentrate on you, rather than searching for things that don't exist.'

'That surprises me,' Wendy said, her lips curling into a small smile. A wise man. What did you want to say about the kids?'

'Oh yes. I went along to the basketball. Both the others were there cheering for their school. Anyway, it was great. Fraser was a star, and he won the game for them.'

'He didn't win the game,' Wendy scoffed.

'He scored a three pointer after the hooter, giving them the game. He also got his nose splattered across his face.'

'You're kidding,' Wendy exclaimed, her eyes wide with surprise. I should have been there for him.'

'No matter. You were no doubt busy with preparations for the dinner.' Wendy turned and gazed out the window, perhaps lost in thought. 'Peter is another matter.'

'Why? What's wrong with him?'

'The federal police identified him as hacking into my ministerial emails. Come to think of it. How did you get those photos?'

'Darling, I know all your passwords,' Wendy said, her tone light and teasing. 'I've been following your messages for ages, trying to keep tabs on what you are up to. When you are asleep at home, I usually get access. I do it discreetly I assure you. I only ever read communication from your slut, and I downloaded files before you deleted them.'

Still confused about this revelation, I didn't know what to feel. Why didn't she ever bring it up? It must have been killing her knowing her husband was being unfaithful, yet she tolerated it.

'Anyway, tell me what Peter did,' Wendy prompted, her voice a little sterner.

'The feds came in this morning and briefed me about it. It's quite a serious matter, and they have left it to me to decide if I want to press charges.'

'What do you want to do?'

'I spoke to him this afternoon and sorted things out. It won't go on any further,' I sighed. 'As if I'm going to get the police to charge him.'

'Will you be in trouble over it?'

'Not likely. The police were very clear, though. This is my decision, and they will record it formally. If it ever goes pear shaped, they will point at me.'

'I'll have a chat with him tomorrow. He can unburden himself a little with his mum. I can guess what he might have seen. Maybe he needs me to help sort out his emotions. It was tawdry stuff she was sending you.' Wendy sterner with her quip.

'Yeah, well, that explains why it would go nowhere.' The thrill of the getting images from Rosemary titillated me, but I should have deleted them. 'I had a word with Sarah this afternoon.'

'Oh yes, what did she say?'

'I think we should let her go.'

'I will not allow her to have a party with a bunch of morons. I know what they're like.'

'No, I'm not talking about the holiday house. I'm talking about next year.'

'You are kidding me? Why have you shifted on this?'

'She is a smart kid. We discussed her plans. She feels she will do better at university if she has a break.'

'I never got a break,' Wendy said; she seemed to have a little resentment. 'Why should she?'

'It's a different world now. I trust her.'

'Have you placed any conditions on her?' she asked.

'I haven't even told her she can go. I wanted to talk to you.'

'That's a first.' Wendy paused for a moment. 'What do you want to do?'

'I will help her get a good job in London, which will mean less partying.'

'I suppose, but will she want to travel to France and Spain?'

'We can discuss her plans and how she will manage once we understand the detail.'

Wendy eyed me, her face a mix of worry and sadness. 'I'm a little scared about letting her go. She's my baby girl.'

'Wends, she is switched on about this. She argues if she went for twelve months now, she would benefit from the trip. She knows what and where she wants to go.'

'Are you sure?'

'I'll have folks look after her. She'll be okay.' I patted her hand. 'I think she'll agree to conditions, so long as they're not too strict.'

'I suppose.' She seemed sad. 'They just grow up so fast. I haven't had enough time with her.'

'It'll be okay. I'll give her enough money and local support to help her. She's a smart kid.'

'Okay, but she is not going down the coast,' Wendy snapped.

'Let her go, she'll be fine.' I laughed. 'You're so beautiful.'

'No, I'm not.' She paused a few moments, gazing out the window. 'I still haven't got my nose right.' I assumed she was joking.

'I'm not talking about your nose, gorgeous. What I'm talking about is Wendy Kennedy, mother of our children. You are beautiful.'

Wendy leaned across and kissed me, then fell back in her seat with a sigh. 'It's been one hell of a day, I can tell ya. I'm glad things worked out for you with the prime minister. It's a relief to know the real Ryan is back.'

'It has been your day, gorgeous. You were unbelievable tonight. You spoke really well.' I smiled as the yellow streetlights flashed across her. 'What happens now?'

'We start again tomorrow and keep doing what we've been doing. If you want to join me and the kids, that would be great. I'm sure you'll work it out.'

I gazed out the window, lost in thought, and wondered why I ever doubted her. What made me think she was not good enough for me? She nailed it when she said I was a dreamer and hadn't woken up, lost in my little world. What a perceptive woman. Maybe it's time for me to get focused and compromise. Maybe it's time to join life as it's offered, rather than constantly dreaming about what might have been.

'I was just thinking, why don't you come to China with me?'

'Are you serious?' Wendy squealed a little. 'You never take me overseas. You're always too busy with meetings and delegation tours. You tell me it's boring as all get out.'

'Beijing will be great this time of year. You can go see the Forbidden City and the Great Wall whilst I'm in meetings. We can even stopover in Hong Kong for a few days.'

Wendy twisted and stretched across my lap and kissed me. 'That would be sensational. Oh gosh, really? I'm so excited.'

'It would be nice to take time out together. This trip would be an excellent opportunity. A perfect opportunity.'

'What will I wear? Will I need formal outfits?'

'I have an even better idea. Why don't we stop over in Singapore? We can do some high-end Asian brand shopping there. Much better than what we offer here.'

Wendy kissed me again, her lips warm and passionate, her body pressed against mine. She pulled back with a gasp, her eyes shining. 'I so love you right now.'

Thirty-Six

11:47 PM

The water thundered into my face as I stood beneath the showerhead, washing away the day. The warmth of the water relieving the tension and stress, which continues to be the bane of my existence. It stretched and shoved me throughout the hours and now melted away with each droplet cascading down my body. I let out a sigh of relief as I looked forward to my bed and sanctuary from the woes of my world.

The towel was soft and plush, a welcome reprieve as I dried my skin. I peered into the mirror to study my beaten face. It wasn't so bad. It was not as bad as some had made it out to be. I shook my head with a minor disappointment as I stroked moisturiser into my skin, as the basketball belly seemed to have grown since the morning. I'll have to do something about that, maybe take up more exercise. The signs of age were showing, particularly around my neck. I wondered for a moment if Wendy's doctor could help, but quickly dismissed the idea. I checked out the damage to my lip before blowing my hair dry. At least I still need a dryer. Plenty of my colleagues don't.

Wendy was yet to step from her ensuite after closing up and

checking the kids, something I seldom do. Maybe I should do more around the house. This brave new world was already changing me for the better I reckon. The sheets were fresh. Today must have been the housekeeper's day. She comes two, or maybe three times a week. On one of those days, she changes the bed-linen and towels, which is why everything is so fresh, or that's what I prefer to think, given Wendy suggested she enjoyed her own fun. I couldn't help but wonder about those strange scratches and the cold water this morning. Why did she apologise?

I shook my head, berating myself for dwelling on such things given my behaviour. It's been a very interesting day and maybe a game changer in many ways. I suspect these concerns about my job and my family do not differ from anyone else my age. This struggle with my identity never seems to be over, but I knew Wendy would always be there to support me through it. Maybe today could puncture this feeling of loneliness I have, and I can begin to enjoy what I do have.

Sometimes, though, I feel as if I'm drowning, overwhelmed by my responsibilities. My mother needs my help, and my brother, that hopeless blockhead, just doesn't seem to understand he needs to step up. I might have to be honest and give him a little nudge. Perhaps speaking your truth is the key to finding your own truth. Maybe I need to speak up more and ignore this idea that I am owed something from people who take advantage of me. Perhaps I should open myself up by giving more of my time to those I care about. Maybe I can do more for mum. I'll drop by for a chat and a cup of tea tomorrow; it would be nice to see her. And maybe I'll bring scones, or perhaps French pastries. She is the security blanket that keeps me grounded. I'm not sure what I would do without her, and yet I still continue to complain about her. Which I guess is a touch selfish. I'll call her tomorrow and organise our tea, and perhaps resolve to put an end to this martyr complex I have.

I now realise I need to stop complaining about what other people weren't doing for me, or maybe I'm just too blind to notice the things happening for me, especially at work. Oh, that reminds me, I better check my emails for the first appointment.

Reaching for my phone, I flipped through emails, opening a note from Joanne. First call at Hancock Media on Good Morning Australia at six thirty, meaning a five o'clock alarm, damn it. I set the alarm, returning the telephone to the side table.

Closing my eyes finding it hard to keep them open, I relaxed into the pillow. Life is good, I suppose. What do I really have to worry about? I feel grateful for having a great family, great job, good friends, and healthy super fund. What more could I need?

I don't know why I thought Selena could have been the answer to my search for love. Why was I bonking Rosemary and ignoring my family? I could feel myself squirm a little, feeling guilty. What is it I'm afraid of? I should be ashamed.

What is this damn thing that I'm searching for? What has been missing in my life? It really can't be love as it surrounds me. It's not sex because it has spoilt me over recent times. I smirked thinking of my duplicity and the lurid images of Rosemary. I'm still a bastard male it seems to be considering those things. But what has life not seriously given me that has made me feel so insecure about commitment?

Fraser said to me today I never tell him I love him. But I do. Why do I hold back from telling him? The more I think about it, the fact is, I don't tell anyone I love them, not even my mother.

Hey, wait, is this the problem?

This inability to express my love to anyone, is that it? Am I love-less because I cannot commit love to others? Who said it today... what you put out; you get back? If I don't tell anyone I love them, especially those I truly love, then how can I feel loved? Is this the ludicrous source of my troubles?

Does my failure to commit to Wendy block me from growing up? Indeed, am I searching for something that doesn't even exist? What did Larry say about diamonds? Something about front yards? He said I should look at what I already have instead of searching for something that doesn't exist. Wise man Larry.

I could hear soft sounds coming from the next room, and a perfumed scent tickled my nose. Wendy was wonderful tonight, quite superb by the way she handled Rose. I was half expecting a punch-on, and the two of them facing off unnerved me a little. She gave Rose the message I had tried to tell her. Let's just hope she gets the message and walks away. I hope so.

Was that a snore? Did I wake myself up again by snoring? It's comfortable, I feel relaxed, and it's been a tough day.

The door slid open, and I opened an eye to see Wendy standing there with the light behind her like some bronzed goddess. Oh my god, she looks fabulous. I roused a little as she slipped into bed and snuggled up for a cuddle. She straddled over me on my chest and kissed me.

It was then an epiphany came upon me so brightly it was like a flash of lightning. It had been sitting behind my mask for way too long and before I knew it; the words were out of my mouth.

'I love you, Wendy.'

DEAR READER

Authors thrive and rely on the opinion of readers, and I wonder if you could help?

I would be extremely grateful if you let other readers know what you thought of SELFISH AMBITIONS by considering leaving an honest review on Amazon or Goodreads or posting a review on your social media including the tag, @852press.

If you would like to communicate with me then please do.

I always respond to emails and enjoy chatting about future projects and seeking opinion about some of the issues raised with my writing.

If you would like to be added to my Advanced Readers list, then please let me know.

readers@richardevans-author.com

Best wishes
Richard Evans

Turn the page for a preview of:

WHAT READERS ARE SAYING ABOUT DECEIT:

Richard Evans' first book, DECEIT, is a five-star thriller that brings the Australian political process to life. – *GOODREADS*

Just finished reading DECEIT and it was gripping; I could not put it down. It was brilliant. I just loved the book and can't wait to read DUPLICITY. – *FORMER CLERK OF VICTORIAN LEGISLATIVE COUNCIL*

Woohoo. Could not put down your book, DECEIT, what a ripper. Kept me up late, then started again at breakfast, in time to read to the end. Better than any whodunit. Waiting for your next instalment. What a delight to read such a great Australian book at last. – *JUDY C, QUEENSLAND*

Former federal politician Richard Evans offers readers a thrilling, twisty ride. A refreshing political thriller with authentic insider knowledge. – *KATHRYN'S INBOX*

From Richard Evans comes one of the most incredible fictional examinations of the Australian political system, an exciting and superb political thriller. – *THE UNSEEN LIBRARY*

For a **FREE eBOOK COPY** of DECEIT and to join my Advanced Readers team is now available from the following link:

richardevans-author.com

PROLOGUE

EIGHT MONTHS EARLIER ...

The two aging politicians sprawled in the leader's soft leather chairs; old friends, comfortable with each other after a slow, four-course dinner in the adjoining dining room. They were enjoying the pungency of expensive cigars, smoke spiraling toward the high ceiling. Both had a tumbler of Irish whiskey, preferring the smooth, refined taste to the harshness of the scotch usually imbibed by the philistines they ruled over.

'I can't do it.' The prime minister stretched his long legs across the heavy coffee table, easing away a pile of books and magazines, his head dropping back onto the green leather. 'It's a generous offer, but I can't.'

'You have nothing to fear, my friend. There will be no trouble for you.' The president blew smoke toward the ceiling. 'It's timing; there's nothing criminal about this.'

'I suspect pocketing a secret commission might be judged criminal.'

'Consider it a gift from me. No-one will ever know.'

'I can't be certain of that – and you can't either.' Prime Minister Gerrard sipped his whiskey and flushed it over his tongue.

'Andrew, you worry far too much. These things happen all the time in my country.'

'To be expected then.'

'Exactly.' The president sharpened his tone. 'All I need to make this happen for you is your bank account – Swiss, of course – and your assurance the money will be released by your government to us before March next year.'

'It's way too risky.'

'You should have little fear; trust me. Legislate the money and perhaps tie it to a condition we start construction at once. Transfer the funds, we start site works, and then you let me do the rest. You will not be involved; I can assure you.' Surriento took a small swig of whiskey. 'You get your detention centres, and we provide jobs to many thousands of my people. It's a win-win for our countries – and us.'

'I suppose I could appropriate the money and release it to you before March, but I'll need compelling evidence of your government's approval for the build well before then.'

'It can be done.'

'I would much prefer to see site works begin before we release any money.'

'It is possible.'

Gerrard drew deeply on his cigar, pondering the deal. The president flicked a lump of ash onto the plush woollen carpet.

'What, you can't reach the ashtray?'

'No problem, rub it in, it's good for the carpet, just as this arrangement is good for you and me.' The toothy salesman's grin prompted a sly smirk from the prime minister.

'You dirty bastard.' Gerrard slowly shook his head, considering the offer. 'I can't just let you have four billion dollars with nothing to show for it.'

'Then don't give me the entire amount; we can do it in stages.' The president began reeling in his catch. 'If you are so worried about how this works, then let's do it in four stages. Four hundred million down before March next year, then one billion for each of the next two years, with a final payment of one point six billion on completion. Just think, in four years you could retire on a high.'

'I reckon if I can convince my colleagues to approve the money in the forward estimates next month, that will leave me enough time to get legislation through both houses of parliament later in the year for the first tranche of ten per cent to be paid, possibly enacted by February next year. Is that enough time to begin work on the first centre?'

'Of course, my friend, more than enough time. Once you legislate, we can start ground works, and once we have the money, you will have your money. Simple as that. We can clear it to you within days of each payment.'

The president knew he was close to a deal: 'You know you deserve it; you have worked hard and sacrificed much. This money will help with your retirement.' The president sat forward, sliding his tumbler toward the prime minister for a refill, knowing silence in these moments was a powerful tool for a negotiator.

The prime minister splashed a handsome dram into his friend's tumbler. 'When do you need to know?'

'Now.'

'The parliament is too finely balanced, and a few of my junior colleagues hate your lot. It may be tricky getting the Appropriation Bill through. We're okay for numbers in the senate, but the house of reps may be a struggle given your insistence on murdering some of our finest citizens.'

'Drug traffickers deserve to die.'

'You know that, I know that, but the great unwashed don't like their own facing a firing squad in the jungle.'

The president picked up his glass, rolled it between his hands and pondered for a moment. 'So, you're telling me, if I do a deal on your two citizens, you will approve the money?'

'No, I'm not saying that at all, but it might be helpful.'

'You get state-of-the-art detention centres in my country, and you want me to breach my own laws?'

'Oh, come on, Amir, you know this project will be good for your economy, and it will shut the fucking humanitarians up. We both need this project.'

'Yes, but if we don't get initial funding by next March, we won't be able to do it.' The president had his own deadlines and financial needs.

'You mean if you don't get your money, you won't do it?'

'I have my own troubles, my own projects that need to be funded.' The president took a larger draw of his whiskey, swallowing hard, stifling a small ref lux before the liquid and vapours disappeared. Suddenly, he felt hot and prickly, wiping his brow with his palm as the whiskey coursed through him. 'I won't deny it will help me, as it will you. I just can't release drug traffickers for no reason.'

'Let me give you a reason. I will approve the four-billion-dollar project on the day you grant them clemency. Not a pardon, but clemency from the death penalty. Let the fuckers rot in jail as far as I'm concerned.'

'I can't; I would lose the next election if I were to do that.'

'Okay, so we agree to disagree.' The prime minister could sense a deal was at hand.

'I can't, Andrew!'

'So, this idea of money was just talk – you had no intention of really doing a deal.'

The politicians sat quietly, not knowing who had the upper

hand in the negotiations. The prime minister, almost asleep with his eyes closed and breathing heavily; the president smirking ever so slightly in recognition of his friend's efforts to force a winning play.

'Here's an idea,' the president said finally, drawing his friend from his sham slumber. 'What say I allow an appeal on the first payment? This then runs for two years, and if I am re-elected, I recommend clemency when the final payment is made.'

'No, my friend. Just the agreed clemency is no longer on the table. The deal now is – you also agree to release them from that hell hole you call a jail when you receive the final payment, then I will consider your plan to embezzle appropriated funds from the Australian government.'

'Clemency and then a pardon?' the president scoffed. 'So, if I agree to this new outrageous demand, you will get me my money?'

'Our money,' the prime minister said, swinging his legs off the table and leaning forward, his tumbler held out in anticipation of a toast.

The president leaned forward and clinked the proffered glass. 'Best you get yourself a bank account, Mr Prime Minister.'

'To a long and prosperous partnership.'

The president brought his glass to his lips but did not drink. With a barely perceptible smile, he recalled his actions of the morning: he had already decided to grant clemency to the two Australians stopped at Jakarta international airport twelve years earlier with ten kilos of heroin strapped to their bodies. Now he could reverse his decision, leaking it to the media to show he was tough on crime, adding further political gravitas to his re-election campaign in two years' time. He loved his Australian friend like a brother. Their wives were friends from university, and he didn't enjoy taking advantage of him, but this was business – and in his culture, business was never personal.

The prime minister lay back and drew heavily on his cigar,

mouthing smoke rings as he slowly exhaled, reflecting on his newfound wealth. It would be a richly deserved legacy for his years of service and sacrifice. 'I've been in this damn business for nearly forty years, and I still have little to show for it.'

'In my country, it is expected our leaders will be looked after. This is the problem with you Australians – you should embrace the political culture of Asia.' The president smiled; his fat cigar stuck in the side of his mouth. 'It is only a small amount to start with, but it will grow and be ready for when you retire. When will you retire, by the way?'

'I am thinking I might do one more term, maybe two. Margaret still has it in her head to move to France.'

'Perhaps there will be room for us as well. Can you imagine both of us retired in the south of France?'

'That's where the shysters go, I suppose. It's an attractive thought, I must say.'

'Get this deal done on time before March next year, and you will be halfway there, my friend.'

CHAPTER

1

MONDAY 4.25 PM

It wasn't unusual for an October storm to hit the coastal city of Newcastle, but the hammering rain belting the corrugated roof of the makeshift airport office troubled Fred Rocher. He needed to be back in Canberra for meetings, and his pilot seemed nervous about flying in the conditions – the smaller the plane the more nervous the aviator, he supposed.

His parliamentary colleagues had been bunkered down in the small, cosy shed – optimistically called a waiting room by Hunter Air Services – for a little under an hour, with no sign of urgency from the inattentive staff, who were working in a much more salubrious shed next door.

Rocher was obliged to get his colleagues back to the national capital the following day to vote on important legislation. The prime minister had insisted on pushing through legislation-approved seed funding for a state-of-the-art offshore immigration detention centre to be built on the Indonesian island of Ambon, the first of similar centres planned throughout the Indonesian archipelago. He wanted it to pass both houses of parliament before the Christmas break because a four-hundred-million-dollar payment to the Indonesians was required as soon as possible to kick-start the project. The government held only a two-seat majority in the House of Representatives, so every vote was important, and Rocher knew they needed him and his colleagues to make sure the bill passed so they could send it to the senate for ratification.

After a hectic day, the group had stretched themselves out across various rickety chairs and benches. A vending machine provided the only amenity, and a poster of sunny beaches partially stuck to a wall provided the only decoration. Each member of the powerful Environment Committee was working diligently, tapping away on social media, reading a book, or flicking through business papers. They'd been up early, travelling from Canberra at 5.30 am, the sky still brilliant with stars and the lush landscape below shrouded in darkness. The ninety-minute flight took them over the Blue Mountains and on to coastal Newcastle to take evidence for a pivotal inquiry into the establishment of a proposed gas facility, the infrastructure of which would affect the region. If the committee approved the project, after hearing evidence from various stakeholders, then it meant jobs for a region struggling with an economic downturn.

Peter Wilson, the committee's long-term secretary and delegation manager, had arranged a bus to transport the parliamentary group throughout their highly structured day of meetings and formal hearings. The first meeting had been with the mayor to garner intelligence on the local politics of the controversial issue, and then a working breakfast with the mayor and the elected members of the city council had provided more insight into the mood of the community and their views about the proposed facility. After meetings with city engineers to discuss planning issues and the complex infrastructure requirements, the committee was transported to the university to hear from a professor explaining the principles of coal seam gas extraction and rebutting the myths about it, with only one politician falling asleep during the forty- minute PowerPoint presentation. The committee then returned to the city's council offices to formally take submissions from residents concerned about their community's safety and water quality if the proposed facility went ahead, the high-ceilinged room echoing with the amplified voices of concerned and emotional citizens. After a lunch of soggy sandwiches and forgettable, watery fruit juice, the committee took supplementary evidence until three o'clock from mining and engineering experts extolling the economic and social advantages of gas extraction for the region, before leaving for their planned 3.45 pm flight.

Clouds started to roll in across the coast during the early afternoon, darkening as they thickened over the nearby mountains, providing an eerily low canopy of cloud cover from the mountains to the coast, lightning flashing high in the blanket of cloud and illuminating through the darkness. What started as a soaking spring shower so typical for the region increased in such intensity during the last hour to build into a wild storm, with no sign of it easing. Gusting wind rattled the building, and the occasional flashes of lightning breaking through the low cloud and accompanying cracks of thunder suggested the storm was travelling slowly, hemmed in by the mountains. The unseen airline staff were yet to venture out of their office.

'Peter, try to see what's happening will you please.' The delay exasperated Rocher. 'We need to get going if we want to be back tonight.'

'I'll try to get hold of the pilot.'

As Peter stood, the door smashed open, rocking the walls. Pelting rain was driven into the room. A soaking, bedraggled pilot rushed through the doorway and struggled to close the door against the wind. Peeling off his inadequate raincoat, he made his way to the counter, then turned and faced his passengers, raising his voice above the din of the rain smashing on the tin roof.

'We're not likely to take off until the storm passes, I'm afraid. It seems to have set in over the mountains, and we would need to get above it to have any chance of getting to Canberra. I'm not sure my kite can do that.'

'Not acceptable, I'm afraid.' Rocher stood and approached the pilot. 'We need to be back tonight.'

'Hey wait up, Fred.' Mark English put aside his iPad and walked over, keen to join the discussion. 'If the pilot says it's too dangerous, then I'm with him.'

English was a government member and understood the necessity of getting back to Canberra that evening, but his reputation for risk aversion was well established.

'He didn't say it was too dangerous. He said we need to get above the storm to get over the mountains.' Rocher was keen to get going. 'What's the weather like on the other side of the mountains?'

'Perfect.' The pilot conceded.

'Well, there you are then. Taking off in a storm is much easier compared to landing in one, so let's go.'

'What do the others think?' English persisted.

'Not sure they have a vote on this, Mark, but if you insist.' Rocher moved to the centre of the room to address his colleagues, most of whom had paid little attention to the pilot. 'Okay folks, listen up. As most of you probably know, we need to be back in Canberra tonight. Well, we government members do at least. We want to leave now, although it's still raining, but we have a small problem. The storm doesn't seem to be abating, so no doubt we will need to take off over the coast, go out to sea and do a slow climb to get above it, first the cloud bank and then the mountains. It will absolutely be a rough ride, but no worse than some of you have already experienced, I'm sure, and then it's smooth flying until Canberra.'

A crack of thunder rattled the unsecured cupboards, and everyone jumped.

'Christ!' yelped English.

'What are our options?' opposition member Nick Trainer asked, a little louder than he would have liked.

'We can get going now and be back around six. We can wait until the storm eases and fly with an unknown ETA into Canberra, or we can stay overnight and fly back on a commercial jet tomorrow morning, but I'm not sure the PM would approve because we will miss a vote,' volunteered Rocher.

'It isn't the worst storm I've flown in,' said the pilot, dragging on a cigarette and blowing out a solid stream of smoke. 'But I'm always nervous about taking passengers up in weather like this. I can tell you; it'll be worse than any roller-coaster, and I suspect some of you will find it frightening... and some of you will be sick.'

'I vote we go now,' said Paul Kress, a government member. 'I have an important dinner at the US embassy I can't miss.'

English swayed slowly from side to side. The others looked about their group, waiting for someone to make a decision.

'Don't forget, we have the retirement presentation for the clerk tonight,' added Catherine Kennedy. 'It'd be nice to get there to acknowledge his service.'

'Stuff the clerk. He's never done much for us,' English blurted.

'Ease up Mark, I'm just saying it would be nice to be there.' Kennedy, the deputy speaker of the parliament, gave him a reassuring smile.

'Let's make it easy. Who doesn't want to go?' Rocher impatiently asked the group, who had fallen silent trying to avoid a decision.

'Me,' the pilot said, sucking hard on his cigarette.

Rocher smirked, shaking his head. 'Anyone else? Mark?' The

heavy drumming of the rain filled the room and English bowed his head, defeated. 'Okay, pack up and let's go.'

'I must formally advise you that you are doing so at your own risk, and you'll need to sign a waiver,' the pilot said as he pulled a folded paper from his jacket and passed it to Rocher. 'The airline will not cover any breakages of either equipment or yourselves, is that understood?'

'What about funerals?' Trainer joked, collecting his papers.

No-one laughed.

'Duly noted. Where do I sign? Oh, and Peter, can you record that advice?' Rocher directed as he signed the waiver and passed it back to the pilot. 'Folks, if anyone is uncertain about taking this flight you can stay and take a flight tomorrow morning. Anybody want to stay? Mark?'

English shrugged and no-one else responded as they packed their briefcases and satchels.

'So be it, you're all nuts.' The pilot headed for the plane, rain whipping into the room through the open door. He tossed his sodden cigarette into the wind.

'Come on boys, this'll be fun.' Catherine Kennedy skipped after the pilot into the rain, holding her satchel on her head to protect her stiff bouffant; her signature developed over twenty years of service in the federal parliament.

The others braced themselves against the wild weather, gripping their suit jackets, shrugging their shoulders, then bolting after her through puddles and driving rain to the plane. Rocher lingered by the door, waiting for his secretary, Wilson, to zip his case and join him.

'It never gets any easier, does it? Remember that flight we had in the Kimberley a few months back?' Rocher's broad smile almost convinced Wilson.

'Yes, but I haven't seen rain like this for a long time,' Wilson responded. 'And I'm not so sure this is a good idea.'

'Nothing to fear, Pete. Our man will take us out over the ocean to get us above this lot. Ten minutes of jumping around and then it'll be smooth as silk all the way home. We can crack open a bottle of wine once we're over the mountains.'

'Let's hope so.' Wilson dashed from the room in a wretched attempt to keep dry.

By the time Rocher reached the plane, the single-engine turbo-prop Cessna was spluttering into action. He climbed aboard, pulling up the steps and sealing the hatch, confirming with the pilot he had done so. He then sank into a leather chair behind the pilot, facing the group, as ground crew in wet weather gear busily secured the plane for take-off and unchocked the wheels.

It was a tight squeeze to get to the back of the plane, the generous leather seats reducing aisle access and movement, but the eight politicians settled in as best they could for a flight, they expected to talk about at future cocktail parties, or when called upon at dinners to recount unusual political experiences. This would be the night they survived potential catastrophe and lived to tell the tale, and the more they told the tale, the more laughs they would get at the expense of their colleagues.

Wet, miserable, and just a little apprehensive, they spread themselves among the fourteen plush seats. The pilot passed back a handful of towels to Wilson, which he distributed to the rest of the group, all keen to wipe themselves down and dry their hands and faces.

Catherine Kennedy seemed the most disordered by the dash to the plane, her trademark bouffant flattened and lopsided, revealing a somewhat sparse patch of scalp. Luckily, she didn't have a mirror; she would not have been pleased if her reputation for perfect grooming was tarnished. Cautiously, she dabbed and prodded at her wet hair, trying to reshape it, while those colleagues sitting behind her smirked and exchanged looks.

Although it was still only late afternoon, the light was grey and ominous under the roof of storm clouds. As the plane moved slowly from the tarmac apron toward the runway, the pilot, visible from the cabin, was working through his pre-flight check, speaking quietly into a microphone attached to oversized headphones. The plane's stability surprised the politicians, feeling only a little buffeting in the gusting wind. Perhaps the anxiety in the cabin was misplaced.

Rocher held up an air sickness bag and asked, 'Anyone want one of these?'

'I've already struggled through those sandwiches once already; I don't want to see them again,' joked Trainer.

'How come you're never this funny in the house?' demanded English.

'The boss always tells me to keep a lid on it, so I behave myself, unlike Harry here.'

'What have I done?'

'Nothing, as usual,' said Trainer.

Harry McMaster, younger than Trainer, squeezed a smile and quipped: 'The trouble with you, Nick, my boy is that you are too predictable. Never a serious word, ever.'

'I'll have some serious words to say about this potential mess, I can tell you.'

'It won't matter,' said English. 'Your team doesn't have the numbers – you'll be in opposition for a long time yet, mate.'

'Oh, I don't know. I reckon Jimmy Harper is the most able man to have entered the parliament since Menzies. He'll take it up to your bloke. Someone has to.' Trainer had reset his political antenna.

'Well, you could be right,' offered McMaster. 'But the PM is not going anywhere, and while he remains in the parliament, you'll never win.'

'You can't be that confident. I'm not so sure your bloke will run at another election. Too old.'

Rocher's phone buzzed, and its shrill alarm startled him. He realised it was the prime minister's call tone.

'Speak of the devil. Hi Andrew.' Rocher had known the prime minister since university and was one of only a few colleagues permitted to call him by name.

'Freddy, where are you?'

'Just about to leave Newcastle. Bad weather has delayed us. It's bucketing down and we're about to take off into it. We should get to Canberra around 6.30.'

'I was just making sure you'll be back for the vote on the Immigration Appropriation Bill tomorrow morning.'

'We'll be there. We understand its importance, and it's the reason we're all flying back. We couldn't afford to wait here any longer. We should be back in time for your function for the clerk – we're looking forward to it.'

'No big deal. The sooner he's gone the better.'

'Now come on, Andrew, you know he's only doing his job.'

'Bastard, as far as I'm concerned.'

'He'll be gone soon enough, cheer up.' Rocher shifted uncomfortably. 'Look, we're about to take off, so I'll ring you when we land. I need to talk to you about this inquiry in Newcastle and the potential trouble ahead with the local community. It could cost us a seat or two at the next election, which means we could lose government. The opposition is taking a tough line on it.' Rocher winked at the two opposition members listening in to his conversation.

'Sure, do that, old friend. I'll be keen to learn more. Take care,' ended the prime minister.

Rocher dropped his phone into the small upper pocket of his damp Armani jacket and looked over to see an apprehensive Wilson gazing at him from the seat opposite. 'Don't worry, Pete, this bird is one of the safest in the air.'

'We'll see.' Wilson seemed unconvinced.

Facing into the wind, the pilot raised the engine revs to a screaming crescendo, building enough force to propel the plane into the air. The travellers sat silently, feeling the plane wobble as it fought against the brake.

'Okay, this is it boys. Hold on,' Rocher joked to his colleagues.

They all looked past him at the pilot, seeking reassurance but getting none.

Just when the engine seemed about to explode, the pilot released the brakes, jumping the Cessna into a fast sprint along the runway to take off. The plane shook and bumped sharply as it drove hard into the wind, laboriously working to reach the required speed of 150 knots. Rocher squeezed the arm of his chair and gnawed at his bottom lip as the plane's nose lifted. Moments later, with a great shudder and creaking shake, they were airborne – cupboard doors popped open and small, untethered knick-knacks tumbled into the cabin. The politicians sat silently.

The climb seemed dangerously slow amidst all the shuddering, banging, and shaking. Rocher continued gnawing on his lip, glancing at Wilson, who stiffened in his chair. Rocher himself was still gripping the arms of his seat, pushing back hard, resisting the uncontrollable movement of the plane. He was already regretting his decision to take the flight as another thud shook the cabin and he looked out his window, seeing nothing but turbulent, grey cloud.

'Fuck!' shouted Kennedy, as the plane jolted heavily to its left.

'Not likely, Cathy,' joked Trainer, seemingly immune to the unease of his comrades.

'It won't be long now,' Rocher said after a few tense minutes. 'Once we're above the cloud band, it should be smooth sailing to Canberra.'

'I've seen worse,' said Kennedy, trying to regain her composure, her hair slipping further as her head jolted with the turbulence.

Thumps and bangs continued to sound throughout the cabin as the plane shuddered and plunged, fighting to climb through the turbulence, and resisting the furious wind. A sudden eerie silence descended on the cabin, and everyone looked at each other for support, hoping for a little relief.

Bam! A colossal thump shuddered through the entire plane, followed abruptly by a thunderous knocking sound from the front, as if a steel-capped boot was rotating in a clothes drier. An urgent, intermittent warning beep sounded from the cockpit, which glowed with a red flashing light. The plane dropped, shuddered, and jerked, groaning as the pilot fought for control. An automated voice from the cockpit warned, 'Terrain ahead, pull out. Terrain ahead, pull out.'

'Brace for impact,' the unruffled voice of the pilot said.

'Terrain ahead, pull out. Terrain ahead, pull out.'

The politicians assumed the brace position as best they could and waited.

CHAPTER
2

MONDAY 5.55 PM

'Is that a rufous whistler?' Gordon O'Brien said to no-one in particular, staring into a leafy maple from his office window. 'It's a bit early to hear them.'

Standing behind his desk, O'Brien often looked for signs of life within the mighty tree beyond his first-floor window. He loved that maple tree. Ever since he had moved into the office following his promotion to clerk of the Australian parliament, he had watched its changing colours and silhouette throughout the seasons. If he was stressed or worried by his parliamentary duties, he was often calmed by the tree's lush green leaves of summer, or the stark, sculpted boughs of winter. He especially loved the colours of autumn – the golds and amber – and always felt refreshed by the new buds and tiny red blossoms of early spring. Finding a bird or some other little creature hopping about the branches captivated him, removing him from the demanding daily grind of parliamentary procedure.

Gordon had stared despondently into the tree many, many times over his seventeen-year career as clerk, often wishing he was else-where, but in a little over two weeks his career would come to an end as he had finally decided to retire. Paradoxically, he realised he would miss all this, even the stress of managing the daily machina-tions of the national parliament and thought with dismay about the uncertain loneliness of retirement, and the fear of living a life unfulfilled.

The distinct black, white, and russet markings of the whistler were a delight – it was not unusual to see whistlers in late spring and summer, but still. 'What a little beauty.'

'Who is?' asked Marjorie Earle, Gordon's long-serving personal assistant, as she entered the office and set a pile of papers on his desk. 'What have you seen now?'

Gordon continued to track the bird as it hopped from branch to branch, searching for food. 'I'm going to miss it, Marjorie,' Gordon sighed. 'All of it.'

'You've done enough, Gordon. You can't keep going forever.'

'I suppose so,' Gordon sighed. 'Still, I'm going to miss it.' He drew a deep breath in through his nose, ballooning his chest, and held it slightly before slowly releasing it in a noisy, dejected sigh.

'Don't you dare change your mind.' Marjorie stopped momen-tarily and studied her boss. 'I've already sold my house, and I'm off in January, so don't expect me to change mine.'

Gordon smiled as the bird fluttered away and he turned from the window. 'You have nothing to worry about.'

'It's almost six. They'll be waiting for you.' The faithful assistant, ever present and confident enough to provide Gordon with advice, even when he didn't want it, straightened the papers.

'Do I have to go?' Gordon dropped into his chair feeling the energy draining from him. The thought of having to mingle with backslapping parliamentary staff and politicians was not one he relished; and he was not looking forward to what he knew he was required to do.

'It's not every day the prime minister throws a party for one of us.' Marjorie slid the first of the files toward him, her bangles hitting the desk.

'I won't miss that one, that's for sure.'

'Come on Gordon, let them celebrate your service. God knows you've sacrificed enough for all of them, so let them thank you.'

'I just want to serve these last two weeks and leave quietly. Frankly, I don't like them that much, and what they've done to this place is disgraceful, so why should I let them celebrate me.'

'Get over yourself, Gordon. Go and enjoy a chardonnay or two and let them fawn over you. You deserve it.'

'What have you got for me?' Gordon carefully scanned each brief for both content and potential errors before signing with his thick fountain pen and sliding it back to Marjorie after blotting his signature. Modern ballpoint pens were yet to touch his much-loved desk.

'Gordon, these things can wait.'

'No, they can't.' Everything had its place and only unimportant items were ever allowed to sit for any length of time awaiting his approval.

Marjorie sighed a little too loudly and bit her lip to stop saying something she might regret. Gordon could flick through a file quickly, scanning the contents, looking for anything out of place, and signing where required. He trained his staff to prepare briefs in plain English on the variety of parliamentary business issues requiring his approval, so there was no confusion with ambiguous language, and clear recommendations for action were set out for him. It made his busy life easier, but he always kept a careful eye on standards.

As Gordon methodically scanned the papers and files, Marjorie stood silently by his side, as she had done for seventeen years. She'd shared his battles with the politicians who had sought to change the protocols and standing orders of the parliament. He often told his staff it was his job to protect the parliament from the political barbarians at the gate.

All parliamentary business crossed Gordon's desk for review and approval. His advice about parliamentary process and procedure was sought by politicians, and he had seen a lot of them come and go. Some were bad, driven by nothing more than self-interest, but most who came to serve their electorates came with good intentions. Gordon knew the rorts, and how to undermine the parliamentary system. He abhorred politicians with a frivolous attitude toward the established historical rules and protocols of the parliament, and often corrected a recalcitrant politician, even the prime minister, when they crossed the line of acceptable parliamentary behaviour. Gordon took it personally if anything untoward happened under his watch and believed that he was the difference between an effective legislative chamber and chaos.

'That's new,' said Marjorie as she admired a small, fluffy object sitting on the brass lamp base.

Gordon paused and picked up his one weakness, a fishing fly. 'Yes, I made it this morning.'

'You really love it, don't you?'

'I'm looking forward to doing more.' Gordon smiled for a moment, twirling the lure in his fingers, studying the orange and green feathers, imagining how a trout might see it, holding it up in the light, his eyes never leaving his creation. 'Could you turn the news on please, Marjorie. I'll listen to the headlines before I go.'

Marjorie moved to the marble coffee table, picked up the remote and flicked on the television. The internal parliamentary telecast from the chamber of the House of Representatives momentarily showed a politician on his feet shouting before she tuned to the local news program. Gordon gently returned his prized possession to the lamp stand and resumed reading a file.

The distinct music of the six o'clock news introduced the headlines, and Gordon listened as he flicked through the final piece of paperwork.

'Prime Minister Gerrard sends a signal to illegal boat people after a meeting with the Indonesian president approving funding for a new immigration detention centre on the Indonesian island of Ambon. Fire disrupts services in the hills, with arson suspected. A teenager struck and killed by a commuter train in Sydney while saving a friend's dog. The Australian cricket team struggles to match England's bowlers in a batting rout in the first test at the Gabba.

'This is National One News, with Sylvia Burns.'

'Good evening. Prime Minister Andrew Gerrard has announced that legislation approving funding for the first offshore detention centre to be built on the Indonesian island of Ambon in the new year will be finalised in the parliament this week. The prime minister made the legislative commitment at a joint press conference after a formal meeting with Indonesian president Doctor Amir Surriento, who is visiting Australia to discuss bilateral foreign policy, intended to reduce the number of illegally smuggled boat people during the summer months. Reporting outside the prime minister's residence is Curtis Jones...'

'You'll miss your old sparring partner, I suspect.'

'I doubt he'll miss me. Turn it down, will you?' Gordon said.

'You really don't like him, do you?'

'If I could leave here and never have to see him again, I would be very grateful. He has upset me so much with his attitude and his changes to standing orders and parliamentary procedure, and the way he mistreats the parliamentary staff is totally unacceptable.' Gordon closed the last file and pushed back from his desk. 'I heard today he's running again at the next election; the man just doesn't know when to give up. You're right, I don't like him.'

'Perhaps you should dismiss him,' Marjorie offered, stifling a laugh.

'If only I could.' Gordon got to his feet. 'Now that I'm going, who will protect the parliament from him?' Just as Marjorie muted the television, the door opened and Paige Alexander, Gordon's diary secretary, entered in a flurry.

'Mr O'Brien, I've just taken a call from the prime minister's office wondering where you are. They're waiting in the speaker's courtyard for you.'

'Yes, okay. I'm coming,' sighed Gordon. Marjorie gathered up the files and papers.

'If I'm not back within forty minutes, please come and get me.'

Gordon collected his jacket, almost identical to the one he'd had on his first day as clerk, and carefully swung it on as he strode from his office.

'Where is the pompous goose?'

'He won't be long, Prime Minister. I just spoke to his office. He's on his way.'

'He's a slimy little bastard. I don't know why I even bothered with this.'

'You bother because you are the prime minister.'

'Get me a drink will you. I'll have a beer. I'm going to have a chat to Zara.' Gerrard smirked and watched his principal private secretary slink off to the drinks table, pushing through the mob of politicians and their staff, more interested in the free hospitality than the honoured guest.

Gerrard scanned the room and saw Speaker Bagshaw in a corner talking to someone he didn't recognise, her elegant black frock complementing her brown skin, her pillar-box red lipstick marking her perfect smile. She was oozing charisma as she listened to the conversation, her thick, curly hair adding to her unique allure. As Gerrard headed for her, she saw him coming and whispered a warning to her colleague.

'You look very attractive this evening, Madam Speaker. I love the way you've done your hair,' Gerrard said, ignoring the other women. He towered over Bagshaw, his stature commanding respect, the greying hair marking his sixty-seven years. His suit looked as if it had come from the finest Italian tailor, the subtle pinstripe of the rich dark blue cloth contrasting with a white shirt and striking orange and grey silk tie.

'Prime Minister? How nice to see you.' Bagshaw straightened her frock, cheeks flushing, as her colleague escaped. 'This was a brilliant idea.'

'Well, the old bastard is finally retiring, so why not?' Gerrard almost spat the words. 'It's the very least I can do for the moron, and thankfully the only celebration I'll need to attend for him. Although there is talk of a parliamentary thing, but I won't be going.'

Bagshaw didn't respond. She didn't share the prime minister's view that the clerk was a handicap to the government. 'It's a nice thought anyway. When would you like to speak?'

'I was just thinking,' Gerrard looked about the room and identified the leader of the opposition examining a food tray offered by a waiter. 'Invite Harper to speak first. Don't let him know, though. Put him on the spot and let's watch him squirm.'

'You're rather devious, aren't you?' smiled Bagshaw.

'You, more than anyone else, should know that my dear Zara.'

Bagshaw stopped and looked at her prime minister, and slowly, suspiciously, said, 'Yes?'

Gerrard played the exotic dance of political banter well, his power absolute; he did whatever he liked, and always got what he wanted. 'How's the new husband?'

'He's good,' replied Bagshaw, looking about the room and nodding to various colleagues. She did not want to encourage Gerrard.

'Giving you what you want?'

'All I need.'

'Surely not everything you need?'

'He makes me happy.'

'Does he? Does he make you truly happy, Zara?' Gerrard mocked.

'He does,' Bagshaw snapped.

'I was just thinking, if you ever want what I know you really need,' Gerrard paused, 'then call me. There is never any harm in someone getting what they really want.'

'It's over, Andrew.' Bagshaw anxiously sipped her wine, scanning to see if anyone was listening.

'Hmm,' Gerrard paused for just a moment. 'Are you planning to retire soon?'

'No.'

'Then perhaps you should reflect upon your career choices.'

'You really are a nasty bastard, aren't you?'

'Not really... I just need what we used to have.'

They looked for any glimmer of understanding in each other's eyes, only to be interrupted by Gerrard's private secretary.

'He's here, Prime Minister.' Miles Fisher passed his boss a glass of beer.

'Why, thank you, young man.' Gerrard took the beer and finalised the conversation. 'We can continue to discuss your career in my suite later, Madam Speaker. Say around nine, after dinner, perhaps?'

'Yes, Prime Minister.' Bagshaw regretted saying it, but the prime minister's authority sent a tingle down her spine.

Gerrard moved away to chat with other colleagues and allow the speaker to host the event, now the guest of honour was present.

The speaker's courtyard, with its beautiful garden, catered for the more than fifty politicians and parliamentary colleagues comfortably. It was a secure, enclosed space outside her office suite with large, open, cantilevered, folding glass doors that allowed the garden and office to merge; a glassed walkway between the foyer of the parliamentary chamber and her office doors had been opened to allow even more room for the guests. Six Australian flags hung limply from a row of masts behind the lectern positioned to one side of the folding doors, as formally dressed waiters delivered drinks and cocktail food on silver trays. The guests chatted and laughed, looking forward to hearing O'Brien speak.

Gordon was warmly welcomed by colleagues from the department as he squeezed through the guests toward his host. Bagshaw was his tenth speaker, and Gordon wanted to get to her quickly so the speeches could start, which would allow him to leave earlier than his forty-minute deadline. He had work to do and legislation to approve for the following day's proceedings in the house. He felt uneasy with the backslapping and overly generous remarks; he was only doing his job, that's all, and saw no reason for a servant of the parliament to be honoured in such a way.

'Gordon, welcome.' Bagshaw extended her hand.

'Madam Speaker.' Gordon took her offered hand and limply acknowledged the welcome.

'Thank you for coming. Everyone has been looking forward to seeing you and wishing you well.'

'Thank you.' Gordon dropped her hand. 'Madam Speaker, I have a number of important tasks I must complete before seven, and I wonder if we could get going.'

'Yes, of course. I'll call everyone together. We have a couple of speeches, and a small gift...'

'Thank you.'

'Will you be able to say a few words? I think your friends would like to hear from you.'

'I haven't prepared anything, but I'm sure I could string a few words together.'

'I'm sure you can, Gordon. Would you like a drink?' The speaker summoned a waiter and Gordon took a glass of white wine from the laden tray.

'Thank you.' Gordon sipped his chardonnay and looked about, ending the conversation.

Speaker Bagshaw moved to the lectern on a small wooden podium, switched on the microphone and called for attention, straightening her notes that had been left there by a dutiful assistant. Her husky tones soon quietened the gathering.

'Good evening, colleagues... good evening. I welcome you all here this evening and thank the prime minister for his generosity in supporting this occasion. As you know, we are all here to recognise and celebrate the career of our long-serving clerk Gordon O'Brien, who is sadly about to retire.

'I was in primary school when Gordon first joined the parliament, almost a lifetime ago. He first started as an administrative assistant to the then clerk Sir Angus Levinstan some forty years ago, and quickly progressed to the ranks of management in various departments. Gordon has served as serjeant-at-arms to the house, deputy clerk and now, of course, he has been clerk for the last seventeen years.

'Gordon has the responsibility for overseeing all departments, from catering – ensuring we are all fed and watered—'

'Hear, hear.' The guests expressed their robust appreciation.

'... to transport, ensuring we all get home to our families safely.

At the same time, he remains responsible for all legislation and the parliamentary process. During his long career, Gordon has served under just two changes of government, and as clerk he has served ten speakers. I am not sure what that means, but I am sure their length of stay in the chair had nothing at all to do with the unequivocal advice provided by Gordon.' Bagshaw waited for the laughter to subside.

'Speaking personally, I admire his respect for the parliament and its rules. He has been vigilant and is respected by all of us, as is his interpretation of standing orders. I have greatly appreciated his advice as I have settled into my role.' Bagshaw smiled at Gordon, who averted his gaze and shifted his weight uncomfortably.

'While we can often disagree on the interpretation of rules and standing orders, only an ignorant or foolish person would ignore his advice. He has assisted many members of the parliament, and his advice on legislative matters has often been sought. His long career has been outstanding, and his service will long be remembered. We are here tonight to assure him we appreciate the professionalism he has brought to his work, and the support he has provided to us all.'

As spontaneous applause erupted, Gordon shook his head slightly as if to challenge the speaker's assertions, before returning his gaze to his feet.

'We have much to say about you this evening, Gordon, so please allow us to show you our respect for the leadership, guidance and support you have provided to us all. Can I first call upon the leader of the opposition, James Harper, to say a few words?'

Gordon registered that Harper had been taken by surprise – he would not have shoved a hot spring roll into his mouth otherwise, just as he was introduced. He struggled to get the food down as he made his way to the podium, took a moment, and breathed deeply.

'I wasn't expecting to speak, and so I'm afraid I'm not prepared.'

Gerrard smiled, and ever so slightly inclined his head toward

Bagshaw, who returned the gesture with a smirk. 'But I do not need a wad of notes to talk about Gordon O'Brien.'

'Hear, hear,' someone yelled, and there was a smattering of applause. Gerrard frowned.

'Gordon is a rock. For over forty years he has been the very foundation stone of our parliament and he deserves the respect we all, as representatives of the wider Australian community, have for him. More importantly, he will be recorded in the annals of parliamentary history as a bulwark who protected the parliament from politicians with too much power, keen to ignore one of the most important institutions of the land.

'We will miss him. I will miss his counsel and the good cheer he provides, despite his rather stern professionalism.' A few chuckles of agreement came from colleagues. 'We all know Gordon has other plans once he leaves this place – he loves the challenge of fishing in the Snowy – but he will always be welcome back here in the corridors of power. We thank him for his distinguished service, his discipline, and his courage to say no. Gordon, I wish you well, and may your days include a memory or two of the folks you leave behind.'

As Harper moved from the podium to shake hands with Gordon, the appreciative applause lasted an embarrassing long time and Gordon was unsure what to do. He nodded his thanks a few times, pulled a disarming face to try to quell the enthusiasm, and looked at his feet yet again. Harper took his hand and shook it with a warmth Gordon respected, and returned to his place, collecting a glass of wine on the way.

'Thank you, James.' Bagshaw resumed her place before the microphone and referred to her notes to check if she was missing anything from her running sheet. 'It is now my pleasure to introduce the prime minister. It is fair to say the prime minister and Gordon have had their differences over the years.' A titter or two sounded among the slight murmur from the guests. 'Please welcome, the prime minister.'

Strong applause greeted Gerrard and he waved away the enthusiasm of his supporters, enjoying the moment.

'Thank you – as the cow said to the farmer one winter morning – for the warm hand.' He had used the joke so many times it was almost a cliché, but his minions laughed obligingly. O'Brien and Harper were not amused.

'Friends, we are here this evening to celebrate a career we all admire. We stand before this gentleman – and Gordon is truly a gentle man; a man to be treasured, a man who is almost an institution.' Heads nodded.

'Gordon was here when most of us – well, at least, some of you – were still at school. He has presided over this great parliament with the zeal of a lion looking after his pride. He has protected the parliament from those who would have torn it down, and from those of us who strive for modernity within the standing orders of the parliament. Not for Gordon a modern Australia. Who could forget his stance during the republican debates?'

Certainly not Gordon: it was one of the highlights of his career, foiling the prime minister's plan to change the entire political system in Australia.

'Australians decided it was not yet time to be a fully independent nation, but no doubt one day we will succeed in convincing our fellow Australians to throw off the shackles of British royalty without worrying about who sits in what chair within the parliament.' Gerrard turned and looked grimly at Gordon.

'Yes, Gordon, you played an important role in the republican debate, but hopefully your sage, if somewhat quaint advice – if I may speak candidly – will not survive long beyond your retirement. I trust that when I raise the issue during my next term in office, the good citizens of Australia will see the choice more clearly and vote accordingly.'

Gordon met Gerrard's gaze, feeling a little irritated by his words. He'd expected as much from one of his fiercest critics.

'It is true, Gordon and I rarely see eye to eye on issues of stuffy parliamentary protocol. He has a reputation for being conventional and conservative and, of course, I am a progressive. Yet ironically, for the last seventeen years, we have managed to work together for the enrichment of our nation and achieve many parliamentary reforms. I point to the recent change to the constitution – parliamentary terms have increased from three years to five – as an example of old structures giving way to new ones. Gordon hated that idea, didn't you, Gordon?' Gerrard turned and casually leaned an elbow on the lectern, triumphantly facing O'Brien as he continued. 'Governments can't govern effectively in only three years; they need five to set out their economic plans and get things done rather than focusing on polls and elections.'

'Hear, hear.' Various government politicians dutifully responded. Gerrard straightened and addressed his audience.

'Gordon also supported the idea of ministers coming to question time each and every day, but I was of the view that it was a waste of time and taxpayers' money. The battles we had over that one, eh Gordon? I could write a book. Indeed, such a book would outdo Prince Machiavelli as a work of political instruction on how to get things done within a parliament.'

Gordon put down his glass and seriously considered walking out on the prime minister, then changed his mind. It would be a serious breach of protocol, but he was sorely tempted.

'We now have progressive and modern standing orders. Prime ministers need only be present for an hour once a week. This is as it should be – there is a government to run, and question time is only ever good for the television news cycle. Let the press gallery go and investigate news I say, rather than report the rather dull questions and unseemly behaviour of the opposition at question time. It was a struggle to get those amendments through, but we did, didn't we, Gordon?'

Gordon endured in silence, letting his anger sweep through him.

'However, Gordon has maintained the balance for all of us. We still have the pomp and pageantry of parliament. As you all know, I am a great supporter of the speaker moving back into the robes and ceremonial wig of times past.' Gerrard acknowledged the murmur of amusement, ignoring the glare from Bagshaw.

'Gordon!' Gerrard paused for a moment to ensure he had everyone's attention. 'You have been a terrific servant to – and for – me. No other has served me as well as you have, and I will miss you and your service.' Gerrard quickly looked about him, searching for something. 'Miles, do you have it?'

Fisher stepped forward with a long, thin colourfully wrapped gift.

'Gordon, on behalf of all those colleagues who work within the parliament and beyond, we wish you well in your retirement. As a measure of our hope you do enjoy your retirement, we would like to present you with this gift.

'The government would like to formally bestow upon you a more significant award in the Great Hall early next year. In the meantime, we think you will get immediate joy from our small gift.'

Gordon stepped forward, ignoring the prime minister's outstretched hand, taking the gift, and ripping at the wrapping paper. It was a Lancaster river rod, the best fly-fishing rod on the market, a valued addition to any serious angler's equipment: two thousand dollars of immediate pleasure, and he stood for a few moments admiring his prized gift before moving to the podium. As he did, he flicked the rod a couple of times and the loud swish satisfied him.

'Madam Speaker, Prime Minister Gerrard, James Harper, colleagues, ladies, and gentlemen. What can I say? I am speechless. This is the most precious gift, and I look forward to standing in the Snowy and casting for a fish or two.' Clapping broke out from a few colleagues, aware of Gordon's passion for fly fishing. 'You have been so kind with your words and your generous applause, and I feel humbled by it all. I am not entitled to feel anything other than humble, because I was only doing my job, my duty. Certainly, I am proud of the work I have done, as any who labours over their work is entitled to feel. Beyond that, I know I am no more special than the next person who works in this fine building.

'We who work here are privileged to serve. We do so because we know that if we did not, anarchy is close at hand. For if the people of Australia do not have authority over their parliament, then what do they have?

'So, we do our job, and we do it to the best of our ability for the people of Australia. We do it not for ego, as perhaps some in this building may believe.' Gordon allowed himself a quick glance at Gerrard. 'We do it because we are patriots to the cause of democracy and its institutions. We do it because we need to do our duty. So, thank you for your warm applause and this generous gift, I truly appreciate them both.'

A text pinged into a smartphone.

> I thank you for the friendships we have developed over the years.

Another ping, and then another.

> I thank you for your respect and support.

Phones were now pinging throughout the gathering. A journalist suddenly appeared at the door to the courtyard.

'And—' Gordon paused, a little distracted by the visitor and the phone tones, clearly something was up. 'I thank you for giving me memories that I will always cherish. I look forward to seeing you all personally before Christmas, as I intend to visit each of you. Thank you, and all the very best.'

Distracted, muted applause broke out, as Fisher whispered into Gerrard's ear the message he'd just received. The prime minister blanched, his mouth dropping open like a fish.

CHAPTER
3

MONDAY 6.45 PM

'A little late this afternoon, Mr Messenger?' The barista at Aussies Cafe tamped the grounds as he prepared another coffee. 'The usual?'

'Thanks, Sam.' Barton Messenger rejected the idea he was a coffee snob; he simply wanted to enjoy his afternoon latte. Melbourne coffee was the world's best in his view, and he never missed an opportunity to remind his parliamentary colleagues. 'Not so hot this time.'

'Busy day?' Sam poured milk into the steel jug and whipped it under the jet of steam.

'Yes, and it doesn't help when the government is yet to set their legislative program. What about you?'

'Ah, you know, always busy, not enough time.'

'You must be a millionaire by now.'

'Ten years I have been working in this place and not one holiday.'

'Didn't you go home to Italy last summer?'

'No holiday for me, family had me working every day.' He slowly poured the heated milk into the glass over a shot of rich espresso coffee, delicately spooning froth to create a rich creme with his signature heart. 'Take me here, Sammy, take me there; no time to put my feet up and enjoy the wine.'

'This is the trouble when you get married, Sam. But, happy wife, happy life.'

'You are so right, Mr Messenger. Enjoy your latte, try, and get a little peace for a few moments.'

'Your coffee is almost as good as I get in Melbourne,' Messenger teased. 'Thank you, Sammy.'

'It's the best, Mr Messenger, you know that.' Sam took the offered coins, tossing them into the cash tray. Messenger smiled, collected his coffee, and walked out into the hall, personal papers under his arm.

Squeezing past the scattered tables, he settled into his favourite chair beside the huge window overlooking the garden courtyard to read a speech he had drafted earlier in the afternoon. Later that evening he was due to speak in the chamber for the opposition in response to the newly introduced Immigration Appropriation Bill. It was no noisier here than sitting in his bustling office.

'Hi Barton, mind if I join you?' Anita Devlin mumbled, pen in mouth, pad under arm, her hands occupied with coffee and a sticky tart. 'I'm doing a story about legislation the government is proposing to bring into the house and I need to talk to you about it.'

Messenger glanced up and smiled at the journalist, turned his papers over quickly and glanced about to see who might be watching.

'Sure, welcome to gossip central.' He quickly leaned forward and moved aside a chair for her to sit on. 'Take a seat, I've been meaning to give you a call.'

'What did you want to talk about?' Anita settled herself. 'Ah, that's better. Do you want some?' She offered the pastry to Messenger.

'No thanks, but I wanted to ask you if you're doing a story on the appointment of the new chairman of the Future Fund.

'Why? It seems uncontroversial to me.' Anita took a bite of her tart. 'Harper has said he'll agree. Don't you agree with your leader?'

'I would've thought the process of appointment could have been better. No-one doubts Lyons is experienced, and possibly the right person, but it is the way this government goes about it. No scrutiny. No checks and balances. Gerrard just does what he wants and to hell with the process.'

'I don't see a problem, it's uncontentious and supported by your lot.'

'You don't think a government should be accountable?' Messenger mocked. 'You lefties are all the same.'

'Of course, I do. I just don't think these minor appointments need reporting though. It's a simple decision, why complicate it?'

'Once we stop scrutiny of government decisions, we relinquish power and the unscrupulous take over. Remember the WA Inc. scandals?'

'That was decades ago, things have changed since then.' Anita broke off a small piece of tart and put it into her mouth. 'And FYI, I'm no lefty.'

'Gerrard just does what he wants, so how do you know he isn't doing something shonky?'

Anita shrugged. 'That's why we have you and your conservative mates, Bart. You have a history of seeking out any misappropriation of funds.'

'You truly are a cynic, aren't you?'

'I have much to be cynical about. You lot just keep giving me the self-interest stories. What about that flake from the senate who got caught taking his girlfriend to Broome for a few nights?'

Messenger smiled, looked at Anita and took a small sip of his coffee, washing it back over his tongue. 'When are we catching up for a dinner?'

Anita paused and delicately put another small piece of tart into her mouth as she watched a woman in stilettos march past, heels clacking on the wooden floor. 'I can never understand why my sisters see the need to wear those hideous things.'

'You are tormenting me.' Messenger smiled.

'You know how I feel about all that, Bart. I think we should cool our jets a little.' Anita waited until the woman had passed. 'Christ, I hate those things, such a ridiculous fashion item.'

Messenger was not distracted by Anita's fashion comment. 'You're being rather mean to me.'

'Not really. You're a big boy. You can get over things. It was a mistake, I told you that. Let's just maintain a professional relationship.'

'Ouch.'

'What did you say once? Something about having a hide as thick as a rhino?'

'Yes, but I meant in politics, you need it. I think you should reconsider.'

Anita sipped her coffee. 'Why aren't you at Gordon O'Brien's party?'

'I don't like him. I'm glad to see the back of him.'

'Why? Is it because he gives you a hard time?'

'He gives Gerrard too much latitude, and he doesn't like me,' Messenger said, sipping his coffee. 'It was his fault we have five-year terms.'

'That's harsh; he tried to stop Gerrard.'

'He didn't try hard enough as far as I'm concerned. The prime minister bullied him, and he weakened.'

'You're not saying this because you were tossed out of question time today, are you?' Anita scoffed. 'I reckon his note to the speaker may have had you ejected.'

'Not really,' replied Messenger, reluctantly. 'I had work to do anyway.'

'I would have thought the manager of opposition business would have been a little sharper on the rules.'

'He doesn't like me. I cause the speaker too much trouble.' Messenger shifted in his seat and took another small sip.

'What do you know about the funding for the immigration detention centres the government is proposing in Indonesia?' Anita took a careful mouthful of tart, to avoid icing sugar falling on her clothes. She worked hard to look professional, but she was always anxious about her choices. It was even harder when black was the only colour she liked.

'We support it.'

'I hear they may be doing something tricky with the funding, bringing a first payment forward to early next year.'

'They tell us nothing.'

'I was told by one of your colleagues you actually do know what's going on.'

Messenger did his look, sip, and smile routine. 'I may have some information.'

'So?'

'Well, it's yet to be confirmed, but I've been advised they will bring it forward this evening for a vote tomorrow morning. They're planning to release funds in four stages with the initial funds as a form of deposit in this first bill. The plan is for the first centre to begin construction in the new year.' Messenger smiled. 'I could disclose more over food. My tongue loosens when food bounces off it. What are you doing for dinner?'

Anita sighed. 'You never give up, do you.'

'No.'

'The government aren't likely to bring it on tonight, given the tragedy.' Anita switched the subject.

'A plane crash is surely not tragic enough to close the parliament. It may be a disaster, but surely not a tragedy. I would have thought a respected journalist and wordsmith like you would know the difference.'

'Christ, you obviously don't know.'

'What?'

'Eight MPs were on the plane.'

'We'll need to make a statement.' Miles Fisher, standing before Gerrard's desk, was working through crisis media management protocol. 'Perhaps we can get a live cross on ABC News. No doubt you can appear on A Current Affair, and the Late News.'

Gerrard didn't respond. He drew long and hard on his cigar, wreathing his face in smoke and sucking it deep into his lungs.

'Boss, we'll need to act soon.' Fisher was more than a little anxious about his lack of direction. 'The nation needs to hear from you.'

'Fuck it.'

'It's a sad day. We've already spoken to the families and arranged for you to speak to them later. Some are in Canberra. I suppose we'll need to have a national day of mourning...'

'Fuck it.'

'We've had calls from the usual suspects, including the president.'

'I lost a great friend today, Miles.'

'We all did, Prime Minister.'

'Fuck it.'

Fisher stood quietly looking down at his boss, waiting for instruction, keen to get moving.

'You know we're stuffed now, don't you?' Gerrard finally said from behind a huge cloud of smoke.

'No. I think this will go well for you in the polls. It's our chance to show leadership.'

'You don't get it, do you?'

'Get what?' Fisher checked his list and flicked a page. 'I think I've covered everything.'

'The numbers change. We lose six votes in the house. That means they now have a majority of two.'

'What do you mean?'

'We can lose government over this – tonight, tomorrow, or whenever the parliament sits again.'

'Oh, shit.'

'Yeah, now you get it, boofhead.'

O'Brien was already back in his office calling department heads – grief could wait. He might only have a few days left to serve, but he was needed more now than at any other time in his career. Extremely tragic for the families and those colleagues directly involved, the accident would mean significant operational demands upon the parliament and the electoral system in the immediate future. Work needed to be done despite the dark cloud descending upon most of the parliament.

'Three days I think would be appropriate.' O'Brien was on the phone to the speaker's office. 'Which means suspension of the parliament for the remainder of the week, then back to work next Monday. A parliamentary memorial service can be arranged for this Friday and perhaps formal state memorials in a few weeks, but this will be up to the prime minister and his department and the leader of the opposition.' O'Brien listened to the response, flicking lint from his trousers.

Marjorie Earle and Paige Alexander, along with Richard Barker the deputy clerk, sat opposite awaiting instructions. 'No, I am yet to speak to either of them.' O'Brien swivelled in his chair and sat upright at his desk, rubbing his temple.

'We should be able to issue writs for the by-elections next week. So that means we can either have the elections next month, if we have time before Christmas, or we wait until February, which is my recommendation. They'll then be sworn in at the first sitting week in March.' He picked up a pen and waited to write something, but nothing came. 'Only if they both agree not to take any votes. If they don't agree, then we could be faced with having a vote of no confidence from the opposition. If the government does not win a no-confidence vote, we can either change government on the floor of the house or be forced immediately into a general election.'

O'Brien listened intently.

'I repeat, only if both the PM and Harper agree not to take any votes. It is only for one more week before the summer recess, so I see no reason why they wouldn't agree. We can assume the numbers will favour the government in the house after the by-elections in March, so it would be a waste of time for the opposition to challenge the current status of the parliament. If we assume the government wins the by-elections, then it would be foolish to change government just for a few weeks.'

O'Brien nodded.

'Okay Madam Speaker, I'll call you back when I have spoken to the leaders and organised events.' He replaced the receiver carefully and sat stroking his chin. 'Paige, the government wants a parliamentary memorial service this Friday in the Great Hall, which will no doubt attract a significant overseas contingent. Gerrard's office has also floated the idea of a religious event in Sydney. I need you to organise the archbishop to make available the cathedral for Friday in, say, four weeks' time.'

'I'll liaise with the government protocol office and ensure we accommodate those dignitaries who want to come to both. What about the funerals?' Paige scribbled into her pad.

'Let's get someone from the PM's office to organise those.' O'Brien suddenly stopped talking. 'God it's terrible, isn't it?'

'The worst, and at the worst time,' said Marjorie, dabbing her eyes with a wad of tissue. 'What do you want me to do about the media? I have already taken a few calls asking about parliamentary procedure.'

'I'll make a statement once I've spoken to the PM and Harper. Are you okay?' O'Brien asked quietly. Marjorie nodded and tears welled again, which she quickly wiped away. 'I see no reason why there should be a parliamentary crisis. The solemnness of it all will ensure politics stays out of it.'

'Well, if there was ever a time for Harper, now he has his opportunity,' said Barker.

'He won't do it,' O'Brien said firmly. 'He knows what he must do.'

'Did you want me to get you something to eat?' Paige asked. 'It's getting late and I want to make sure you're not neglecting yourself.'

'No, I couldn't, thanks. I'm too stressed to eat anything right now. Now, please leave me to do my job.' O'Brien picked up the phone to call the leader of the opposition before being connected to the prime minister.

After completing his call to James Harper, Marjorie's voice came through the handset on his desk: 'The prime minister, Gordon, line six.'

'Good evening, Prime Minister,' Gordon said as he stabbed a button on the phone to put the prime minister on speaker, allowing Richard Barker to quietly listen in.

'Gordon, how are you holding up?' Gerrard said. 'Such a tragedy.'

'Prime Minister, I've just spoken to Mr Harper and explained the possible legislative scenarios for him to consider. I put before him a recommendation.'

'And that is?' Gerrard was curious.

'There are two clear scenarios. We can either issue writs for by-elections next week and the status quo remains until the end of parliamentary sittings next week, or the opposition can force the government to a vote of no confidence. If we do that, we are likely to have a change of government.'

'What did he say?'

'I explained it would be likely the parliamentary numbers would revert to the status quo in March after the by-elections. Therefore, I told him there was little point in achieving a political advantage for so little return by forcing a no-confidence motion in the parliament.'

'And what was your recommendation?'

'I recommended to him to retain the status quo.'

'Good man, Gordon. I knew I could depend on you to do the right thing.'

'Yes, Prime Minister.'

'Is everything else in order?'

'As far as the funerals and memorial services go?'

'No. That's not my priority at the moment. Are we sitting next week? I want to be sure we do.'

'Why is this so important to you, Prime Minister?' Gordon was a little surprised by the request.

'I have government business to complete, and the Immigration Appropriation Bill needs to move through the parliament before the recess. We were going to bring it into the house tonight for a vote tomorrow.'

'This surely can wait until next year, Prime Minister. The money is not due until March, so there is plenty of time.'

'Listen here, Gordon, my government has made promises to the Indonesians, and we need to release funds this year,' Gerrard's voice was louder. 'Do not stop this bill from being passed next week, do you understand?'

'Yes, Prime Minister.'

'Good work. Goodbye Gordon.'

On the second floor of the senate wing, in the Hancock Media offices within the parliamentary press gallery, Anita Devlin worked at her desk, tapping at her computer surrounded by notes and papers. Her filing system was uniquely hers, and she abused anyone who touched anything or disturbed its order. She had her most controversial stories clipped and pinned to the walls like trophy wallpaper. Various coloured sticky notes were stuck to the sides of her computer screen with phone numbers and information that could not be filed.

'Hi,' Messenger stood at her cubicle waggling two wine glasses, tapping an opened bottle on the frame.

'What can I do for you, Barton? I'm just a little busy at the moment.' Anita didn't spend long looking at him and turned back to her computer keyboard. 'Who let you in?'

'I wanted to apologise for storming off, and I thought you might like to share a drink with me.'

'I've got to finish this last piece, I'm on a deadline.'

'I can wait.' He assumed he was welcome and took a chair beside her desk. 'What is it?'

'I've had to do four obituaries.'

'Bummer.' There was no room for glasses and bottle on her desk, so he put them carefully on the floor.

'It's been a little distressing. What do you think will happen?'

'Well, there is a cornucopia of opportunities.'

Anita stopped typing and looked at Messenger with a wry smile. 'Cornucopia? Not just opportunities, but a cornucopia of opportunities?'

'Yes. Do you forgive me?'

'I need to talk to you anyway. Pour me a drink and I'll send this off.'

'Yes ma'am.'

A flick of a few keys and she was done. 'So, what do you think will happen?'

Messenger poured as he spoke. 'Well, I actually know what will happen. I've already spoken with the leader. Basically, nothing. We have by-elections proposed for next February and we will continue as normal next week. We have the rest of this week off, a memorial service on Friday, and come back for legislation next week.'

'You couldn't expect him to do anything else. I've read the PM's release, and it seems the most appropriate course of action.'

'Cheers.' They both said together as they clinked glasses.

'My only problem with all that is that we have the numbers now, so why not use them?' Messenger took a generous mouthful.

'The government will get them back in March after the by-elections, surely.'

'Not if we prorogue the parliament and call a general election.'

'That's an interesting suggestion, an early election...' Anita sipped and studied the politician at her desk. 'Surely Harper would not allow that. He has already agreed not to take any action that will disturb the current parliament.'

They sat quietly for a moment. Messenger swigged his wine, wrestling with something he wanted to say. 'If we change the leader, then it could be game on.'

'Can I quote you?' Anita picked up her pen and flicked to a new page of her notebook.

'Ease up, Anita, I'm only joking,' Messenger said. 'Not everything I say should be taken literally, politically speaking of course.'

'Of course. You are a politician, after all.'

CHAPTER
4

MONDAY 10.55 PM

The prime minister's car rolled into Yarralumla, his official Canberra residence, gravel crunching as it moved slowly to the portico. Gerrard smiled, pleased with what he saw; there had been an extremely negative public reaction to his decision to upgrade the governor-general's residence and move in himself. He used the need to host international dignitaries as the reason for the redevelopment, but many insiders reported it was the loss of the republican vote at the referendum that motivated a vengeful prime minister.

'The president has the White House. The British prime minister has Chequers,' Gerrard explained during an interview. 'We need a similar stately building for our nation's leader, not a rundown shoebox like the Lodge.'

Gerrard wanted the Australian people to know exactly who was running the country, even though they had voted for the retention of the antiquated constitutional monarchy. 'If the governor-general

RICHARD EVANS

wanted improved living quarters, let the King pay for renovations. She is, after all, his representative.'

The prime minister directed the governor-general to vacate the heritage-listed house and heavily renovated the property, ignoring the public and political outcry. He wanted a grander residence, so he moved the governor to a much smaller residence in an obscure Canberra suburb.

A small administration wing was added to house the estate's management, providing accommodation for the prime minister's staff. He also insisted his wife Margaret had her own staffed office within the wing. Essential house staff lived in separate quarters over the expansive garage. One or two staff had children who were some-times seen, but never heard, within the main compound.

It was a chilly night. Spring in Canberra was colourful and attracted many thousands of tourists to the renowned Floriade. The weather was normally pleasant at this time of year, but this October day had been unusually chilly, and Gerrard shivered as he left the car. His butler had anticipated his arrival, having received advice from the security gatehouse as the prime minister's car swung into the residence. He opened the large, heavy white door and took the prime minister's briefcase as he entered.

'Thanks, Edmond. Is Mrs Gerrard still up?'

'No sir, she retired around thirty minutes ago. Would you like anything?'

'I'll have a shower and take some brandy to bed. Pour two. I'm sure madam would like one.'

Gerrard walked through the darkened marble hall to the stairs and padded up the thick woollen carpet to his suite. He had insisted on a separate retreat with a private dressing room and bathroom, so as not to disturb his wife. It was a secure private retreat with a comfortable lounge fitted with all modern communication devices and cable television and served as a soundproof anteroom to the bedroom. This was the area of the house in which he felt most secure. No-one but Edmond ever entered, not even Margaret, his wife.

Gerrard entered the dressing room and kicked off his shoes. He hung up his Zegna jacket and draped his trousers carefully over a chair, tossed his shirt and socks into a cane basket and entered his bathroom, turning on the shower with the pre-set temperature. He walked into the vast marble cubical and stood under the broad stream of water. He insisted on a waterfall stream shower as opposed to the little shower heads so common in hotels; small units were good for small people, but not for him. As he soaked under the warm stream he removed his underpants, soaped them with his imported French body wash, and washed away any evidence – he had learned over the years to be careful.

Ninety minutes earlier, Speaker Bagshaw had not arrived at his office at the agreed time and Gerrard phoned her office insisting she attend an immediate meeting to discuss the tragedy. Bagshaw obeyed and arrived at nine forty-five with Gerrard already two glasses into a bottle of French champagne.

'You can't be serious, Andrew,' Zara said, as he passed her a sparkling flute and resumed his seat with Bagshaw sitting on the other side of the desk. 'This is not a time to celebrate.'

'It has been a trying time for all of us over the last few hours, especially for you and me. I thought we should talk about what to do next, and at the same time have a relaxing drink.' Gerrard raised his glass. 'Cheers, in memory of our sadly departed comrades.'

'Cheers.' Bagshaw took a mouthful. 'I have decided not to reopen parliament until next Monday. We should then have a few days of condolences.'

'Bullshit, we will,' Gerrard almost spat the words as he sat up, slapping the desk with his open hand. 'We open for business as soon as we can. I want a few things through before Christmas, and we only have a week to do them.'

'I can't promise we will not have demands for marks of respect and a need to express that in the parliament.'

'Let them do that crap in the Federation Chamber for the entire week for all I care. We will have the Reps open again on Monday.'

'O'Brien is keen for protocols to be followed. It's his last week, and he wants to ensure the parliament does not carry-on business while the voting numbers are skewed against you.'

'He can get stuffed. We work through. Harper has already agreed not to bring on a division.'

'Prime Minister, are you really sure? This could cause some major challenges for us. Nothing could be that important.' Bagshaw drained her glass. 'The opposition has the numbers so you can't afford any divisions – there is no guarantee the opposition would support us. If they don't support us, they can call a no-confidence motion and we are gone.'

'We must push the Immigration Appropriation Bill through next week. My meeting with Surriento this morning confirmed the government would release the first tranche of funds to Indonesia this year, which would allow work to begin on building the first detention centre. I promised him we would vote on it tomorrow and money would follow immediately after; they are expecting it. Now we have closed the place for a few days, it is absolutely vital that it goes through the parliament next week. We don't need any crap from O'Brien, or Harper for that matter, and we need to sit next week.'

'Why do you need this to go through? Surely it can wait.'

'Never you mind why, just ensure we get it through without any controversy. I certainly don't want any votes taken to a division when we don't have the numbers.'

'What we need is a formal agreement from him not to take a division to count votes.'

'Harper wouldn't do it, he would be stupid to sign a formal agreement, no-one would.' Gerrard retained little respect for the opposition. 'Just make sure we maintain control of the chamber when we are back next week. If there are any problems from Harper, just squash him with parliamentary procedure.' Gerrard drained his glass. 'I am relying on you, Zara. This is an opportunity for you to shine and make sure the government gets its first Indonesian detention centre.'

'I'll do my best.' Bagshaw waggled her empty glass at Gerrard, encouraging a refill. 'I always do.'

'I remember,' smiled Gerrard, as he got up from his desk and walked to the expansive leather lounge, beckoning Bagshaw to follow. She refilled her glass from the bottle in the ice bucket and sank into the soft leather lounge close enough to Gerrard to give him permission.

An hour later, Gerrard was examining his neck and chest for any signs of passion. Satisfied there was no evidence, and smiling at the memory, his long gaze took in his ageing body. He was happy he was still in shape, although when he stood sideways, he slapped his protruding stomach, acknowledging he was getting an oldies' belly. Thin legs, zero arse and a burgeoning belly was the image he'd been fighting against since his days as a talented basketball player. Still, he was pleased with his tanned body – and pleased he was still capable of romancing a woman as he had in his youth.

He wrapped his underpants in a towel and tossed them in the basket, slipped on an overly large silk robe and walked into his suite. As he did, a gentle tap on the door signalled the arrival of his brandy.

Edmond's timing was impeccable, as always. He took the tray and moved to the bedroom.

Margaret was propped up among a galaxy of different-shaped pillows, grey hair pinned back off her face and reading glasses positioned on the end of her nose. Age had brought her a mature beauty, and she dressed in a sophisticated style, even to bed. Her long, green satin slip hugged her trim form, the result of constant exercise and care.

She looked up from her book, pleased to see her husband. 'Everything under control, darling?'

'Yes, my sweet. I have a brandy for you. I'm glad you're awake; I need to talk to you.' Gerrard respected his wife's opinion and sought it whenever he had unresolved issues that worried him.

He had been seduced by her when he first heard her laugh and promised he would always keep her happy and laughing. When they first met, he kept her out into the early morning talking about the future and his strategy for the country. She was smitten by his plans and his larger-than-life charismatic nature and knew before she invited him home for dinner with her parents that she would marry him. Three months later he proposed, and they married twelve months after their first meeting. They had been a formidable political team for the forty-five years since.

'How are you feeling?'

'A little upset actually, I insisted Freddy come back to Canberra tonight. I spoke to him when he was in the plane on the tarmac just prior to take-off. I feel responsible ... he was a great mate.'

'Do you want to talk about it?' Margaret took her drink as Andrew sat at her feet.

'I needed them for a vote tomorrow, and now we've lost them, and the vote.'

'I only spoke to Sonja this morning about his retirement at the next election. She was saying they were pleased to be getting out and encouraged us to think about it.'

'It all has to end sometime, I suppose.' Gerrard didn't want to think about his trusted friend and adviser who had entered parliament at the same election he had. 'He only had eighteen months to go.' He took a gulp of brandy to collect himself.

'It got me thinking though, darling. Why don't we take this opportunity to get out now? To step aside so we can go to Paris.' Margaret had been suggesting for many months that it was time to think about retiring. 'This is a great opportunity to do it, you have nothing more left to do and your announcement before Christmas would mean a by-election at the same time as the others.'

'Go easy on the brandy, darling. We'll win the by-elections and then the general election.' Gerrard stretched and dragged a large pillow to prop his head as he lay back across the bed. 'My plan is to do one more term.'

'No, Drew, listen, please darling. If we make a move now, we don't have to face another two years of speculation. What happens if Harper tries to take over? He has the numbers now.'

'He won't do it, the weak bastard. He's already committed to not moving against the government.'

'And you believe him?'

'Harper is a weak prick. He'll do what he's told. He won't want the aggravation.'

'I'm just saying, this is the perfect opportunity. We leave on top and with honour.'

'And go to Paris?' Gerrard mocked.

'You know we've been planning it.'

'You've been planning it, darling. We don't have the money to live in Paris. We live the high life here, but Paris would be very different.'

'I've been thinking about that.'

'And?'

'That could have been you today, darling. You have done enough. You have rewarded your friends and they have a comfortable life. It's now time for us.'

'What are you suggesting?'

'Increase the commission from the Indonesians.'

'You must be kidding.' Gerrard sat up and drained his glass. 'I'm already very nervous about the deal I've done with Amir. This first one was to be a trial.'

'Surriento suggested the deal, so why not ask for more?'

Gerrard didn't speak as he considered the proposition. Surriento was a friend and had counselled him many times on how to personally benefit from the transfer of international funds between governments. Gerrard had not been tempted previously – until this one time over a few too many whiskeys. Still, the secret commission wasn't enough to fund a retirement in Paris.

Finally, Gerrard smiled. 'You have been busy, haven't you?' He loved her assertive nature; she always got what she wanted, or rather she got it most of the time, depending on how he felt. He also knew she was a realist. She understood his flaws and knew of his weaknesses and temptations. He smoked too much, he drank too much, and he shared himself with others too much. But he would always come home to her, and that was why she loved him – and why he loved her.

'I'm just saying, he opened the door for you. Why not take full advantage and ask for more? Everyone else does, so why not us?'

'You could be right. Let me sleep on it.' Gerrard stood and walked to his side of the bed, slipping off his robe and dropping it to the floor.

'What do you think you're going to do with that?' Margaret purred, tossed her glasses to the side table, and opened her arms as he slipped into bed beside her.

Early morning in Canberra is nearly always cold, but Yarralumla's kitchen was warm from the ovens preparing various treats to be consumed throughout the day, including the usual cooked breakfast for the prime minister. Gerrard sat at the stone kitchen bench; his breakfast always formally presented on a stiff cotton napkin with highly polished silver. A three-egg omelette, Earl Grey tea and a small bowl of fruit, cut to spoon-sized pieces. Toast, with a curled tab of butter in a ceramic dish, and a separate one of jam; different every day. Today was his favourite: apricot.

Gerrard was dressed for early media interviews in a blue Italian suit, navy blue silk tie and crisply ironed white shirt. He scanned the Financial Review, flicking past the editorials and obituaries; looking for any political leaks that should worry him. He zeroed in on an article about his meeting with the Indonesian president, then a smiling Margaret joined him, slinging an arm over his shoulder, and kissing his cheek.

'Hello, handsome.'

'Sleep well, gorgeous?'

'Eventually.' She picked at his fruit and smiled.

'I've been thinking about your idea, and I reckon I've worked out a plan.'

'Go on.' Margaret, in her nightgown and silk robe, straddled a stool and joined her husband as Janette, Yarralumla's chef, poured her tea into her favourite over large, colourful china cup.

'Freddy's death has hit me a little bit and maybe you're right, it could be time for me to let go.' Gerrard sipped his tea. 'I was planning to hang around until I hit seventy, and then we could get a job overseas and live comfortably forever.'

'How nice.'

'But now I'm not so sure.'

'I keep asking you to retire, Drew, and this thing with Sonja has sent a shiver through me. I don't know how I feel, but suddenly all of this doesn't seem as important to me anymore.'

'I tend to agree, so I have a plan.'

'Can you tell me, or will it be a secret like some of the other things you do?'

'Well, historically, after significant tragic national events, there is usually a period of community mourning. Don't ask me why, but consumers leave the market for a significant period, leading to an economic downturn. This could be bad news for the retailers during the Christmas trading season. We can't afford to have a consumer-led downturn right now. This could affect the by-elections and the vote could move against us. It may even mean we lose government.'

'Like I said, darling, it might be time to go.'

'You could be right, so I have an idea.'

Margaret turned to the chef. 'Janette, would you mind giving us a few moments.'

The chef wiped her hands and left the kitchen.

'Thank you.'

Gerrard paused for maximum impact. 'We release a Christmas bonus to the punters.'

'How much?'

'I'm thinking six to seven billion.'

'How does that help us?'

'Well, we put an urgent Appropriation Bill into the house. We tie this legislation to the deal with the Indonesians. Not just the first tranche we were planning to vote on today, but the whole lot.'

'Can you do that? How much would it be?'

'The total appropriation would be around ten billion. The media would normally have gone ape-shit over a four-billion-dollar deal with the Indonesians; they've already given me a tough time with the millions in this first lot.'

'Four billion is a lot of money, how can you get it through?'

'Well, if cabinet agree, we tie it to the stimulus package and hopefully it will be lost in the excitement of the announcement. I mean, you would have to be dumb not to see the change, but the politics is so beautiful. Get the punters onside and the Indonesian money will be lost in all the excitement.

'You hope.'

'It will be if it goes through next week.'

'So what?'

'It means paper trails offshore would be harder to follow if we get it done before Christmas. And, anyway, the money would have already gone to Indonesia – too late to get it back.'

'How much more will you add for us?' Margaret took her own selection of fruit from a dish.

'I'll need to talk to Amir.'

'Will he be okay with the changes?'

'I don't know,' Gerrard picked out a piece of rockmelon and slipped it into his mouth, wiping his fingers on his serviette. 'He is such a wheeler and dealer on anything that has a sniff of opportunity for him, but with this idea, I'm not so sure.'

'He wants the money by March, right?'

'It would be difficult to hide, but yes, it would be possible to get the money to him within days of the legislation passing the parliament.'

'What are you really saying?'

'We potentially expose ourselves. I'm concerned about how it will look.'

'It'll be okay, it always is.' Margaret leaned forward and reassuringly stroked her despondent husband's shoulder then eventually said, 'So, if we give him the entire amount, why wouldn't he reward us?'

'I trust him, and it was his idea in the first place, so I'm confident he will agree to increasing our payout.' Gerrard perked up and scooped omelette into his mouth. 'We send the funds to Amir, hopefully, late next week. He then starts developing the first centre on Ambon but skims off a commission to a bank in Switzerland via his normal laundering channels as previously agreed. By my reckoning, if we take one per cent, that should set us up with forty million.'

'Are you serious?'

'No-one will miss one per cent if we do it right.'

'Do you really trust him?'

Gerrard smiled. 'As much as I trust you, gorgeous. So, you'll have to set up the bank account a little earlier than we expected.'

'How much earlier?'

'This week if you can.'

'Will you get it up?' Margaret was staring at her smirking husband. 'The bill, I mean.'

'I'll tell the department to begin work on the roll-out of Christmas stimulus funds today. I'll put it on the agenda for cabinet this morning, and hopefully announce the handout to the punters on Thursday. If Amir comes to the memorial on Friday, I'll confirm the deal. We then put it into the house on Monday and get it into the senate and back to the house by Thursday for final approval. We recess for Christmas Thursday evening, and I could announce my resignation and immediate retirement then in the House, or on Friday.'

'Will you get the numbers to pass it?'

'Harper will be okay. It's O'Brien I'm worried about. I don't need any delays from him, and we can't afford any extra scrutiny by the parliament, so Zara needs to step up and keep him under control.'

'Zara will do what she's advised by O'Brien, surely?' Margaret knew the clerk supervised the legislative program and would determine what was added to the parliamentary notice paper.

'I have her under control, and she will ignore O'Brien. Her parliamentary career relies on her doing what I need her to do next week.' Gerrard took a gulp of tea. Margaret did not miss the momentary hesitation. 'I have lost too many speakers because of O'Brien. She'll be okay, and she'll do what I tell her.'

'O'Brien won't cause much grief. He's out of the parliament in a week,' Margaret said, as she finished picking at the fruit bowl. 'Zara knows what she wants, but just be careful, darling. She may cut you loose if it gets too hot for her.'

Gerrard began quickly tucking into the remains of the omelette; he needed to get moving. He was scheduled to appear on early-morning television.

'I'll keep you advised as I get through it all. Worst-case scenario is we only get the original four million next February, and I don't retire,' Gerrard said before rinsing his mouth with tea. 'Can you begin some research for a bank? Remember, we don't want to leave a paper trail.'

'Leave it to me. I know exactly who I'll talk to.'

'Who?'

'No trails, darling. This is good news, the punters get a Christmas bonus, Immigration gets their offshore detention centres, Indonesia creates jobs for their people, and we retire. It's time. I've just about had enough. I may have been a socialist most of my life, but I can't ignore my own needs.' Margaret rubbed herself against her husband as they stood and kissed him so he would remember. 'I'm so proud of you.'

'Saucy minx. See you tonight. Talk soon.'

Gerrard headed for the waiting car.

A message from Richard

BUILDING A RELATIONSHIP WITH MY READERS IS THE VERY BEST THING ABOUT WRITING.

Join my Advanced Readers team for information on new books and news from my journal about Plots Publishing Politics and Personal news; plus a **FREE** eBook copy of Deceit now available from the following link:

richardevans-author.com

ABOUT THE AUTHOR

As a political insider, Richard Evans served as a federal member of parliament for Cowan in Western Australia during the turbulent 1990s. He now specializes in writing crime thrillers, writing about the exotic characters in the mysterious world of the Australian Parliament. He lives in the coastal village of Airlie Beach, the gateway to the Whitsunday islands, with a view from his writing desk overlooking the Coral Sea.

For more information about his other books, or to contact Richard visit:

richardevans-author.com

Visit Instagram for updates on
Plots, Publishing, Politics and Personal news.

instagram.com/richardevans_author

EPISODE 1 DEMOCRACY TRILOGY

The last thing Gordon needs this week is an abuse of political power.

A plane crash begins a sequence of events which leads corrupt Prime Minister Andrew Gerrard, after a long political career, to rush through legislation designed to secure his ill-gotten gains for his retirement. Stalwart – and soon retired – Clerk of the Parliament, Gordon O'Brien, sets out to foil the Prime Minister's plan with the help of investigative journalist, Anita Devlin.

O'Brien, a stickler for correct parliamentary process is concerned by the rush to legislate and becomes aware of various incidents, which by themselves would mean little but collectively shape a conspiracy to defraud the government.

The Clerk anticipates there is a potential fraud upon the government being enacted, he has run out of time and now must act. He forces the Speaker to resign, and O'Brien takes her place, causing the parliament to prorogue, imposing a general election, preventing the fraud.

A **FREE COPY** of Deceit and to join the advanced readers team is now available from the following link:

www.richardevans-author.com

For more information and purchasing options visit

852 Press.com.au

EPISODE 2 DEMOCRACY TRILOGY

Anita uncovers political corruption; will she survive to tell the story?

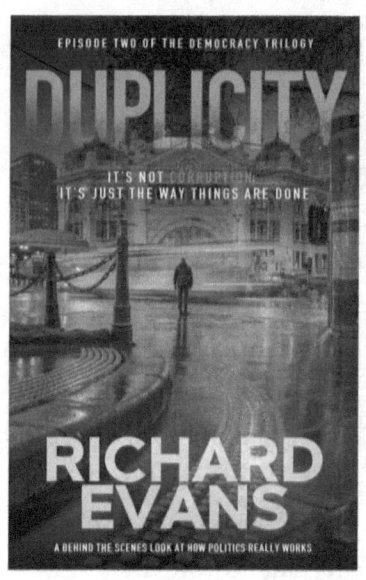

The Mercantiles, a long-established, clandestine group of high-taxpaying business owners have grown frustrated by Prime Minister Andrew Gerrard's failure to meet promises, and decide the nation needs a change of government at the upcoming election. They call upon experienced and ruthless political operative Jonathan Wolff to organise their election campaign and defeat the prime minister.

Realising he cannot win the election his way, Wolff initiates an explosive campaign designed to remove the prime minister by defeating him in his own electorate using an independent candidate.

Investigative journalist Anita Devlin is appointed by her editor to promote the Stanley campaign as the publishing owner, unknown to her, is a member of the Mercantiles. She discovers the nefarious Wolff strategically working the campaign, and endeavours to expose his influence and manipulation.

For more information and purchasing options visit

852 Press.com.au

EPISODE 3 DEMOCRACY TRILOGY

She will do whatever it takes; her ambition will be deadly.

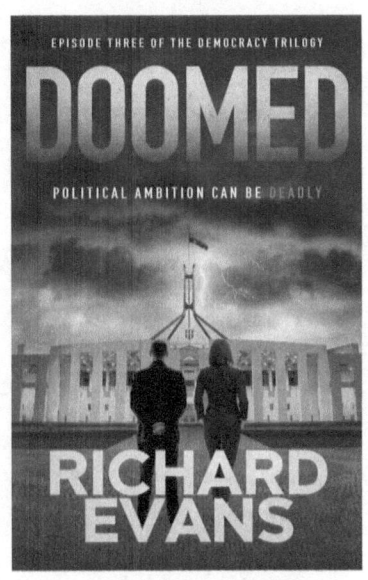

Three years after a change of government, the nation is facing huge social, policy, and environmental-related disasters yet the Australian government seems paralyzed on how to proceed. Two senior ministers resolve that a change of prime minister is essential for Australia's future and begin to lay the foundations for his dismissal.

Meanwhile, the parliament is held in a balance of power by the independent, Jaya Rukhmani, who can decide at any time if government legislation will be approved. Upon hearing the news that former prime minister Andrew Gerrard wishes to re-enter parliament, Jaya turns to Barton Messenger as an ally.

Doomed takes us behind the scenes of a parliament unaware of how ambition and political manipulation affect the everyday Australian. When the environment and economy are brought into the mix, which will be the one to flourish, and which one is doomed?

For more information and purchasing options visit

852 Press.com.au

FIRST NATIONS HAVE NEVER CEDED SOVEREIGNTY.

She wants her culture and country back. Independence was never ceded, and she will do whatever it takes to get it back, including the ultimate sacrifice. When government peace talks stop, revolution begins.

Revolutionary leader, Nellie Millergoorra, campaigns for an aboriginal homeland to preserve indigenous culture by advocating the prohibition of mining in Arnhem Land using a United Nations declaration to convince a disrespectful government to sign a treaty. Nellie will do whatever it takes to finally gain independence and end government regulation over her people.

When there is no agreement, she recruits mercenary special forces to inflame community chaos establishing an explosive aboriginal revolutionary movement.

In a surprising confrontation with a reluctant prime minister, who is threatened with an ultimatum he can't ignore, Millergoorra negotiates a treaty whilst facing her own battle for survival.

Forgotten People is gripping political thriller featuring surprising plot twists, compelling characters, and a kick-arse female heroine.

**For more information and purchasing options visit
852Press.com.au**

EUTHANASIA, A BLACK POPE, AND AUSTRALIAN POLITICS COLLIDE IN THIS INTENSE THRILLER.

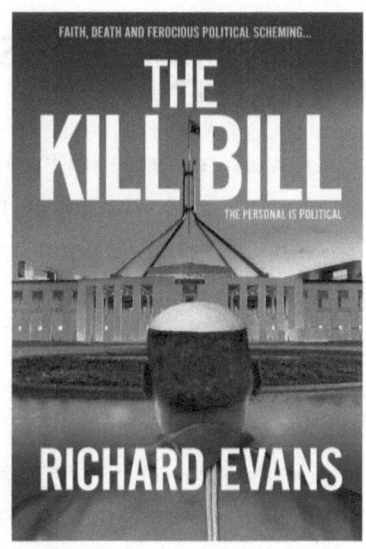

He's the nation's chief law maker. His daughter is fighting for her life in intensive care, a victim of a terrible crime. Will he ignore the prime minister's demands and his own laws to save her? Or will politics and the Catholic Church prevent him from doing his job?

Treasurer, Parker Osborne, initiates a covert plan, in partnership with Vatican emissary, Cardinal Rosseau, to guarantee proposed euthanasia legislation is destined for failure in the national parliament triggering a leadership challenge.

In a surprising development, the prime minister makes a decision which changes everything.

The Kill Bill is a gripping political thriller featuring emotional and surprising plot twists, convincing characters, and exposes the black-art of politics that will have you questioning the ethics of assisted dying. If you like fast-paced, page-turning thrillers that draw you into the story then Richard Evans' fourth book will not disappoint you.

Buy The Kill Bill today and learn how the black arts of politics really works.

A CRIME, A TRIAL, A PUNISHMENT. IS IT JUSTICE?

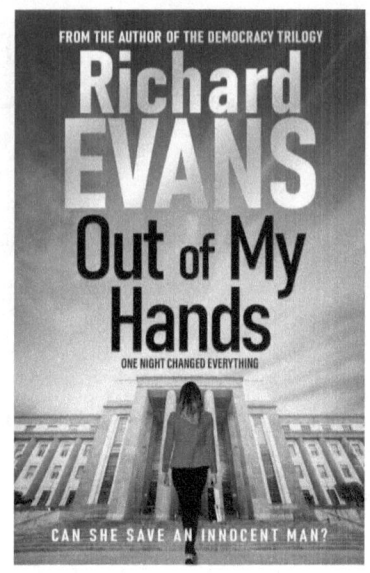

They were in the wrong place at the wrong time and will regret it forever. Nothing can change what happened, but only the lawyer can provide justice for them both. Will Anna Booth do it or will it be out of her hands?

A teenager is looking for a good time and meets a young woman who has no interest in him or his friends. Their worlds collide again when walking home. His mistake was not helping her.

After a police investigation exposing his friends, Billy Brown faces his day in court. He knows he is innocent and has little fear of the justice system. But the justice system wants a guilty accused and Billy is their patsy.

Three trials and a media storm later, his lawyer Anna Booth fights for justice for her client and the victim.

Buy OUT OF MY HANDS today and bring to light the reality of the American justice system and its faults.

Trigger warning: Out of my Hands is a gritty crime thriller and reader 18+ recommended.

For more information and purchasing options visit 852 Press.com.au

SHE CHANGES HER NAME BUT NOT HER ATTITUDE.

A streetwise opportunist escapes despair and abuse in the big city by seeking opportunities in the mallee. She changes her name but not her attitude when she discovers wealth and privilege ripe for the taking from the influential Dowerin family of the mallee.

Rose Dowerin replaces her husband as the local federal politician. The subsequent trappings of influence and power as a minister in the federal government suit her ambitions. It's a privileged life, a life very different from the abusive streets of Melbourne from where she escaped and the dry dusty heat of the mallee.

A crack appears in her perfect world when the mallee agonises over prolonged drought. Farmers question her influence on water policy and concede they need a more dynamic politician to represent them in Canberra.

Under threat Rose falls back into her malevolent ways to overcome the forces against her until an unexpected family twist changes everything.

THE MALLEE is an action-packed thriller with a strong female lead featuring emotional and surprising plot twists, convincing characters, and exposes the dark-arts of politics that will have you questioning the system.

If you like fast-paced, page-turning thrillers that draw you into the story then Richard Evans' seventh book will not disappoint you.

For more information and purchasing options visit
852 Press.com.au

852

PRESS

We are an independent publisher, helping Australians tell their story.

We are keen to share our experiences and processes with Australian writers so they can self-publish their own works. We will be launching a range of resources, services, and events for those with a story to tell.

Visit our website for more information.

WWW.852Press.com.au